TRADED

Blood Ties Series

A.K. ROSE

ATLAS ROSE

To my readers...I seriously love you guys. Your support and love for this series just blows me away.

Atlas, xxx

Warnings

Grab the playlist here on Spotify

ONE

London

Tires squealed when I took the corner sideways as we raced for home. Colt rocked in the seat behind me, pale and terrified, while Carven was unflinching beside me, staring straight ahead, his fist clenched around the grip of the gun.

All I saw was that contract illuminated in King's apartment. The one where Vivienne was sold behind my goddamn back...*to Macoy Daniels.*

COME ON! I strangled the wheel.

"He's mine," I warned, my focus fixed on the street ahead. "You got that? Macoy Daniels *is mine...*"

I pushed the car harder, driving the accelerator all the way to the floor as the sight of my house rose in the distance. The rear door of the car cracked open as I barely touched the brake, pumping the damn thing to bring us to a stop. But the son was already moving, charging out of the car with his brother close behind.

White steam billowed from the engine as I shoved the car into park and threw open my door. Footsteps boomed, swallowing the thunder in my chest as I raced for the house. Bodies lay in the front yard. I caught the wide, unblinking eyes of the guards assigned to protect us before I fixed on the open door of my house, listening to the thud of boots on the stairs.

Blood...that's all I saw as I raced inside and skidded on the splattered mess in the foyer. Bright red across the stark white tiles. I followed the smear and found Guild lying face down.

"Vivienne!" Carven roared. *"VIVIENNE!"*

"Hey!" I lunged and dropped to my knees, pulling my closest goddamn friend over and into my arms. "I'm right here. *Guild, I'm right here."*

Tight, shallow breaths. Wide, shimmering eyes. But he was still alive...*he was still alive. Jesus...*

Upstairs, doors crashed against walls as the sons tore their way through every room, making their way from their floor to mine, before descending on me like the wrath of the gods.

"Tried...to...get...her...to basement," Guild whispered as Colt skidded to a stop in front of me.

He jerked his head toward the kitchen, then lunged, with his twin right behind him. *"Where?"* Carven barked, his eyes full of terror. *"WHERE?"*

"They...took her," Guild forced, then he coughed, splattering blood against my arm.

Cold plunged all the way to my core. "They took her?"

"The Order," he whispered, his face turning gray. *"I...failed you."*

I winced and shoved my hand into my pocket. "You didn't goddamn fail me, Guild." I scanned the bloom of blood at his side and swiped my thumb across the screen of my phone, pulling up the only person who could help me now...

The Director of Emergency Medicine, Doctor Lucas DeLuca.

"DeLuca," he answered, sounding calm while chaos reigned in the background.

People screamed. Machines howled. But I didn't care about any of that. I didn't care about a goddamn thing other than what was mine. "DeLuca, this is the man who spared your life." I stared as Guild slowly closed his eyes. "Now it's your turn to spare one for me."

He went quiet at the other end of the line, then spoke carefully. "Don't suppose I have a choice here?"

"No," I answered. "You don't." Then I gave him the address of my house.

"I'll be there in thirty minutes," he responded.

I winced as the sons came up from the basement carrying vests, guns, and a whole arsenal in a duffel bag.

"Hold the fuck on," I growled as I grabbed the sniper rifle Carven shoved toward me.

"Go." Guild shook his head and whispered. "*Save...her.*"

I eased his head back to the floor, gripped the weapon, and rose. I didn't want to leave. But I pulled on a vest as I stared down at him, then turned and headed for the door.

I didn't stop, didn't even look back, just forced myself to move and pushed into a sprint. The engine was still running, the steam no longer pouring from the engine.

"The tracker, Colt." I slipped in behind the wheel and threw it into drive. *"Find the goddamn tracker."*

My pulse was pounding. I swore the sound screamed her goddamn name. I barely waited for them as they flung themselves into the seats, just drove my foot all the way to the floor and jerked the wheel, whipping us around, and headed for the city once more.

It all came rushing back to me.

The hunt.

The violence.

I was trained for this…

I was born for this.

I looked over as I took the corner hard and headed for where I knew Daniels's place was. The rifle was pointed muzzle down against the floor as Colt punched the details into his phone and waited.

"Do you have it?" I snapped, jerking my gaze from the road to him. He scowled and pulled the GPS out wider. Even from the driver's seat I saw the tiny red light blinking. I turned back to the road, pushing the car through the city streets. He was silent…*too silent.* *"Well?"* I snarled. *"What the fuck is wrong?"*

"It's gone."

Rage punched through me. "What do you mean it's *gone?*"

"It just fucking disappeared."

I reached over, grabbed the damn phone, and turned it. That tiny crimson marker was no longer illuminated, leaving the map as dark as the goddamn night.

"It's fucking broken," he growled through clenched teeth.

"It's not broken," I said coldly. "It has interference."

That contract burned inside my goddamn head. *Permanent right to possess/use:*

Permanent right...

Permanent right.

Hale sold her.

He FUCKING SOLD HER!

I gripped the wheel until my knuckles turned white.

She'd be terrified. Hurt. She'd be goddamn savage. I knew my Wildcat better than she knew herself. She'd fight with all she had...and they'd hurt her for it. *The things that fucking cocksucker will do to her because of me...*

"It can't be broken." Carven reached over and snatched the phone, then swiped his thumb to close the app, then opened it back up. "Or we have interference. The only way that tracker can be stopped is if they enclosed it in a metal box."

I stared ahead blankly, terror blooming as I envisioned all the fucking things they'd do to someone so fucking pure. "Exactly."

TWO

Vivienne

BOOM!

The steel lid slammed closed over my face, trapping me inside. *"NO! NOOOOO!"* I threw myself forward, slamming my head against the steel barrier until stars collided behind my eyes.

I couldn't breathe...*I couldn't breathe! I* COULDN'T—

THUMP! I sucked in hard gasps as the sound detonated in my ears.

"Stop fighting and you might just make it," Daniels snarled and gave a chuff, sounding almost *amused.*

"Stop...*stop, please!"* I closed my eyes, holding on to the last traces of my sanity. "Let me out...*just let me out of here!"*

But there was no scrape of steel.

No glimpse of moonlight.

No breath of cold winter air.

Just this *suffocating space.*

Shallow breaths bounced back from the metal, warming my face.

"Thirty minutes, Vivienne. I think you can manage thirty minutes, after all...you survived worse."

Survived worse.

Survived...worse.

My mind howled and raged, the screams consuming. *I'm going to die in here. I'm going to die—*

No.

Carven's cold, guttural snarl cut through my screaming mind.

No, you won't.

Because you're a daughter...

Now start acting like one.

My breaths deepened, enough to slow the unraveling inside my head. I was jerked sideways and slammed against the side with a *crack!* Stars blazed to life behind my eyes as the steel box shifted and bounced, jostling me as we moved.

"Just until we can cut it out of her," Ashwood's sickening voice was muffled, but I heard the words.

My scalp burned from his cruel fist and my cheek had its own savage, throbbing heartbeat, a remnant from his fist when I'd tried to run. But it was Macoy Daniels's words that gripped me. I could still feel the bastard's hand around my neck as he drove my face into the seat of his limousine.

I was thrown sideways again, only this time I had enough time to jerk my hands up and push against the walls, cushioning the blow. Still, it hurt. *Everything hurt.*

"Move," Daniels's slimy voice sounded as I was thrown from side to side, then slid upwards before I stopped.

Were they burying me?

Leaving me to suffocate and rot in the ground?

You're coming home with me...

Those words echoed from earlier, when he'd driven somewhere and forced me into this...*this hell.*

BANG! A car door closed before an engine started. I cried out as we moved, pressing my hands against the steel enclosure. The heat of my breath blew back at me, caressing the burning outline of Daniels's hand.

I'm going to enjoy the fuck out of you. His words were all I heard, resounding over and over like my own personal torment. *London won't want you at all...by the time I'm done.*

London.

London...

"Where are you when I need you the most?" I whispered out loud.

The vehicle sped up, making me press hard against the metal walls. "Think," I whispered in answer to myself. "Come on, just think."

I needed a way out of this. Whatever *this* was.

Hot, thick tears slid down my cheeks, stinging against the burn. I needed a plan. Just a chance—I swiped the tears away with my thumb and lowered my head, pressing against the cold steel— just one goddamn chance to get out of here, and I'll run.

To where? London's voice surfaced. *Where are you going to run to, Vivienne?*

"To you, asshole," I whispered, forcing the words through my tight throat. "I'm going to run to you."

I didn't know how long we'd driven for when we slowed, then turned sharply. It could've been minutes, it could've been hours. It felt like an eternity. I squeezed my eyes closed, desperate to pull myself together, as the vehicle skidded to a stop, before I opened them. Car doors opened.

"You need to hurry up and get her out before the signal is triggered," Daniels muttered.

"Don't worry," someone answered. "It won't even be a blip on the radar."

"Good," the piece of shit added as I was jerked forward. "She's quiet...it'll make it easier now she's broken."

Now she's broken...

Now...she's bro—

The metal lid opened and sparks danced in front of my eyes. But then I blinked and they were gone.

"There you go," Daniels's ugly fucking face moved into view as he leaned over the box. "Nice and quiet now, aren't you?"

*Fight, Wildcat...*Carven's words pushed in once more.

He wasn't the son I wanted to hear. Not comforting. Not kind. But he was here.

Snap the fuck out of it!

I flinched as Daniels's man reached in, grabbed me around the arm, and jerked me upward. My head snapped forward. Cold night air danced across my bare skin. The pajama shorts and thin satin camisole rode high as they yanked me from the steel coffin they'd shoved me into.

"Get her inside. I want that *thing* cut out of her and her naked in my study in an hour."

Now that she's broken...

Are you broken, Wildcat? Carven's savage growl reverberated in my head as they dragged me from the van.

Those blue eyes burned in my mind. Hateful. Demanding. A monster at any other time.

My own personal monster.

Just not right now.

I snapped my head upwards a second before my feet hit the ground. Instead of falling, I yanked my knees to my chest, then kicked out with all I had. The guard took the full force of the blow right in the center of his chest, knocking him backwards until he hit the ground.

I didn't stop, didn't even look around. I just saw darkness and trees and ran.

"*Get her!*" Daniels's roar rose from behind me.

I sucked in the cold, night air and tasted freedom. I wanted more...*I wanted so much more.* Outlines of looming dark trees shifted with every jarring step as I ran. I headed for them, for the road...and *London.* The crunch of gravel came from behind me. I didn't dare look, just unleashed a cry and drove my bare feet into the cold winter ground.

My feet stung and my chest was on fire as I pumped my arms and zig-zagged, racing for the road.

"No, the fuck you don't," a grunt came behind me.

I was hit and driven forward, headfirst to the ground. Agony unleashed along my face as cruel hands gripped the back of my head before he turned me around. But I wasn't done fighting. I wasn't *anywhere* near done.

I unleashed a scream and swung my fists, clawing anything I could get my hands on. I raked my nails down the bastard's face as his hot breath drove into my open mouth. My scream seared along the back of my throat as I kicked and thrashed.

"Enough!" he roared, sounding far too much like London.

Only London wasn't brutal...London wasn't cruel.

Not like this.

His fist was a blur as it drove into my cheek, snapping my head backwards. Stunned, I tried to hang on, but my world was dimming and growing darker by the second.

"*No*," I croaked. "*No!*"

The fist came again and smashed into my mouth. *Crack!* Blood bloomed across my tongue. The sting at the corner of my lips was as nothing as those bloody knuckles came once more.

Crack!

My head was thrown back and impacted the cold earth with a *thud. A* shadow shifted over me as my attacker rose.

"Tried to warn you, you fucking bitch," he grunted as he reached down, grabbed a fistful of my hair, and yanked.

Pain roared through my head and poured out of my mouth. I reached for his hand, unable to do anything but shove to my feet, even as my world blurred.

Others raced toward me. Two guards, their faces indistinct through my tears.

"Hold her still," one demanded.

A sting came at my arm, one I'd felt far too many times to count. I looked down at the syringe in my abductor's hand and tried to hold on to the only thing that mattered...the memory of London and the sons. They were going to take me now. They were going to take me back to The Order.

I waited for darkness. I waited to be numb. Only, whatever they'd given me didn't knock me out. Instead, my head swam as they hauled me upwards, carrying me by my arms and legs toward that van once more.

"Get her inside, for fuck's *sake!*" Daniels roared.

My lips curled. The sting was savage, carving deeper even as laughter spilled from my mouth. I couldn't stop it, even if I wanted to—*and I didn't want to.* "Did I mess up your *widdle plan?*" I grinned, watching rage settle into his eyes.

He strode closer, grabbed my jaw and stilled the laughter. "I'm going to really enjoy tonight, Vivienne. Pity I can't say the same for you."

"Bring it the fuck on, you pathetic excuse for a man," I muttered.

He clenched tight, pain tearing through my jaw. But I didn't give him the satisfaction of seeing me wince. No, I held his stare, even if in that moment the bastard had three pairs of eyes.

The world swam as they carried me along a path and through a massive open door. *It looked familiar.* I tried to think. Tried to remember. *Trees...long driveway...towering mansion.* Something about a fire? But my head swam, swirling and darkening the moment I came close.

Boots thundered as they carried me along a hallway toward the rear of the house. The damn thing seemed to go forever. "I can't wait for London to find me," I croaked. "Or Colt and Carven. You know about them, don't you?" A giggle rose as images of blood and carnage filled my mind. "They call them *sons*."

The asshole who had hold of one leg lifted his gaze and looked at the other. "I don't give a fuck who they are."

"Not *who* they are, motherfucker...*what...they...are.*" I stared at his face, making sure I burned it into my mind.

"They're going to come," I whispered, grinning like a damn fool. "They're going to tear you apart."

"*Shut the fuck up!*" The one who gripped me under the arms snapped as they dragged me into what looked like a massive sitting room.

My vision blurred, but I caught the rows and rows of hardback books stacked in towering bookshelves. "Why is it that all the spineless pricks think they're so fucking smart?" The question came from out of nowhere...and right now, I had no filter.

With a grunt from the scumbags around me, they threw me toward the high-backed brown leather sofa. I hit the hard seat with a *thump*. Splitting shards of agony resounded through me like a drum as the assholes stepped away.

"Get the doctor in here, now," Daniels commanded.

From the corner of my eye, he stepped into view, shifting his gaze over me.

"You look at me with all that disappointment," I spat. "You think you can just take me and I won't fight back?" I pushed upwards. "I don't think you're used to that, are you, Daniels? *Women fighting back?*"

Those soulless eyes glinted.

I glanced at his pathetic boy-toy army as they slipped from the room. "You like them meek and mild, don't you? You like them drugged so they can't fight while you can do all the filthy, degrading things you want to them, don't you?" I swung my gaze to him. "Or is it so they don't really notice how *pathetically* small your prick is?" I lowered my gaze. "I bet it's so fucking small they don't even feel it. I bet it's *so fucking tiny that—*"

"Shut. Your. Fucking. Mouth."

"Hit a nerve, did I?" I whispered, lifting my gaze to his. I could barely see him through the tiny slit of my only open eye.

He stepped closer and I fought a tremor of fear. I wouldn't give him the satisfaction of seeing me cower. *It'd take bigger and badder sonsofbitches to break me.*

"You know, you remind me of something…" I whispered, staring up into his eyes, still talking even though my mouth hurt like a bitch. "A slug," I added as he loomed over me and leaned down. "A slimy, cold, crawling slug. That's what—"

SLAP!

I flew sideways and hit the side of the sofa when the blow landed. Layers and layers of pain. Cutting. Torturing. *Punishing.*

"You *will not* talk to me like that, do I make myself clear?" he snarled as he stood over me. "I own you, you fucking cunt. Do you get that? I can hit you. I can hurt you. I can do whatever the fuck I want with you. I can fuck you myself, and I can whore you out to whomever I want. What do you think about that? I might like to sit back and watch your body be torn apart over and over again. Stretch your pussy. Split your ass. I bet that mouth of yours will take so much cock. Maybe I'll make you eat pussy, how about that? I can think of a few women who like to be licked." He leaned closer. "How about I hold your head down and make you eat cunt while my men take their turns?"

Revulsion clenched my belly. Tight. Twisting. Agony stabbed inside.

"You mean *nothing to me, do you understand?*" he spat, his eyes soulless. "I got what I wanted when I took you from *him*."

Terror filled me, making my arms tremble and my body quake. I tried to stop the tears from coming, but my body had a mind of its own.

"That's better."

My gut clenched with the words. I didn't know what hurt worse, his palm or his satisfaction at my cowering silence. The rage that had driven me a second ago had frozen, leaving me reeling.

"Don't make me have to break that pretty face." He gripped my jaw, turning my gaze to his. "Because I will. I'll beat you until you're unrecognizable...then I'll send a photo to the man you seem to have grown quite attached to. Let's see if he wants you then."

Unmerciful breaths consumed me. I hated him at that moment, hated his beady fucking eyes and the flabbiness of his drooping jawline. I hated the graying hair on his head and the pudgy fucking hand that gripped me. But I hated his power most of all...and the way he wielded it.

"It's about time," he snarled as the door opened and someone entered the room. He straightened as he released my jaw. "The tracker in her. I want it out."

Wretched waves of pain ripped through my head as I turned to the man who strode into the room. Déjà vu hit me, but instead of the older doctor with his black tuxedo and annoyed expression who strode closer, I saw a kid. A fumbling young idiot who barely knew my nipple from my clit. That kid might have looked at me and seen someone in need of saving. That kid might've even interjected himself.

But not this man. Oh, no. He strode in, set his small black leather case on the small table beside the sofa, and unbuttoned his jacket. "You'll need to hold her down for this."

Daniels motioned to his men near the doorway. "That won't be a problem."

I shoved backwards as fear grew talons and tore me apart from the inside. "No...*no...no...no*."

Daniels just looked down at me. "Grab her."

They came for me, all three of them, and there wasn't a damn thing I could do. I fought and kicked, scurrying over the arm of the sofa. But they were all around me, closing in around the rear of the seat to grab me. My spine bowed as I kicked and thrashed, the drug making me slow and weak.

"Over here," the doctor ordered.

He was a blur at the corner of my eye, striding toward a desk pushed against the far wall of the room. I clenched my jaw, kicking and bucking, even though it was useless.

You want to be a victim? Carven's empty tone blared through my terror. *Then keep acting like one. You are a byproduct of what they created. You...are...a...daughter.*

I went limp as they jerked and pulled, straining the tendons in my arms until they screamed.

"On the desk. Hold her."

I hit the top of the wooden desk with a *crack*. Hands gripped me, slamming my wrists and my ankles to the surface.

"Her top," the doctor demanded.

My camisole was ripped. The thin strings snapped and tore. I cried out, bucking as they snatched it from me. Not because I was bare for their sick stares. But because London had bought that for me...

"Give it back!" I roared. *"Give it back to me!"*

They cast aside the torn garment. I jerked my head to the side, watching the pale peach remnant fall to the floor. The outline of the guard's body blurred as he moved. I just knew he was treading on it, crushing the fabric under his boots.

"That's mine," I cried as a hand closed over my breast.

"There's the previous incision," the doctor muttered.

Stabbing pain came and it was...*relentless.* I screamed, unleashing a savage cry. One that ripped along my throat and filled my mouth with blood. Those fingers pinched. Those fingers squeezed. Those fingers bore down until it felt like he was driving through my ribs and into my chest.

"There," the doctor snarled, and suddenly let me go. Bloody fingers swam in my vision as the room turned dark.

"No, you don't." Daniels slapped my cheek, driving away the darkness. "You want to be fucking mouthy, then I want you conscious for this."

He turned his head and gave a nod...and the sight of that chilled me to the bone.

Hands gripped the waistband of my pajamas and jerked down. I kicked out, screaming and howling.

"I did try to warn you," Daniels sneered as he stepped backwards and reached for the buckle of his belt. "You wanted this the hard way...then the hard way it is."

THREE

London

Betrayal. I tasted it in the air before I even got there. The sickening, rancid tang ran down the back of my throat as I swallowed. My boots were silent. But my pulse was a goddamn freight train thundering in my head. Carven flanked me on one side, Colt on the other as we skirted the long drive and headed for the dark brown expansive Tudor mansion at the end.

The tracker had come to life barely ten minutes ago...

It was only a minute.

But it was all we'd needed.

I glanced at Carven and gave a nod, unleashing the son like a bloodthirsty beast. He gave a chilling smile and rushed forward, leaving Colt with me as we neared the van parked in front of the house. I scanned the grounds as Carven disappeared, then looked inside the rear door of the van...

My steps stuttered as I took in the long metal box they'd shoved her in. It was barely big enough to hold anything, let alone a person. But they'd shoved her in there, sliding that steel cover

over her face, nearly suffocating her. *Jesus...the hell she must've endured...*

I ground my teeth as hate burned inside me.

I wasn't the only one who flinched with anguish at the sight.

I glanced at Colt as he turned away, those dark blue eyes were black with primal rage as he lifted his gaze to movement.

Carven appeared from around the corner, his face splattered with blood and a knife in his hand, dripping. I froze, my gaze fixed on the two eyeballs that hung from the optic nerves gripped in his hand. I met his stare, my brow rising. "Isn't that excessive?"

It wasn't rage I saw in those blazing blue eyes...it was *revenge.* "He looked at her, didn't he?"

Jesus.

This wasn't just any kill for us.

This was personal...

I lifted my hand and motioned toward the doorway before pushing forward. But before I could even give the signal, Colt was already moving, charging ahead. I'd trained them to attack and to obey. I gritted my teeth and raced after the son. It looked like he was done following commands, especially where Vivienne was concerned.

The movement wiped the smile from Carven's face as his twin disappeared through the towering wooden door and slipped inside.

"Sonofabitch," he hissed before lunging after Colt.

We were barely a few steps behind, but even that was too much, especially when three guards moved out from an expansive living room and into the hall in front of him.

"Carven," I managed.

But I didn't need to. They'd bred these sons to be silent, terrifying savages—and that's exactly what they were, rushing forward in chilling silence. Carven tossed the knife in his hand up in the air, flipping it end over end, before he clenched his fist around the hilt and drove the blade into a guard's chest.

I lifted my weapon, found Colt as I rushed forward, and took aim at the third asshole charging toward them.

Pft!

The suppressor smothered the sound, leaving nothing more than the rush of air and the bite of gunpowder in its wake. The bastard dropped where his last step landed. The bloom of blood at the front of his head was nothing compared to the blowout on the other side. Carven unleashed a snarl, ripped his blade free, then grabbed the bastard around the throat and drove him against the wall with a *thud*.

Blood was everywhere, streaming from the bastard's chest and his throat as Carven lifted the weapon, but a piercing scream unleashed from deeper in the house.

"That's mine!"

I froze.

We *all* froze.

Vivienne...

The bastard against the wall gasped, then shoved forward, eyes blazing as he fought for his life. But Carven wasn't looking at him anymore. In fact, he barely registered the mercenary at all when he cocked his hand and drove the knife straight into the bastard's belly. Two terrifying upward jerks, and he turned that chilling glare back to the dead man in his grasp. "You don't get to survive this...*none of you do.*"

Blood spewed from the gash as Carven sliced him all the way from navel to collarbone before he stepped away, leaving the guard's body to slump to the floor. The son stepped over the body as Colt rushed forward. I lunged too, swinging the muzzle of my rifle upwards as he rushed toward the sound.

"*NO!*" Vivienne screamed from a room further along the hall.

That sound punched all the way through my heart.

But as brutal as the sound was to me...it was *destroying* to Colt. The son didn't stop as we raced toward the heavy wooden door where her screams came from. He didn't even slow, just dropped his shoulder as he charged, and slammed his body against the ornate barrier.

CRACK! The door shuddered and gave way under the force, leaving it to bounce against the wall with a resounding *boom* as we rushed inside.

Eight men...I scanned the room, searching for weapons, finding the kill angles.

Eight men...and three of us.

Colt moved right as we entered, vaulting clear over a large brown sofa. The son didn't roar. He didn't even utter a damn sound. He let the sickening *thump* of his fists as he attacked with savage ferocity do all the screaming for him. His blows were brutal, driving into the guard's face over and over again until there was a gut-wrenching *crunch*.

The body dropped to the floor before Colt took a slow step forward, his chest rising and falling with consuming breaths.

But my focus wasn't on him...it was on the others.

The six men crowding around the desk at the far end of the room.

Before movement came between them.

Thin arms.

Long legs.

Thrashing.

Vivienne...

Colt drove his fist into a male's face before the guard fell to the floor.

I lifted my rifle as Carven hurled his knife through the air, hitting the center of a guard's chest as he turned at the intrusion. In the span of a slow-booming heartbeat, the room was filled with a vacuum of violence. One that sucked all the sound away with it.

There was nothing.

Nothing but a tsunami of merciless rage.

One they'd created when they'd taken her.

I lifted my rifle and took aim, my reflexes taking over as I squeezed the trigger, taking out one...two...*three of them*, before I advanced. I felt nothing but emptiness as I narrowed in on the bastard standing at the end of the desk...and between her thighs. Daniels was a dead man...and I didn't give a fuck about the consequences.

His pants were open, his zipper all the way down. But it was those fucking hands around her thighs that sickened me... touching what wasn't his to touch.

Thump! Thump! THUMP! Colt unleashed a roar. *CRUNCH!* Then he lifted his gaze, his focus on the desk before he lunged. Vivienne unleashed a cry and kicked out with frenzied movements. I was already striding forward, swallowing the icy sting of rage. The burn was all I felt as I risked a glance at her and froze.

Fuck...

Her face was a fucking mess. One cheek was red and blazing, darkening with an agonizing-looking bruise that was going to be a bitch tomorrow. Her lips were bloody and split. But that was nothing compared to her eyes. One was badly swollen, with only a blank stare visible, the other was swollen closed. She slipped and fell as she tried desperately to escape. But Colt was there, lunging through the air to catch her before she hit the floor.

Then she was in the son's arms.

She was safe.

I swung my gaze back to the piece of fucking shit who'd done that and lifted my gun. The small red light from my scope found the center of his forehead. I could almost see the blowout and the crimson mist blooming with one...*gentle*...squeeze...

"*No!*" Daniels roared, lifting his hands up to cover his face, and dropped to his knees. "*Wait...WAIT!* You need me...*you FUCKING NEED ME!*"

I stepped forward, carving my way through the violence.

Screams punctured the air as Carven drove another attacker to the floor beside me and wrenched his blade into the air. I'd never seen him so frenzied as he stabbed and stabbed...*and stabbed.*

I'd never seen him...so...*terrifying.* Not even when he fought for me. But he was now. Consumed with bloodlust and vengeance and when he was done, he turned that chilling gaze to her...

Vivienne.

I caught his flinch in the corner of my eye as I advanced, sucking in hard breaths. I didn't speak, because there was nothing left to say.

"You d-don't know what I know," the slimy motherfucker cried as I pressed the muzzle of the sniper rifle to his forehead. *"I do...I DO!"*

In the corner of my eye, Colt slipped his tactical vest free and pulled off his black t-shirt before he slipped it over Vivienne, covering her as best as he could.

"There is nothing you could tell me that'd spare you from this," I answered coldly.

But there was that tiny voice inside my head that whispered, *what if...*

"You need me," the bastard blubbered, his eyes filled with tears as he looked from the sons to me. He shook his head, as though it finally hit him just what she meant to us, then lowered his stare, cowering. "I didn't know—"

He barely got the words out before Vivienne lunged, tearing from Colt's arms. His t-shirt flapped as she lifted her hand and slapped Daniels's cheek with a *crack!*

"You *bastard!*" She hit him again and again, leaving him to cover his head with his hands. "You...*fucking*...BASTARD!"

I just stepped back, leaving her to do her worst.

"I didn't know," the slimy fuck muttered over and over.

Until Vivienne stopped sucking in hard breaths as she towered over him. She looked so fierce, even beaten to hell, she was a goddamn force, looking down at him.

"You didn't know?" The words were hollow and strange." I lowered my gun and squeezed the trigger. *Pft!* The bullet found its mark in the back of his hand.

Shrill, blood-curdling screams erupted from the filthy piece of shit as he gripped his wrist, staring at the neat bullet wound through his hand. His skin turned gray, his eyes wide and bloodshot as I took a slow step closer, until I met that horrified stare. "Now you do," I finished. "Now you know the lengths we will go to to protect her."

Daniels jerked his gaze from Vivienne to me. Red welts were rising on his pasty-as-fuck cheeks. "Y-you d-don't know what he's p-planned," he stuttered. "I do. I can help you. I can tell you everything."

I shook my head until Vivienne looked my way. All I saw was her swollen, darkening eyes and the bloody strands of her hair. "Wildcat," I answered and handed the sniper rifle her way.

She knew.

Even as tortured and terrified as she was, she knew what I was saying...*the choice is yours.*

She reached out with a trembling hand, three fingernails broken and bleeding. All I saw was that metal fucking coffin in the back of that van, and I knew instantly how they'd been broken. She gripped the weapon and turned back.

"No," Daniels's eyes widened as he stared at her. *"No!"*

She lifted the rifle, gripped the barrel, and with a savage scream, she brought the butt down hard against the side of his head with a loud *crack!* Daniels flew sideways as Colt stepped closer, watching as she stumbled then righted herself.

But the motherfucker didn't slump. Dazed, he swayed on his knees, bracing his uninjured hand against the floor.

"Didn't knock him out, pet," I muttered, staring down at him. "Maybe try one more time?"

She found me through the slit of her barely open eye and gave a slow nod before lifting the weapon high once more.

"Wait!" Daniels shrieked as my damn phone rang in my pocket.

She drove the rifle down, hitting him again, only this time even harder. He slumped to the floor hard, knocked out cold, as I reached into my pocket and pulled my phone free.

Daniels never moved, but the sonofabitch was alive, and he had Vivienne to thank for that. I never took my eyes off her as she looked my way. "If he knows what Hale is planning, then we're going to need him."

I gave her a smile, then glanced at the caller ID, unleashed a snarl, and answered. "This better be good."

"We have a problem," Mickie growled. "I wouldn't have called, but...the damn place is a mess."

"What do you mean, *a damn mess?*"

"The emergency sprinkler system went off and flooded the entire east wing. We've had to close the whole wing down...and that means moving bodies. So you're going to get here...*and fast.*"

"Fuck!" I barked, glaring at Daniels, my mind racing. It couldn't be a coincidence that this happened on the same goddamn night they tried to take her. Because I didn't believe in them. "I'll be there as soon as I can."

"You're going to need to make it soon, London—"

I clenched my jaw, forcing the words through gritted teeth. "Don't push me, Mickie. Not tonight, understand?"

He went quiet on the other end of the line. "Yes, sir."

"Good. Keep everything contained until I get there." By every*thing*, I meant every*one*.

The east wing housed not just Jack Castlemaine, but also Dominic Petrov, one of Killion's security detail. He came in handy when I needed access to setting up not only cameras for spying on the scumbag, but he was the one who had helped to protect Ryth.

I ended the call and turned to the mess of dead bodies. "Take Vivienne back to the warehouse," I ordered, turning to her. "She doesn't leave your sight, understand me?" I swung back to the sons, knowing the words weren't needed.

"No." She shook her head. "I'm coming with you."

I winced, thinking of the mess waiting for me. It wasn't somewhere I wanted her, not like this. "Vivienne, I don't—"

Even bleeding and busted, there was defiance in her stare. "Don't you think I've proven my loyalty by now?"

A pang tore across my chest. "It's not a question of your loyalty."

She held my stare. I knew in an instant there was no budging her. My mind raced, hunting down all the implications of her coming face to face with Ryth's father, I then slowly nodded. "If you insist."

"I do."

A smile tugged at the corner of my mouth as I stared at the t-shirt barely reaching her thighs. "Colt, find her something to wear. Carven," I glanced at him. "Tear the place apart. I want to know everything this rapist piece of shit knows."

One nod and he glanced at Viv. Something passed between them, a look, one that had the son scowling as he turned and followed his brother out of the study. The air was different when they left, quieter, strained.

"Vivienne."

She shook her head. "Don't." She shifted that busted up, beautiful face my way. "I don't need words. I need action. I *need* you to fucking end this once and for all."

My pulse pounded, and the desperation crawled out of the hole where it lived. "I will. I promise."

She gave a nod and turned away, looking at the dead bodies that littered the room. "Good. Because these men cannot live, not in this world."

That was all that drove me.

All that kept me awake at night.

All that had me hunting, trying to protect those I loved.

Footsteps resounded from out in the hall. I knew Colt's gait, even if the son was more frantic than I'd ever heard him. He strode back into the room carrying a handful of red lace lingerie.

"This was all I could find." He looked sickened, lifting the cheap, disgusting garments.

Vivienne just stared at what was in his hand, then slowly reached out, taking the lingerie. "I'd rather walk naked down the fucking streets than wear red for him."

Colt looked away, following her gaze to Daniels, still slumped on the floor. "There's nothing else."

"If I don't have pants, then neither should he." Vivienne stared at where Daniels's pants were open under his gut. "Or a cock, for that matter."

She glanced my way. "Now, where did Carven disappear to?" she murmured and a tiny smirk tugged the corner of her mouth before she winced with the sting.

FOUR

London

"You know what?" she whispered, staring at Daniels slumped over on his side. "Never mind. I wouldn't want Carven getting some filthy fucking disease from touching it, anyway."

The way her eyes glazed made rage burn deeper inside me. Did he touch her? Did the filthy fucking *worm...rape her?* Colt's shirt barely reached her thighs, but all I could see was Daniels's hands on her thighs, and I shook with the need to kill as Carven entered the room.

"Get him into the car before he wakes up," I snarled. "I'm taking this sonofabitch to the warehouse."

"Don't worry." Carven strode forward, then bent and heaved the fat bastard onto his shoulders. "He won't be conscious for a while."

There was that look again, the tortured stare as Carven met Vivienne's gaze then turned away. I locked that memory away, because right now I didn't have time to unpack the dangerous range of emotions that came with either of them.

I slid my arm around her, leading her out of that room littered with bodies. "Don't look," I urged.

But telling Vivienne not to do anything was like pissing into the goddamn wind. Of course she looked, and froze, staring down at the white entrails of the gutted guard Carven had left behind in his murderous rage.

I expected tears.

And screaming.

Lots and lots of screaming.

But there was nothing from this...*wildcat.* She just shifted her focus from the goddamn bloody mess that ran along the grouted cracks of the tiles and kept on walking. Each step was excruciating. I saw it in the way she stiffened and limped. Still, there was no damn way she wasn't walking out of there on her own.

Carven walked ahead, carrying Daniels.

Smack!

The piece of shit's head collided with the edge of the doorway as Carven carried him outside and down the stairs at the front of the house. Headlights glared, blinding me for a second, but I knew the familiar growl of the Mercedes's engine when I heard it as Colt pulled the car alongside the van, leaving the engine running as he hit the button for the trunk and climbed out.

"I'll be at the warehouse." I headed around the rear of the car and opened the back door, finding my suit jacket where I'd tossed it earlier tonight. "Organize the cleaners. I want this house spotless...and empty by sunrise."

Carven gave a nod and dropped Daniels into the trunk...*hard.*

Thump!

I glanced at the body, then lifted my gaze. "We still need him alive."

"He's breathing, isn't he?" the son muttered as he stepped back and closed the trunk.

I wrapped my jacket around Vivienne as she headed for the passenger side, helping her slide her arms in. "I'll call when we're almost done."

I hated leaving them, especially not knowing how this was going to go down. We had a small window of opportunity here, one that was closing fast. Any moment now, Hale would find out this had gone south...then the game would be out in the open for all to see...

Him against me...

And it'd be brutal.

I opened the car door and helped her inside, hating how she winced when she sat, until she jerked her gaze upwards, that one eye widening. "Wait...Guild..."

I flinched, hating that sinking feeling. "He's alive...well, he was when I left him. I have a doctor working on him now."

"Good." She gave a slow nod and tugged the seatbelt across. "Good."

I closed the car door, and my thoughts returned to Hale. He'd never been an ally, just a fucking snake. I'd stayed around in the hopes he'd lead me to the nest. *His nest.* Him and all his sick, spineless friends.

Looked like that wouldn't happen.

Not anymore.

I climbed in and shoved the car into drive, pulled us around, and headed back down the drive. Vivienne watched the reflection in the side mirror. I didn't need to look to know Colt was still standing there, watching us as we drove away.

"You're safe with me." I glanced her way, meeting her stare. "I want you to know that."

"I know," she answered. "I'm not scared. But anyone who steps between us should be."

By *us*, she meant me, her, and the sons.

I gave a small chuff, then turned the wheel as we replaced pebbles for pavement. The drive was quiet. Too quiet. I glanced over, hating that comforting was never easy for me. I protected. I hunted. *I killed.* But in the quiet hours of the morning, when there was a need for more than sex, I found myself...*lacking.*

Touch her, you idiot.

I swallowed hard and divided my focus between her and the road. But in the corner of my eye, I saw her grasp the edges of my jacket and pull them tight around her. All the way tight, almost like it became a second skin.

It took me twenty minutes to get to the warehouse.

I both hated and needed that twenty minutes.

I cursed the sight of those lights in the middle of nowhere. Headlights flared in the distance. I glanced at that car and then the turnoff, with the warehouse waiting in the distance. As that car drove past, I stared at the young woman behind the wheel. She never looked my way, just kept her focus on the road as she drove by.

Red brake lights flared in the rear-view mirror behind us. I forced my attention back, slowly anyway, until the sedan was long gone before I pulled up at the set of gates. A second was all it took before the gates slowly opened and I pulled the Mercedes in.

Thump!

The thud came from the trunk. I stilled, my brows rose as it came again. *Thud.* "At least he's still alive," I muttered. "For now."

I climbed out, leaving her to follow. The frigid air carved all the way under my vest. She must be freezing. If she was, she never said a word. The thud of boots echoed. I rounded the rear of the Mercedes and stopped at the trunk as Mickie headed toward me.

"Get that piece of shit out," I growled as I moved closer to Vivienne. "And take him inside."

Thud!

A muffled scream came from inside the trunk. A pathetic sound that fit the man. But I held her tight as I led her forward, pushed through the double doors, and stepped inside.

"So this is what this place looks like. It's nice," she muttered. "What I can see."

I shook my head, the tight curl of my lips more of a wince. "Always the jokester."

"Get the fuck off me!" Daniels squealed.

Two of the armed guards strode along the hallway toward us, both soaked to the skin and pissed off. One swiped his forehead, muttering a string of obscenities, until he lifted his gaze and saw me.

"Sir." He gave a slow nod, then looked panicked as his gaze settled on Vivienne.

"Damage?" I asked.

He said nothing, just stared.

"Hey!" I barked, and he flinched hard and his eyes widened, finding mine. *"Do you have an answer for me or not?"*

"Y-yes, sir," he stuttered. "The east wing...it's ruined. We had to move the...move the items to the west wing."

I lowered my arm from around her shoulders and took a step forward as the memory of that sedan we'd just passed rose in my head. "Jack Castlemaine."

"Safe. Wet, but safe." He glanced at her once more.

"Take me to him."

He gave a nod. I turned, meeting that dark stare behind the slit of her eye. "You want to do this?"

She nodded, looking so fucking innocent under the bruising and the blood.

"Fuck you, St. James!" Daniels spat. *"FUCK YOU!"*

I lifted my hand, my curled fingers barely brushing the swollen flesh of her cheek. "I will kill him for what he's done to you, whether it's now or later. He *will* die screaming, I want you to know that.

"FUCKING COCKSUCKER!"

"Sounds like he's screaming now." She held my stare.

I gave her a smile. "That's not screaming, pet. That's called clarity."

Mickie shoved the slimy piece of shit forward, causing Daniels to stumble. I turned, following them along the hallway to where the corridor branched off into blocks of storage compartments that housed all my dirty secrets...some now dirtier than others.

Our footsteps resounded through the corridor until Daniels slipped on the slick floor.

"Jesus!" he screamed, wrenching his dazed gaze to my guard. *"Are you trying to kill me?"*

"Death is too kind for you," I snarled. "Believe me, what I have planned will make you wish you'd never been born."

He stiffened at the low growl and risked a panicked look over his shoulder. Those dark beady eyes met mine before he looked behind me.

"Eyes on me, motherfucker," I growled. "You don't get to look at her. Never again."

He looked at her…

Carven's words surfaced, as did the image of those hanging eyeballs in his grasp.

They don't get to survive this.

Daniels flinched, then turned back as our steps slapped through the puddles of water left behind. We headed deeper, to the west wing. The smaller wing…that was mostly taken up with not just warm bodies but my own rooms, filled with weapons, money, and equipment I didn't dare leave at the house.

But everything, I had paled compared to King's reach.

The ruthless bastard had it all.

He had everything I wanted.

And I had everything of his.

"Here." Mickie stopped outside the door of W312, the larger space fitted with living quarters.

He opened the door and pushed it wide, leaving me to stare into the murky depths until movement came from the edges.

"What the fuck is this?" Daniels barked, jerking his gaze toward mine.

"Your cell…for the time being," I answered as Jack Castlemaine stepped into view.

His hair was still wet, his clothes somewhat dry as he buttoned a fresh shirt and stared at Daniels being shoved into the room. "London?"

"It's temporary," I answered. "Until we can figure out what the fuck set the sprinkler system off."

"Jack?" Vivienne whispered and my pulse jumped as she stepped around me.

His eyes widened at the sight of her and, for a second, I saw something flicker in those depths. A desperation. A *hunger*. One that was smothered as he winced, then slowly shifted his gaze to Daniels. "You did that?"

"Fuck you, Castlemaine." Daniels barged his way inside the room. "Let's get this over and fucking done. You want the bitch and I want to live. So, bring me the goddamn contract and I'll give her to you."

He spun, wobbling on his feet as he stared at her. "The cunt wasn't worth what I paid."

I tried to keep my rage leashed, but the shit just blew out. With a roar, I lunged, knocking Castlemaine aside. Daniels unleashed a cry and stumbled backwards. But it was too late. I grabbed his shirt and lashed out, driving my fist into his face hard enough for his head to snap back with a sickening crack.

Dazed, his eyes widened…but he was still alive.

I sucked in a hard breath. "You will *never* speak about her again. Do you understand me? *Or you won't speak again.*"

Specks of blood flew as he coughed and spluttered. I released his shirt, letting the bastard fall to the floor in a blubbering mess.

That's all he was…a blubbering, filthy, fucking mess. One I was desperate to wipe from the face of this Earth.

"I spoke to Ryth," Vivienne murmured.

I inhaled hard and turned at the sound, watching as Vivienne stepped closer to Ryth's father. "She's okay."

Jack gave a slow nod, his gaze never shifting from her face. "But are you?" he asked softly.

She shifted her gaze my way. That stare never flinched as she answered. "I am now."

Beep.

The sound came from behind me. Anger flared.

"Fuck!" I spun on my heel and lunged, grabbing Daniels as he reached into his pocket for his phone.

The thing rang as I snatched it from his hand…and the name on the caller ID chilled me to the bone.

Hale.

"Mickie," I said carefully. "Make sure Daniels isn't heard."

"My fucking pleasure," the guard muttered and crossed the room, slamming his hand over Daniels's mouth as I answered the call without speaking.

"How's London's little bitch?" Hale chuckled in my ear. "I hope you didn't completely ruin that cunt. I plan on taking my sweet time with her tomorrow after our little celebration. Christ, I bet she can scream."

I stiffened.

Unable to move.

Or think.

All I did was consume, swallowing down every word until it was etched into my soul.

The low chuckle on the other end slowly died away, leaving nothing but silence.

The kind that was a beast of its own.

Cold.

So fucking cold.

Then quietly, "London?" Hale murmured.

I lowered my hand and ended the call.

FIVE

Carven

I WINCED AND LIFTED MY GAZE FROM THE CELL. THE clean-up crew would be here in thirty minutes, which meant we had that long to get what we wanted and get the hell out of here. "You ready for this?"

I lifted my gaze to Colt, who just stood there staring down at the bodies in the sitting room. He didn't say a word. His gaze was focused on the men who'd crowded around her on that desk. I knew what he pictured. I knew how much he hurt.

"Colt."

He lifted his head and turned toward me. Rage darkened his blue eyes. Rage and an unquenchable need for revenge, as I said, "They're dead."

"Are they?" That was all he said.

Two goddamn words. *Are they?* I looked away, finding the unfocused stare of the asshole in front of me. I lifted my foot, cocked my leg and kicked the fucker in the face. His head snapped backwards with a *crunch* and there it stayed. Blood oozing, life non-existent.

Then we started tearing the place apart, just like London wanted.

I strode around the desk, staring at the dislodged green leather desk pad.

They'd tried to rape her...

I stared at the mat and the pristine lacquered wood, then I dropped my hand, drew my gun, and emptied the fucking clip into the thing. *Crack. Crack. Crack crack crackcrackcrack!* The gun kicked in my hands and the sharp stench of gunpowder filled my nose. I squeezed the trigger until there was only the empty *click* left.

Bullet holes peppered the wood.

The mat was a shredded mess.

"THERE!" I turned my head and snapped at my brother, my cheeks blazing. *"Better now?"*

Hard, consuming breaths punched through my chest. I met his gaze until I couldn't look at him anymore and turned away. To appease the need for revenge, I wanted to scream at him...at all of them. I thought it was because it was *her.* The woman my brother and London craved.

Only it wasn't compassion that tore through me like wildfire. It was worse. The emotion *I* didn't battle. Because I wasn't weak and needy...*like them.*

My face burned even hotter when I turned back to that ruined desk and its ugly damn mat.

"They fucking took her. Carven, they took her. They took her, and she's *ours.*"

Jesus...

I winced at the emptiness in his tone. There was nothing in there. Nothing but hate. Nothing but that ten-year-old fucking kid almost beaten to death. I bent, yanked open the draw and started destroying the place.

Drawer after drawer.

Bookcase after bookcase.

I decimated the goddamn room.

There was nothing there.

Nothing anywhere.

Nothing—

Goosebumps raced along my arms. My senses sharpened, honed like a fucking blade. I cocked my head, listening.

"What?"

I sank all the way down into the dark pit where my past waited. The terror we'd tried to leave behind rippled, echoing until it reached into the present. I knew this feeling. It was the same gut-clenching feeling I'd had last night when I'd driven out to the ruins of the orphanage. The feeling that whispered another of us was stalking me.

He'd waited for me then, lingering in the shadows outside the decrepit remnant of our past, waiting for the moment to step outside the shadows. I tried to think, to replay everything about last night.

Do you hunt alone? My own words came back to me now.

No, he'd answered behind me. I hadn't turned around then, hadn't looked him in the eye. If I had, would I be standing here now? I wasn't so sure.

Are you looking for someone in particular? I'd asked the Son.

A daughter, Clair Murdoch. He warned. *You're to stay away if you find her, do you understand me?*

I had stayed away, hadn't made so much as an inquiry about the daughter, so then why the fuck was he here? I turned and headed for the study door, leaving Colt to snarl. "What is it?"

"Nothing," I answered.

But it wasn't nothing. It wasn't nothing at all. I left the bodies and the carnage behind and made my way out of the house, where the tire marks from London's car were still fresh. The frigid December air stung as I inhaled deep. I tasted the faint tang of smoke as I looked around, scanning the front of the house. We weren't far from that foul fucking cunt's mansion. The one we'd tried to burn to the ground. Figures. All those vile fucks gravitated to each other.

But I wasn't here for her...I was here for *them.*

The ones I knew were watching me right now.

The sons.

I waited for them to show, to tell me what they fucking wanted. But there was no movement from the shadows, no voice in the dark. There was just the white of my breath billowing out in front of me, until finally I turned and made my way inside and found Colt upstairs, destroying a bedroom.

Only it wasn't just a bedroom...they'd designed it for hell.

Crack! He unleashed his fury, driving his boot down on the end of a bed in silent rage. He never screamed, never howled his fury, just bent and grabbed the foot of the bed, fitted with shackles and an extender bar, designed to keep her legs spread far apart, and hurled it across the room to smash against the wall before he straightened, gulping in harsh breaths.

I stopped in the doorway, staring at him as he met my eyes. "Find anything?" I asked.

He shook his head, concern creasing his brow before he turned to the ruined room.

"Then let's go," I muttered, staring at the destruction. "The cleaners can do the rest."

He turned away from the extender bar impaled in the wall and stepped over the mess. I couldn't wait to get out of there, couldn't wait to scrub the filth of this place from my skin, even if it would be useless. That shit was branded in my soul, seared into my memory. But not like she was....

This...*daughter.*

A tremor rose as I made my way back out with my brother, knowing he'd fallen for the daughter and he'd fallen hard. My cheeks blazed as I thought about her. No one touched her, not while either of us was alive.

Headlights shone at the entrance of the driveway. Two sets of headlights. I watched as a van and a black Explorer pulled up. Four men climbed out of the van, one from the driver's side of the four-wheel drive, leaving the engine running.

"Your ride," the cleaner declared as he rounded the front of the vehicle before heading to the rear of the van in front of him.

I didn't speak, just took my place behind the wheel and waited for Colt to climb into the passenger side. I'd send the crew a text where they could pick it up at a later time. After they were done with the bodies, that was.

"I want to be there when she gets home," Colt muttered, then glanced my way. "I need to see her."

I winced at the desperation in his tone. I should've expected it. The way he fucking fought for her was like nothing I'd ever seen. My heart thundered as I pulled the four-wheel drive onto the road, headed across the city toward the house, and shifted in my seat.

Because the truth was…he wasn't the only one who'd turned savage for her. We *all* had, and I didn't know how to deal with that. I grabbed my phone, punched the number, and listened to it ring three times before it was answered.

"It's me," I started. "Is the team in place?"

I could hear the thud of heavy boots before Hunter answered. "All good on our end. I have a team of six men at the house and four more on standby. If they're going to attack, it won't be tonight."

I gave a nod. "Good. We'll be there soon."

The rest of the ride was in silence. We both knew what kind of war waited for us. It was a war we'd been preparing for our entire lives, ever since London carried two broken and bleeding young boys from that place after having made a deal with the devil herself.

Any other time, I might've welcomed the war…craved it, almost. I winced, shifted gears, and glanced into the rear-view mirror for anyone following. But there was a shift inside me. A clarity that hadn't been there before. One where I was aware I could lose everything…

Vivienne's brown eyes rose inside my mind, and my pulse picked up in response. I tried to shove her away as I pulled the four-wheel drive into the driveway and stopped. Colt glanced my way. He didn't say a word. One look said it all.

"I'll be back later," I muttered, shifting my gaze to the armed mercenaries now patrolling the grounds.

He climbed out and shoved the door closed harder than normal. He was pissed. He should be. *Hell, I was pissed, and I was me.*

Still, I shoved the Explorer into gear and punched the accelerator, swung the car around and headed for the warehouse. By the time I got there, my mood hadn't improved. If anything, it'd darkened. I parked the Explorer out front and texted the cleaning crew the address. The vehicle would be gone by sunrise, as well as the bodies and the blood we'd left behind.

I made my way through the coded locks on the warehouse door and went inside. Cars, guns, walls and walls of information and a goddamn cold room, of all the fucking things. I glared at the thing, then turned and hit the overhead lights.

That icy tremble came out of nowhere, the same one I'd felt at the orphanage and the same one I'd felt tonight. I turned and scanned the space, but found every gun in its place. Still, there was *something*. I stepped forward, my senses screaming as I tried to find what felt *wrong*.

I couldn't see it. Couldn't get a fix on it. *I couldn't…*

Reflex made me lower my hand to the knife tucked into my belt. But the moment I did, I saw it…a knife, driven hilt deep into the drywall. I didn't put it there. I *swear* I didn't put it there. But they had not impaled it for nothing. It was pinning a card to the wall.

I gripped the handle and wrenched it free. It wasn't my blade, nor was it Colt's. The white card dropped to the bench, its belly torn free. There was a name of a bar on one side. I caught the writing before it landed on its front…the writing on the back face up for me to see.

We want the daughter.

Sons.

We want the daughter? *We want the daughter?* That chilling rage swept through me as I picked up the business card and stared at the address. I knew what that cold was now, that stinging rage in the pit of my stomach when I stood at the edge of that hell last night, and I knew it now.

It was fear.

SIX

Vivienne

LONDON PALED IN FRONT OF ME AS HE LOWERED THE
phone in his hand.

"What?" I whispered, lifting my gaze.

"London?" I heard his name come from the other end of the
line.

But he didn't answer. He wasn't speaking at all. Just pressed his
thumb against the screen and ended the call. Those dark eyes
fixed on Daniels. I'd never seen a look so...*murderous*. Daniels
felt the full force, taking a slow step backwards, past Jack and
deeper into the darkness.

"You're to keep him in your sight at all times," London said
slowly, his tone devoid of emotion. "I don't want a damn hair on
his head harmed. Do I make myself clear?"

"Yes, sir," the guard murmured behind him.

One slow nod and London responded. "Good, because I want to
be the one who makes this motherfucker scream and beg for his
life. If anyone robs me of that, I'll gut them where they stand."
He glanced at Jack. "Jack, we'll have you out of here and back in

your own room as soon as we can get the mess cleaned up and the problem fixed."

Jack's stare was stony, never once taking his eyes off me as he answered. "Take your time."

I licked my lip and winced. My damn head was pulsing and howling, but it was nothing compared to the punishing agony in my eye.

"You should get that looked at," Jack spoke, his voice full of concern.

I lifted my head, finding him through the slit of my eye. "Yeah, maybe," I answered as London turned, glared at Jack, then shifted that stare to me...and winced.

"Let's go." He nodded, lifting his hand to the middle of my back.

I stole one more glance at Jack, lingering for a second. A tremor tore through me, stealing my breath. Was it the fact he was my only contact with Ryth that nailed me to the spot? Or was it something else...some kind of ache that fluttered in my chest.

"Vivienne," London urged, his hand forceful on my back.

I didn't have time to put into words the chaotic mess inside my head. I let London guide me out, taking one last look over my shoulder at the man who watched me with a careful stare, until the guard closed the door, locking Jack Castlemaine inside once more.

"Are we going home?" I asked, my steps fast under London's guiding hand.

"No."

I scowled. *No?* "Then where are we going?" I demanded as we went back along the hallway to the foyer of the storage yard.

"To see a goddamn doctor," he growled.

He never spoke to the guards again, not even a bark of a command. Just...*nothing*. I resisted, pulling away with a jerk the moment we were out of the building. "Hey!"

London kept walking, the heavy *thud...thud...thud...*of his steps echoing in the night.

"HEY!" I barked. He stopped, freezing with his back to me. Anger burned as I closed the distance. "You don't get to do that...not with me."

He spun and leveled that dangerous stare on me. "I don't get to do *what,* Vivienne?"

"Freeze me out." I stepped around him until he had no choice but to give me his undivided attention. "You don't get to do that, London. You don't get to be all up *here.*" I tapped my finger in the center of his forehead *hard.* Hard enough to shove his head backwards.

I doubt he'd ever been stabbed by a finger in the middle of his head in his entire goddamn life. But he had now...

His brow creased as his lips twitched. There was a flare of anger, one he quickly swallowed. Because it was me, right? Still, I waited for the bark of anger, or for him to grab me and haul me inside the car. He did neither. Just stared down into my eyes and said carefully. "What would you like me to say?"

"Oh, I dunno," I growled, wincing at the goddamn sting in my lips. "How about, *are you okay?* How about we start with that? I mean...*Jesus,* London. You could show me you at least care *a little bit, can't you?*"

That fucking twitch came at the corner of his eye. Christ, he was a cold sonofa—

"You think I don't care that you're hurt?" he said carefully as he took a step forward, then another, forcing me backwards until I hit the rear of the car. "You think I can look at your face and not want to destroy the whole fucking world?"

My breaths were hard, my pulse even harder, shuddering. This wasn't what I—

He leaned down, those bottomless eyes staring all the way into my soul. His tone was low, husky and unmerciful. "You think I wouldn't love to turn around, walk back in there, and put a bullet into that lowlife motherfucker?" Torture crossed his face. "I want it so much I can't think straight. I can't — I can't get it out of my head. I want to tear him apart. I want his blood on my hands. I want *all* their blood on my hands. I wanted to tear the entire world apart when they took you from me. I would if I could. I'd torch it all until there was only you, me...and the sons left."

I tried to swallow the lump in the back of my throat, but it wouldn't go down.

"So when you ask me if I care, then the answer is yes, Vivienne. I care very much. I care...too much."

Too much?

That tremor in my chest was full of shudders. Did London St. James just tell me he loved me?

"So right now, we're going to get into that car and drive out of here. Because if I'm here a second longer, that's what I'll do. I'll walk back in there and make good on my promise. I'll kill Daniels...I'll kill him and then I'll start killing all of them and I won't stop. We *all* will. There will be no end to this carnage, you understand that, right? You understand that once we start there is no stopping and, once we do, then we've lost the opportunity to find them. All the men who run Orders of their own. All those *daughters* out there. Ones who have no protectors. Ones who have nothing but terror and despair. Those are the ones who stop me from unleashing all the wrath I have burning inside me. They are the ones who keep me from ending it all right now."

My heart lunged, slamming against the confines of my chest.

"So, now you know," he murmured, his gaze boring into mine.

"Now I know," I repeated.

Some part of me reeled with the level of his aggression...and obsession with me. And, another part—the part that had *needed* that level barely an hour ago, howled with satisfaction.

"Are you ready to leave?" he asked and even that sounded awkward for London.

He asked no one. But he asked me...

My chest swelled with the heady rush as I nodded. "Yes."

"Good." He stepped around me, headed to the passenger door, and opened it. "Then get in, so we can get the hell out of this place."

I did, sliding slowly into the seat and waited for him to lean down and tug the seatbelt across. Dark seduction washed over me. I inhaled the scent of him, letting it flow through every inch of my body. What if what Daniels had done changed me? What if just the thought of London, or Colt, or even Carven, touching me was too much to bear? Would they discard me? Would they take me back to The Order?

I closed my eyes, letting the fear ripple and find a hold as the belt clasp went *click.*

"Vivienne," London's deep, throaty tone hit me like a sledgehammer.

I opened my eyes to find his stare and I didn't know why I'd even thought I'd feel anything different as the tsunami hit me so hard it snatched the air from my lungs. An ache bloomed in my chest as I met his stare. "Yes?"

"You're mine, Wildcat. Never forget that."

Then he pulled away, leaving me aching for the brush of those hard lips on mine, and closed the door. I watched the movement as he headed around the car and climbed behind the wheel. The car started before we backed up and made our way out of the gate. London reached into his pocket and pressed a button, letting it ring through the speakers of the car.

"You're alive, how disappointing," came the voice on the other end of the line. My breath caught at the snarl, watching London as a roar of agony came from the background, loud enough to boom through the car, before it slowly died away.

"Where are you?" London growled.

"Why...don't think you're bringing anymore of your goddamn mess to my door."

London's hands clenched around the wheel. "Address, doctor," he forced through clenched teeth, staring at the road ahead. "Don't make me ask twice."

"*Fine*," the dead man snapped. Because if he wasn't before, he was about to be. No one spoke to London like that. "I'll text it to you," he muttered as those screams of agony came once more in the background.

I fixed on that howl as I realized. That was Guild...*that was Guild.* I snapped my focus to London as the call went dead. Two seconds later a message appeared on the screen.

London hit a button, turning the address into a map on the screen. I was pushed backwards into the seat as he punched the accelerator, taking us through the city streets as we followed the directions.

"Stay close to me." I turned my head and met his gaze. "I don't trust anyone who isn't us," he added. "Not tonight."

I gave a small nod as he pulled into the driveway of a small brown brick house at the end of a cul-de-sac. I barely saw the damn thing, let alone the streets that led us here. Second by second, my eye was closing, leaving me without a good eye and a thumping headache.

London pulled the car up against the house and climbed out, taking his time before opening my door.

"We're heading around to the back," he urged as he watched the street before turning back. "Take my hand."

I did, sliding my fingers between his like it was the most normal thing in the world, until a flare of jealousy rose. How many other women had he held like this? How many lovers had he taken care of?

My steps stuttered, pulling away from him. Please don't tell me it was her...that fucking *bitch, Ophelia.*

Anyone else but her.

Anyone else—

"What is it?" Panic deepened his snarl as London turned to me. My heart thundered so fucking much, my whole chest hurt. No matter how hard I tried, I couldn't shake that consuming wave. I doubled over, unable to catch my breath as thick tears slipped from one eye and oozed from the other.

A cry tore free.

Cruel.

Stinging.

Like someone had reached into my chest and ripped my heart free. "Y-you...you and *h-her*," I blubbered like some love-struck teenager and lifted my head. "You...you and her."

Torment filled those eyes, just a taste of the pain he gave me.

"That's all behind us." He dropped my hand to cup my face with both hands and gently tilted my gaze upwards. "You hear me? That was done before this night existed. There's only us now. Only *us*."

I tried to hear the words.

I tried to swallow it down.

But I couldn't seem to let it go, even when my knees buckled.

London was there, catching me before I hit the cold concrete path. Strong arms lifted and carried me around the edge of the building toward the back door. *Thump!* He kicked the door and the sound of heavy footsteps followed. The door was yanked open. I barely caught the darkened, blurred outline through the sheen of my tears before we were striding inside without an invitation.

"Jesus Christ," the doctor muttered. "In here."

London never said a word, just followed the guy into a room that was toward the back of the house and eased me gently onto a table.

"What the fuck happened to her?" The bark came with a tiny *click*.

Bright light blinded me. I let out a moan and shied away, hiding the tears that ran down my cheeks.

"You really are a bastard, aren't you, St. James?" he snarled, turning off the light. "Easy now. I'm not going to hurt you. I'm a doctor."

"I know," I answered, then slowly turned and lifted my head until I found him through the slit in my eye. "And this wasn't London, so you can stop the tirade."

He stilled, then slowly straightened, his focus fixed on me. "Okay, want to tell me what happened?"

"Would you believe I slipped?" His lips flattened and his jaw clenched, the muscles flaring. "I guess not," I muttered. "Let's just say London didn't do this. He saved me from the assholes who did."

There was a second where I didn't think he was going to believe me. But then he slowly exhaled and his tone became a little softer. "Then how about we lay you back so I can get a good look at you?"

My body trembled, shuddering with the quakes that gnashed my teeth. Still, I gave a nod and gripped the edge of the table. The doctor helped me, easing me down until I lay flat. London's jacket rode up, revealing Colt's t-shirt I wore.

The doc took one look at that and froze for barely a second before he turned around and grabbed his stethoscope. "Want to give us a little privacy?" he sort of ordered.

"No," London answered, forcing the doctor to meet his stare.

He fixed those dark eyes on mine. All I saw was loyalty and pain...and a dangerous desperation that made a shiver tear through me.

"Not a request," the doc pushed. "Besides, you can see to your buddy."

"Guild?" I turned toward the hallway.

"Don't *you* worry about him," the doc urged. "Right now, your focus is on yourself. London will check on Guild. God knows it looks like you both have had a helluva night."

"You can say that again," I muttered, licking my lip at the fresh sting.

London's phone gave a *beep*. I knew instantly it was one of the twins. "Go," I murmured. "I'll be okay."

He didn't want to leave, I knew that, knew it by the stubborn scowl that settled on his face until a low moan came from out in the hallway.

"London," Guild called.

"Go," I ordered. "I'll be fine."

He left reluctantly, but not before he gave the doc a look that spoke volumes...volumes of violence, that was.

"Looks like you have a fan," I groaned, shifting against the hard surface under me.

"Lucky me." The doc turned and went to work, shining the light in my better eye once more, before forcing my other eye open and pressed his fingers against the agony until I hissed. "It doesn't appear to be broken. But you have some pretty severe hemorrhaging."

"Lucky me," I repeated.

He didn't flinch, didn't stop. Just started from the top, finding each gash in my scalp before he worked his way down, lingering on the bruises on my arms before asking. "Do you feel okay with me pulling up your shirt?"

I gave a slow nod. His fingers didn't linger, his focus was fixed on my injuries alone. I waited for the revulsion of his touch. But the man was so damn respectful, only probing what he needed to check my injuries. I turned my head as he probed my belly, crying out and stiffening when he found the deepest of my pain.

"I need to ask," he breathed, his tone commanding my gaze. "Were you sexually violated?"

My pulse thundered, smothering out the sound of advancing steps. But I held his stare and slowly shook my head.

I don't know if he believed me. I didn't have a chance to find out. The doc pulled the shirt down, covering me as best he could as London entered the room. Those dark eyes missed nothing, fixed on the doctor's hand as he moved from my thigh to around my back, helping me to sit up.

"When can Guild leave?" London's voice was threatening.

"A gunshot like that? A week. He needs medical care, London."

"He needs to get back to work." London fixed his stare on me. "Can you give her something for the pain?"

The doc didn't like the intrusion one little bit. "Of course."

He moved, stepping to a counter on the other side of the room and reached into a glass cabinet, rifling through it to pull out a vial. Not once did London look away from me. There was no softness in his stare, no flicker of embarrassment. Just that savage glare that turned to the doc as he handed me a couple of white pills. "These will help the pain. They might make you feel a little drowsy, but a good sleep is what you need right now. That's if she's safe..." He aimed that last part at London.

"Vivienne," London said carefully. "How about you wait outside for a second while the doctor and I have a word?"

"How about no," I answered, knowing full well only one man would make it out alive if I did that, and it wouldn't be the doc.

"It's fine." The doctor held London's stare while I slipped from the bench and my feet hit the floor.

I left them to their pissing contest and headed out with the pills in my hand. I didn't search for a drink. Instead, I slowly made my way along the hallway to the doorway of another room...and to the man who'd risked his life to save mine.

Guild glanced my way. His eyes widened for a second as a look of anguish hit home. "Jesus, Viv." He shoved upwards, rising with a wince and a guttural snarl.

His chest was bandaged, his arm strapped across. I stared, then slowly lifted my gaze. "Will you be okay?"

"Better than you, by the looks of it." He reached up, yanked the electrodes from his chest and cast them aside, before he stumbled toward me. "Fuck, they did a number on you." He gently grabbed my chin, tilting my face.

"It looks worse than it is," I mumbled.

"I doubt that." He released his hold, the concern in his eyes hardening. "Are they dead?"

"All but one."

He scowled. "Who?"

"Daniels."

He swore under his breath and took a step. "Where the fuck is he?"

I grabbed him when he wobbled. "Wait. He's...he's in London's storage unit."

Guild stopped, grabbed hold of the doorway and met my stare. "He's keeping him alive?"

I nodded. "He needs him."

He searched my gaze, fixed on the swell of my eye. "Not that fucking much. I'll kill him myself."

"Like hell you will," London barked from outside the door as he stepped into the room.

He took one look at me before turning to Guild. "Good, you're up. We can get back to the house."

God, he was an unfeeling bastard. So fucking cold, all the way to his core. Still, he held out his hand for me. "Vivienne."

I shook my head, but it was useless fighting him. It was useless fighting either of them. Guild followed with a steely determined stare as London took my arm and led me to the rear of the house.

"*Wait!*" The doc pushed through the door behind us.

His expression was thunderous, narrowing in on London. "You can't do this."

I watched him over my shoulder as London dragged me out of there, never once stopping.

"*Think of the goddamn complications!*"

"I am," London growled as he rounded the car to the passenger side, opened the door, and ushered me in.

Guild climbed into the back, grunting with pain.

But it was the doc's stare that gripped me as London climbed in behind the wheel. Because he wasn't staring at London anymore...he was staring at me.

"What complications?" I asked as London started the Mercedes and backed out of the driveway. "*London.*" I jerked my gaze to him. "What complications?"

SEVEN

Carven

I TYPED OUT A MESSAGE:

Status update?

Then hit send.

I didn't look up, didn't focus on anything other than the screen as I waited. I didn't have to wait long.

Beep.

London: Heading home now.

I typed again:

I'll be back later. I have something I need to take care of.

I waited a second after the screen died before I moved, lifting my gaze to the darkened alley on the seedy west side of the city. The business card buckled in my fist as I clenched. I didn't need to read the words because I'd engraved them into my mind.

We want the daughter.

I clenched my jaw, shoved open my door, and climbed out of the car. They could want all they wanted. I was here to give them an answer…son to son. I closed the door and locked the car behind me as I headed to the address printed on the card. It was some kind of cannery that'd long gone out of business and was now used for illegal rave parties the cops stayed far away from.

I headed along the alley to a steel door. Movement came from the corner of my eye as a big dude slid from the front of a black Mustang.

"Looking for something?" he inquired.

"Yeah." I held up the card. "This. Know it?"

He barely glanced at my hand before he stepped toward the doorway, turned the handle and yanked. Hinges squealed as the door opened and the heavy thud of the music spilled out.

"Good luck," he muttered as I stepped in, leaving him to close the door behind me.

I didn't need fucking luck. I needed a goddamn shower and a solid eight hours of sleep—I scanned the darkened warehouse of packed partygoers, finding a DJ standing on a podium up front, waving his hand like a damn idiot as he blasted some heavy metal track through the speaker—I wouldn't find either of those here.

I kept my focus on those around me as panicked thoughts tried to push in. *How the fuck was I supposed to find some jackass in here?* Some asshole shoved into me. I jerked my gaze toward him, finding a stoned-out stare before I shoved the bastard back, watching him topple and disappear amongst the head-banging bodies once more.

Think…

My pulse thundered, driving that frustration deeper. *Fuck.*

I couldn't get a handle on this, not after the fucking night I'd had. My fingers were still bloody, my mind still dialed into the need to *hunt*.

Until the slamming bodies and the guttural screams faded away.

That's it...

Hunt.

Instinct took over, dulling everything else around me. I didn't care about the rave or the music. I didn't care about anything but that honed hunger inside me. The one which wanted me to strangle, shatter...and gut every motherfucker around me. I stopped walking, staring at a point straight ahead as I sank into the darkness.

I wasn't like them. I wasn't like any of them. I was broken and rebuilt...*different*.

Not just a hunter...or a killer. I was a fucking machine. Cold. Empty...detached. My brother and London were the only two people in existence who made me flick the switch to human. Right now, I needed that emotionless part of my nature more than anything. It was that coldness I turned to...that cruel part of my nature that took over, leaving me to scan the blurred faces of the lambs all around me.

I was a hunter now...only it wasn't *them* I hunted. It was my own kind—*a son*. I turned away and kept on walking. He wasn't out here, not amongst the drugged idiots sweating and sleeping, oblivious to the war waging around them. I headed to the rear of the old warehouse.

The darkness called me.

Hidden.

Quiet.

That's where I'd find him.

Because that's where I'd be.

I pushed forward, sinking down into the dark depths. My strides lengthened. Shoulders hunched slightly. My eyes low, scanning those around me as I slipped along the side of the podium. The DJ turned his head, finding my gaze before he scowled and looked away.

He should...

His music was shit.

Another bouncer stepped out of the crowd as I neared the rear door. One glare and he gave a jerk of his head. I knew the drill by now. Not that it'd help them. I stopped in front of him and lifted my arms. The pat down was fast, finding nothing. The bouncer nodded, stepped aside, and opened a door behind him.

I stepped in and closed the door behind me, finding dark murky lighting and a makeshift bar filling the space. I sensed the son the moment I stepped in, cold, secretive, his gaze narrowing in on me like a laser.

Careful gazes cut my way. Silas Ares sat at a small round table in the middle of the room, eyefucking someone in the corner before he turned to me.

We weren't friends. Fuck, we weren't even allies, but he gave a slow, careful nod, acknowledging me. I returned the same before movement came in the corner of my eye and, what do you know...Nathaniel Wolf made his presence known.

He took one glaring look at Silas and chuckled.

Silas paled, and rage cut across his face before he winced. Then he rose, grabbed the bottle of Scotch, and pushed past, shouldering Wolf hard as he went. I stepped around them. Their bad blood was their bad blood. The last thing I needed was to get involved. I'd spilled enough of the shit just keeping my family safe.

My thoughts turned to *her*. The reason for all of this.

London should've never brought her into our home.

He should've never—

Carven! Her cry invaded my mind as I stepped around the table and made my way to the bar. *CARVEN!*

My damn pulse thundered with the sound as I pulled out my wallet, slipped a twenty on the bar and gave a nod to the grungy fucking asshole who grabbed a glass and poured.

I didn't give a fuck about the drink. I was here for a different reason.

I turned and scanned the shadows that clung to the edges of the room, finding other familiar faces. Lazarus Rossi was there with some gorgeous redhead. He watched as I scanned her and moved on, feeling not even a flicker of interest. Instead, it was Wildcat that filled my head, remembering the way she'd covered my brother's body with her own when I'd burst into that changing room when we'd come under attack.

It was always her...

Always fucking her.

I grabbed my glass and drained the Scotch as some asshole rose from the far end of the room. My senses came alive. Goosebumps rose, the hair standing on the nape of my neck. I scanned the rest of the room as the guy slowly made his way toward me.

My heart thundered, booming in my ears as he slid his empty glass along the bar in front of me, chewing a toothpick in the corner of his mouth.

"Carven," he said carefully, and the panic grew until it was screaming inside me.

I searched the bastard's face, trying to find a flicker of anything familiar. But there was none. He was older...older than us, hard jaw, the same cold, deadpan stare.

"The daughter," he spoke quietly and casually as the bartender took his empty glass. "I want her."

I clenched my jaw and waited for him to meet my gaze. "Not going to happen," I answered.

All I could see was Colt as he'd fucked her. My brother was involved. *Very...fucking...involved.* That was the only reason I slowly rose from my seat, standing face-to-face with the motherfucker.

He leaned close to murmur against my ear. "It will if I say it will. She doesn't belong to you."

My heart punched against my ribs as that unmerciful need for blood rose. "You think she belongs to you?"

"She's a daughter, isn't she? They *all* belong to me."

He straightened, meeting my stare as I answered. "Good fucking luck getting this one."

A slow nod and he took a step backward. "Around you, or through you." He gave a shrug. "Makes no difference to me. One way or another, the daughter will be mine."

My breath caught as cold plunged through me. I wanted to stab the motherfucker. I wanted to stab and keep on stabbing until there was nothing left, but the moment he moved, so did another, stepping from the shadows behind me.

My pulse thundered as he followed the first asshole toward the door. Then another at my side moved, pushing off the wall.

Jesus, I'd never even seen him. He was nothing but shadows... shadows with that bleak, vacant stare. One that fixed on mine before he turned and went to the door.

That chilling fear swept through me.

It wasn't just one Son who was after Vivienne...*it was three.*

Three cold, fucking killers.

Around you or through you. Makes no difference to me.

We were in trouble...big fucking trouble. I knew that now. If we lost our daughter again, it would devastate Colt and London—a pang tore across my chest as her face filled my mind—yeah, they'd be fucking murderous.

I didn't wait, just pushed forward and strode toward the door.

"Carven." Someone called my name. *"Hey!"*

But I didn't stop, I didn't even slow. I just yanked open the door and plunged into the crowd and the music once more—desperate to find those who wanted to take what was ours.

EIGHT

Vivienne

THE SIDE OF MY FACE THROBBED, DRIVING PUNISHING blows through my head until I thought it was splitting apart. I cupped my cheek as Guild and London went at it. I winced at their roaring.

Any damn moment London was about to explode. When it did...it was going to be bad.

"You can't be serious," the bodyguard muttered as we pulled into the street where we lived.

My heart boomed, driving home the punishing blows in my head.

"You're really taking her back here? For Christ's sake, London. *It's not safe!"*

London cut me a glare. I saw the movement, but I couldn't look at him. I was frozen, as one hand gripped the door handle and the other clenched around the seat next to me.

"I don't fucking run." London turned back to the street, slowing the car before we pulled into the driveway. "Not from them.

Not from *anyone*. The moment you do, you're dead. You know that."

That was all he said as he killed the engine.

"You *don't run?*" Guild grunted as he shoved open the door, carefully following London out of the car. "*You. Don't. Fucking. Run?*"

Boom!

The door slammed closed behind me. I winced, holding onto my head as London rounded the car and opened my door. "That's what I said." He held out his hand for me, those dark eyes fixed on mine. "I stand and fight."

London held onto my hand as I climbed out. I knew what he was saying. I saw it in that dangerous, dark stare. He was going to war over this...he was going to war over me.

Hunger bloomed like a deadly rose inside me. If London St. James was a dangerous man before...he was about to get a lot worse.

"Take a goddamn look. *There's no fucking door!*"

But London didn't say a word. His stare was a heavy weight on my shoulders as I made my way toward the house. The moment I neared, memories slammed into me and terror followed. My steps stuttered and my breath caught. All I saw was the busted open door and the blood that seeped into the concrete path leading to the front steps. All I saw was death.

"She can't stay here, London. You know that," Guild urged, coming up behind me.

But still, I forced myself to walk. I'd been through worse, I reminded myself...*much worse.*

I swallowed hard and forced myself past those splattered crimson stains as London snapped. "The safehouse hasn't been checked. I can't be sure that's safe. So where the fuck do you suggest we go, The Four fucking Seasons?"

My fingers shook as I gripped the doorway and stepped inside. But it wasn't a foyer covered with Guild's blood I saw...it was Colt striding down the stairs carrying two bags that looked like they were stuffed...*with my clothes.*

He dropped them at the entrance with a *thud,* next to two others stuffed with the same, before he met my gaze. My body trembled at the sight of him. Tears welled in my eyes.

"What the fuck is this?" London growled behind me.

I lowered my focus to the bags, then to the quiet resignation in the son's stare.

"Her things, by the looks of it," Guild commented. "At least *someone* gives a shit about protecting her."

In the corner of my better eye, London cut him a deadly stare. "You're lucky you're wounded, or I'd shoot you myself."

I took a slow step forward, finding pink chiffon and black denim sticking out of a half-closed zipper. "These are all my clothes."

Colt gave a slow nod.

Those piercing blue eyes searched my face as I spoke. "And none of yours."

He scowled, then slowly shook his head, as though it hadn't occurred to him he'd need them.

"You did all this for me?" I croaked.

Desperation fluttered as he took a step closer and lifted his hand to skim his thumb across my cheek. I winced at the throb, hating it when he pulled away. But he grabbed my hand, gave London a glare, then gently pulled me with him.

We made our way upstairs with me holding onto the railing, wincing with every step. But I forced myself to move until I stepped onto the landing, stared at the open door of my bedroom, and froze. Hours. That's all it'd been...hours since I was in there, tucked in my bed, trying my best to sleep off the hell we'd endured from the attack at the shopping center.

Then it all hit me.

With a thunderous, heart-shattering roar.

A wounded sound tore free as my knees buckled. But I didn't hit the floor. Strong hands grabbed me. I was lifted and pulled against a powerful, warm chest and I turned my face, pressing my agony against his strength. My arms went around his neck as my silent captor moved, carrying me into my room. He held me, not wanting to let me go...not just *yet*.

I clung to him, holding on like he was my life raft in this unmerciful sea of terror, until his quiet voice broke through.

"Vivienne."

I trembled and shook, unable to do anything but fall into the chasm of despair waiting for me.

"Vivienne."

The deep, dulcet tone made me lift my head. I opened my barely functional eye, finding him blurred behind my stinging tears.

Those dark blue eyes gripped mine. "We don't do this," he murmured.

"Do w-what?" I forced around the boulder wedged in the back of my throat.

"We don't lose ourselves."

I stilled, my heart hammering…trying to process his words.

"We might shatter…" His thumb caressed my hand as he lifted it and turned it over. "We might break." That gentle touch skimmed the gash across the middle of my palm. The gash I'd received when I'd wielded the broken mirror like a weapon. "But broken pieces cut too."

My body shuddered as my knees locked in tight.

"They cut, baby," he urged. He lifted his focus to me. "They cut so fucking deep, especially when we sharpen them."

What was he trying to say to me? I tried to find meaning between the shudders. He turned his head to the clothes laid out on the neatly made bed. Clothes meant for me. *Because we were leaving…*

Just like Guild said.

We were leaving this house, and we weren't coming back.

"W-where?" I whispered. That word burned like fire in the back of my throat. Those edges were cutting alright…only they were cutting *me*. "Where will we go?"

Colt gave a slow shrug, those perfect lips curling. "The Four fucking Seasons sounds nice, doesn't it?"

I let out a ridiculous bark of laughter. Still, it was like those edges finally cut right through, breaking me away from the heavy weight of fear. I surged to the surface, kicking and clawing, the weight of all this falling away as I finally broke through.

I inhaled deeply, swallowed the air, and exhaled hard, finally understanding what Colt meant.

I was the honed edge.

I was the weapon.

I was the thing they'd tried to destroy.

But they hadn't, had they?

Because I was here. I was right fucking here, staring up into those endless dark depths of those knowing eyes. The eyes that shimmered with depths. I wasn't drowning anymore. I was carried, swept away in the current of his love. My pulse thundered as that rushed through me.

Those hard shudders eased as Colt leaned forward and gently, without touching me, kissed me. I closed my eyes at the warmth of his lips and under the rush came the need that burned like fire in my veins. I surged forward, wrapping my arms around him tight, pressing my body against his until I ached.

I didn't care about the pain.

Not anymore. Instead, I welcomed it.

He never touched me, never wrapped those powerful arms around my body to pull me in tight. He let me take what I wanted, sliding one hand until I cupped the back of his neck. That familiar hunger rose with it. My mouth opened, the kiss deepening. He gave me everything, without lifting a goddamn finger to touch me. It both infuriated and drove me wild and, with a low, guttural moan, I broke away.

His perfect lips were reddened and parted, that ravenous stare fixed on me. But still, he didn't speak, leaving me to glance at those clothes lying splayed out on the bed once more. "The Four fucking Seasons, huh?"

The moment I said the words, I knew that's what I wanted. I'd never been to a fancy hotel, never sashayed through a foyer with men turning to stare at me. I'd had nothing for me in my entire life. Everything I'd ever experienced was at the hands of, and controlled by, men.

A movie rose inside my mind. My favorite movie of all time. One made especially for me, even if it came out years before I was even born. As I looked at those clothes on the bed, I relived that movie. I was *that* Vivienne, courted by Richard Gere with beautiful clothes and a whole new life laid out neatly in front of me. I was that woman whose life was suddenly filled with potential.

My broken nails ached. My body still trembled and hurt.

But it didn't have to be this way.

I didn't have to succumb to the pain.

I undressed and dropped London's jacket to the floor with a soft *thud*, then I pulled Colt's shirt off, wincing with the ache in my breast as I dropped it as well. Pink panties lay neatly in front of me. I reached out, lifted them from the bed, and slid them on. Black jeans and a thick blue turtleneck sweater were next. By the time I tugged on my boots and straightened my spine, I felt *better*.

Colt had known exactly what I needed, even if I hadn't. "Thank you," I whispered, listening to the growls and snarls from London and Guild filtering up from downstairs. "Thank you for saving me...*again*."

He gave a slow nod and smiled.

That smile was *everything*. I channeled that inner Vivienne and headed for the doorway, leaving my bedroom behind. I made my way back down to where Guild and London were locked in a glaring competition, with neither a clear winner.

The moment I came down, London turned to me. "The Four S-seasons." I ignored the tremble in my voice. "I'd like to go there now."

He didn't speak, just searched my eye, then gave a slow nod. "Guild, I want the men close. By close, I mean camped on our fucking doorstep." He swung his gaze to the mercenary.

"She'll be protected, London. You have my word on that. I'll have the rest of your things packed and sent ahead to the safehouse," Guild acknowledged.

"Thank you," London answered carefully as he lifted his hand to the small of my back. "Vivienne."

The heavy thud of footsteps rang out in the night as we headed back to the car. London opened my door and waited, but before I eased back in, I stilled, lifted my gaze to his...and slid my hand along the back of his.

He was so damn stubborn, unmovable.

I knew he didn't like this.

Then I slowly sank, leaving him to close my door behind me.

Colt was silent as he climbed into the car. London followed, sliding behind the wheel and starting the engine. With my two protectors, we backed out of the driveway and left the only place that'd ever felt remotely like my home behind.

It was early, still dark, when we headed into the city. London watched the rear-view mirror like a hawk as bright lights of the late-night clubs drew my gaze as we passed. Colt was still behind me. I didn't need to turn my head to know his gun was in his hand.

Because we still couldn't trust the night.

Maybe never again.

London turned the Mercedes into the driveway of the Four Seasons and pulled up hard. "Keep close, Vivienne," he murmured and cracked open his door.

I glanced at the sparkling bright foyer and my stomach dropped. "Wait."

I met his gaze, shook my head, and lifted my hand, touching my swollen, throbbing eye. "I can't...I can't go in there like this."

He shifted his gaze to the nearly empty foyer of the hotel, then leaned toward me, hit the button on the glove compartment, and pulled out a pair of aviator sunglasses. "Here."

I stared at the glasses. "Won't they stare?"

"Not if they want to keep their jobs, they won't."

NINE

Vivienne

Headlights splashed along the expensive hotel's
driveway as I climbed out and glanced behind me at a dark
sedan as it stopped behind us. London adjusted his jacket and
glanced its way as he rounded the car and placed his hand
carefully against my back. "It's okay. They're here for us."

My pulse sped...of course they were.

I swallowed, trying to work some moisture into my mouth, and
gave a nod. We were protected...within an inch of our lives.
Hadn't stopped them before, though, had it? London's hand
against my back guided me toward the towering glass doors as
he watched the street.

No, it hadn't stopped them.

I only hoped Guild was right, that The Order wouldn't come for
us, not out in the open like this. The trunk closed with a *thud*. I
jumped at the sound, still hearing the *boom* of the metal coffin
closing over me. Colt was two steps behind us as we made our
way inside, the dark sunglasses dulling the sparkle of the lights
in the foyer.

I tried to keep my panic under control as the desk clerk raised his head, smiled, then took one look at me. The smile died instantly. Still, he held his composure and turned to London instead, who slid a credit card across the desk. I glimpsed the name printed on the front, it sure as Hell wasn't London's. "Whatever you have available."

"Sir..." he gave a careful nod but glanced my way once more before he started typing. "Let me have a look for you. It is rather late."

"I'm well aware of the time."

He winced at the edge in London's tone. "Of course you are, sir. My apologies. It seems we only have one opening, the executive suite."

"I'll take it."

"At five thousand dollars a night," the clerk continued. London said nothing, just held the poor guy's stare until he paled and reached for the card. "I'll have someone come for your bags."

"No need," London murmured. "Just the key is fine."

The guy hurried, punching London's details into the system as he gave them. I risked a glance over my shoulder and saw Colt standing right behind me, watching the glass walls and the world outside until he turned back to me.

"There you go," the clerk murmured as he handed over two keycards. "Please enjoy your stay at the Four Seasons. If you require anything—"

"We will let you know," London finished for him as he slid his hand against my back once more. "Vivienne."

I let him steer me toward the elevator, not feeling the *Pretty Woman* vibe at all. Instead, this felt more like *The Bodyguard.* The elevator doors closed in front of me and the shine of the steel triggered that panic all over again, until Colt brushed my arm with his.

The movement was subtle. With London's sure hand at my back, it spoke volumes. I was safe with them. I was protected. Only it made me think of Carven...*where was he?* The doors opened with a whoosh. Colt left my side and stepped out first, one hand gripping my bag of clothes, the other a gun, one I hadn't even seen him grab.

London waited for a heartbeat before he followed. Surely The Order wouldn't be so fucking bold. As soon as the thought rose, I knew it was a lie. Of course they were that bold...because they were desperate.

Colt turned and met London's gaze as we stopped outside the white double doors. One swipe of the card in London's hand and he pushed through, urging me forward. I lowered the dark sunglasses as I stepped inside and stopped in the middle of the entrance.

"Oh my *God.*"

"God has nothing to do with it," London muttered, stepping past me to head toward the wall of windows. "It's money, Vivienne, pure and simple. Money and power, that's all."

Money and power. That's what I was looking at now. The door closed behind me and I turned to give Colt a grin that stung like a bitch. "It's stunning."

He grinned right back and giving me a nod toward another set of closed double doors at the end of the expansive living room. Elation punched through me as I hustled forward, wincing at the pain. "I call shotgun on the master bed!"

London turned from the glittering city below as I hobbled for the doors, turned the handle, and pushed through. Colt just, stood outside and watched me, grinning like an idiot as I took in the massive king-sized bed and the surrounding room.

For a second, I felt like *her*.

The other Vivienne...

And not me.

I stumbled forward, clutched my side, and launched myself into the air to hit the comforter with a *big oof!* It was like diving headlong into heaven. I landed on a soft pillow and slowly sank down. Colt placed my bag on the foot of the bed and just watched me as London's deep snarl filtered in.

He was pissed.

Growly.

Demanding.

Cruel.

But I didn't let that touch me, not now...not here. I rolled and stretched as far as I dared until that throbbing ache inside me grew fangs, then I pushed upwards and froze as I caught sight of the mammoth open bathroom. Even in the dark, I saw it. Hulking, dark...*magnificent*.

I pushed, slid off the bed, and went to the doorway before I reached inside and hit the switch. The lights didn't just come on...*they caressed.* Dark amber stone, with a bathtub the size of the Grand Canyon. I stepped inside and stopped at the edge, trying to think if I'd ever sunk into something so glorious.

"I want it," I declared. Colt was in the doorway. "I want *that*."

A nod, and he came toward me, bent down, flipped the drain lever closed, and turned on the faucets. Water rushed from the waterfall spout at the end and soft lights lit up behind it, making it look like some private rock pool. I kicked off my boots, then slowly tugged off my sweater and dropped it beside the tub.

Colt watched me carefully while London's growl continued in the other room. I tried to ignore him, just slid down my jeans, but stopped. "My bra," I sighed. "I can't reach—"

He stepped close. Gentle hands worked the clasp of my bra, then slowly slid the straps down my shoulder before his lips followed. I closed my eyes at the brush of his lips, listening to the cascading water in front of me. The rush and the kiss were an anchor I held on to.

My bra fell to the floor and the soft graze of a curled finger skimmed my side until his big hand closed around my hip. He was so quiet. If it wasn't for the slide of his fingers under the edge of my panties as he dragged them down, I'd never know he was here.

I opened my eyes and turned to meet those blue eyes.

"Fine, Ares. You want to meet, then let's meet," London's voice growled outside the bedroom. "You knew one day there was a damn chance of this. I told you once before I'm not here to pick sides. Fine...*I said, fine.*"

The shine dulled.

The warmth grew cold.

Still, I stepped out of my panties onto the floor and lifted my foot to test the warmth before I stepped in and sank down. A moan tore free, soul-deep and aching, as I closed my eyes and sank back against the molded headrest. "This," I whispered. "I would kill to have this."

"Good," London grunted, making me open my eyes to find him standing over me. "By the time this week is done, I'm sure we'll kill for less."

If it was anyone else, I'd have thought they were joking. But there was no amusement in London's tone and after the night we'd just endured, murdering for a bath wasn't out of the question. I held his stare as I let the warm water lick my breasts until my nipples pinched tight.

He stared.

My breath caught.

The slow rise of his chest made my pulse skip.

"Vivienne," he murmured, then met my gaze. "I need to ask... did they, when they took you? Did they—"

I looked away and curled my shoulders as I covered myself with my arms. "No," my voice was cold, emotionless. Christ, I sounded just like him. "They didn't, but they intended to."

The powerful chest sank with a sigh. "That's good. That's... really good."

"No shit." I held myself tighter as I watched him turn and walk away.

I lay there while the water lost its warmth and the hotel room lost its gleam, and all I wanted to do—all I *craved* to do was forget tonight ever happened. I just wanted it over...I just wanted it—

Thick tears flowed once more.

I pressed my fingers against my swollen eyes as Colt's words rose...*we don't do that. We don't succumb.*

I may not succumb, but that didn't mean this didn't hurt like hell. I dragged the washcloth along my arms and watched the dried blood splatter melt away, until my skin was red and the scratches no longer stung. By the time I climbed out, my tears tasted like water and I felt like I could sleep like the dead.

I tugged on the thick bathrobe hanging behind the door and climbed into the expansive bed all on my own, robe and all. The lights were out in the living room. The tiny *clink* of a glass echoed. I knew he was out there, sitting in the plush lounge, drinking Scotch and scheming.

Always scheming.

My eyes closed on their own as I lay down against the soft pillows.

Clink.

I exhaled, sighed...and drifted.

GET OFF ME! *NOOOOO!*

I jerked upwards, heart pounding, a scream trapped in the back of my throat. All I saw was the darkness. The cold, empty darkness. With my pulse thudding in my ears, I lifted my hand and reached out with trembling fingers, expecting to touch metal.

But I didn't touch metal...I touched nothing.

Nothing...

I curled my fingers and my shoulders with it. I was alone...my body shuddered as grief savaged me on the inside until I saw it... the shadow at the foot of my bed. Thick shoulders, head tilted as he stared toward the quiet living room.

Colt.

I slid over the side, my body shaking and fear trapped like a boulder in my chest, and stumbled around the bed to face him. Steel gleamed in the moonlight, bouncing off the shotgun lying across his lap. Silently, he stared straight ahead, then slowly turned and lifted those blue eyes that looked almost black to me now.

"Colt…" His name ripped from me. "I—I…"

He slid the gun from his lap and rose, coming soundlessly toward me. I lurched forward, slammed into him, and buried my face against his chest. His strong arms wrapped around me, but then he bent and placed the gun within reach on the bed.

We said nothing.

Because no words were needed.

I lifted my head to his, sliding my hand along his neck until he tilted his mouth to mine. I ignored the stinging of my lips as we kissed, until the memory of cold steel filled me and the *bang* when they'd trapped me inside the metal box followed. Panic thundered through me like a freight train as I pulled away enough to whisper. "I need you…Colt, I need you."

His hands fell away, then he bent, lifted me, and carried me back to the rumpled sheets. My robe parted as he eased me backwards. One slow swipe of his hand and the tie unraveled, leaving me bare to his gaze.

"They didn't…" I started before my throat closed.

He lifted his head. Shadows and sorrow were all I saw.

"They didn't—"

He shook his head. "It wouldn't matter," he whispered. "You're mine, anyway." A quake tore through me as he lowered his head, kissed between my breasts, and moved upwards. "All mine."

I slid my arms around him, closed my eyes, and narrowed in on the feel of his lips and his body. His big hands slid along my body. I was safe here. Safe with him…my silent protector. As that realization hit home, the walls I'd built inside me came crashing down.

There was only him.

Only this…

Us.

He lifted his head and rose to tower over me. One glance at the gun on the foot of the bed, then to the quiet living room, and he moved to drag the weapon closer with one hand and reached over his shoulder with the other to drag his shirt off.

I stared up at him, then ran my hands over the thick ridges of his stomach muscles until I touched the scars. He stiffened and watched as I stopped. The tips of my fingers skimmed the thick, raised edges that glimmered pale in the night.

"Mine," I declared, and rose to slide my hands down to cup his ass through his jeans. "All mine."

Pain fused us together.

Terror and The Order.

I kissed his healed wounds and took my time to feel every inch of him as I worked the button of his jeans before I reached in. He closed his eyes and dropped his head back. This powerful, deadly male was throbbing in my grasp. Even after all I'd endured, I still wanted him…

I wanted all of them, maybe more than ever.

Memories rose swiftly to fill my head. But this time they weren't the cruel, confining terror of being trapped in that steel coffin… they were him. The way he'd launched himself over the sofa toward me. The way he'd beaten a man to death with his bare hands.

I cupped his cock and lifted my gaze as he met my stare. So silent. So utterly silent. His lips parted. The rush of his breath was loud in the space between us.

"Wildcat," he whispered.

He spoke...this silent protector spoke...

For me.

I slid my hand free so he could ease back off the bed and push his jeans low. He kicked off his boots and shed the rest of his clothes until he stood naked in front of me, with thick, powerful thighs, the hard ridges of his abdomen, and a chest you could lay your head on and sleep forever.

Only sleep was the last thing on my mind—he stepped closer, climbed onto the bed, and pushed me back down—and it seemed like it was the last thing on his mind, as well.

He lowered his head, his mouth finding the peak of my breast. I lifted my hand and cupped his face. I needed this...to touch and be touched. I wanted to drown myself in him, in all of them. Anything to push the events of tonight back into the darkness of my mind where they belonged.

He crawled higher and bent his head to kiss me softly. Warm lips claimed me. His gentle hand pushed me backwards.

"Let me take care of you," he murmured, his tone husky.

My body trembled as I slowly nodded, and he sank lower. I lifted my gaze to the ceiling, shoving away Daniels's ugly fucking face when it rose.

And softly...a hum rose in the air.

The sound pulled me from the memory and made me look down.

Throaty, gentle, the faint sound drifted from him as he ran his hand over my thigh and leaned close to kiss my mound.

"What are you doing?" I whispered as I glanced at the darkened living room. "You'll wake London."

He stopped humming long enough to answer. "No, I won't. He's not here."

Not here?

He focused again, his hand insistent as it parted my thighs. That sound continued and drew my focus to him and away from the terror in my head. I guess that's what he wanted. My pulse skipped as I glanced toward that dark living room.

"You worry too much." Colt grazed the back of one finger along my slit. "Do you think we wouldn't protect you?"

That pounding in my chest grew louder as I turned back to him.

"Protection and revenge. That's all that drives us now, Wildcat," he insisted, and pushed my legs wider apart to kiss the top of my slit. "All there is for us now."

Because of me.

And what they'd done.

He lifted my knee and lowered his head to lick my core. I unleashed a moan and slid my fingers through his thick hair. He licked, slid his fingers along the outside lips of my pussy, and rubbed me until that heat quivered.

His warm tongue slipped deeper and the tip danced around my clit as he rubbed and rubbed. We'd done this before, he and I, my virgin protector who'd had to be shown what to do. I dragged my teeth across my lip and this time, I relished the sting. He didn't need to be shown now.

I lifted my head and watched as his finger slipped into my crease to follow the slick trail his tongue had left behind. His hands slid under my knees and lifted, as he tilted my hips to meet his mouth. His deep blue eyes were fixed on mine as he sucked my clit.

He liked to watch me, those ocean-blue eyes twinkling as I dropped my head back and closed my eyes. I gave in to him, his hunger, his desire...his love. Urgency thrummed in my veins, then spiked as he pulled away and rose upward, the blunt head of his cock pressed against my entrance.

I wanted this.

I wanted him.

I wanted to forget everything else existed.

As he pushed, sliding the thick head inside, everything else disappeared.

"Mine," he groaned as he slid back out, then just barely eased in and out, stoking the fire. *"Mine."*

The word resounded as my throat thickened and ached. But this wasn't a time for tears or heartbreak. This moment was for us. Nothing touched us here. Not pain or terror, not The fucking Order. I lost myself in the rush of desire and answered. "Yours... all yours."

And he thrust and drove all the way inside. I bucked with the force, and held on to him. My hands skimmed over the hard muscles of his arms, which flexed as he held his weight and slammed his hips against mine. Even though my eye was terribly swollen and the entire side of my face was darkened with bruises, he still looked at me like I was the most beautiful woman on Earth.

I didn't need a movie to make me feel pretty.

I sure as hell didn't need Richard Gere.

I had everything I wanted right here.

With them.

Colt lowered his head and kissed me before pulling out and sliding back down. I lifted my head, concern flaring. "It's okay. You don't—" His mouth met my clit as he sucked and replaced his cock with his fingers. "Oh my *God.*"

My legs widened on their own, my body trembled for a whole other reason, and it swept me away in the rush. Like a defiant reflex of its own, that desperate need for release slammed into me. I cried out and my body jerked as I came hard against his mouth.

With a threatening-sounding snarl, Colt rose swiftly, and his lips glistened with my release as he drove his cock home once more. I unleashed a moan as I pulled him down to kiss me. Slaps of flesh filled the room. He was thunderous as he threw his head back and unleashed a guttural sound as he came...hard.

Warmth spread through me. Deep breaths consumed me as Colt slowly met my gaze and eased out of me. Those dark blue eyes twinkled as he fixed me with a look that sent a charge of worry through me. "You okay?"

"I..." he started, then pulled away enough to sit on the bed beside me. "I think I might love you."

My pulse skipped...*then thundered.*

"You do?"

He gave a careful nod and dragged his fingers through his hair. "Yeah. Is that going to be a problem?"

I swallowed as my heart swelled with desire. I could barely speak as I answered. "No. That will not be a problem at all."

One thoughtful nod and my silent protector slid from the bed, grabbed his clothes, and pulled them on. In an instant, he changed right in front of me as he morphed from my lover to my guardian once more. He grabbed the shotgun from the bed and pushed his feet back into his boots as he looked down at me.

I saw that love now.

Maybe I always had.

"Sleep, baby," he murmured. "I'll keep watch."

TEN

Vivienne

My belly snarled, low and demanding, dragging me from the darkness. I cracked open one eye to the spill of soft sunlight around the edge of blackout blinds. For a moment, that's all there was, nothing but that hint of daylight. Hope waited with it. Until a deep throb in the side of my face made me wince...and in an instant, the terror of the last twenty-four hours came flooding back.

The mall.

The attack in the dressing room.

And the abduction.

I closed my eyes with a shudder. My throat thickened and forced me to swallow. *Bang!* That clash of steel echoed in my head. I dragged my knees higher and curled my body as the memory of their hands followed, clawing me...*pawing me,* until my belly growled again, only louder this time, and I smelled food.

I lifted my head and pushed upwards. Through my better eye, I stared at the open bedroom door and the glimpse of the living room before I glanced at the foot of the bed. Colt had been there last night, sitting and watching—protecting me. But he wasn't there now. I scanned the room. He wasn't anywhere.

I pushed the covers aside, slid out of bed, and retrieved the robe from where Colt had dropped it. The silence in the apartment was deafening. The pounding of my pulse drove through me as I tugged the tie around my waist. Had they left me? Had they...

Been killed?

I stumbled forward until I stopped two steps into the soft white living room and stared at London, who sat on the sofa. His legs were crossed, one arm was casually lying along the back of the sofa. Those dark, unflinching eyes were fixed on me.

He slowly turned his head and motioned to the cart against the counter in the kitchen. "I figured you'd be hungry, so I took the liberty."

"You seem to do that a lot," I grumbled as I glanced toward the food. From the corner of my eye, I saw him smirk. I ignored that as I looked at the bedroom opposite mine, with the double doors open and the room silent. "Where are the others?"

"Busy."

The way he said it made the hair at the nape of my neck stand on end.

"I bet they are," I muttered. Busy spilling blood, that is.

I was so hungry, the smell of bacon was nearly overwhelming. I moved carefully over to the counter and lifted the cover before I picked up a plate and turned to him. "Are you not eating?"

The corners of his lips twitched. "I ate hours ago, Vivienne. The food is for you."

I grabbed the last two pieces of bacon, bit the end of one and headed back to take a seat on the sofa opposite him. My robe gaped as I flopped down, opening to expose my thigh and breast. I didn't cover them. He'd seen it all before. *Touched it and kissed it too.* Hunger glinted in his eyes, only it wasn't for the food that was piled on my plate.

He wanted me. Even battered and bruised, he still wanted to take me down to his basement and fuck me with his machine. Only he didn't need to do that now, did he? Because there was no contract stopping him from taking me whenever and however he wanted.

London St. James was the one I ran to.

They all were.

His gaze skimmed my breast, then lowered to my bare thigh, and to the diamonds that glinted around my ankle. Diamonds he'd bought for me.

I tore the bacon in half and chewed, relishing his attention just as much as the food. "So, what's the plan?"

"You mean, apart from finding the name of every person who betrayed me and slaughtering them?"

I stopped chewing as the bacon turned dry in my mouth. I swallowed again and again, forcing it down. "Yeah, that."

"Then my *plan* is to make sure you and the sons are safe the only way I know how."

I didn't have to think hard. "King?"

He gave a slow nod as his attention lowered to my bare breast. "King."

I shifted and opened my thighs. "You still think that guy is the way to end all of this?"

He was silent as I bit off part of the last piece, my hunger returning with a vengeance as I did. He uncrossed his legs and rose slowly, moving with the grace that made me feel so insignificant. Because I was insignificant in London St. James's shadow...*everyone was.*

He was the man who was an enigma, holding more darkness and power than flesh and bones should allow. He took a step closer and loomed over me as he stopped beside the sofa.

Just for a moment, I wanted to know what was behind that bottomless stare. Just once, I wanted to taste his soul. He reached out and brushed his curled finger along my jaw. "You know everything I do is to keep you safe, don't you?"

My breath stilled as my pulse leaped.

I searched that callous stare, but found no trace of a smile. Because his words weren't meant for comfort or joy. His words were threatening, the kind that should terrify his enemies... because they terrified me.

Still, he held my stare. "Don't you?" he urged.

I swallowed to wet my mouth and answered. "Yes, Daddy."

One slow, careful nod and he glanced at my plate. "After you're finished, you'll need to shower and get ready. We're leaving."

"Leaving?" I repeated as he turned and adjusted his jacket as he headed for the hallway. "Where?"

He didn't answer, just left me with the soft thud of his footsteps until the sound of a door opening came. I rose and followed, sliding my plate onto the counter. Voices spilled out before the door was closed once more, leaving me out of whatever they were planning.

That spark of anger rose, but it was quickly snuffed out as a deep throb came at the side of my face, reminding me what this was for.

You know everything I do is to keep you safe...don't you?

Those words haunted me as I turned away from the hallway, my gaze moving to the plate still piled high with food. My belly clenched with hunger, but it was a sickening hunger, until the ache moved lower, blooming low down in my abdomen.

I winced and caught my breath as that pain expanded. "Great," I growled. "As if this day can't get any damn worse, now I get my period."

A throb came in my cheek, hurting like hell as it hit home. I was going to get my damn period...confined with three goddamn controlling assholes and I had no necessities. I scanned the room and found a beautiful ornate wooden desk at the far side of the living room, with a phone sitting to one side.

I fixed my robe and crossed the space, picked up the handset, and called the number listed for the reception desk. I spoke fast when it was answered, giving instructions for the things I needed and how I wanted them wrapped before I hung up. One embarrassing conversation over...now for another goddamn battle. I steeled myself and made for the other bedroom door.

"This is dangerous territory." London shook his head as I yanked the door open. "The last thing we need is to piss Dante off, so we listen to his thinly veiled threats before we go to—"

Carven swung that savage glare toward me, fresh blood splatter marking his face. "Need something, *daughter?*"

I flinched at the sting of his tone and my cheeks burned. *What the fuck had I done now?*

They all stared. Colt, London...and Carven. Especially Carven.

My face throbbed, my belly hurt, and now rage bubbled up as I glared back at him. Still, I bit down on that anger and forced my words through clenched teeth. "I have a package coming up from downstairs. Would you let them in?"

"Package?" Carven snarled as he turned to face me. "What kind of *fucking package?*"

Christ, there was blood *everywhere,* splattered across his shirt and up his neck. I froze, fixed on that gruesome mess, until I looked away. "That's *none* of your business, is it?"

"None of my—" Carven lunged, but he was stopped by Colt's hand on his arm before he shook his head.

The sight of him fuming suddenly made me feel a lot better. "Be a good *son* and let him in, will you?"

He unleashed a growl and yanked his arm from Colt's hold before he stepped closer. Those blue eyes chilled me as he leaned close. "You better be worth it." He sneered. "Because if *daddy dearest* doesn't want you, we're as good as dead. You get that, right?"

My world narrowed into that second. To the rage in his eyes and the hate in his tone. His words had no trace of love, not that I expected any from Carven. "What is he talking about, London?"

I turned to the only man who wanted me to call him *daddy* and searched his gaze.

"Nothing," London snarled and cut Carven a glare. "Nothing at all."

A pang ripped across my chest as I remembered it had been *Carven's* voice I'd heard as I fought. His voice that drove me to kick and fight even when hope had gone. The threat of tears shimmered as London gave a slow shake of his head.

"Carven," London warned. "That's enough."

I didn't look away, just gave a slow nod, riveted by the power of his hate. My chest was a wall of fire as I croaked. "No, it's fine. I know where I stand."

Those piercing blue eyes widened, taking in every flinch, until I turned and headed back through the door. The moment I closed it behind me, the tears came sliding steadily down my cheeks.

I swiped them away and cursed the ache in my belly, and not just for the pain. I hated being emotional. Hated it more now that I lived with the most callous fucking assholes God ever put breath into. I clenched my jaw and headed for the bedroom, tearing the robe off before I stalked into the open shower and hit the faucets.

A sob resounded in my chest, burning like a brand. I touched my breast and the cut underneath but my fingers came away bloody and I washed it away in the shower's stream. I hurt... Jesus, I hurt. Warmth spilled over the ache of my body, plastering my hair to my face. I faintly heard a sound coming from outside the apartment. But I turned around, shielded my tears from them, and set to work pulling myself together.

By the time I'd washed, I was better. My face still throbbed, but I could open my eyes a little wider, enough to see a bit more, at least. I stepped out, avoiding the mirror for as long as I could, until I raised my eyes to the reflection and took a good look.

My breath caught as the world stood still.

"Jesus," I whispered as I gently probed the deep purple bruise that spread across the side of my face.

My damaged eye was bloodshot, and my lower lip was a damn mess. I looked like I'd been in a car wreck. It was the only answer I'd want to give, because the truth was too fucking terrifying to believe.

I took my time drying my hair, then applied what little makeup I could and headed out to the bedroom. Clothes were laid out neatly on the foot of the bed, just like always. I jerked my gaze to the living room, but heard no movement.

I dressed in the clothes he wanted, neat black slacks and a high-necked bronze cashmere sweater, with a soft black bomber jacket lying next to it. The boots were carefully chosen and stunning. I tugged them on, zipped them up midway along my calf, and rose from the bed just as pain tore across my belly.

The wave of agony rocked me. I clenched my jaw and hunched over for a minute, then stepped into the apartment to find the package wrapped in plastic waiting for me on the kitchen counter. I grabbed it and found the end torn open, with the contents exposed. "Motherfucker." I lifted my gaze, picturing Carven's eagerness to tear my shit open. "Is nothing fucking off limits here?"

Well, I hoped it was worth it. I was about to make his goddamn week miserable. I strode back into the bathroom, inserted a tampon, and stowed some in my purse before gathering my things. Nothing was private with them, not even my goddamn menstrual cycle.

The apartment door opened, and the thud of footsteps headed my way. London was first, instantly scanning my clothes before he lowered his gaze to the purse in my hands. He glanced at the counter. "I see you found your package."

Heat rushed to my cheeks. Great, so they *all* knew now.

"Yes," I forced through clenched teeth. "You can tell Carven—"

"It wasn't Carven."

I froze, my mind racing. "You?"

Of course it was him. Why wouldn't it be? He knew everything else there was to know about me. Why should my bodily functions be any goddamn different? Goddamn men and their fucking needs. They wanted to pluck at my edges and tear me apart. They wanted to shove their greedy fingers and hungry tongues into the very center of me just to find out what made me shudder and tick. I hated them for it and craved them all at the same time.

He searched my eyes. "Ready?"

"Yes," I snapped. *"Thank you."*

One careful nod and Colt came closer and gave me a soft smile before he grabbed my things and carried them with him as he turned toward the door.

"Vivienne." London held out his hand.

I took one look at the offer and walked right past him, my head down and shoulders hunched, and headed for the hallway. I steeled myself and yanked open the door, expecting to walk right into a wall of hate. But Carven wasn't there, just Colt as he headed for the elevator and London behind me.

I followed Colt, my pulse thrumming furiously.

"Head up, Vivienne."

I jerked my gaze to London. His long strides made little work of the distance between us. "What?"

He met my gaze. "Always walk with your head up, watching everyone around you. Meet their gazes. It makes you less of a victim."

Victim.

The word hit me like a blow. My steps stuttered and my shoulders curled even more. He stopped and came closer to stare down at me. "No one will ever try to take you again," he murmured. I saw it now. Under the mask, he was scared...no, he was *terrified*. He lifted his hand and that curled finger lifted my chin. "Never again. Do you understand me? *Never...again.*"

The faint *ding* of the elevator sounded, and we were alone. I gave a slow nod.

"So, you'll walk with your head up, aware of your surroundings at all times. You'll lengthen your stride, with your shoulders straight. You'll look every motherfucker in the eyes, and be the woman no one will dare touch ever again, not unless you want them to."

"Why are you telling me this now?"

He searched my gaze, then lowered his hand. "Because we're about to walk into a fucking lion's den, pet. I need them to not only see you as a warning for what happens to *anyone* who touches what's mine, but to see that this didn't break you, it only strengthened you."

I wanted to tell him that was a lie.

That inside I was on very shaky fucking ground.

"Because you are stronger for it. Look inside, find the fury. Use it to rebuild yourself into a goddamn force."

I inhaled and dragged his words deep into the clinking pieces of my shattered spirit. I found that taste of rage, that seething hunger for retribution.

"I'll be right beside you," he added. "Every step of the goddamn way."

I gave a slow nod as he motioned toward the elevator, and this time, when I took a step...I straightened my goddamn spine.

ELEVEN

Vivienne

LONDON'S AVIATORS WEREN'T DARK ENOUGH OR BIG enough to hide the mess of my face. Nothing was, but they would help shield me from the scrutiny we were about to endure as the elevator doors to the Four Seasons foyer opened and the rush of voices spilled in.

I automatically turned my head to shield myself, until the soft brush against my arm stopped me. London adjusted his jacket before he placed his hand on the small of my back. In an instant, he changed. There was no hint of the smile he'd given me or the gleam of amusement that had been in his eyes when I'd snapped back at him. No, this wasn't the private London, this was the cold, merciless male, the one no one would dare to cross. Not without consequences, at least...

As those who'd taken me were about to find out.

He met my gaze.

Raise your head, Vivienne. His words resounded in my head. I had no choice but to obey. Spine straight, hands by my sides, I stepped out to match his stride. Heads turned our way as we headed for the front doors. Men watched him with envy.

Women glared at me with jealousy. I didn't glance their way just walked through the open glass doors into the pitch-black night to the waiting Mercedes and climbed inside.

London hadn't been joking when he said we were protected. A black Explorer idled in front of us and another waited at the rear. Not to mention that somewhere around here Colt and Carven watched every move we made.

Muffled voices drew my focus. I turned my head and watched London out the rear window as he rounded the car and climbed in the other side. A lion's den, that's what he'd called the place we were headed to. I could tell he was nervous as he stared straight ahead. That alone made me nervous too.

"Who are these people?" I asked as we pulled out and headed east.

"Someone you don't want on your bad side" he answered carefully.

Dante, that's who he'd said. I wondered how he fit into all this.

"What did Carven mean before…when he was pissed? He said, I'd better *be worth it* and he wasn't talking about the money you paid for me either, was he?"

He didn't look my way. "Nothing." He shook his head, staring out the window. "He was out of line."

"Out of line maybe, but he wasn't lying. Not like you are now."

Only then did he meet my stare. "This isn't the time, Vivienne."

There he was, chastising me like I was five. I wasn't five. It was about time he started treating me like I was one of the team. "Fine."

"Fine," he repeated.

"But just so you know, this conversation isn't over, not by a long shot. I *will* figure out the truth."

His brow rose. "Will you?"

"Yeah," I said, finding a little more defiance than I'd thought I was capable of.

"Then I'll look forward to the challenge."

A charge of excitement filled me, and the heat of desire followed. This, whatever this was between us, wasn't over, not by a long shot.

Beep.

The sound of his phone ruined the moment. He held my gaze and reached into his pocket before he looked down.

"Problem?" I asked.

"Nothing I can't handle," he answered as he typed and hit send. "When we get to this house, I want you to stay right by my side, Vivienne, and try not to...piss anyone off, okay?"

Jesus, he said it like I always rubbed people the wrong way. But his tone was deep and careful, because he was *being* careful. Who the hell were these people, anyway? The thought stayed with me as we rode in silence, allowing me to watch the city give way to houses until we took a turn and slowed.

Men leaned against beefed up Camaros and other sports cars and watched us as we passed. I stared back, taking in the glint of expensive watches around their wrists before I turned away. Quiet streets and neat houses gave way to more opulent playthings. Maseratis, Ferraris, and Lamborghinis sat parked out on the streets.

"Jesus," I whispered, and lifted my gaze as the car slowed and turned into another quiet street.

A brown brick Tudor mansion sat at the end of the cul-de-sac with a gleaming black Bentley parked in the drive and an Audi behind it on the street.

Our driver slowed, then pulled into the driveway and stopped as three men stepped out, each carrying a semi-automatic weapon. Two moved in, but they didn't open our doors and usher us inside. No, they extended a pole attached to a mirror to check under the car. Barely a few seconds later, the one in charge stepped toward the front and gave a nod, allowing our driver to get out and open London's door.

"Stay close," London murmured quietly to him. "You know what to do if this goes south."

The driver glanced my way. "Yes, sir."

What? I wanted to ask. What was he to do? Only I didn't need the answer, did I? I saw it all in the way London, Colt, and Carven protected me. I knew if it went south, the driver would get me out first. For a second, I didn't want to move, frozen by fear and apprehension, until I met London's stare and he lifted his hand for mine. Trust drove me out of the car.

Trust and love. It was all I had now.

All I fought for...*and all that fought for me.*

Doors closed behind us with *thuds.* But I was already lifting my gaze to the opulent, ivy-covered home. Twisted black wrought iron grates covered the windows and doors. I took it all in, from the concrete path to the immaculate hedges of the garden filled with thick white gardenias that perfumed the air with the most beautiful scent. It was all so...*beautiful.* Beautiful and deadly.

Movement caught my eye from a window on the top floor. Soft sheer curtains moved as I followed London along the side of the house until I lost sight. More men with guns waited at the back.

My pulse sped at the thought that if this went south, there was no way London could get us out of there alive.

I glanced his way but found that mask firmly in place as the back door of the house was opened by a guard. "He's waiting in the sitting room. I trust you know the way?"

London gave a nod. "I do."

His grip tightened around mine as he stepped through. The last thing I wanted was to remove the sunglasses, but the moment we stepped into what looked like a mudroom of the lethal kind, I felt the need for as much visibility as I could manage. Guns were fixed against the walls, a lot of guns.

My pulse beat louder at the sight before we left the room behind and headed along a wide hallway. Exposed dark brown slate and black iron were the common theme as we stepped into a massive room with a carpeted wooden staircase that swept upwards.

I lifted my gaze, my mind returning to the movement in the window above. But we'd moved along before I could dwell on whoever it might've been. Two men dressed in black suits stood in the middle of the hallway, watching us as we neared. One motioned for us to enter a room to the side.

The sitting room they called it? It may as well be a house inside a damn house. High, exposed-beam ceilings drew my gaze upwards. There was so much to take in, from the multiple bookshelves that towered higher than anyone could ever reach to the enormous lush rugs my heels sank into as I followed London inside.

"Dante," he murmured beside me.

"London," the husky growl came from a high-backed leather sofa in the middle of the room. "Nice of you to come."

His stare fixed on us as we neared before he slowly rose, then stepped forward and reached out his hand. A lion's den. That's what London had called this place. If this was a den, then this man...Dante was the lion.

He was older, the same age as London maybe, but where my captor-turned-protector was cold, unemotional, and refined, this man was a barbarian. Battle-scars marred one side of his face, cutting through the eyebrow before ending with a jagged mess under his eye. Dante looked like a man who'd fought for everything he had...I looked around at the opulence of this place —which meant he'd won a lot of fights.

"I appreciate the invitation," London lied beside me. "I'm sure the last thing you wanted was me taking up your time."

The *lion* smiled. "Not at all." But the smile never reached his eyes.

Instead, he swung that gaze my way, cutting right through me to scan the room behind us. It was as though he didn't see me, like I totally didn't exist. Maybe I didn't to a man like him?

"The sons?" Dante asked, that scarred brow rising.

"Right behind us." London answered, holding his stare.

The thud of footsteps rose before the low mutter of the bodyguards in the hall. Carven's glare swept the room first before moving to Dante. But as he came closer, he flicked that menacing stare at me.

"Ah, here they are," Dante nodded. "The boys said they'd noticed you around."

London said nothing, leaving Dante to smile at the lack of response before waving to the doorway. "Silas."

From the corner of the room came a man who was the spitting image of a younger Dante. One who was tattooed and scarred.

He strode in wearing black jeans, a black t-shirt, and a stony stare that descended on Carven.

"I heard you're moving into the Parker Street residence," Dante said.

"Yes," London answered. "Is that going to be a problem?"

I had no idea *how* it could be an issue. Surely someone living in their own house wasn't against the law?

"Not a problem at all," Dante responded, that dangerous gaze shifting my way before returning to London. "I just like to know what mess is landing on my doorstep, that's all."

I understood this play now. London's safehouse was in this guy's vicinity and so this was what? A reprimand...*a warning?*

"If you think your presence here is going to influence my standing or threaten my family, then we're not going to be very neighborly, if you get what I mean?"

So this *was* a threat.

London stiffened and the room seemed to plunge in temperature, raising the hairs on the back of my neck. London inhaled hard. This was going to be bad...*this was going to be—*

"Dante!" The cry came from somewhere in the house, tearing through the sitting room to make the man in front of us take notice. His breathing deepened as his head turned toward the sound. In the blink of an eye, a woman came rushing into the room, her floor-length yellow dress billowing behind her and her eyes alight with satisfaction. "We *got it! We got the VAN GO—"*

Her eyes widened the moment she saw us. Her steps slowed as she glanced from London and the Sons back to the man who was obviously her husband. "I'm sorry." She shook her head, her cheeks reddening. "I didn't realize we had company."

But Dante wasn't angry at the interruption. Instead, his lips curled into a grin filled with pride as he chuckled and held his arm out to her. "It's fine, honey. An informal chat is all."

Another woman entered from same direction. Only, this one was quiet and careful, slinking into the room behind the woman who still beamed. But she looked nothing like the woman she followed. Maybe she was an assistant, or a niece? Someone close...but not blood.

The closer she came, the more clearly I saw her. She was my age, maybe a year or two younger. Long caramel-colored hair fell in soft waves. She was beautiful...stunningly beautiful. But she was also frightened.

She fixed her gaze on me. The longer she stared, the bolder that charge of panic grew.

My pulse thundered.

My world narrowed in on those faint green eyes and cautious stare.

I knew her somehow...

"I apologize anyway. I was just so excited," I woman gushed. "I've been in a damn bidding war for the Skull and Cigarette for the past five years and we finally won."

"Congratulations, Meredith," London murmured, giving her his best grin. "That is quite a feat. Not even I would attempt something like that."

But it was fake. It was all fake, wasn't it? Everything but the threats. No, those were very real.

"Thank you." She smoothed down her yellow dress, as her gaze moved to mine.

But I couldn't look away from the woman at her side as Meredith stepped forward, cutting off my view. "I don't think we've met."

"My apologies." Dante placed a protective arm around her waist. "Meredith, baby, this is London St. James."

Her eyes widened before she caught herself, then glanced my way. "Nice to meet you," she said carefully as she reached behind her protectively for the young woman's hand. "My daughter, Angelica."

Only then did it hit me.

I knew her...*I fucking* knew *her.*

I turned my head as London stepped forward and took her hand. My pulse was booming, my mind was screaming. There was something wrong here. Something very...*very wrong.*

He knew. I didn't know how he did, but he turned and motioned Carven forward. "My sons, Carven and Colt."

The moment Meredith's focus was elsewhere, London looked my way. He saw it all, the catch in my breath and the way I was transfixed. Carven played the game as he came closer to step in front of London and shake her hand as Colt hovered closer to the doorway. If they noticed his reluctance, they didn't say a word.

"Nice to meet you," Carven muttered. "I'd introduce you to my brother, but he doesn't speak."

"Oh." Meredith's eyes widened. "Not at all?"

Carven shrugged. "Sometimes, he's just very selective."

She looked at London, then at me. "That's strange."

"Angelica." Carven extended his hand. "I wasn't aware you had a sister, Silas."

"I don't," the tight-lipped son answered, his attention fixed elsewhere.

There was rage in his eyes and hate in his tone. Not once did he look at her, neither him nor Dante.

"Angelica is adopted," Meredith added, her cheeks flushing red.

It hit me...*adopted...adopted...just like Ryth.*

London shifted closer, sliding his fingers along my arm, his touch whispering *easy...*

But my mind was racing, replaying every second of that hell called The Order. I knew I'd seen her...I was *sure of it.*

Meredith knew, too, her face paling as she took in the way London touched me before she turned to her husband and beamed. "Honey, I think I'll leave you to it. Angel and I have a lot to prepare."

Dante was oblivious to whatever had just happened. He'd hardly spoken since his 'daughter' had stepped into the room. Whatever went on with them, there was definitely no love lost between them, and suddenly I wanted to remember just where I knew her from.

But I didn't have time to ask either of them before Meredith stretched up and kissed her husband on his cheek, then reached for her daughter's hand and slipped toward the door.

While London stepped closer to Dante, I watched them. Before they disappeared through the doorway, Angelica turned her head and her gaze found mine. And with a careful shake of her head, she mouthed the word, *Please...*

London's low chuckle spilled out. "You've got your hands full with that one."

Dante grinned and shook his head as his focus moved to the paintings that adorned the sitting room walls. With a wave of his hand, he muttered. "A goddamn Van Gogh, London? The woman is going to send me broke by the time I'm forty."

"I doubt that very much." London shot me a cautioning glance, that intense stare had missed nothing. "It'll sting a little, but for a smile like that, it'll be worth it."

I pulled away from the banter and glanced toward the door where the two women had left. Carven strode forward but left Colt behind. It was as though I didn't exist, as though *none* of what just happened existed. I glanced at Colt. But he wasn't there.

He was gone...

Disappearing without a sound.

That icy shiver raced along my spine as I turned back to the men, my mind racing. Why would London willingly step into the lion's den and bring us with him?

What game were we playing here?

And what were the stakes?

I turned to that empty doorway as my belly sank.

Whatever they were...they weren't good.

TWELVE

Colt

———

The guards glanced at me, then looked away as I headed for the hallway. Their focus shifted back to the ones who mattered, the ones they saw and heard. I was nothing, silent, invisible, and not a threat.

I kept my head down and walked slowly, catching movement up ahead. Theo Ares strode along the hallway, his black tuxedo jacket hooked around his finger and slung over one shoulder. Not even he saw me. But I sure as hell saw him.

Bloodshot eyes.

A faint dusting of white powder on his top lip.

He lifted his gaze the moment he sensed me, that raw stare narrowing in. "What the fuck are you doing here?"

I said nothing, just stepped to the side to pass, until the asshole grabbed my shirt, fisted it, and shoved me against the wall. "I said, *what the fuck are you doing here?*"

His focus narrowed as he searched my eyes, then shifted to my hair. I said nothing, just stood there. Not a threat, remember?

"You," he slurred, leaning closer.

I smothered the urge to wince and turn away. He stank of sweat and sex and god knew what else he'd gotten up to last night.

"You're the mute, right?"

I scowled.

"Yeah, the fucking mute Son." He shoved me, releasing his hold as he looked back to the hallway.

The faint sounds of London and Dante drifted in from the sitting room.

"Figures," he muttered, his lip curling. "It's all bullshit anyway. Fucking bullshit, the lot of it."

His eyes glazed for a second before he suddenly saw me again. "Want a drink? Of course you do, we *all* fucking do. Come on."

He gave a jerk of his head and stepped away, heading toward the other side of the massive house. I followed, because that's what ghosts do. We wound up at a darkened den. Amber lights glowed as he stepped inside and switched on the lights.

"I'll get a fire started."

I said nothing, just hovered near the armrest of the black leather sofa, taking in the doorway at the far end of the room. A desk sat behind us. I glanced at Theo, crouched over the fireplace, before I turned to that desk and the paperwork spread across the surface, trying to narrow in on the words printed on top.

"As it we don't have enough fucking trouble? Goddamn Wolf up our ass. They're gonna go to war, you get that, right? Fucking Wolves. Motherfucking bastards."

I turned back as he tipped, falling face first into the goddamn fireplace as he reached to light it. But the paperwork called. The fucking paperwork that could give us the information we—

Theo unleashed a moan and tried to push upwards.

Sonofabich...

I tore my gaze from the desk and strode forward, grabbed the stoned, drunk asshole, and hauled him to his feet. Anger ignited in his eyes before I bent, grabbed the starter, and set the shit alight. Feeble flames grew bolder as they licked the kindling before the warmth grew.

"Fuck, it's cold," Theo muttered as I rose. "I don't think I've ever felt it this cold before."

He stared at me, those brown eyes boring into mine. "You don't speak, do you? You don't fucking speak, so you can't tell."

He licked his lips, seeming to like that.

They all did.

People said shit around me. Shit they shouldn't normally say.

I just stared at him.

"There's going to be a war. You get that, right? There is going to be a motherfucking war and I want no part of it. I want no part of...*this*." He waved his hand through the air. "I want no part of it. Silas can have it all. He can have every fucking foul bit of it."

Footsteps came from the door at the end of the room. Softer. Lighter. He swung his gaze, narrowing in as his sister stepped into the room. In an instant, he changed to the lion...no, not the lion...the goddamn hyena.

"You?" he snarled as she kept walking, cutting through the room on her way out.

But he wasn't having that. Drunk and high, he stumbled toward her, blocking her way. "There she is...mom's little *Angel*."

She jerked her gaze to his golden, blazing eyes. Anger grew bolder and hotter by the second, mirroring the fire. She was pretty...real fucking pretty. Expensive, too. You only had to look at her to know she was out of your league. She had that look. Defiant, but not like our Wildcat. No, she was a fighter, like us, whereas this one...this one was the woman you never turned your back on. She was poison, this one, beautiful poison. Her golden hair shimmered as she moved. I was sure it'd smell like honey if you came close. Instinct made me take a slow step backwards as she tried to step around him, her black thigh-high dress swishing as she moved.

"You've got coke under your nose, Theo," she whispered. But it wasn't just quiet, was she? She stepped closer until she met his stare. "Way to go, you should be so proud. I know mom and dad are."

His lips curled into a sneer. That was no sibling rivalry...that was hate. He pushed forward, to tower over her. "They aren't *your* mom and dad, are they?" He stabbed his finger into her shoulder hard enough to drive her backwards with every hard jab. "Never forget that."

She jutted her chin upwards. "How can I? When you remind me all the time?"

She glanced my way and for a second, I was hit with a wave of... kinship, familiarity almost. I looked away and broke the contact, my cheeks burning. Theo didn't move as she stepped around him and walked out of the room.

I just stood there as he lowered his gaze to the floor and listened to the sound of her heels as she left.

"Goddam her," he muttered before he turned around and left, exiting through the door she'd come in...leaving me behind as though I had never been there in the first place.

I turned to the desk as the fire crackled and popped. This was why I was here, right? The one they talked over. The one they ignored. The goddamn ghost. I moved closer, pushing aside the papers. Land development contracts. Contractors, warehouses. I took snapshots of what I needed before a muffled voice caught my attention.

"You understand what's happening here, right? What do you mean? They *aren't our problem* and we can't be caught in the middle of this." The soft feminine voice spilled through the doorway.

I narrowed in on the one-sided conversation. It wasn't the young woman. No...it was the wife.

My steps were silent as I hovered inside the doorway.

"Ophelia will go after her. You just wait and see. She won't stop until she takes the daughter from London. It won't matter how many men he has watching her. It won't matter a goddamn thing. She won't stop, not until she ruins him. We can't be around them if she notices us. Yes, thank you. Yes, I feel a little better now. I just worry. I know you understand."

My stomach clenched. My pulse was pounding.

Who was she...who the fuck was she, and what did she know?

"I have to go," the wife murmured. "I want us to distance ourselves as much as possible. They're on their own. Dante will see to that...no, he isn't aware of what we are doing. If he found out." Her words turned throaty. "If he found out, he'd kill me. He'd kill us all."

THIRTEEN

London

CAR DOORS CLOSED BEHIND US WITH A *THUD* BEFORE WE pulled away from the Ares' residence and I dared release the breath burning in my lungs. Vivienne stared out the window, lost in her thoughts. It was those thoughts which gripped me. Those thoughts which had made my pulse frantic the moment Dante's wife and daughter reacted at the sight of her.

Vivienne knew them.

And *they knew her*.

Which only meant one thing. They were connected to The Order. How or why was still a mystery. One I planned on figuring out. Just as soon as we were out of here. I glanced at Gus, catching him glancing at the rear-view mirror. Even with the sons in the car behind us, I didn't trust Dante not to take his threat to the next level before we made it to the end of his goddamn driveway.

I pressed my spine against the seat, my mind racing, replaying what the hell had just happened. Not taking sides, my ass. The moment Dante decided to step out of this, it had made him a target. He knew that. So if he knew and did it anyway, then something else was going on here.

Vivienne adjusted the sunglasses nervously as the car turned, taking us a block away. The ugly purple bruise looked even worse in the daylight. The longer I stared, the more savage I felt. I'd make her forget what those bastards had done to her. I'd make her forget...right before I tore them apart with my bare hands.

My murderous thoughts turned to Daniels, and I clenched my jaw, inhaling deep.

That piece of shit didn't deserve to live a second longer than necessary, not after what he'd done. A nerve twitched in the corner of my eye as I replayed Hale's call in my head. *How's London's little bitch? I plan on taking my sweet time with her tomorrow after our little celebration. Christ, I bet she can scream.*

Vivienne glanced my way, giving me a nervous smile.

Christ, I bet she can scream.

I forced an awkward smile of my own, trying my best to ease her worry.

She didn't need to anymore. I'd make sure she was safe. I lowered my gaze, taking in her body and stilled at her belly. I'd make sure she was safe...*and mine.*

The ominous Victorian mansion rose at the end of the street, drawing my focus, and Vivienne's as well.

Moving trucks were parked outside. One was backing into the service entrance while we slowed and pulled into the main driveway that ran along the side of the house. She turned her head, taking in the towering gables of the gothic mansion as Gus pulled the car in front of the garage that was separate from the house.

"You...own this?" she whispered, turning back to me in surprise. Then she corrected herself, "Of course you do. What a stupid question. You own everything."

The moment Gus opened my door, I gave her a laugh, but it died. "I'd like you to move into the driver's quarters for the time being," I murmured.

His nod was instant. "Whatever you need."

I adjusted my jacket and went to the rear of the car. This wasn't about a need for a driver, only the need to survive. The more men I had around protecting her, the safer she was. The landscape was shifting around us, casting shadows where there had been none before. I needed to get a handle on this...more than ever before.

I rounded the car, opened her door, and held out my hand. She eased out slowly, wincing as she straightened. I didn't enjoy seeing her in pain. It made me feel...*violent*.

The good doctor was about to make house calls...if he wanted to stay alive, that was.

As Carven and Colt climbed out of the Explorer, I led her to the side entrance of the house. I'd bought this place after viewing the place from photos alone. I didn't care about the house, not really. It was the location that mattered.

It'd be suicidal to attempt open war in a Mafia stronghold. So if Hale couldn't go to war with me, then that left a stealth attack, one we'd be ready for. But as Vivienne lowered those aviators and took in the grandeur of the old place with its cathedral ceilings, I realized the effect this place had.

"Holy shit," she whispered, staring. "This place is gorgeous."

The moving men grunted as they heaved boxes through the towering ornate front door with Guild limping in after them.

"Through there into the kitchen," he ordered, drawing our gazes.

I watched Vivienne's eyes widen and fought a flare of jealousy as she smiled at him. *Easy*...that savage part of my nature lingered too close to the surface where she was concerned. Guild glanced our way and met her gaze, then mine, before he gave a nod and shuffled away, holding his arm against his side.

I knew there wasn't anything romantic between them. He'd risked his life to save her, that was the extent of her appreciation. But still, seeing her watch him as he limped away stung.

"Let me show you to the east wing and our bedrooms," I urged.

We walked through the entrance and past the stairs that would lead to the two levels of stately bedrooms above. But there was no way in hell I'd make that mistake twice. No more bedrooms upstairs for us, from now on we slept where we could escape.

The shriek of a drill rang out behind us. Most exterior doors were welded shut, and I'd installed grates on every door and window in the place. The moment we'd booked into the hotel last night I'd started making phone calls. From now on, this place would be guarded twenty-four-seven, one way or another.

Vivienne glanced at the sitting room with its moody dark wood grain and stunning herringbone wooden floor. The place grew even more mysterious and consuming as it spilled into the elegant dining room we passed.

The mammoth fifteen-seater black table barely made an impact in the massive dining room. This place was even bigger than the city residence and half the price, considering the neighborhood.

"That's different." She stared at the table.

"It came with the house," I offered.

She smiled at me, and this time it was genuine, curling those beautiful lips.

I leaned close to her ear. "You should see your bedroom."

Her eyes widened before she carefully dragged her teeth across her lip. It was all I could do not to kiss her.

"Come on." I tugged her hand, leading her further along the hallway to the east wing of the house. "Let me show you our wing."

"A wing, huh?" She glanced over her shoulder at the stairs. "Not upstairs."

"No. Not upstairs."

There was an audible exhale. "Good."

I curled her arm around mine, leading her past the open double doors. Moody dark grays darkened the hallway as we switched from the original hardwoods to new plush dark carpet. "My bedroom is first on the left." I nodded to the closed black door, then Carven's on the right. "Yours is the black door next on the left and Colt's is on the right directly opposite yours."

My pulse kicked at the words, but instead of jealousy, there was a wave of relief with her wedged among all three of us. We'd keep her secure...*and busy*.

"Colt's bedroom?" she whispered. "He's not sharing one with Carven?"

I met her surprised stare. "Apparently not."

Her cheeks reddened under the bruise, making me smile, until she shifted her gaze to the last door beyond hers. "And that? Whose bedroom is that?"

The kick of my pulse boomed even louder. "It's not a bedroom."

"Oh, what is it?"

I strode past our bedrooms, stopped outside the black painted door, and turned to her. Secure grates and trip switches on the windows weren't the only things I'd had secured in the house overnight. She stared at that door and I could almost see that perfect, headstrong mind ticking overtime.

I reached out and grabbed the handle but I didn't turn it, not yet. Instead, I met the excitement in her eyes. "You know what they say about curiosity, Wildcat?"

There was a flicker of concern before that defiant spark ignited. We were back there, the push and pull, neither of us wanting to succumb to that goddamn inferno blazing between us. She jutted that adorable chin higher. "No, what do they say, London?"

My lips curled higher as I twisted the handle and shoved the door wide. I didn't need to look at the room. I saw it all in the widening of her eyes and the catch of her breath. She pressed against the door frame as I moved closer. "She gets fucked by the machine."

Her breaths raced as she turned those beautiful brown eyes to mine.

I lowered my head to whisper against her ear. "What, no witty retort? Don't tell me I finally silenced you."

I lifted my hand and dragged the back of a curled finger down her arm. She slowly turned her head, our lips so...damn...close...

"You in need, pet?"

Those lips parted. Her breath became mine. "Maybe."

I leaned in, gently kissing the corners of her split lip. Desire and rage swirled inside me. The violence felt...soothing.

"Are we safe here?" she whispered against my mouth.

I pulled away, staring into her eyes. "The truth?"

She nodded.

"Then no. We're not safe anywhere, not until this is over. But you can damn well believe we're not taking another risk. Not with you. You're going to be guarded twenty-four-seven." I moved my finger to the outside of her breast. "Think you can handle that, pet?"

She licked her lips. "I'm sure I can make do."

I smiled until my phone vibrated in my pocket, wrenching me back to reality. My happiness turned to rage when I looked at the caller ID. I was aware of everything about her, including the way her eyes darted to my hands as I answered the call, before they shifted to me.

"Is he dead?"

I clenched my jaw so hard my teeth nearly cracked.

"At least tell me that, *for fuck's sake.*"

"No," I answered Hale.

I concentrated on the silence on the other end of the line, waiting for the slow exhale. But it didn't come, making me turn away from her. The hairs on the nape of my neck rose as Hale spoke once more. "In that case, I'd like to propose a trade, his life for the contract."

My gut clenched.

"Fuck you," I forced. "How about that?"

"They're my most lucrative possessions. But I wanted your whore for myself." The bastard kept talking, digging himself deeper. "The moment Daniels had his fill and fucked the scent of you off her, she was to be mine."

My fist tightened around the phone until it crackled. Harsh, consuming breaths filled the speaker and there wasn't a damn thing I could do to stifle the sound.

"Fifteen minutes and I'd ruin her."

"I'm going to kill you," my voice was devoid of emotion as I murmured. "I hope you realize that. One day, you'll open your eyes and I'm going to have a gun to your head. I want to look into your eyes when I pull the trigger."

The response was slow and careful. "Until then," Hale answered. "Daniels for the contract and we leave her alone."

I lifted my gaze to the only one I'd make a deal with the devil for. "Fine," I answered, then lowered the phone and ended the call...with my heart in the back of my throat.

The only question was...

Why the fuck did he want Daniels that bad?

I pushed the question to the back of my mind as I closed the distance, pressed her against that doorway, and kissed her.

FOURTEEN

Vivienne

I'M GOING TO KILL YOU. I HOPE YOU REALIZE THAT...

A moan rumbled in the back of my throat, tearing from me like a whimper.

London's threat rang in my head as he kissed me. My pulse thundered in response to both those words and the feel of his hunger, one that consumed both of us as we stood in the bedroom's doorway.

My spine was pressed against the doorjamb. His fingers slid through my hair to grip my neck, holding me in place as he took my mouth with such ferocity that it stole my breath.

Our teeth gnashed, stinging my lips as he claimed my mouth before he pulled away. His eyes were dangerous, all dark and no stars. There was nothing but violence in him at that moment, nothing but wrath. Still, he clung to me like I was a tether to his soul, one he desperately fought for.

I *was* his tether, and he was mine.

A tether for my survival, and of my heart.

All three of us were connected, whether or not we wanted it.

His breath was a rush against my ear and his hands were frantic as they tugged my shirt up to cup my breast in one big hand.

"London," I whispered, breathless as I glanced toward the double doors at the end of the hall.

He didn't stop, just curled his spine and tugged the straps of my bra low. "This wing is off limits," he whispered as he licked my nipple. "No one will see us."

Still, it didn't ease the fear until his teeth grazed that puckered, sensitive flesh, and drew me away. "Oh, God." I closed my eyes and shuddered.

His hand delved between my legs and those strong fingers grazed along my slit. "Mine," he murmured. "You're fucking mine, you get that? Everyone will fucking know by the time I'm done...*they'll...all...fucking...know.*"

Heat tore through me at those possessive words. My hips thrust forward as I met his hunger with my own. I drove my fingers through his hair and clenched tight, fisting the strands to drag his mouth to mine once more. I'd never wanted to belong to someone so desperately as I did right then, to him and the twins.

One day you'll open your eyes and I'm going to have a gun to your head. I want to look into your eyes when I pull the trigger.

He broke the kiss and pulled away just enough to stare into my eyes. All I saw was desperation and the terrifying need for revenge. "I won't fucking lose you. Do you hear me? I won't lose you."

He lowered his head and gently cupped my breast. "The tracker..."

I shook my head. "No. No more fucking trackers. You want to protect me, then you'll treat me like the sons. Give me a phone...

but no more goddamn trackers. No more *things* inserted in me against my will. Do you hear me, London? *No. More.*"

He went still. So still I waited for that monster to rear his head, to control and force and bend me to his will until I had no choice but to give in to him. London St. James was a monster.

He'd had to be.

Because it took a monster to destroy one.

But as I waited for that dominating force to consume me, a flicker of something else rose in his eyes. Something that snatched the breath from my lungs. His grip tightened around the back of my neck as he pulled me closer, so our lips touched. "*I. Cannot. Lose. You. Again...it will destroy me. It will destroy all of us.*"

This was as close to the truth as I'd ever come to his true feelings.

The closest he'd *allowed* me.

I saw it now.

London didn't just love me.

He was consumed by me.

Just as I was consumed by him.

I kissed him, taking those hard, gorgeous lips until *he* gave into *me*. He palmed my breast, then dropped his hands to the button of my pants as a cramp ripped through my belly. Agony descended and tore through my belly until I rocked forward and moaned.

It was like a switch tripped inside him. His hands dropped as he pulled away. I opened my eyes to find his fixed on mine. "It's okay." I forced a smile that was more of a wince. "Just a cramp."

That fist low down in my belly clenched tight, strangling something inside before it slowly eased. *Jesus...*I tried to catch my breath as the dark hallway brightened once more. London said nothing, just watched my breaths deepen as I straightened once more.

"You get many of those?" he asked.

Surprise flared as I nodded. "Yeah, some. Not usually as bad as this, though."

One careful nod and he adjusted my bra, gently sliding it back upwards to tug my shirt low. He was tender and nervous. Was he worried that whatever they'd done to me had damaged me somehow? If he was, he didn't voice his concern, just glanced behind me, then turned back. "I meant what I said before, none of the guards or the staff are allowed back here. It's just us...to do whatever we need."

Whatever we need...

"After I stop bleeding." It was both a question and a statement, however he wanted to take it.

He gave a shrug. "I've had more than my fair share of blood on my hands, Vivienne. A little of yours will not rock me, as long as it's this kind of blood, that is."

"Oh?" My eyes widened in surprise.

His response was vastly differed from the disgust my foster father had displayed. He couldn't wait for me to be out of his sight when I started bleeding, as though somehow this monthly curse was catching.

But London gave a shrug, those dark eyes narrowing on me. "Nothing that comes from you offends or disgusts me, pet. Everything is beautiful. Remember that."

He gave a tight smile before glancing at the open door to the room. "But maybe we leave the exploration of this room for another day, shall we?"

I smiled, adjusted my clothes, and pushed off the doorjamb. "Yeah, it might be best."

"But that doesn't mean I don't want to fuck you, pet." He dragged his teeth across his lip. "They say an orgasm or two helps with the cramping."

My clit pulsed in response. Christ, even his voice made me throb, making me bolder than what I felt. "I think I'd like that."

His deep chuckle resounded as he held out his hand. "How about I show you your bedroom?"

I met his grin with my own as I slid my fingers between his. He led me back to the doorway beside this one.

"I'll make a call." He pushed the brass handle and opened the ornate black bedroom door, pushing it wide as he finished. "And have the doctor visit just to make sure you're okay."

"There's really no—" I started, to tell him everything was fine, but the noir majesty of the expansive bedroom stopped me. "Oh my God, London," I whispered and stepped inside.

The size of the room dwarfed the massive bed. Black walls and ox-blood-colored furnishings filled the space. I stepped forward, moved to the bed first, and leaned over. Velvet and faux fur adorned the bottom.

"It's not red," he whispered. "I made sure they knew that, but I wanted to keep in tone with the—" I turned and lunged, to slam into him to wrap my arms around his neck.

I hadn't realized how terrified I'd been to go back to that house and look at the same walls I'd stared at right before I—

Right before I—

I pressed my face against his chest as my throat thickened. My body trembled, and I knew the tears had come. My body jerked and shuddered as thick sobs tore free. I clung to him and felt him slowly slide his hands around me as though he didn't know what to do.

I will kill you...

Those words clung in my mind. I was wrong. He knew *exactly* what to do.

Still, he held me as my chest heaved and my breaths sawed. My tears flowed onto his chest as he held me. He didn't speak, didn't move. He was here, pulling me against his powerful body until my chest burned from the violence...and that was all I felt.

When I slowly straightened and lifted my head, there was only one face that burned a brand in my mind and it wasn't Daniels'. It was *her,* that fucking bitch, Ophelia.

"They need to die, London." I lifted my gaze to find him through the blur. "They need to fucking die. If not for me, then for all the other daughters."

He looked down and held my stare, then slowly hooked my hair behind my ear. "I know, pet. Believe me...I know."

I swallowed hard as he leaned lower and kissed the tears from my cheeks. I'd never felt safe in my life, never felt wanted or protected...not like I did now. They might've taken me, they might've done...*this* to my face and my body—a quake cut through me as I stared into the dark depths of his gaze—but there was no doubt retribution was coming...in the guise of this man.

Beep.

His phone ruined the moment. I saw the flicker of anger before he slowly pulled away and I left him to turn back to the creepy, glorious grandeur of the room.

His indistinct murmur came behind me as I walked back to the bed and bent low to drag my fingers along the plush bedding. The ache stabbed deep into my belly before I lifted my head to the cathedral doorway to a darkened room.

"The leak is secure?" London murmured. "Good. I'll be there as soon as I can. Keep an eye on Daniels. I need him alive and talking...for a while, at least."

While London spoke of that wrath he so desperately wanted, I reached in and skimmed my fingers along cold tiles, found the light switch, and flicked it on.

Blood red, black, and gold captured me as I stood nailed to the spot. My things were here. The same expensive bottles of perfume and makeup were lined along the black stone cabinet, but that's where the past ended. I glanced at the massive black clawfoot bath to my left, then took in the expansive shower that took up most of the space on my right. Black subway tiles were accentuated with...what looked like a snake.

I stepped closer and reached out to touch the cool surface and dragged my finger along the pattern.

"If you hate it..." London started behind me.

I turned, to find him in the doorway, and shook my head. "No." My pulse thundered. "No, I don't hate it."

He exhaled with relief. "They say snakes are a symbol of rebirth, transformation, and healing. So the moment I saw this room, I knew it was for you."

"The others don't have this?"

He smiled. "No, pet. This one is special."

I turned back to that symbol of rebirth and touched it once more. "I love it."

Beep.

His phone chimed once more. "I have to go," he said. "But the sons are here and I'll be back as soon as I can. You and I need to talk about what happened at the Ares' meeting."

I tried to nod, but my belly tightened as a cramp caught my breath. I braced my hand against the wall and doubled over.

The heavy thuds of his steps came behind me. The brush of his finger along my back came as I closed my eyes with the pain. "The doc will be here to give you something for the pain, and Colt is anxious. Use him, pet. Give him a purpose and take what you need."

My pain mingled with desperation as his hand fell away, and I heard the sound of his steps again, this time retreating. My thoughts turned to Carven and the hostile way he looked at me.

You better be worth it. Those words came back to me as I turned around to watch London walk out the bathroom door. *Because if daddy dearest doesn't want you, we're as good as dead. You get that, right?*

He wasn't talking about London, was he? My pulse boomed. Was he talking about... "Who is King to me?"

London stopped, standing at the foot of that majestic bed. But he didn't turn.

I took a step just outside the bathroom doorway. "Answer me, London. Who is he?"

His shoulders sank with a sigh. "He's your father," he answered before he went out the door.

Leaving me behind...

With my cheeks burning.

He's your father.

Anguish filled my chest. Deep down, I'd suspected. I mean, why else would a man like London St. James want someone like me if not to use me for my bloodline? It stung to actually hear the words. Then the tears threatened again.

But I was all cried out. I was empty, so fucking empty, nothing more than a hollow shell of the person I'd once been. I wanted to hate him. I wanted to hate them all. But there was no end to that hate because it had started well before London.

It had started with my father.

King.

I stumbled toward the bed and climbed up onto the plush bedding. But I barely felt it, just the booming in my chest. I stayed like that, legs curled underneath me, staring into nothing as my belly cramped and ached.

Hours passed until finally a soft knock came at my door.

Was it London? "Yeah."

The handle tilted and Colt stepped in. Those dark blue eyes scanned the room before settling on me with my hand fisted at my belly. Concern flared as he stepped in, carrying a plate of sandwiches in one hand and a bottle of juice in the other.

"Hungry?" he questioned.

Tears came as I shook my head. I turned away as he stepped closer and hovered at the foot of the bed.

"He hurt you?" The question was a snarl.

I jerked back, to find him staring at me with a look of pure rage on his face. What could I say? Yes, no...maybe? Maybe they all had, or maybe I'd just hurt myself?

In the end, I slowly shook my head. "No, it's just my period. It makes me emotional as fuck until I stop bleeding."

Colt stiffened. His face turned pale as he glanced at the fist pressed against my abdomen. "He *did* fucking hurt you. That *motherfucker*."

He turned before I knew it and placed the wrapped plate of sandwiches on the foot of the bed. The bottle of juice slipped from his hold to drop to the floor as he strode to the door. I lunged from the bed, scurrying to get to him before he hit the door. "No, Colt...*wait!*" I yanked his arm, forcing his gaze to mine. "He didn't hurt me."

He scowled, searching my gaze. "You said you're bleeding."

Heat rushed to my cheeks and I readied myself for disgust. "I have my period, that's all."

"Period?"

I flinched, narrowing in on that confused stare. "Yeah, my period. You know, where I bleed every month?"

He stepped closer until he towered over me. "You bleed...*every month?*"

God, he was so close...towering over the top of me, confused, angry...a powder keg ready to explode. "Yeah, I do."

"Show me."

I jerked my gaze to his, my eyes widening. "What?"

His jaw flared in anger, searching my gaze. "I said, *show me.*"

I shook my head and took a step backwards. "You can't be serious?"

Oh, but he was...deadly serious, in fact. Rage simmered just under the surface. "You're trying to tell me you're bleeding and London had nothing to do with it. So I want to see...I want to see what he didn't do to you."

My stomach sank.

The dark, moody room seemed to sway. "You can't see."

He stilled, then turned to the door. "Then I'll take the bastard out now."

"*Wait!*" I roared as he grabbed the handle. "*Wait, okay!*"

He stopped, his hand on the handle but he didn't turn back. "*Show. Me.*"

"You don't understand," I whispered. "The blood comes from inside me."

His head snapped to mine. Rage turned those blue eyes almost black. "*Inside* you?"

Jesus, I couldn't believe I was explaining this. Surely he knew about a woman's *body?* I winced, remembering how terrified he'd been after our first time, when he wasn't the only virgin. He'd reacted badly, his eyes were wide and screaming as he shoved those blood-flecked sheets at me and shouted, *I broke you!*

But he hadn't broken me.

I licked my lips and inhaled, knowing there was no other way out of this. "Fine." His gaze bored into mine. "I said *fine.*" I looked away, my cheeks burning. "You want to see? Then I'll show you."

I grabbed his hand and pulled him with me.

God, I couldn't believe I was doing this. My heart pounded as I pulled him with me toward the bathroom. "I swear to Christ, Colt. If you barf, or wince, or freak the hell out, I will *never* tell you anything like this ever again." I swung around to face him. "Get it?"

He didn't speak, those wide eyes still fixed on me as he gave a slow nod.

My heart hammered as I glanced at the door. London had said no one came to this wing. Still, I couldn't take the chance. If anyone else walked in while I was doing this, I'd be mortified...*even more than I was right now*. I left him there, strode to the arched black door of the bathroom, and closed it, just in case.

He'd seen blood. There was no question about that.

But he hadn't seen *this* blood.

My breaths raced as I made my way back to stand in front of the vanity. With my gaze fixed on his, I unbuttoned my slacks and pushed them low before I stepped out, leaving me in my panties. He scowled, then jerked his gaze to mine.

"You wanted to know," I forced the words through clenched teeth. With my heart in the back of my throat, I slid my fingers under the waistband of my panties and shoved them down till they hit the tile floor. I froze, standing there naked from the waist down. I knew what I had to do now...but I couldn't move.

Colt just stared between my legs, then met the panic in my stare. He wasn't freaking out...not yet, anyway.

With all the courage I had, I widened my legs and reached down, grasped the string of the tampon, and gently tugged it free. Bright blood shone neon in the white bathroom lights. I watched his every reaction and took in the widening of his eyes, then the panic as he lifted his gaze.

Then...he moved.

He stepped forward and gently grabbed my hand with the string.

"You wanted to know," my voice was a hoarse whisper. "So now you know."

"You hurt?" He lifted my hand and gently took the string from my grasp.

I shook my head. "No. I mean, yes, but not in the way you think. I'm not injured, Colt. This happens to a woman when she... when she can get pregnant."

"Pregnant?" There was panic in his stare.

Jesus, I did *not* know someone his age could be this...*sheltered.*

"Yes," I answered. "I could have gotten pregnant every time we...every time we fucked."

Heat moved through me with the words. He grabbed the tampon soaked with blood at the tip and stared at it. It did not horrify him like I'd expected. There was no gagging, no moans of disgust. There wasn't even a flicker of revulsion in those blue eyes.

Instead, there was...intrigue.

"You bleed where I want to be." He moved closer. I flinched as he slid his fingers between my legs and brushed my slit. "It hurts where you bleed?"

"Not exactly," I whispered, unable to move as his fingers delved into the top of my slit and moved down to find my clit.

"Where do you hurt?"

"My uterus cramps to get rid of the blood."

"Cramps?"

I slowly nodded as his fingers danced around that sensitive nub.

"So, this doesn't hurt?"

I pinned my lip with my teeth and shook my head. "No, I sometimes...touch myself. It helps with the cramps."

His brows shot high. "It helps?"

It was like I'd given him a green light. His fingers drove deeper until they reached toward my entrance.

I lashed out and grasped his big wrist to stop him. "You don't understand," I whispered. "I'm bleeding in there."

He moved closer, so close our bodies pressed against each other. My heart was booming, driving all that heat straight to my core as he slipped his fingers inside me. My hand was still wrapped around his wrist and I felt his tendons flex as he pushed in deeper.

"You're...different," he whispered, his chest rising and falling hard.

"I swell," I answered. "All the blood makes me..."

"Sensitive," he finished for me as he slowly twisted his fingers inside.

I reached out, braced my other hand against the vanity, and moaned.

"So sensitive, Wildcat." He pushed another finger inside.

It was all I could do to hold on. Long, languid strokes made me rock my hips to the movement until that throbbing need swept me away.

"Help you," he murmured.

I panted and bucked against his bloody fingers and stared into those big blue eyes, eyes that seemed ancient and naïve all rolled into one. He'd known violence his entire life...now he knew pleasure...now he knew *me*.

I whimpered, gripped his wrist tightly, drove those big fingers all the way inside until they stopped. My body pulsed and opened, then sparks danced behind my eyelids as I clamped around those fingers...and came...hard.

"Colt...oh, *God*," I moaned as I lowered my head against his chest.

That hard chest rose with a heavy breath. I slowly came floating back to reality and lifted my gaze to his...to find a *smile*. I should've known...I should've—

"I want to see again." He searched my eyes. "Next time I want my cock here." He pushed his fingers in a little deeper.

I trembled, my body plump and sated...for the moment. "Okay," I answered meekly. "Whatever you want."

His smile widened as he slipped his fingers free and looked down at the mess coating his fingers. I expected a little uneasiness at the sight. But then again, the sons were a breed of their own.

He clenched his fist instead, smearing the blood into his palm as I pulled his hand upwards and over to the sink. "Let's get you cleaned up."

He didn't want to. I saw that, but he didn't fight me either. In fact, Colt *never* fought me. He seemed like he was the only one. I hit the faucets and washed his hand before I grabbed a wad of toilet paper, wet it, and cleaned myself up.

Colt watched every second, not once looking away as I flushed the mess down the toilet and pulled my clothes back on.

"Need to eat," he urged. "And drink."

It was his turn to capture my hand and lead me back to the bed. My body was spent and my feet throbbed, still bruised from the rocks when I'd tried to escape. So I let him lift me back onto the bed and move around the foot to find the bottle of juice on the floor and grab the wrapped plate of sandwiches.

"Go on," he urged as he pushed the plate toward me. "Let me take care of you."

FIFTEEN

Carven

THE DOC STEPPED INTO THE SIDE DOOR OF THE NEW HOUSE
and glanced around before he saw me with my arms crossed,
standing against the wall. His eyes widened for a second before
he gave a slight nod. But I didn't return the greeting, just stared
at him until he flinched and strode away to follow my brother to
the east wing and the *daughter*.

I glanced at Colt, then back to the doctor.

Fuck him.

Fuck all of them.

I shoved off the wall. I needed to hunt. To fight, to do anything
but watch day turn to night in this fucking prison. The
goddamn walls were closing in even in this monstrosity of a
house. What the fuck kind of place was this, anyway?
Everything was black...and grotesque. Everything was
so...confining.

I headed along the empty halls, the air ringing with silence after
the last of the workmen had finished. London's guttural growl
echoed from the door along the hall, so I slowed.

"Look harder," he demanded. "I want every fucking rock turned over. I want to know everything there is to know about that asshole, Daniels, and I want it within the hour."

My gut clenched at the name.

Maybe that's why I was so fucking savage.

Daniels didn't deserve to live. Yet, there he was...*living*. My jaw tightened as I slowed my steps and took in the bare study. London's stuff was still in boxes, the towering black shelves still empty. But he was working, pacing the floor as I passed, that commanding growl following me.

An ache came at the nape of my neck. I worked my head from side to side and massaged the muscles, trying to work the knot free. But it wasn't budging. If anything, it was sinking deeper, triggering paranoia. I made my way through the massive kitchen. Guild was there, loading supplies into the refrigerator. He turned as I headed through, but there was no greeting now. Just a stony stare as though he finally, after all these years, saw what I was.

Good...

I was tired of pretending.

My breathing deepened as I swung my focus back to the endless fucking hallways and headed for the rear of the house, then to the mudroom, where the steel grate covered the back door. I punched in the code, and watched it open automatically. Movement came from the hedges at my left. Two of the additional guards London had hired came my way as they scanned the back area of the property. Only, their guns were holstered.

I scowled at their empty hands. "Guns out, we don't pay you for a leisurely fucking stroll."

One asshole scowled and opened his mouth like he wanted to say something. His buddy, on the other hand, was smart, watching me as I strode toward them, hate seething in my veins.

I couldn't help it. Rage didn't just live inside me.

It was created there.

Spawned like some fetid rot.

And he sensed it somehow.

The asshole moved his hand to his holster and drew his gun. I didn't turn away, just held the motherfucker's stare as I passed. Those goddamn chumps were gonna get us all fucking killed, I just knew it. I moved to the outside doors and the new grates that had been installed, yanked the metal bars to test the locks, then made my way around the house, checking every damn window.

Her face pushed into my mind, freckled and fucking beautiful.

The daughter.

Wildcat.

My pulse sped with the thought.

I goddamn resented her, even after she'd protected Colt with her own life. None of that mattered now. She was a goddamn liability, one I was tired of defending. *They all belong to me.* I clenched my jaw and that muscle in the back of my neck throbbed as the hairs rose.

I stilled, sensing...scanning...

Those words resounded in my head.

As I turned around, I scanned the darkness along the side of the house and the garage. The four-wheel drives were there, as well as the doctor's Range Rover, but there was something else. Something that reminded me of the Son's words. I scanned the grounds further out before I shifted my focus to the front of the house, and that feeling of being watched grew stronger.

Instantly, I lifted my Sig and moved. My boots were silent, my breaths shallow, if only my goddamn pulse would quieten, but it seemed deafening as a low *moan* came from somewhere ahead of me. I stilled and cocked my head, *listening.*

And that wounded groan came once more, only this time it was louder.

What the fuck?

I lunged and tore around the corner of the house, scanned the front and caught movement at the edge of the bushes. A hand reached out and clawed the grass as a guard crawled out from underneath them.

The side of his head was a dark, bloody mess. I stared at the sight, then jerked my gaze to the dark street, to the streetlights further along the block.

Beneath their glow was a man. My gut clenched in warning as he raised his head. My senses were a fucking siren in my head. I didn't have to linger to know who it was...

It was him.

The Son.

"Get the *fuck up now!*" I screamed at the guard, who rocked on his hands and knees.

But I didn't have time to care about him. I swung back around, but the asshole was gone from under the streetlight. A car's engine started and brake lights flared neon red in the night as I turned and lunged for the side of the house. Her face was all I saw. Her screams howled in my mind. I drove my body harder, and barreled toward the side door as the doctor stepped out and jerked his gaze toward me.

Panic flared in his eyes as he glanced behind me. "Everything okay?"

"Get the fuck out of the way." I grabbed his shirt and yanked him forward.

The dude was strong, and resisted for a second until I tore him out of my goddamn way and shoved past.

The daughter belongs to me...

The daughter belongs. To. Me.

I lengthened my stride, heading for the east wing. Black doors were a blur. I didn't stop, didn't slow. Just bore down on the handle of her bedroom door and threw it open to the sound of the shower in the bathroom.

And a guttural grunt of *my brother*.

I stepped forward, drawn by the sounds and the need to see. Through the steam and the drops on the glass, I saw them. Her ass was pressed against the glass as my brother thrust deep into her cunt. My heart thundered as I watched them.

I flicked my gaze to him and stepped into the doorway, my gun in my hand. The *slap...slap...slap...*of flesh on flesh resounded, making my cock twitch. I wanted her and hated her all at the same time.

"Oh, God...*Colt,*" she moaned.

But my brother stopped mid thrust and his head turned. Through the blurred glass, his blue eyes found mine. "Brother?"

Her gaze snapped to mine as he slipped free of her body and lowered her feet to the shower floor. Water dripped from his body as he stepped out, those blue eyes saying far more than words ever could. I scanned the familiar scars across his chest and along his hard stomach before my gaze stopped at his cock.

There was blood.

Blood on his cock.

I jerked my gaze to her as Vivienne stepped out of the shower and grabbed a towel. "Is everything okay?"

No. I wanted to tell her. *No, it wasn't anywhere near okay.*

But that *boom...boom...boom* was a freight train in my head.

"Carven?" she murmured.

"What?" I snapped as she wrapped a black towel around her body and stepped closer.

"Is everything okay?"

I couldn't answer. I was riveted by the strands of her hair stuck against her neck and my cock was harder than it'd ever been before, so fucking hard it ached.

"Do you need me?" she asked, her tone soft, her movements slow as she carefully approached.

I took a step backwards, staring as the light bounced off her bare shoulders.

"If you need me, Carven, I'm right here." She slowly lowered the towel from around her body.

I froze, staring at her body with my cock throbbing in both need and anger. She looked at the gun in my hand, her voice strained and desperate. "You think I don't know you have my life in your hands here?"

I clenched my jaw, unable to look away.

"You don't think I see how you battle yourself?" She slowly rounded the foot of the bed to stand dripping on the plush bedroom carpet. "How you want me." She lifted her hand and placed her palm against the thunder in my chest.

I was sure she could catch lightning, because that's what ripped through my veins. A bead of water dropped from the end of her nose to catch on her lip. Christ, I'd never seen anything so goddamn beautiful. She splayed her hand wider over my chest, turning the thunder in my head into a deafening roar.

"What are you so afraid of?" She pressed her body against me.

I lashed out and grasped her wrist. "You don't know a goddamn thing, *daughter.*"

"No?" Her eyes widened. "Then kiss me."

Kiss me?

Desperation collided with rage. I grabbed her other hand despite the gun in my hand and shoved her backwards as I kicked her feet out from under her. She had no choice but to fall...against the bed. That savage part of my nature reared its head.

All I saw was gray.

Gray where her face should've been.

Gray where there should've been blinding light.

I yanked her upwards, listened as her teeth gnashed, and flipped her over, driving her facefirst into the mattress. "You want me to fucking *kiss you?*"

She didn't fight, didn't buck, just lay there as I dragged my gaze over the yellowing bruise on her fucking side, knowing I was no better than the fucking animals who'd done that.

No better than a...

Son.

I drove my body against her, my hips thrusting to meet the curve of her ass. "This is what you fucking want? Because this is *all* you'll get from me."

My brother was a blur, driving his fist against my shoulder, those dark blue eyes blazing with rage as he snarled, "Get the *fuck off her.*"

I stared at him.

At the man who was part of me.

The man who knew me better than anyone.

The man who'd die for me.

But the way he looked at me in that moment wasn't one of love, or sadness.

No, this was a man who looked like someone who'd take me out if I hurt her.

I eased my hold, leaving her to jerk her face from the soft comforter to gasp for air. I tore my gaze from my brother to her as she twisted and turned over.

I sucked in a harsh breath as I looked down at her. "Be careful what you wish for, Wildcat, and do yourself a favor. Stick with my brother. He's a far better man than I could ever be. You don't want this."

Her chest heaved, but her eyes didn't waver as I eased back, the gun still in my hand.

"I do," she said, and licked her lips as she answered. "I do want this. I want *you.* Carven, I'll take *whatev*er you give me. *However,* you give it, too. You think I can't take the pain, then you're wrong. I know what that darkness looks like. I saw it when they took me." Her eyes blazed as they connected with mine. "So, if that's all you can give me, then I'll take it."

I flinched at the words and took a step backwards, staring at her as she turned on the bed, naked.

A sickening wave of revulsion swept through me.

She thought I was...*like them,* like those sick fucks who'd taken her. I took another step backwards from the bed as I stared at that sick desperation in her stare. She'd let me do that to her. I knew that now. She'd let me fuck her the cold, callous way I fucked, and I was betting she wouldn't whimper, either. No, I bet she'd swallow every fucking cry along with my cum. Then I turned and headed for the open door.

The daughter is mine.

The daughter is mine.

The daughter...is...mine.

My footsteps punctuated the words as I pushed into a run and tore along the hallway of the east wing.

Beep.

My phone beeped as I hit the side door of the house and stumbled out into the night. I stopped, grabbed my phone, and stared at the message from London.

I'm out, will be home as soon as I can. Protect her.

Protect her?

Protect her?

I clenched my fists, one around the phone and the other around the gun as that fucking message blazed in my mind. *Protect her...* I sucked in hard breaths as I stared at the gun in my hand. If we weren't in the middle of a fucking war, I'd end it right here and now. Because, in this very second, the only thing I needed to protect her from was me.

But without me, they were dead, and I knew it.

It wasn't a stroke of ego. It was a cold, hard fact. They needed a machine. They needed a *Son.* One to hunt. One to kill. One to keep them safe. If that was all I could be for her, then that's what I'd give.

My balls clenched and my dick ached. But I ignored the hunger, swallowed it down, and glanced at the garage, to see that the doctor's Range Rover and London's car were gone. I needed to get out of here. I needed to hunt...I turned my head to where that piece of shit had stood under the streetlight. The guard hadn't been an attack; it was a warning. One I heard loud and fucking clear.

The daughter is mine.

His words resounded.

Almost as deafening as the sound of my heart.

She was all I saw. All I craved.

"I don't fucking think so, asshole," I whispered. "This time, I'm coming for you."

SIXTEEN

Vivienne

I STARED AT THE BOTTLES OF VITAMINS THE DOC HAD GIVEN me, then lifted my gaze to the mirror. The bathroom lights bounced off the yellowing bruises along the side of my face and made them look sallow and ugly. But I didn't really care about those bruises. I probed the fresh red marks on the sides of my throat and winced.

Those I did.

A thumb mark on one side and a mess on the other in the shape of his fingers. I grimaced and turned my head to stare at what Carven had done last night. Any other time, I'd want them to darken, just so I could shove them in *his* face. But not this time.

Instead, I picked up my concealer and squeezed enough on my finger to smooth it over the blemishes. The last thing he needed was a reminder of what he'd done. I wanted that as far from his mind as possible.

I spread the liquid over the middle and smoothed out the edges before I picked up a brush and set to work blending. Last night had shown me the son was far too close to the edge. One wrong move and I'd push him too far from me. But I *knew* there was still a kinder man inside.

I just had to hold on to the hope I'd get to him. If I couldn't, what then?

My hand stopped before I dropped the brush to the counter. I didn't know. Because losing him wasn't an option, I knew that now. I could still see the pain in Colt's eyes after Carven had stormed out of the bedroom. You didn't just get three-quarters of a package with them...you got the whole thing. Or you got the brothers torn apart, and there was no way that was about to happen.

I titled my head to check the blended concealer before I grabbed the vitamins and made my way out of the bedroom and the east wing of this moody, gothic mansion as I headed to the kitchen. My belly grumbled with urgency, only this time from hunger. My cramps were gone and I was almost done bleeding. Thank fuck for that.

Having a damn period was a literal pain, especially now I was living with three grown men...with serious appetites. Two of them at least, the other...well, that was still up for debate. Those neon blue eyes lingered in my head. He was so fucking savage. So ruthless...so angry when it came to me. I needed to change that. No, I *wanted* to change that.

The clatter of a drawer came from the kitchen as I stepped inside. Guild lifted his gaze as I entered and gave me a small smile before he saw the bottles in my hand.

Then the butler turned chef but was really a bodyguard, scowled.

"I see you're following the rules," he muttered as he turned away.

I glanced at the gun next to the knife block. "And I see you're not taking any chances."

He followed my gaze and gave a shrug. "Not after last time."

I plonked the bottles on the counter and moved around to the row of upper cabinets before I stopped.

"Second on your right." He reminded me for the fourth time.

I pulled the cabinet open and grabbed a glass before I made my way to the refrigerator. "Still no chef?"

"Still no chef," he answered as he scribbled a list on a piece of paper.

I poured a glass of juice and set the container down. "Maybe better that way, fewer bodies to clean up."

He met my gaze as his brows rose. "*We* were almost *those* bodies."

I lifted my glass in salute. "Here's to *never* being one, either."

He clinked the crystal with his pen. "A-men." Then he placed it down before he moved back to the refrigerator. "I was about to make some pancakes. You hungry?" My belly let out a howl, which stopped him and caused a small chuckle. "I'll take that as a yes."

I settled against the counter and observed as he got to work, gathered the ingredients, and set a skillet on the stove. He glanced my way and watched me swallow my pills one by one before he turned back. I remembered the first real moment I'd seen Guild, right as London drove his fist into his cheek for letting me escape. I carried the guilt of that encounter with me to this day. Still, it didn't stop me questioning everything and everyone...especially now.

The black-and-white tiles in the kitchen seemed to tilt and shift as I remembered what London had told me. My pulse spiked and thumped in my ears. But I needed more information, and right now there was only one person who I knew I could trust to tell me the truth...and he was standing right in front of me.

"Did you know King was my father?"

He froze with his back to me, his hand still pressing the ignition on the stove as the gas burner came to life. There was a heartbeat of silence, followed by another, until the emptiness strained.

"I'll take that as a yes," I said slowly, repeating his own words back to him.

He turned around, but looked away. I saw the truth right then. What a fucking idiot I was. Of course he knew, they *all* knew. Everyone but me. Deep down, I was always a captive. I nodded slowly as I finished the pills, along with a healthy dose of pain, before I chased both with the OJ.

"I'm sorry."

My smile was more like a wince. "Why? It's not like you could betray him, right? We both know how he reacts."

"He's not a bad man, Vivienne."

"But he's not a good man either, is he?"

Guild just held my stare. "Are any of us?"

I slowly shook my head. "I guess not." But I had an opportunity here, maybe the best one I'd ever had to find out as much information as I could. "So I was always what, the bait?"

Panic filled his eyes as he shook his head. "That was one thing you never were to London."

I leaned over the counter a bit. "Then what was I?"

He cracked an egg into the flour and added a dash of vanilla. The sweet smell permeated the air and reminded me of Ryth as a pang tore across my chest. Christ, I missed her. Maybe more now than ever. I hoped she was safe where she was...and happy. God, I hoped she was happy.

"An opportunity at first," Guild answered, drawing me back as he whisked the ingredients together before plopping a cube of butter into the pan. "But that was short-lived."

My pulse sped as he spoke about London's feelings.

"Then you became an obsession," he added. "And his salvation."

That ache in my chest grew at the words. "I did?"

He glanced over his shoulder and gave a nod. "No, you *are*."

Heat rushed through me as he turned back and spooned the mixture into the skillet. There was a hiss as it hit the butter, instantly searing the edges. As it filled the kitchen with that delicious scent, I turned my focus back to the questions as I carried the juice back to the refrigerator.

"So, Hale runs The Order, which is some sick breeding, trafficking facility. The girls...I mean, *daughters*. They're born from the women they have there, but do they all know who their fathers are?"

He turned back for a second. "You really should ask London those questions."

I gave a chuff and pulled strawberries, blueberries, and a canister of cream out of the refrigerator. "Do you think he'd honestly tell me?"

He had to think for a moment before he turned back and flipped the pancakes. "Probably not."

I closed the refrigerator and set about opening every cupboard until I found the plates. "So, who else do I have to ask?"

"No one."

"Exactly."

There was a heavy sigh before he answered. "I don't know about the fathers. I guess no one would know. As far as I knew, each of the *founders* bred with the women they initially kept there."

"Jesus." Revulsion hit me when I thought of Daniels and the others breeding...until I remembered London was part of that sick facility, even if it was just to infiltrate. He was still there. Had he *bred* with any of them?

My cheeks burned with the thought. "Like Ryth's mom?"

He swallowed hard. "Yeah, like Ryth's mom."

I tried to shake away the image, forcing myself back to the information. "And her dad, is Jack involved somehow?"

"He isn't her dad, Vivienne," he said carefully and turned around to face me. There was a panicked glance at the doorway behind me, which made me nervous enough to follow his stare, but I found nothing.

I turned back. "Then who is?"

Tension crackled in the air. *Jesus, please let it not be Daniels or London...please let it not be—*

"The same man who's yours."

I jerked, and my eyes widened. "King?"

He gave a slow nod as memories of Ryth flooded back. Every second we'd been together I'd felt a connection, from that first moment I'd snuck into her room and pressed my hand across her mouth. Somehow, I'd known it...I'd *felt* it.

King was her father...and mine. I'd never been so happy to have a fucked-up bloodline. Tears welled in my eyes as my throat thickened. My voice was hoarse as I forced the word around the painful lump in my throat. "She's my...*she's my...*"

"Sister," he finished for me as he set the plate of pancakes in front of me. "Ryth is your sister by your father. Your mom, well, we lost track of her. We suspected The Order."

Agony bloomed at the thought of the woman who was my mother. I didn't know her. But I knew Ryth. I knew my...*sister...*

I strode forward and rounded the counter to rise up on toes and plant a kiss on Guild's cheek. He flinched, and his eyes widened with surprise. But before he could say anything, I reached out and grabbed a pancake from the top of the stack. "Oh, *hot,*" I winced as I juggled the searing cake between my hands. "I... owe you, Guild. *Thank you.*"

I *floated* around the counter, tearing off pieces of the pancake as I went...chewed and swallowed, then I realized I didn't know where the hell I was. I scanned the hallways and started to head down the nearest one, only to stop and double back, only to find empty rooms.

Each step felt purposeful as I ate the rest of the pancake and passed an open door. Stacks of boxes drew my gaze, making me stop and stare inside London's new study.

This was it...

I glanced at the Mac as I rounded the desk and pulled out the chair. Excitement filled me as I sat and hit the power button. *Sister,* the word rose as I wiggled the mouse and brought the screen to life, then logged into the account London had set up for me.

Think, I urged myself as I tried to remember what I'd done to connect the last time. Then I hit the icon to load up the program he'd used and started typing.

Ryth, are you there?

....

I WAITED with my heart in my throat. Still the cursor blinked and blinked while my knees bounced and my breath turned shallow. Seconds felt like hours...I licked my lips with nervous tension. "You know what? *Fuck it.*"

I started typing.

I DON'T KNOW *if you're there, or even if you're okay. But I really hope you are because I just found out the best news and I really need to share it with you.*

I STOPPED, my fingers resting on the keyboard. It was now or never...now or I'd be the only one who knew this secret. The only one who knew how important we really were to each other. Important enough to fight for. Important enough to...

Come back for.

My heart kicked in my chest. Would she do that? Would she come back to *this* if she knew? I remembered the way she'd fought when we ran from that place. The way she'd given it all, fighting next to her stepbrothers. She loved hard and completely. She'd be tempted if she knew about us. There was no doubt about that. She'd be tempted...

And that was all that mattered.

I closed my eyes and inhaled, dragging the agony deep inside before I opened my eyes and pulled my fingers back from the keyboard. I couldn't have that, not even in the slightest. If she even contemplated coming back here to this war, then she'd be in danger.

I stared at that cursor as my throat ached and before I changed my mind I typed.

I KNOW WHAT LOVE IS. *Real love. The kind that lasts a lifetime.*

TEARS SLIPPED from my eyes as I hit the key and logged out of the program. The heavy thud of my heart boomed louder until I realized it wasn't my pulse. I quickly swiped the tears off my cheeks with the back of my hand just as London strode into the study, his attention fixed on the phone in his hand as he scowled.

He stopped and glanced my way, then his eyes widened for a second before they flicked to the darkened screen of the Mac in front of me.

"Everything okay?"

I leaned backwards and crossed my arms. "I was looking for you."

"Really?" He tossed his jacket over the top of the stacked boxes and something hit with a heavy *thud*. But he didn't stop, just turned around as he worked the sleeves of his shirt to roll them along his muscular forearms. "And to what do I owe the pleasure?"

He was wary, testing me. Maybe he thought I was angry knowing King was my father? Maybe I had been before Guild spoke to me. But not now. Now was different.

You're his salvation...

I pushed off the chair and rose to stride around the desk toward him. "Three million dollars, huh?" I whispered as I stopped in front of him.

His dark eyes flared as he pursed those perfect lips. Jesus, he was sexy, and dangerous. Dangerously sexy, that's what he was. My pulse fluttered as I stood in front of him. I reached up and grazed those lips with my thumb. "Did you buy King's daughter, or did you buy me?"

He held my stare, those lips moving under my touch. "You."

My pulse quickened as I stepped closer and pressed my body against his. He didn't make a move to touch me, just stood there, stoic and calm. So fucking calm as I looked up at him and slowly rubbed my thumb back and forth over that soft flesh. "Three million dollars is a lot of money, London, even for you. But it wasn't just money, was it? How many deaths were there? How many men have you killed to get to me?"

He opened his mouth and allowed my thumb inside before I eased it out. Stars sparkled in his eyes. But he didn't answer, just held my stare. I was fixed on my movement as I thrust my thumb inside again, only to have him suck it deeper. Desire slammed into me. I wanted him so much it fucking hurt.

I slowly pulled my thumb out and lowered my hands. The buckle clacked as I slipped his leather belt free. He didn't say a word. But he didn't need to. I saw London St. James now. Saw him more clearly than I'd ever seen anyone else in my entire life.

He loved. He loved so fucking hard it was choking.

You're his salvation.

I might be his salvation, but he was my wet, erotic dream.

"Pet," he warned as I worked the button of his pants. He was hard, straining against his fly I couldn't stop myself as I slid my hand over the bulge and cupped hard.

His brow pinched with torment. I craved that reaction and continued to massage him through his pants until he unleashed a guttural groan and grabbed the back of my neck. Those hard fingers slid through my hair until they clenched.

"Just giving daddy what he paid for," I whispered as I slowly sank to my knees.

I unbuttoned his pants and slowly lowered his zipper. His cock was already pushing through the gap in his black boxers. The thick, veined shaft twitched as I closed my fist around it and drew him all the way out.

Fuck, he was beautiful.

Thick, smooth, and all mine.

That ravenous stare found me as I opened my mouth and slipped the head of his cock inside. My lips met smooth flesh as my tongue trailed along the edge and chased that pulse, which throbbed even harder.

"Jesus fucking *Christ.*"

"Vivienne," I mouthed as I slid him back out to lick the eye. "My name is Vivienne."

That heavy stare drew my gaze. "Vivienne," he murmured, and the sound of my name was like a drug as it tore through my veins.

I opened my mouth wider as his hold tightened on the back of my neck. He thrust slowly at first, but then I watched that spark give way to the monster inside. London wasn't a good man...nor was he kind. He was brutal and dangerous, taking exactly what he wanted...and what he wanted was me.

"My good little pet, aren't you?" he muttered, and thrust deep.

So deep my breath caught and built in my chest with the pressure. But it was like a switch had tripped inside him.

No, it was more like the monster was fighting to get to the surface.

The kind of monster who killed without question, who controlled, who confined.

Who claimed.

His lips curled to bare his teeth as he eased back out, let me gasp, and thrust back in once more. "My perfect little pet. I'm going to destroy you in the most beautiful, tragic way possible, and you will to crave every moment, won't you?"

My core clenched as I worked his shaft with one hand and held onto his hip with the other.

"I'll kill them all..." he grunted as he drove into my mouth. "I'll kill *them. All.*"

He would, too.

I knew it.

Because it wasn't a threat.

But a promise...

"Wider," he commanded.

I opened until the corners of my mouth burned.

"Wider, pet."

Those soulless eyes gripped mine. I let out a whimper and *stretched.*

He eased inside slowly, so fucking slowly until his head rubbed the back of my throat.

"That's a good fucking girl..." his voice was husky and raw. "Now I'm going to come down this beautiful throat and you're going to swallow it like the good girl you are, aren't you, *Vivienne?*"

My thighs clenched together as the pulse throbbed even bolder between my legs as I slowly nodded. Those cruel lips curled at the edges. "I'm going to use you." He shifted his focus to my mouth. "Then later, I'm going to take you to our room..." he licked his lips. "And fuck you with my machine until you're nothing but a quivering, wet mess." He thrust again, hard. "I'll take care of you, pet. I'll take care of what's mine."

I tried to hold on, even when he stepped forward and made me fall hard on my ass. His fisted hand in my hair was the only thing holding me in place.

"My. *Good...little toy.*" He thrust hard as he stared down at me. His pace quickened until my breaths were choked around the intrusions. Desperation creased his brow. In my panic, those words rushed back to me.

I know what real love is...

I did. It looked like this man...this man and his sons.

"*Fuck,*" he grunted as he drove in hard one last time.

Warmth splashed against the back of my throat as he groaned. I sucked in hard breaths through my nose. His chest rose and fell as he slowly pulled away, leaving a trail of saliva behind. I swallowed and eased my aching jaw closed.

"Wait," he murmured as he slid his thumb along the corner of my lip. "Every drop, pet."

I held his stare, opened my mouth, and sucked his thumb. His hold against my hair eased.

"So proud of you." He slipped his thumb out, grazing my lip. "So very proud."

My pussy quivered at the praise. I swear I was going to come by those words alone.

But I didn't, just watched as he stepped away and held out his hand for mine. I took it and let him help me stand. In an instant, I was yanked forward and his hand slid around my waist to press me against him as he growled into my ear. "You fucking consume me, do you know that?"

I didn't answer, just dropped my head forward as his hand smoothed the strands of my hair. "You asked me how many men have I killed to have you? The answer is not enough, Vivienne. Because they still tried to take you. But I plan to rectify that...I plan on teaching them a very valuable lesson. By the time I'm done, there won't be a man standing. I can promise you that. Only us...*always us.*"

Always us...

I eased back and found the terrifying truth in his eyes. The darkness shone as he searched mine and cupped the back of my head, gently this time, then, with the softest brush of his lips, he leaned forward and kissed me.

This man would destroy them all.

And himself in the process.

I closed my eyes gave into him, and opened my mouth once more as he kissed me until he gently eased back. Hunger roared between us. Consuming. Terrifying. Hunger. He searched my eyes before he slowly lowered his hand and fixed his pants. "I have a gift for you."

"You do?"

He nodded, buckled his belt, and went to his jacket, then lifted it from the boxes and reached into the pocket. "Rose gold," he murmured, and handed me a white box with an image of a cell phone on top.

"No way," I whispered as I opened it.

"It's already programmed with my number, Carven's, and Colt's. You'll need to charge it fully tonight, but the battery should last you until then. You wanted no more track—"

My very own phone.

I stared at the thing for a moment before I lunged forward, slammed against him, and wrapped my arms around his waist.

"—ing," he finished with a grunt. "I'm going to trust you that you won't go anywhere unless it's with one of us," he cautioned. "If you get into trouble, or if you need any of us, then I expect you'll call."

"Or text," I added.

"Or text," he agreed.

I smiled, swiped my thumb across the screen, and hit the app for the contacts. They were all there, all of them...even Guild. But it wasn't Guild's number I cared about. I lifted my gaze to Carven's...

It was his.

My way to get to him.

And capture a son...

SEVENTEEN

London

My phone vibrated on the desk in front of me and drew my gaze. I lifted my head, snatched the thing as it shuddered, and glanced at the caller ID.

Hale...

I clenched my jaw and stared as the number flashed over and over and over until it went to voicemail. He wouldn't leave a message, that I knew. No, he'd wait until tomorrow, then he'd call again and wait for the moment I gave in and answered. I shoved my chair back and rose from the desk while I rubbed the corded tension in the back of my neck.

Unreadable files.

The words were a thorn in my goddamn side. It'd taken the hackers days to pick apart the computer system we'd found in King's apartment, only for them to come back with that. I ground my teeth and tore my gaze from the words as my phone vibrated on the desk once more.

"Sonofa—" I snarled and snatched it, ready to hit the button and answer the bastard's call. But he wouldn't like the outcome, I was damn sure of that.

But the moment I snatched up my phone and saw the number on the screen, I stopped. Because it wasn't Hale's. I lift it to my ear and answered the call.

"We have him. *We have the bastard!*" Harper barked in my ear.

"King?"

"No, Daniels. We have Daniels."

I winced and braced my hand on the edge of the desk. It wasn't really the information I was hoping for, but I'd take it. "Give it to me."

"Ever heard of *the Vault?*"

"The black-market facility for information."

"Yeah, the one we use from time to time. Men we pay to access certain information. Well, Mr. Daniels is one of the key players."

I jerked my head upward. "He is?"

My mind raced as I tried to think of how that fit.

"And according to my source, he has not just information on Hale, but on the other splinter cells, as well."

My heart hammered at the words. "Daniels? Macoy Daniels."

"Macoy Daniels," Harper repeated. "Hale didn't just keep him around for his vile need to destroy you, but for the weasel's ability to hide information."

Maybe I don't need King?

The thought filled me. "Fuck."

"Fuck, indeed. I'll send you what we found. The rest is up to you."

I gave a nod. "Thanks for this."

"Just promise me one thing. When you find the information you need, tear that bastard to the ground."

In my head, I saw the piece of shit standing between her legs with his hands on her thighs and the fly of his pants undone. "Oh, believe me…there will not be a damn thing left of him by the time I'm done."

"Good," Harper answered before he ended the call.

It floored me for a second. I'd always thought Daniels was a slimy piece of shit, but I hadn't thought he actually had a purpose, let alone a purpose that'd been kept hidden from me. That nerve twitched in the corner of my eye as I straightened. I snatched my keys from the corner of the desk as I rounded it and grabbed my jacket.

Carven…

I lifted my phone and typed a message, but I stopped before I hit send. I needed him here, protecting her. Even if I had another way to get the information I wanted, she was still the only thing worth protecting. I backspaced instead, then typed:

I'm out. I'll be back later.

Then I slipped the phone into my pocket. Whatever information Daniels had, it was something I needed to find out alone. I strode from the study and out of the house, then climbed into my Audi, now that it was fixed. The entire front had needed to be replaced after Vivienne's little joyride. Still, I loved her damn spirit.

I started the engine and backed out, left the house behind, and went the long way around to the storage yard. By the time I got there, my mind was a damn mess trying to piece it all together. I watched my rear-view mirror as I slowly turned and pulled into the street.

My chest tightened at the sight of the warehouse. I was risking too much, gambling too lightly. Not only did I have Castlemaine here, I had Daniels, as well. In the same goddamn room, too. That random water leak wore at me as I pulled into the driveway, entered the code, and waited for the towering gates to open.

Razor wire drew my gaze. It took my mind back to that night, the one when Vivienne had crashed my damn car into the gate in front of me. I shifted my gaze to the slight buckle that remained in the damn thing. The woman had left a lasting impact...

Just giving daddy what he paid for

My hands clenched around the wheel. I glanced at my phone, but I didn't yet have the cameras set up in her new room. No, now I had something new to track. I lifted my gaze to the gate as it rolled open, then pulled the car into the parking space before I killed the engine and snatched my phone from the console.

A swipe of my thumb unlocked the thing and I opened up the app.

13 days.

Thirteen days until I made good on my promise and claimed her, body, mind, and soul. I glanced at the app, the one which tracked her cycle.

Think of the implications!

The doctor's roar resounded in my mind as I strode to the entrance and unlocked the door with my code. Two armed men stood in the foyer, one obviously waiting for me.

"Status?" I demanded.

"The leak has been fixed. It was some problem within the sprinkler system, somehow it was overridden. But we've fixed that and all rooms have been checked. We were just transferring Mr. Castlemaine back to his room."

I followed him along the corridor to the room Jack shared with the vile fucking bastard who was now a lot more useful to me than I'd realized. If it hadn't been for Vivienne, I would never have known how damn important the piece of shit really was.

We stopped outside the door and as I waited for the guard to unlock it, a chill swept through me, raising the hairs on the back of my neck. The door to the room swung open and movement came from inside. But the edges of my vision were nothing but a blur. One that made my heart boom as I slowly stepped inside.

Jack Castlemaine stood at one end of the room, glaring at Daniels.

"No...*no*..." Daniels shook his head the moment he saw me and stepped backwards as his eyes widened.

The guard followed me in and closed the door behind us.

"The Vault," I said carefully. "I want you to tell me about it."

Daniels froze, which was more telling than anything else, and as I watched, he changed in front of me. Gone was the whimpering mess he'd portrayed himself to be. His spine straightened, not that he had a lot of that in the first place. I held his stare as I watched him relax, those pale lips barely curling at the edges.

"You want to threaten me?" he murmured as he glanced behind me at the guard with a shrug. "Go ahead. You won't find out a damn thing."

I said nothing, just fixated on every flinch he tried to hide as I moved closer. Jack didn't move in the corner of my eye, just watched as I stopped in front of the...pathetic excuse for a human.

No... NO!

Vivienne's screams resounded in my head as I stared into the depths of his rotten soul. "There are no threats from me, Daniels. That's one thing you should know. It was a hard lesson Killion learned."

There was a twitch in his cheek.

His breaths deepened.

"But he did," I continued. "Right before Ryth shoved a knife into his groin and sliced through his artery, then her stepbrother pressed a gun to his head...and blew his brains out."

Then there were no breaths from Daniels.

No color, either.

It drained from his face, to leave him ashen and empty.

"I could replay it for you," I offered. "Or I could give you a blow-by-blow recount of how he begged for his life. After all, I not only set up the entire thing, but I recorded it, as well. Every. Perfect. Moment...of his end."

"You..." he panted. "You bastard."

He saw me then, saw me for what I truly was.

I was a result.

And the end for all their vile fucking games.

"But you won't have that end," I continued softly. "No. I have something special planned for you, unless you decide to change my mind. Now." I stepped closer, so close I almost touched him. "I'd like you to tell me about *the Vault*."

Daniels shook his head, his chest rising and falling rapidly.

"No," he denied. "No..."

"There's always Pen though, right, Daniels?" Jack Castlemaine broke his silence.

I slowly looked over my shoulder. "What did you say?"

His gaze was unflinching. "His sister, Penelope Brooks, he calls her Pen." He shifted his eyes to Daniels.

"No..." Daniels hissed. "No, you fucking don't."

But Jack didn't stop. "She's his sister, currently living in an assisted living community near here in Green Acres."

Daniels released a moan.

"A place Daniels visits every other Thursday," Jack continued. "And he pays her bills. He loves her, as much as someone like Daniels could love." He shifted that icy stare my way. "You could always start there."

Adrenaline raced through my veins.

It was what I'd needed.

A way to break him.

I gave a slow nod and stepped backwards as I reached for my phone.

"No," Daniels forced through clenched teeth as I swiped my phone open and selected my contacts. *"NO"!"*

I pressed the number and lifted the phone to my ear. It was answered on the second ring. "I have a job for you," I stated.

"NO! NO, YOU SONOFABITCH!" Daniels roared.

"Penelope Brooks, living in an assisted living facility in Green Acres."

"*OKAY!*" he broke, and slowly crumbled to the floor. "*I'll tell you...I'll fucking tell you!*"

I stopped and turned my head.

"I'll fucking tell you!"

He sounded broken. A pity. I would've loved to watch real agony descend for the bastard. Daniels shook his head. "I'll tell you whatever you want."

"The Vault," I pushed.

"Fine." He looked up at me. Were there fucking tears in his eyes? "I'll tell you."

"No," I answered coldly. "You'll do better than that. You'll take me."

He just nodded as tears slipped down his cheeks. "Fine, whatever you want."

My gut clenched at the sight of his blubbering. Hale trusted this piece of shit with his fucking information? I don't know which one of them disgusted me more. I lifted my phone. "Stand down for now. I'll let you know if I need you."

"Will do," came the voice on the other end right as I ended the call.

I glanced at the guard behind me, a guard I trusted with the storage yard, that was all. But I couldn't call Carven, or Colt. I needed them right where they were, guarding the only thing in my life worth protecting.

"Use me," Jack said. "Let me come with you. You trusted me before, so trust me now."

I turned back to the man who'd been useful to a point. A man I'd used and manipulated and kept like a prisoner in this place, waiting for the moment I could use him again.

Trust.

It was such a fragile thing.

"How did you know about the sister?"

Jack just gave a shrug. "You have your sources and I have mine."

I fought the quirk in the corners of my lips.

"You do this and you'll start a war you can't bluff your way out of," Daniels warned.

But I didn't look away from Jack. "Who said I was bluffing?" In an instant, I knew. This was what I'd felt right before I stepped in here. This was what I was meant to find. "Can I trust you, Castlemaine?"

"As much as I can trust you," he answered.

Damn if that wasn't the truth.

"You'll all die for this," Daniels barked as I turned to the guard behind me. "Gather what weapons you'll need, we're taking a road trip."

The Vault was exactly what it promised. I stared at the black mirrored-glass front wall of the building as I sat in the vehicle. From what I could see, there was only one way in and out, and that way was fitted with electronic locks and cameras. No doubt there'd be a swift and deadly reaction the moment we gained access. At least Daniels was right about one thing...this was...suicide.

"You sure you're ready for this?" Jack asked beside me as he stared at the same damn problem I had.

I waited for my racing thoughts to slow as I tried to pick apart every damn scenario of how this might play out.

But there were no thoughts. There was no planning...

There was just a face.

And those commanding brown eyes as she looked up at me from her knees. "No, but I'll do it anyway."

He followed as I strode to the Explorer parked in front. The driver's door cracked open and the guard climbed out.

"Watch our backs, Seb." I opened the hatchback of the four-wheel drive, pulled out the drawer, and grabbed the bolt cutter. "This could turn ugly fast."

"Will do." He pulled his gun as I closed the back and strode around to the vehicle's back door.

"Out," I commanded as I opened the door and scanned the street.

Green Acres turned out to be the perfect location, an hour's drive from the city in a quieter but more exclusive town. There was money here, and it showed, from the Bentleys and Range Rovers which lined the streets to the suits at midday on the men who passed. They kept their heads down, their focus not on our business as they passed. Which was a good thing. Because today our business was violence.

Daniels slipped out, still glaring at me. I ignored the heat of his stare, grabbed his arm, and shoved him forward. "Move."

He stumbled as we cut across the street toward the building. Jack was behind me, not running, not causing any concern. He wanted this as much as I did. I felt it in him, that same hunger that drove me. Not for the first time, that surge of confusion rose where he was concerned. But I pushed that aside and drove Daniels ahead of me across the street.

A pang cut across my chest as I lifted my gaze to the cameras. "Get us inside."

"He's watching," the bastard said as he followed my stare. "He'll come for you."

"Not if I come for him first," I responded. "Inside, *now*."

He stepped up to the access pad and punched in a sequence of eight digits. I didn't watch him; it didn't matter. I had no intention of coming back to this place after I'd taken what I came for.

The locks clicked open and Daniels pushed the mirrored door inward. The moment I was inside, I realized it wasn't just mirrored glass, but reinforced, as well. Bulletproof. Fireproof. But not London-proof. Right now, that was all that mattered.

I shoved him forward as the interior lights came on automatically. Jack's steps were strangely comforting behind me, even though I missed the ruthlessness of the sons.

That pang in my chest grew savage. As the lights came on, illuminating the hallway to a set of steel doors in the back of the building, I recognized the ache for what it was...fear.

Beep.

My phone chimed. I pulled it from my pocket.

Hale:

What the fuck are you doing, London?

I stared at the message as my pulse pounded. "Get us inside, Daniels."

His eyes were wide as he met my stare. He knew. He fucking knew.

There was nothing I wouldn't do to keep my family safe. I gripped the cutters in one hand and clenched the other, my thumb moving to massage the faint mark around my finger. Desperation filled me as Daniels stepped up to a keypad and pressed his thumb to the screen.

A green light came on the sensor a second later and the heavy vault door unlocked with a *click*. In front of me, the three-inch steel door swung open. No one moved, not for a second, until Daniels glanced at me. "I tried to warn you."

With my heart thudding, I stepped forward and pushed the heavy door further open. The room was a giant safe. Numbered steel boxes lined the walls. My breath caught at the sheer number of them, and I scanned the rest of the room as the lights above brightened.

"Jesus," I whispered as I stepped further into the vault.

"You wanted the information, then here it is," Daniels muttered. "But it won't help you."

I jerked my gaze toward him.

"It's all encrypted," he said, but when he said it, his focus shifted.

"What do you mean *encrypted?*"

Daniels just fixed me with a cold-blooded stare. "You didn't think he'd just hand it all over, did you?"

That same panic rose. But I swallowed it as I watched his eyes flick to a drawer on our right.

"Hale is the other person you'll want," Daniels added as he smirked. "He is the key to unlock all this."

I shifted my gaze to Jack, who said nothing, just stared.

"That was why he wanted you," I said, as the pieces fell into place. "Because you were one half of a key."

Of course it was. Hale did nothing unless it served him. All I had to do was to look around to know that. Rage tore through me as I fixed on this vile...sick...bastard. "So, let's make good on our deal and send you to him."

I gripped the bolt cutters and stepped forward.

"London..." Jack started.

But it was too late.

Far too late.

No...NO!

Vivienne's screams resounded inside my head as I grasped the bastard by the shirt and drove him backwards. I was that hunter, that killer...that ruthless empty shell of a man I once more. Daniels stumbled under the sheer force of my thrust. He windmilled his arms as he tripped and slammed back against the steel boxes along the wall.

"If he wants you back," I snarled as I reached down and grabbed his hand. "Then that's what I'll give him."

"*NO!*" the bastard screamed. "*NO!!*"

I lifted his hand and closed the jaws of the cutters around his thumb. Emptiness consumed me as I forced my weight onto the steel and bore down.

Daniels screamed and howled, his eyes wide.

Inside my head, the thrashing of the woman I loved drowned out his sounds of agony.

Crunch.

Blood flew, sliding down the tool until it hit the floor at the same time as the thumb. He clutched his wrist as I released him and fell to the floor. I was so calm, so utterly fucking empty as I bent and picked up the thumb from the floor. I dropped the cutters and reached into my pocket with the other hand.

I wrapped the thumb in my handkerchief and glanced around at the steel drawers. "Encrypted, huh?" I muttered as I stepped forward and pressed the drawer for it to slide open. The small chip inside gleamed under the overhead lights. "I bet this one isn't."

"Fuck YOU!" Daniels screamed, until the glint of the chip caught his eye.

Fear made him gasp and widen his stare as I lifted the thumb toward the tiny chip. "Whose is this, Daniels?" I shifted my gaze and bored into his. "Answer the question...*whose...is...this?*"

EIGHTEEN

Colt

OPHELIA WILL GO AFTER HER, JUST YOU WAIT AND SEE…

I jerked awake with the voice's words in my head.

Shadows…

Shadows and the faint sound of a moan.

Instantly, I turned my head to look at the bed. The crumpled sheets were still draped where I'd left them, but she was there, her breaths deep and steady, still asleep. *Good.* I lowered my hand to the gun at my side and leaned my head back until it hit the wall with a soft *thud.* Let her rest. She needed it. God, did she need it.

She shifted, tossing and turning, and one bare leg escaped the comforter. She was naked underneath the sheets. Beautiful, warm, spent, and naked. Her bruises were now all but faded.

"*No,*" she whimpered.

The bruises would fade, but the wounds of the memories were left behind. I knew those wounds. I carried those wounds. I'd carry more for her.

Ophelia will go after her, just you wait and see.

My pulse kicked with those words. I gripped the gun and pushed up from the floor before I took a step toward her. Strands of her hair were fanned across the pillow. Her arm was outstretched, her fingers curled. Was she reaching for me? Searching the darkest depths of her mind for someone to keep her safe?

That heavy thud in my chest grew louder as I looked down at her. Need swirled inside me like a gathering storm. I turned away, my steps silent until I was outside her room. Darkness greeted me. I blinked and rubbed my gritty eyes with the back of my hand as I made my way to the spill of light that came from the kitchen. But there was no one in sight.

I winced at the glare and went to the refrigerator to grab a bottle of water before I turned around. I swallowed, letting the cold liquid slide down my throat as I leaned back against the counter. Mentally, I sank down into the place where Carven waited, sensing that connection that thrummed like a live wire between us.

He wasn't here.

He hadn't been here all night.

I'd felt the moment he left, sensed the distance between us somehow. Only this time, the distance felt different, heavier, hollower. It wasn't as powerful as it normally was, like he was keeping things from me. No, like he was keeping things from *us*.

You want me to fucking kiss you?

I saw them in my head, Vivienne still dripping from the shower.

My brother's rage still echoed in my head. I'd known he resented her, but I hadn't realized how much. After the other night, I knew now, and the thought of it was eating at me. But not as much as it was eating at her. I headed out of the kitchen and turned along the hall to the lights in London's study.

But I didn't need to step inside the room to know he was gone. London was also slipping away from us, consumed by his own need for revenge. There was only me now. I was the one who watched her wrestle demons in her sleep. I was the one who saw the real picture.

The old house creaked and groaned as I stopped in the open doorway of his study and the front door opened. I didn't need him to tell me whatever happened today had been bad. I saw it in his unflinching gaze as he walked in with blood on his shirt and closed the door behind him.

He'd been shut in here all day. More than once, I'd walked by to hear him roaring at someone on the other end of the phone. The old London was back and it looked like this time he was here to stay. I glanced along the hallway toward the rear of the house, then turned back to the printed sheets splayed out on his desk.

Instinct called me, forced me to step inside.

I headed for the desk and picked up the first page, finding a printed conversation between Hale and that bastard who'd taken Vivienne. Rage pricked the edges of my vision, making me see stars. I glanced at the tiny chip inserted into the reader in front of me. But it was the Mac's screen I turned to, and found it unlocked. I braced my hands on the desktop and leaned over.

Hale: Daniels has the contract now. Whatever happens after this will be the decider. If he wants to go to war, then it's war he'll get.

Ophelia: The bitch. I want her.

Hale: We may need her alive to make him heel, so don't get carried away.

Ophelia: I don't have to kill her to hurt her. But you never know what happens when my artist's muse takes hold. I wonder if London would like a special canvas made out of the whore's skin?

Hale: If it's a reaction you're after, then that just might do it. The man is unpredictable at best. Pity you couldn't control him.

Ophelia: No one can control him.

Hale: Except for her.

Ophelia: Yes, except for her.

EXCEPT FOR HER.

I could almost hear the contempt in her tone. Hate plunged deep inside me. It wasn't Hale's words I stared at...it was hers. The woman who'd tormented us, the woman who'd tortured me. London's steps followed the sound of a thud from outside. I straightened and took a step backwards before I made my way around the desk to the doorway.

"Colt, everything okay?"

I turned toward the darkened hallway and watched him appear from the shadows...like he was one of them. I gave a nod and waited for him to step inside the room.

"Is she..." he started, then met my stare.

I flinched, then caught my breath, unable to look away.

"Is she okay?" he murmured.

But the man in front of me wasn't the London I knew. He was... a casing, a shell. The man I knew was gone, buried somewhere under his rage. I glanced at the desk and the papers splayed out on top. Whatever he'd read there had changed him, and not for the better, either. I glanced at the desk once more and took a step to the side.

My heart was thundering as the walls closed in.

And all I could see were those paintings. Charcoal bodies with blue eyes going up in flames.

"Colt..." London stepped closer.

I snapped my gaze to him and moved back.

Ophelia will go after her, just you wait and see...

Those words haunted me as I turned and left London standing there, staring at me. *She would...she would...she...would.* I headed for the east wing, my steps automatically slowing when I neared her room. But I forced myself to keep walking, headed to my bedroom, and flicked on the light as I stepped inside.

I moved fast as I slipped on a dark hoodie and black boots before I slipped my gun against the small of my back and walked out. One glance at her door and I turned away, left the hallway behind and headed for the rear of the house. I lingered long enough to snatch the keys to the Ranger from the hook and shoved through the back door.

The two guards patrolling snapped their gazes my way. Their eyes widened as one of them made a show of the gun in his hand before the other gave him a soft smack on the shoulder and shook his head. "It's not him. It's the deaf one."

The deaf one...

I kept walking, not giving them a second glance and pressed the remote for the four-wheel drive before I climbed in. The connection burned between me and Carven. I could sense it now as it burned brighter. I started the engine and shoved the vehicle into gear.

Headlights spilled along the side of the house and the front of the driveway as I drove out. I turned the wheel as the bright shine of the familiar oncoming car headed toward me. My brother snapped his gaze my way and scowled as I passed.

A second was all it took for my phone to ring.

But I didn't answer, just drove on, turned at the end of the street and headed for the city. My brother was on his own path at this moment, one that was taking him away from the only thing that was important.

Keeping her safe.

I gripped the steering wheel, my hands slippery with sweat as I lifted my gaze to the roundabout in my rear-view mirror and veered back onto the right side of the road.

"Don't you say a goddamn word, Carven," I muttered, but I still heard his goddamn laughter echoing in my head. I wasn't shit at roundabouts. They were just...confusing as hell.

I focused on the darkened streets as rain started to smack the windshield. My pulse skipped at the sight as I leaned forward and peered up at the sky, waiting for the white flash and thunder to follow. But they didn't come and there was just the steady thud of raindrops on the car to fill the silence.

I eased back, focused on the streets, and slowly made my way to the executive house where she was staying. I knew she was there, because parts of the sprawling house in the countryside were closed off and still under investigation from the fire we'd started.

I only wished I'd burned it all down...and her along with it.

Maybe if I had Vivienne wouldn't have been taken?

Maybe we'd all be safe.

I pulled the Ford into the street across from the two-story house and turned around, parking in the shadows. Soft lights shone on the second floor, hidden behind the curtains. I couldn't see movement, but I knew she was there.

Movement drew my gaze to the garage door as it lifted and a sleek black Mercedes pulled out. I waited before I followed. The wipers moved back and forth, a damn distraction as we headed into the city. The Mercedes pulled up outside Hungerford's, an exclusive restaurant in the bustling nightlife, and parked before the driver climbed out.

But there wasn't just the driver. As I watched, another car pulled up and three more armed men in suits climbed out, swarming around the Mercedes as Ophelia exited. I pulled the Explorer into an alley two streets away and parked, my heart booming in my chest as I climbed out.

The gun wore at the small of my back as I tugged the hoodie down low, stepped out of the darkened alley, and made for the restaurant across the street. Cars passed as I quickly scanned the bodyguards surrounding her as Ophelia climbed the steps and disappeared inside.

Ophelia will go after her, just you wait and see...

I lifted my gaze to the two bodyguards who went inside with her, then shifted to the two outside, knowing there would be no walking away from this for me. I waited for the panic and the fear but none of that came.

Instead, it was her face.

Her eyes closed in ecstasy.

My name on those perfect lips.

Do it...

Do it...

Do...it.

I reached around to the small of my back as I stepped up from the street to the sidewalk. The two bodyguards turned around and started back down the stairs. In my head, I could already see it.

The restaurant in chaos.

People screaming everywhere.

Me standing there shot, bleeding. The gun trembling in my hand as I lifted it to her head.

Beep.

My phone beeped.

Beep.

The damn thing hummed and buzzed, drawing the bouncer's stare as I stepped closer.

I knew it was my brother calling, but it wasn't his face I saw.

It was the woman who held my heart in the delicate palm of her hand.

The woman I'd die protecting. The woman I'd make sure was safe.

Ophelia will go after her...

She'll go after her.

No, she wouldn't. Not if I could stop it.

Not if I could save the only one who mattered.

NINETEEN

Carven

W*HERE THE FUCK ARE YOU?* I PUSHED THE CAR HARDER, tearing through the city streets as the rain unleashed a torrent while I looked for the goddamn...stubborn, *asshole.*

I clenched my jaw and gripped the wheel. "It should be goddamn easy, right? Any direction which didn't have a goddamn roundabout?"

But it wasn't easy, no matter how many non-roundabout-filled streets I went to, trying to fucking think what might've set him off. I'd checked the warehouse. I'd even checked our other house, still damaged after the attack. But the guards we still had patrolling hadn't seen the moody fucker.

Now I just felt...*lost.*

Lost and pissed off.

Beep.

"About goddamn time!" I snarled as I snatched the phone from the console and glared at the screen.

Vivienne: Carven, I can't find Colt.

I stared at the message, then lifted my gaze to the traffic as I wove through the busy downtown streets. She had a phone now, that I knew. But I hadn't thought she'd...

What? You didn't think she'd look to you for anything? You don't deserve it. You don't deserve—

Beep.

I winced, then looked back down.

London isn't in his study, either. I'm starting to get a little worried.

Worried, my ass.

There was no way the daughter would message me if she was *worried.*

She was scared.

Real goddamn scared.

"Fuck!" I jerked the wheel.

Tires howled as they skidded along the street as I swung back the way I'd come. The engine roared as I punched the accelerator and tore past the same alley where I'd met the other Sons. It was one thing to go hunting for the one fucking person who was always by my side, but it was a whole other thing to—

Beep.

I tore my focus from the street.

Are you even getting these? I don't know if I'm doing this right.

Jesus. "Yeah, yeah, I'm getting them," I growled.

But I didn't text back. I didn't reassure her in the slightest. It was better that way.

Better she didn't look to me for anything...except this. A muscle twitched at the back of my neck as I tore around the roundabout and accelerated. Yeah, except for this. It took me less time to get back as I took the corners sideways and scanned the assholes who watched the Ares' streets as I passed.

I kept going, then jerked the wheel and turned into our new street.

Beep.

"What the fuck is it now?" I snatched the phone and read her latest text.

He's home now, and Carven...he's...he's acting strange.

"Strange?" Panic filled me. *"What the fuck does that mean?"*

The other Sons pushed into my mind. If they were hunting me, then they could be...

"The fuck they are." I braked hard, and hit the entrance to the driveway.

My headlights splashed over the Ranger my brother had left in. I searched for bullet holes as I pulled up alongside it and climbed out. I was already racing for the rear entrance of the house before the *thud* came from my driver's door.

"Gun out," the asshole guarding the place muttered as I neared.

I jerked a savage glare at the bastard and clenched my fists. I'd never wanted to hurt someone so fucking bad as I did right then. So the motherfucker was tempting fate. But I focused on the house, yanked the handle, and tore through the door. My pulse was out of control, erratic and thundering as I lengthened my stride almost into a run.

London's study door was open. The light was switched on but the room was empty. I glanced inside and kept going, headed to the east wing and our rooms.

"Colt, *please talk to me,*" Vivienne's voice spilled into the hall. "You're scaring me."

But the sound didn't come from her bedroom, where he spent most of his time now. Instead, it came from his room. I strode inside and scanned the room, to find him crouched in the corner. His eyes were wide, his skin pale. There was a blood smear on his cheek and a gun clutched in his hand.

I knew that look. I knew it well.

It was bad.

"Baby..." Vivienne knelt in front of him, gently touching his knee.

"He's not listening," I told her as I stepped around the bed. "Because he can't hear you."

She jerked her gaze my way. Fresh tears shone in her eyes, shimmering under the lights. "I don't know what happened. I thought he was asleep, then when I woke up, he was gone."

I turned my attention back to my brother as she kept talking.

"When I couldn't find him, I got worried."

"I'm here now," I answered as I stared into my brother's terror-filled eyes.

But the words were as much for her as they were for him. I just couldn't tell her. Instead, I focused on the only one who mattered right now. "What the fuck have you done?" I asked as I gently reached out and took the gun from his hand.

I'd only seen him like this once, shut down, close to comatose. That'd been the moment we'd come face to face with Hale for the first time. He's been bad...but I'd been able to bring him around.

Only I didn't know about tonight.

This time, it felt different.

"Hey, you gonna ignore me?" I pushed the gun behind me, scanned his face for wounds, and caught the deep gouge on the side of his face. It looked like a graze, like someone had shoved his head against a wall. My stomach tightened as I quickly sank into that rage. "Wanna tell me where you were tonight?"

My tone was forceful and dangerous as I glanced at the wet hoodie he was wearing. "Out in the rain, huh?"

"I did something, didn't I?" Her voice was barely audible.

There was pain in her voice, real pain, and he heard it. His breath caught at the sound and I used that, driving it all the way home. "You gonna sit there and listen to her like that, brother?"

Those wide blue eyes flinched.

"She was so fucking scared, she texted me."

He turned his head at that and stared at her.

"Yeah, that's what I thought, too. The woman had to be desperate, right? So next time you feel like disappearing in the middle of the night, you might wanna let me know, huh?"

So I can fucking stop you. But the words never reached my lips. Anguish ripped me on the inside. I would destroy the fucking world just to keep him safe...like he'd done for me all those years.

Through all the beatings.

And all the scars.

I lowered my gaze to the thick scars that cut across his body. A reminder of what *they'd* done. I had to stop them. I had to stop them all.

"I'm sorry," Colt croaked, looking at her.

But the daughter never flinched, she just fell forward, right into him. "It's okay. It's all going to be okay."

It didn't matter that he was sodden. She drew him against her and cupped his jaw to kiss him. His hard lips met hers and the contact transfixed me, unable to look away. He grabbed her arm and pulled her hard against him, but then he broke away.

He seemed to come back to himself then and glanced around the room, before slowly pushing to stand up. I followed, scanning his clothes. "Where did you go tonight?"

Those dark pupils searched mine, but he didn't answer.

"You're soaked," Vivienne exclaimed as she tugged his sweater over his head.

The moment felt *off* and yet blindingly clear. He was here, and she was with him, helping him, his anchor in the storm, just like I'd been for like...*forever*. Yet there he was, lifting his goddamn arms like a child for her to drag his sweater off and drop it on the floor.

Goosebumps raced up my arms as she removed his t-shirt as well, which left him standing there with wet damn jeans and a bare chest. Her hands raced over the hard muscles of his arms and I swore I could feel the connection. I flinched and my heart hammered. Somehow she noticed, and glanced my way before she turned her focus back to my brother and stepped closer to him.

The thin fucking nightie molded to her body as she pressed against him. Colt held my stare as the tight peaks of her nipples brushed his arm. He turned her on. No, it was more than turned on. I saw it in the way she looked at him…it was the same way she looked at London.

"Never scare me like that again, understand?" she murmured as she slid her hand along the back of his neck and pulled his mouth to hers.

My breath caught and my lips parted as hers took my brother's.

Mine…

My cock twitched in response. She broke the kiss and turned to move against me. That same feeling ignited and blazed to life under the featherlight graze of her fingers. So careful…so very careful as her hand snaked around the back of my neck.

"It's just us," she whispered as she pulled me down.

Unable to fight at that moment, I let her. The scent of her invaded my lungs and forced me to close my eyes. I reached up and my hand slid around her throat. But she didn't flinch, nor did she pull away, not even when my grip tightened and our mouths collided. No, the *daughter* gave in to me.

Thump…thump…thump…thump…thumpthumpthump.

The panicked beat fluttered under my thumb. I opened my mouth as I tasted her and licked her, then dragged my teeth across her plump lips. My cock strained against my fucking jeans, desperate to take her to the bed. I'd bend her over and press her head against the pillow. I'd take her…*hard*.

Would she scream?

They all screamed…*eventually*.

That moment was all I saw. Her as she thrashed and her nails tore at the sheets as I ripped her nightie off and showed her what kind of son I was. I broke the kiss, my breaths deep and consuming. Still, that thrumming under my thumb grew to a crescendo. "Are you afraid of me?" I asked, and searched those brown eyes for the truth.

She swallowed and slowly shook her head. Her lower lip was red and marked from my teeth.

"No?" I leaned down until I whispered hoarsely into her ear. "Your body is telling me something different."

"I'm...I'm just really turned on," she answered, her voice a whisper.

I closed my eyes. She wouldn't fight me.

Not this one.

I clenched my jaw, hating how that hunger rose inside me, that savage need to *destroy* overwhelming.

"You think you want what I have to give, Wildcat, but you don't know what you're asking for. Stick with the son that actually gives a shit."

Pain came in the back of my throat. I tried to swallow, to drive that agony into the empty pit of my chest. But I couldn't do it. I couldn't force it away or pretend it didn't exist. I couldn't be mean and hope like hell I made her hate me.

In the end, there was only one thing I *could* do. I lowered my hand and stepped backwards.

The daughter belongs to me. She belongs to me. She belongsshebelongsshebelongs...

Those words were all I heard now, all that raced inside my head.

"Carven?" she whispered.

But I couldn't help her, not the way she wanted me to. Instead, I lifted my gaze to my brother and saw the scars and the desperation in his eyes. I was letting him down. I knew that, letting him down when he needed me the most. His brow creased and pain flared for a second before anger came.

That connection between us roared to life. Only it wasn't with loyalty or love, it was anger...

Which I deserved.

The bright smear of blood on his cheek shone under the lights. The sight of that turned my anguish into white fiery rage. He'd been somewhere tonight, doing things he didn't want to tell me...because he didn't trust me.

He...didn't...trust...me.

I couldn't fix that. Not yet, anyway. So I turned my attention to the one thing I *could* fix, the thing that would fuel me, that would give me more than a purpose. But would give me an opportunity to give my brother the thing he deserved most in this world.

I'd give him...her.

Yeah.

I'd give him *her*.

I turned around and strode for the open door, my boots thudding, mirroring the panicked booming of my heart. But I wasn't running this time, not like I had before.

Clarity cut through me like a knife and made that dead thing inside my chest clench. My brother didn't need me to pull him from the darkness anymore. He didn't need me to strap his hands down or stand guard while he slept. He had what I could never be part of. I was too broken, too savage. But I could damn well make sure he kept the only one who mattered to him.

The other Sons thought they owned her, thought they could take her.

I'd show them just how wrong they were.

I shoved through the back door and made my way back to the Raptor with the engine still warm. The asshole was there, striding around from the corner of the house. He made a show of his gun. He didn't even make a snide comment. But he didn't need to. The fact he was in my fucking face was enough.

I snapped my gaze toward him, and that craving for violence rolled through me. He flinched as our gazes collided and stopped, his buddy oblivious at his side.

"What is it?" the second guard asked as he scanned the grounds.

I tore my focus away, rounded the rear of the car, and yanked open the door.

"Nothing," the asshole muttered as I climbed back in.

Still, that hunger was there, urging me forward as I started the engine and shoved the four-wheel drive into reverse. Movement came from the corner of my eye as I left the garage behind.

Vivienne raced forward, still wearing that barely-there nightie that made my breath catch. My headlights spilled across her body, outlining every fucking curve. I stared a heartbeat too long, then turned my gaze to the face which haunted me.

"Carven!" she called.

Her lips moved with my name, and my foot eased off the accelerator. The four-wheel drive slowed, the desperation an animal inside until I snapped myself back to reality.

She wasn't meant for me, no matter what I wanted. I had to be smart about this. I had to put her first when it came to me. Especially when it came to me.

The daughter deserved better.

And kinder.

That sure as hell wasn't what I could give.

It took all my strength to turn away from her, but I did, looking over my shoulder instead until I bounced and braked in front of the house, then shoved the Raptor into gear.

I didn't see her as I drove away, my gaze moving along the driveway before I left them all behind.

I headed back to the city, to the darkened alley where the rave was coming to an end. I parked the car and sat, watching.

Partygoers spilled out, some stumbling, acting both drunk and high. But it wasn't them I cared about...

The engine of the Raptor had turned cold as the faint blush of the rising sun kissed the darkened sky. Still, I waited...until that hum inside me sparked and drew my focus as two guys dressed in black jeans and leather jackets stepped out of the crowd and turned left.

I hadn't noticed them before, but I didn't need to.

I knew instantly what they were.

They were Sons...

An Ares brother followed. I watched him glance their way before he turned right. I scowled as I divided my focus between them. If he knew who they were, then either he didn't care, or he was planning on following. The Mafia had no beef with the Sons, just like they had no beef with London. Still, it wouldn't stop them using us when the need arose.

Not tonight.

I shoved open the door and climbed out.

Tonight was my need.

It was time to go hunting.

This time for Sons.

I'd waited long enough, making sure the Ares asshole was long gone before I followed, keeping to the opposite sides of the streets. Faint sunlight spilled along the tops of the buildings. I followed them for what felt like goddamn hours until my eyes were gritty and my patience had all but run out. Until they disappeared down a darkened alley that looked like it ran toward the homeless shelters.

Loaded carts sat outside the entrance, with an older man asleep next to it, his arm wrapped around a busted wheel. I glanced into the darkness, then followed.

I kept my head down, hands fisted in my pockets as I cut across the street and sank into the dark. The smell hit me, fetid and stale, and the closer I got to the end of the alley, the more rank it became. I turned my focus to movement and caught the Sons as they slipped through the torn gaps of a fence where the back street spilled out to what looked like a forgotten area of the city.

I scanned the busted tents and ripped tarpaulins before I ducked and slipped through a gash in the chainlink fence. The Sons were gone, disappeared into the gloom. So I tuned into that hunger and that connection we shared, hating it even more than I had before.

Son...

The word was a slur and a brand. One I knew I'd never get out of and, as I caught movement up ahead at the entrance to an abandoned warehouse, I knew this was my fate. But it didn't need to be my brother's.

He could get away from the name.

He could have something real.

I'd give it to him.

I slowed to watch the darkness and the cracked open door, then reached around and dragged my gun free. My boots crunched on dirt and rocks. I stopped at the open door, peered inside, and scanned the shadows. The place was filled with the homeless. I moved inside as my phone vibrated against my thigh.

My pulse skipped, then raced, and I knew on some level it was *her*.

I didn't answer, just slipped further inside, careful as I moved between sleeping bodies. Grunts and snores rang out. The whites of eyes were neon from those who watched me. But they weren't who I wanted. I kept moving toward the rear of the warehouse until I came to the back wall.

I scowled and turned around to scan the mess of bodies again. My senses were screaming, but they weren't calling me here. I turned back around to face the far wall and spotted a cracked open door. There was no one lying close to the exit, which left a path of a sort. That's where I headed as I followed that innate compass inside me and grabbed the handle, peering into the gloom before I moved ahead.

But the moment I stepped inside, something hit me...*hard*.

I stumbled backwards and slammed against the door with a *crack*.

"It's about fucking time you showed," a deep snarl came from my right. "Been waiting for you, asshole."

I unleashed a roar as I drove my gun upwards and connected to something with a grunt. Hard breaths sawed through my chest. This was what I'd wanted...this was what I'd *craved*.

I swung again as movement came all around me. Black on black shifted. Instinct kicked in, only it wasn't the need to survive that howled inside me. It was the craving to destroy. I swung, connected again, and drove forward, unleashing blows in a savage onslaught.

Crunch.

The sound was music to my fucking ears as I turned to the next asshole and lunged.

Crack! The blow came at the side of my head and knocked me sideways.

I stumbled and my knee grazed the dirt floor, but I used the momentum to drive myself forward toward the darkened blur and hit him hard.

Hands gripped me, the rush of air instant. My heart pounded as I moved, jerked my head sideways, and swung my fist high in the air. A grunt came, low and guttural, which sounded not just pissed off but surprised.

Good.

He should be.

The daughter belongs to me...

She belongs.

She belongs.

She...crack...belongs.

Those words drove me and pushed me harder into the kind of place that scared even me.

With a savage snarl, I drove my head forward to crack against bone with a sickening sound. My smile grew as I swept my foot out and took the bastard to the ground. He hit hard, with a grunt. I was on top of him in an instant, driving the muzzle of my gun under his jaw.

Blood bloomed in my mouth, the tang bitter and metallic. Lucky I enjoyed the taste.

"You wanted me..." I growled as I shoved the muzzle harder against his skin. "Here I am, asshole."

The rush of his breath was brutal when it pushed against me as he lay on the ground. Movement came from all around me. I didn't need to hear the clicks to know they aimed at least three weapons at me.

My finger curled around the trigger of my gun.

Looked like we were at a standstill.

"Hand her over, Carven. Don't make me take out your cozy little family just to get to her."

Agony plunged deep into my chest at the words. "Come near my family, motherfucker, and I'll be the one taking you out...you and your girl band."

"You think I don't know about you?" the dead man grunted under me. "The self-destructive asshole with a mute brother. I know *everything* there is to know."

"Good," I answered, my focus on the surrounding movement. "Then it won't come as a surprise when I blow your fucking head off."

He just laughed. That low chuckle vibrating against my thigh made me fucking uncomfortable. "I say something funny to you?"

"Funny? No." I caught the motion as he shook his head. "If this was any other circumstance, I might invite you to join our *'girl band'*."

Invite me? The words stopped me cold.

I flinched at the movement as the one above us lowered his hand, the gesture clearer as the warehouse slowly brightened.

"She's not worth it," the asshole underneath me urged. "Why risk your brother's life...and your own? They'll come for her eventually. If not us, then there are others out there."

They'll come for her.

The. Fuck. They. Will.

Terror filled me at the words. I didn't know the feeling...and I didn't like it. Still, it came from that merciless need inside me, that sick, bloodthirsty desire to rip apart the entire world...*to protect her.*

I turned my attention to the Son underneath me. "You don't touch a fucking hair on their heads, you got me? Not London, not my brother..." I leaned down to stare into those empty, soulless eyes, and saw my own. "And *especially* not hers. She doesn't belong to you, asshole...she belongs *to me.*"

The words hit me.

But it was too late to pull them back.

Too late to undo the spell.

Because that's what it was...

No, not a spell...*but a compulsion.*

She was *mine.*

The prospect of that was terrifying.

I rose and stared down at him. They pointed their guns at me, even as I lowered mine. They wouldn't shoot...not now. I took a step backwards, still holding the Son's gaze.

"Where the fuck are you going?" he demanded.

My lips curled at the question. He expected me to answer, to fall into line like the rest of the Spice Girls here. But I didn't owe him a goddamn thing. The memory of her standing there in the middle of the driveway filled my mind. I knew where I was going.

The only place I could...*home*.

TWENTY

Vivienne

"*Carven!*" I yelled and winced at the blinding headlights from the four-wheel drive.

Still, I stared into the glare as I prayed that somehow, he'd stop running...and he'd come back to me. But he didn't. Sparks danced in my eyes as the darkness gave way and left me standing in the middle of the driveway, shivering.

The scuff of a boot sounded and I jerked my gaze toward the two guards who'd been patrolling the grounds. One of them turned away the moment I faced them. But the other one didn't. I suddenly became very aware of how little I wore, and how, in that moment, I was vulnerable.

Vulnerable in ways I never wanted to be again. I forced myself to breathe and hold his stare. "What the fuck are you looking at?"

I wasn't scared, not really.

But I didn't like the shiver of fear that worked its way along my spine. The guard didn't answer as his gaze took in every curve of my body, until I crossed my arms over my chest. Movement came from the corner of my eye and a low, familiar, protective growl came.

"Vivienne," Guild called as he stepped out of the back door and held it open.

I turned to him, thankful for his presence. The guards turned toward him as I headed for the door. He gave the asshole guard a slow nod and kept his stare as I slipped under his arm and back inside. I didn't stop, just headed back along the endless hallways. The soles of my feet stung from the cold as I pushed into a run.

By the time I hit the east wing, I was panting. I tore past the open door of my bedroom and raced to his. Colt was still standing there, staring at a spot in the middle of the queen-sized bed.

"Colt," I murmured as I crept closer. "Baby?"

He didn't answer, gave no sign he heard me at all. I stared at the blood splatter on his shirt and lifted my hand gently to skim the graze on his cheek with my thumb. "Talk to me. Grunt at me. Hell, push me away for all I care. Just please come back to me."

His brow creased. There was a flicker in the depths of those blue eyes. Still, he didn't answer. I moved closer and ran my hands along his arms. What should I do? What the *hell* should I do?

Carven would know...

But he wasn't here.

I licked my lip, still feeling the warmth of Carven's kiss.

Warmth. I flicked my focus back to Colt and saw his body shiver. That's what he needed. A reminder I was here. I took his hand. "Come on, big guy," I murmured and pulled him forward.

His gaze met mine, but he didn't fight me, just let me lead him toward the bed.

"Let's get you warm." I pulled him down to the bed and dropped to my knees, tugged the zipper of his boots, and pulled them free.

His muscles trembled, his nipples were tight peaks. I dropped his boots and nuzzled his shoulder until he lay back against the pillows. I tugged the comforter up, hating that the sheets were cold under his body.

"I'm right here." I moved against him, molded myself against him, and slid my arm across his middle. "You'll be warm soon."

This reminded me of the first night we were together, with the storm raging outside and his wrists shackled to the bed to stop him from hurting himself or me. I gently slid his hands around my waist. I couldn't shackle him, but I'd give him something to hold on to.

That I could do.

He shifted closer, his big body caging me in. My pulse sped at the contact as he felt the power of my touch. I was fascinated by the movement of my hands as I dragged my fingers along his powerful arms. He wasn't talking, but I knew he was here. Goosebumps raced along his arms under my touch. His breathing eased and became deeper.

He was so tired.

So spent.

Within minutes, his breaths deepened even more. Now it was my turn to watch over him. "Sleep, baby," I whispered, mirroring his echo in my head. "I'll watch over you."

I was the one who couldn't sleep now. I wanted to close my eyes and give into that oblivion, but I couldn't. My thoughts tethered me to the waking world as I relived the feel of Carven's mouth against mine. I'd almost had him...almost felt the terrifying son yield.

Are you afraid of me?

My pulse sped now, just as it had then. I lost myself as I drifted into the fantasy, then I glanced at Colt and found his breathing steady. He was still asleep...while I fantasized about his brother. I grazed my teeth across my lip.

No.

My own voice echoed in response.

No? Your body is telling me something different.

My core clenched and my thighs tightened. I glanced at Colt once more, then inched my hand lower to between my thighs. Christ, I was wet. I closed my eyes and relived the moment. His hard lips, the way he'd refused to touch me. He was so...fucking cruel.

His hands.

His words.

His *hunger*.

My body shuddered and warmed under my touch, until a faint *thud* sounded somewhere in the wing. I froze, and my fingers slipped from inside me as an icy shiver raced through my body. Somewhere underneath the heavy thudding of my heart, panic rose and I raised my head.

Colt's eyes snapped open and fixed on mine. But he didn't reach for his gun, not even when those heavy thuds grew louder...and closer. No, he stared, transfixed on me as though he were under some kind of spell. I shoved upwards as a shadow filled the doorway.

Carven wore a mask of menace. His eyes blazed and his lips were curled, to bare his teeth. Panicked, I looked at Colt's gun sitting on the nightstand beside the bed. Carven took a step inside, but his gaze didn't once move to his brother.

He moved closer, soundless, just like the night. "You just won't quit, will you, *daughter?*"

I shook my head and kicked the comforter free. Cold air swept all around me as I stood, stealing the warmth in an instant. "I—I didn't mean..."

"You didn't mean," he growled and kept coming, rounding the foot of the bed.

My heart was in my throat as I stepped backwards.

"You think this is what...*love?*"

He spat the word as he advanced. I hadn't ever seen him so...*unhinged.* Colt watched this all play out, but didn't lift a finger. My body both trembled with fear and thrummed with desire. "No."

"No?" He stepped closer and pushed me against the wall. "Then what the fuck do you think this is?"

I shook my head. "I—"

Words left me. I lost the ability to speak or move. But it wasn't terror which gripped me. It was *him.* This...son whose voice hadn't ever left me in my darkest moments. Was that love? I didn't know...I didn't know what that felt like.

But I knew what my heart screamed for...and it was him.

"Whatever you want it to be," I whispered.

He froze, and his forehead creased. He hadn't expected that. I saw it now. I didn't know what he thought I wanted, but it sure as hell wasn't words of devotion.

He narrowed his gaze and reached up to close his hand around my throat. "What did you say?"

"I...I said, *whatever you want it to be.*" I gasped at the pressure of his grip.

But it wasn't cruel, just enough for me to know who was in charge here. Panic flared in his eyes. He was reeling, unable to put whatever this was between us into a neat box complete with a perfect bow tie.

"You want to hate me, then hate me," I whispered and slowly licked my lips. "You want to fuck me, then we can do that too."

His grip eased, then fell. He took a step backwards and shook his head. "You don't want that, *daughter.*"

Daughter.

There was that word again.

Like he didn't want to see me for me.

I was just a *thing,* right? Just a problem. A target. A pain in his ass.

"Vivienne."

He scowled. "What?"

This time, I was the one who stepped closer. "My name is Vivienne."

His lips curled. "I know what your goddamn name is."

"Then use it," I demanded. "Use *me.*" I reached out, slowly took his hand, and lifted it. "You want to wrap your hands around my throat, then consider this my explicit consent. You want to push my head into the pillow so you don't have to look at me while you fuck me, then we can do that too. As long as you don't hurt me, as long as there is a level of pain we never reach."

He paled in front of me. Anguish collided with disgust as he jerked his hand from me as though I'd burned him. "No." He stepped backwards. "*No.*"

But I wasn't losing this moment. I wasn't losing him. "I'm here to stay, Carven." I moved forward. "I'm not going anywhere. You can either watch your brother and London fuck me or you can take what you need from my body...and my heart. This is me offering all I have to offer."

"And what if what I need you can't give me?" he snapped. "What if—" He raked his fingers through his peroxide-blond hair. "What if I don't want you to?"

"Then what do you want?" I whispered as I slid the thin strap of my nightie off my shoulder. "All you have to do is tell me. You want me on my knees? You want me splayed out on the table in front of you? You want to control the machine?" I moved to the other strap and let my nightie fall to the floor. "All I ask is that you use me...and only me. When you want release, come to me. When you want other things, too, then I'm your girl."

He shook his head. "You don't want that."

"Don't I?" I moved closer and took his hand, only this time I closed it over my breast and clenched tight. "Let me show you what I can handle."

It wasn't me who looked to his brother for salvation this time, it was him...

My tortured, broken...son.

"I'm a daughter. You are a son. I was made for you. I was made *only for you.*"

He moved instantly, surged forward, grabbed me around the waist, and drove me backwards. My hair flew into my face before I hit the middle of Colt's bed *hard.*

I bounced, and my teeth gnashed with the impact. The blur in front of me sharpened as Colt yanked his shirt over his head. Colt slid from the bed to stand and watched us before he took a step backward.

"You. Stay." Carven stopped him instantly.

The silence was deafening.

The slow slide of a zipper was followed by the thud of Carven's boots. "Last chance to run, *dau*—Vivienne," he corrected himself. "Last chance."

I pushed up onto my elbows with my heart in my throat. Footsteps sounded out in the hallway. Heat flushed across my skin as London stopped at the doorway to Colt's room, his gaze fixed on Carven before he shifted it to me, and watched this all play out.

Fear raced through me as Carven's jeans hit the floor and he stepped closer. "Want to fight me, Wildcat?"

Mesmerized by him, I shook my head.

He stalked up from the foot of the bed and pushed me backward. "Want to kick and claw?"

"No."

"No?"

"No," I whispered, and lay down.

He lowered his gaze. I shivered under his focus, but he didn't once touch me, not until his lips twitched. Only then did he grab me by my waist and flip me over on the bed. I landed facefirst, my heavy breaths swallowed by the soft bedding. He was on me in an instant as he yanked my hips up into the air and then back hard to slam me against him.

His hard cock pressed against my core. Terror swept through me. All I could feel were the hands of all those men pawing at me, desperate to hurt. All I could feel was Daniels. I closed my eyes and fisted the sheets, trying my best not to fight.

This was what I wanted, right?

This was the only way I'd have him...

This was the only way I'd have them all.

I braced myself for the intrusion, but it didn't matter.

He rammed inside and filled me until I bucked and moaned.

"Not yet, Wildcat," he grunted. "Not...fucking...*yet*."

He pulled out, only to thrust back in harder. Pain flared between my legs. I bit down on the inside of my cheek to keep from crying out.

"You wanted me. You wanted *this?*" He pulled out quickly and left me panting and shaking.

He was shaking, too...I heard it in his tone.

"Say it," he forced through clenched teeth. "*Say it.*"

"What?" I whispered, opening my eyes to stare at the crumpled sheets.

"Say no, say stop. Say *stay the fuck away from me.*"

My body was clenching and trembling. My teeth pinned my lip into place.

"Say it, *Vivienne,*" he demanded.

I slowly shook my head.

With a snarl, he lunged, his cruel hand gripping the back of my neck. "I said, *say it!*"

"No," I groaned as agony flared from his fingers. "I *won't.*"

His hard breaths were savage in the air. I knew the others were there. They wouldn't let him hurt me. I also knew something they didn't...I knew Carven was scared.

Not just scared. He was *terrified.*

This wasn't just an act of dominance. This was him pushing me away, desperate for me to see him as the soulless bastard he considered himself. He *was* that bastard. I knew that better than anyone...but that wasn't all he was. Deep down, there was a man in there. A man who'd rested his head on my shoulder as I fucked his brother, grateful I was loving Colt in ways he couldn't. And a man who'd seen me risk my own life for those who mattered.

His grip eased from my neck to slide down my spine and stop in the middle of my back. I closed my eyes at the sensation, too terrified to move in case I scared him.

"You're not going to say it, are you?" His words were quiet....

"No."

"You'd let me...hurt you like that?'

"If that's what it took to have you, then yes."

I stiffened as he lowered his head to rest his forehead between my shoulder blades. Warmth from his breath was a blast against my back. "You would do that...for me?"

I swallowed. "I would do that for you."

"Jesus fucking Christ."

"He isn't going to help us," I whispered. "I don't think I could handle another male, anyway."

His breath caught before a low, quiet rumble of laughter spilled out. His hand moved and slowly slipped to the side to cup my waist. Only this time, the touch wasn't cruel. It was gentle, his thumb brushing my skin.

I was drawn to the heat of his exhale, fixed on the rush, and that's when it happened...

He kissed me.

Not just robotically yielding, like he had before. But he softly kissed the small of my back, then moved lower and ran a faint trail of his lips down the curve of my ass.

"I don't know what to do here," he murmured.

I was too scared to say a thing.

"Do what feels right...for the both of you," London urged, his voice close.

"For the both of us," Carven repeated, his hands moving to my waist.

He gripped me and moved to toss me over once more, but stopped. "Wait...do you like that? Like when I...*manhandle* you?"

"Yes," I answered truthfully. "Although, seeing as how we're getting used to each other, we might take it a little slower. If that's okay with you?"

I didn't wait for him to answer, just eased to the side and rolled over, sliding one leg around him. He looked down at me as though he was finally seeing me for the first time. Maybe he was. I glanced at Colt. I'd thought he was the broken one...but he was nothing compared to his brother.

Carven slid his hand along my waist, then dragged his gaze higher as he cupped my breast. "How's this?"

That calloused thumb skimmed the hardening peak of my breast.

My body trembled.

He saw the shiver and ran his thumb across again. "That feel good, Wildcat?"

His voice was husky and raw, and my body heated with the sound. I nodded. "Yes, but I like your tone more."

He leaned down. "Like this?"

I closed my eyes and nodded. "Yeah. Like that."

"Then let me tell you what I plan on doing here," he started, and I quaked at the sound. There was something about his voice, his tone, his tenderness in the face of the need to be cruel. "I'm going to move lower, spread those perfect thighs, and kiss what I hurt. How does that sound, Wildcat?"

Oh, Christ...I was going to come.

I could only nod.

That same chuckle came again. "At least I know now how to shut you the hell up."

He didn't just move down my body...he kissed his way there and took his time over the swell of my belly until he stopped and looked down. My senses were humming, desperation and fear choking me. *What,* I wanted to ask...*why are you stopping?*

Then he slid his finger down my slit and pushed in. My hips rolled and my back arched, just at the feel of him inside tenderly this time.

"I hurt you before." He lifted his gaze to mine. "You're different...drier."

The muscles of his throat worked as he pushed my thighs apart and leaned down...then *spat*.

My pussy clenched at the splattering.

Saliva dribbled down his lips before he swiped it free with his finger, then pushed that finger inside.

"Hmm...almost," he declared as he lowered his head again.

It was all I could do to hold on as I watched his white-blond hair between my thighs. He took his time licking. "My brother likes this..." He spread his fingers on either side of my clit. "I was always jealous of him for it."

Colt flinched and jerked his gaze to his brother, but Carven didn't say anything more. Delicious heat rolled through my body as he sucked my nub. I clenched my fists in the sheets, then lifted my head to watch as he moved down, licked my core, and moved his fingers there to splay my pussy wide.

"Still dry, Wildcat," he clucked before spitting all the way inside me.

I unleashed a moan and dropped my head back. His fingers pushed inside me. I knew damn well I wasn't dry, not anymore. Still, I croaked, "Again."

"Such a needy fucking whore," he growled.

My breath caught and my pussy trembled.

"You like that, don't you? Like being my fucking whore. Christ, I'm gonna treat you like one, too. I'm gonna take out my frustration on this cunt." He shoved his fingers in and fucked me before he leaned back.

I lifted my head and watched as he fisted his hard cock and guided it to me. One hard thrust and he was all the way inside. Those blue eyes connected with mine. No words were needed.

He bucked his hips and thrust deep. I lifted my leg and hooked it around his waist.

I expected him to pull away. Instead, he reached around and captured my ankle. The diamonds London had given me pressed against my skin as Carven held me against him.

"No going back now, Wildcat." Carven closed his eyes and groaned. "You're mine."

I drove down with the thrust. Stars collided behind my eyes. "About fucking time," I gasped, and my body throbbed in response. "About time."

He leaned forward and his cock slammed inside until he dropped his head, unleashed a moan, and filled me with warmth.

The air was filled with the harsh sounds of our breaths. My pulse was erratic and booming.

I couldn't think...

Couldn't move.

Still, I sensed movement as London stepped closer. Those dark eyes, filled with hunger, drifted over me. He slapped his hand gently on Carven's shoulder. "You should've known it was a losing battle when it came to her. Easy, pet. This one will fuck you raw."

Then he gave Colt a nod and left us.

TWENTY-ONE

Vivienne

CARVEN LOOKED DOWN AT ME, NAKED AND SPLAYED OUT ON the bed.

"You good?" he asked, his voice quiet and careful...but the question wasn't aimed at me, it was for his brother, Colt.

I glanced at my silent protector and shoved upwards. "Colt?" I called as I slid out from under his twin and moved toward him. Fear surged inside me at his silence. But there wasn't a spark of jealousy or anger in his deep blue eyes. There was just relief.

"He'll protect you now." He slowly shifted his gaze from me to his brother. "He'll keep you safe."

I caught Carven's flinch as the words hit home, like he hadn't understood the true implications of what we'd just done, and now he did. But before either of us could speak, Colt headed for the open door. I shoved forward to head after him.

"Don't." Carven stopped me as he slowly glanced toward the empty doorway. "Let him go. He'll come to us when he's ready."

I hated the anguish between us. I'd thought that once we were together, somehow our connection would be strong enough to insulate us from anything. I just hadn't counted on the pain from within. But the horror out there still waited, even more ravenous than it'd been before. Only this time it wasn't after its pound of flesh.

Now it was after my heart...and it was sharpening its teeth.

Carven stepped backward and turned his attention to me. He bent slowly, snatched my nightie from the floor, and held it up. "You won't be needing this."

He fisted the garment and surged forward, but that unflinching stare didn't move from mine as he grabbed me around the waist and lifted. My legs went around him and my hands slid over his strong shoulders. He didn't speak, just carried me from his brother's room.

The dull bathroom light spilled into the hallway and the low hiss of the shower caught my attention. I wanted to go to him, but Carven was right. He needed to come to us. To trust us. To let us in...

Still, Colt's haunted stare stayed with me as Carven strode to his bedroom, stepped inside, and kicked the door closed. I wanted to know what had happened to Colt tonight because, whatever it was, it had been bad.

That empty stare stayed with me as I took in Carven's darkened room. I hadn't ever been in here, not because I hadn't wanted to, but because I hadn't been welcome. Everything about this brother had been off-limits. He'd made that abundantly clear...until now.

He'll protect you now.

Those words echoed as I took in the guns and knives scattered across his bed and cabinets. But he was gentle as he shoved aside handguns and a machete to lay me in the middle of the bed. He didn't speak, just looked down at me as he stepped backward.

Bright light spilled from a small refrigerator in the corner of his room as he cracked open the door and reached inside. He grabbed two bottles of water, came back, and handed me one. I took it and watched him carefully as he removed the lid of his and drank.

Those piercing blue eyes didn't waver, just stayed fixed on mine.

Feeling awkward, I opened my water and drank some. He gave a nod when I stopped, urging me to keep going. I did until the cold water spread through my belly and sloshed. Only then did he take it from my hand and placed both of them on the dresser before he slowly turned back.

Prey...

That's what I felt like.

And he was the predator as he stalked forward to stop in front of me.

One who gripped me around the waist and turned me over. Only this time he was gentle. I let him move me while I stared at the gleaming edge of the blade in front of me. A tender touch came against my ass and made my breath catch.

"You scared of me now, Wildcat?"

His hand trailed over the swell of my cheek, then slipped between my thighs.

"No," I forced the word.

"No?" he repeated softly, as if he wanted to double check.

I closed my eyes as he reached between my thighs and spread the slick remnants of his cum along the crease of my ass. "No," I repeated. "I'm not scared of you, Carven."

That touch pressed against the ring of muscle and drove the slick inside. "Maybe you should be. London is right, Wildcat. I *will* fuck you raw...and you'll enjoy every fucking moment of it, won't you?"

I fisted the sheets at the invasion and held on. "Yes. Jesus Christ, *yes.*"

"I won't hold your hand." He thrust in, then eased out before he slowly pushed in two fingers until the muscle burned with the stretch, then slipped free again. "I won't buy you flowers. But what I will do." He turned to press his face against my pussy, and licked. "Is bring you the hands of every motherfucker who hurt you."

I closed my eyes as he drove in again, my body stretching under the intrusion.

"That is the one thing I'm good at. So tonight, Wildcat, it's this. Then in the morning, I want names and faces. You think you can do that?"

I splayed my knees wider, swept away by the softness of his tongue and the deadly implications of his promise. "Yes."

"Good." He pushed his fingers all the way inside, then spread them. "That's real good."

Splat.

He unleashed a cheekful of saliva that dribbled between his fingers onto my skin. I pushed back against him. This was what it meant to be cared for by this son. I wasn't just protected.

I was going to be *avenged.*

"Kill them." The memory of their cruel hands invaded. "Kill them all."

"Oh, I plan on it, Wildcat." He slid his fingers from my ass and gave it a sharp *slap!*

I bucked as panic tore free.

Memories of London's spanking flooded my mind.

But this assault wasn't in anger, nor was it a surprise. I trembled and my pussy fluttered as his demanding grip clenched around the flesh of my ass and then eased.

The slick trail of his saliva came again and trickled against the searing heat of my body. I fisted the sheets as the thick head of his cock pressed against the ring of muscle and pulled away as he invaded. But he wrapped one strong arm around my waist and held me in place.

"Say it," he demanded as he pushed...pushed...and *pushed.* "Say stop."

I shook my head and clenched the sheets tighter. "Harder," I moaned.

He was so fucking big...*too big.* I wasn't going to be able to take him, not like this...not like...

"Oh fuck," he moaned. "I'm going to fucking use you, fuck your pussy every chance I get and stretch this ass until you're begging me to fill it. Then I'm going to wrap my hand around your throat and watch you choke on my cock."

Then he eased back out. I panted and focused on the burn as he slowly pushed in again, just past the thick head. His arm tightened around me. "Just until you...get...used to it," he groaned as he held me in place and slowly thrust his cock all the way in.

I whimpered, my breaths panting.

"My good little whore," he moaned, and pulled me back against him. *"Such a good whore."*

Panic boomed as it fought a battle inside me. I both wanted that *thing* out of my ass...and it in deeper. "Oh, God." I released the bedding and reached around to grab his waist instead.

"That's the way," he grunted as he thrust so hard it made me buck. "Hold on to me."

I dug in my nails, which only made him growl in response. His thrusts picked up until my pussy throbbed. But before I could climax, he unleashed a grunt and then stilled, deep inside.

"Oh...*fuck...fuck!*"

His cock pulsed as it sent warmth deep inside me.

"Wildcat..." he started.

I slid my hands from his waist. "It's okay."

He pulled free from me. "What do you mean?"

"It doesn't matter that I didn't climax."

His chest pressed against my back. "Yet."

I looked over my shoulder and found that icy stare, which was very much *unspent*.

"On your back," he ordered. "We're only done when I say we're done..."

I couldn't think, only obeyed, lowered myself, and turned over.

"That's the way," he praised. "Look how obliging you are. Spread your legs, Wildcat. I want to take a good look at what I'm about to eat."

I could barely lift my legs. When I did, he rose above me like some ravenous, bloodthirsty god and caught my trembling leg in one hand before he sank down.

"I'm gonna use you, Wildcat," he murmured throatily as he spread me wide before he dragged his teeth over my clit.

I twitched and bucked at the sensation. It took all my strength to lift my head and watch as he nipped that plump and swollen hood, then spread my pussy open with those calloused hands.

Hands I knew would be bathed in the blood of my enemies tomorrow.

The thought of that turned me on.

"You'll kill them all, won't you?"

He lifted his head until that icy stare met mine. "I'll do more than kill them, Wildcat. I'll wipe their fucking existences from the face of the Earth."

My arm was heavy, but I managed to cup the back of his head and gently pushed him back down. "Yes," I whispered. "Yes, you will."

His mouth covered my pussy and he sucked slowly, then drove that tongue deep inside.

My hips rolled, desperate for the friction.

Yes, he used me...

But I used him, too.

Driving his face harder where I needed it the most.

And he obliged greedily.

Until the low, drugging waves slammed brutally into me. I came hard, my hand fisted in that white-blond hair until slowly, the son lifted his head, his mouth glistening.

My hands fell back down to the sheets, my legs still spread wide. I couldn't have fought him even if I'd wanted to. "If you want to fuck again, help yourself," I whispered as I closed my eyes. "I need to sleep."

I floated, rising and falling, but surfaced when he lifted me higher in his bed and eased my head against the pillows. The clatter of guns and knives came until darkness stole me away and pulled me all the way down.

"I'll be back soon," he whispered as he slid from the bed. "Just going to shower."

I woke sometime later as hands gently rolled me over and spread my legs, making me crack open my eyelids.

In the darkness, I found him.

"Not gonna hurt you," he assured me, his voice laden with sleep. "I just need to feel you one more time."

I said nothing as he slid inside and thrust slowly. Drops from his wet hair hit my back. I felt the tickle at my side as his cock filled me.

"You truly were made for me," he murmured.

My body jolted with his thrusts, so I opened my legs wider. "Yes," I whispered. "As you were made for me."

TWENTY-TWO

Vivienne

"You sure these are all there were?" Carven growled behind me.

My pulse pounded and my hands were sweaty as they gripped the armrests of the chair as I stared at the screen in London's study, like I'd been for the last three hours. "I think so."

"You...think so," he repeated coldly.

I winced, then jerked my gaze to his. "It was a little hard to take a mental snapshot when I was fighting for my life."

My words stopped him cold. He straightened slowly, then shifted his focus to the screen, etching to memory every name and face I'd picked out from The Order. But I no longer looked at the faces of my attackers. Not because I was sickened by the sight, but something else had captured my attention. Something that sat perched on the end of London's desk...and seeped blood.

I flinched as Carven leaned across and hit the key to exit the screen. My reaction wasn't lost on him, but he said nothing.

"You make sure you stay here." He shifted his shoulder holster. "Text me if you need, otherwise I'll be home later."

Home.

We'd barely been here two weeks and already he was calling it home. Was this our life now? Moving around from safehouse to safehouse in a desperate attempt to survive? "I will," I answered as familiar heavy footfalls sounded out in the hallway.

But it wasn't Colt.

He'd been long gone when I woke up.

I'd searched his room, but found the sheets the same way I'd left them last night.

He hadn't slept in his bed and he hadn't slept in mine.

So where had he slept? And what the hell had happened last night?

Carven rounded the end of the desk and didn't glance once at the package seeping blood. He was gone before I knew it, and left the frigid sting of retribution behind. I was under no illusion that it'd be any different with us.

We'd fuck.

We might even talk in stilted conversation.

But he wasn't about to connect with me on any deep level.

That just wasn't who he was.

Then I stared at the box, swallowed hard, and slowly reached out.

The brown wrapping paper was so...*plain.* I skimmed the taped down flap and gripped the thing, tilting it.

"Vivienne." London stepped into the room.

I flinched and dropped the box as he came around the desk and opened the top drawer, then tucked an envelope inside.

"London." I pushed up. "Sorry, I'm in your way."

"Not at all." He stepped back around and tossed his jacket across the back of the black leather sofa they'd brought from the other house.

It looked like Colt hadn't been the only one up all night. There was a heaviness about him, one I'd never seen before. Gone was the stoic, unflinching male. His shoulders were curled, his breaths deeper.

I moved around the desk risked a glance at the box before I went to him. "London."

He glanced my way and I saw fear...fear and worry.

Dark circles under his eyes made my heart ache. I reached up and touched the deep creases at the side of his face. "What have you been up to, London?'

He didn't answer...but he didn't need to.

I saw it all in the weariness of his eyes...and the blood that seeped from the box.

He was up to whatever it took.

"Did Carven...did he hurt you?"

Did he hurt me? Yes, a little. But I couldn't tell him that, not with the way he looked at me. London was on his own rampage of revenge, one that was taking its toll. "Let's just say we have an understanding."

There was a tight twitch at the corner of his mouth. "Good."

Still, those dark eyes pinned me in place. Heat rose instantly to drive away the ache between my thighs. He took a step and slid his fingers along my temple and through my hair. "Have you been taking your vitamins?"

I nodded.

"Good." He moved until his powerful body pressed against me. Slowly, he leaned down and murmured into my ear. "Carven fucked you all night, but still you want me, pet?"

Now *that* was a question which deserved an answer. "Yes."

Under some kind of spell, I trembled in front of the man.

"There's no one like daddy, hmm?"

My core clenched as I licked my lips, mesmerized by his mouth so close to mine. Carefully, I turned my head and answered, "No."

His grip on my head tightened. "Good girl."

He picked me up and let me wrap my legs around his powerful waist. Carven and Colt were young and hungry, determined to ruthlessly fuck me every chance they got. But London...what he lacked in fervor he made up with depth.

I wrapped my arms around his shoulders and lowered my mouth to his. His hard lips were gentle at first, until, in an instant, he consumed me and drove me backwards until we hit the desk.

I forgot all about the box with the blood.

I forgot all about Colt and Carven.

All I knew was him.

He lifted his head and met my stare, then looked down to where my hands were fisted in his shirt and my legs were wide, desperate for him.

"You are such a daddy's girl, aren't you, pet?" He reached down and those strong fingers ran a trail along the ache.

I clenched my ass and thrust against his touch. "Yes," I whispered breathlessly. "Such a daddy's girl."

He let out a chuckle and that deep, rumbling sound did things to me no body part could. My nipples tightened and my core clenched. I knew without a doubt I was wet.

"Take me to the room with the machine, London." I whispered, staring into eyes. "Take me to the room and fuck me."

His chest rose with a deep breath...but then he shifted his gaze to the desk behind me.

"What the fuck..." he exclaimed, then stepped forward to set me on the desk. "The chip that was here, where is it?"

"Chip?" I slid off the desk and stared at the unopened bloody box and the paperwork still scattered near the monitor. "I didn't see a chip."

He jerked a pissed off glare my way and pointed to the mess. "It was right there."

I shook my head. "There was no chip when I came in."

With a savage growl, he shoved the paperwork aside and lifted the keyboard, then searched every inch of the desk before he yanked open the top drawer. "It was here last night."

I moved closer, watching him turn frantic. "What was it?"

He jerked that panicked glare to me. "Everything there is on Ophelia."

"Ophelia?" I whispered.

My stomach sank with the name. But under the fear was rage. I clenched my jaw as he tore the drawer apart, dumping the contents on the desk.

"What was on the chip, London?"

He stilled, his head bowed. Only this time he didn't look at me when he answered. "Nothing."

I flinched with the words. London St. James had been cruel when he invaded my life, tearing me from that place and holding me captive. He'd been brutal, demanding, obsessive. But the one thing he'd *never* been was a liar.

Until now…

His dark eyes were stricken as he grabbed his cell phone. He didn't once look at me, just turned on his heel and strode from the room.

I stared at the mess, then the bloody box on his desk. "You fucking bitch," I whispered. "You goddamn fucking *bitch*."

TWENTY-THREE

Carven

THE TIRES OF THE EXPLORER SQUEALED AS I PULLED INTO the parking lot of the exclusive Hale Club. Sleek, dark sedans filled some of the otherwise empty spaces, with the drivers huddled inside to escape the brutal January wind. I pulled the four-wheel drive near the back entrance before I killed the engine and climbed out.

I pulled the dark hoodie low to shield my face. But the wind still lashed my hair into my eyes, so I lowered my head further as I strode toward the back door.

I knew this place probably better than anyone, knew the men who came here, their names, and where they lived. I knew who their families were, if they were married, had kids...and even where those kids went to school. Not that I wanted to need that knowledge. But you never knew with those slimy motherfuckers. Everyone was fucking collateral.

Glancing over my shoulder at the gunmetal gray Bentley, I checked the driver before I turned back, punched the code into the lock, and yanked open the door. The howling wind was quickly silenced by the *thud* of the door. Then there was only the quiet, until I headed deeper into the vile fucking club.

Laughter rang out. Deep, booming...masculine. I scanned the expansive room to search the occupied tables in the dim, discreet areas designed for the kind of secrets these men kept. Movement drew my gaze as one of the men rose and buttoned his jacket. His laughter was infectious as it spread across the table. He lifted his hand in an *I'll be right back* motion.

I narrowed in on him and searched his face...*he was one of them.*

One of those who'd taken her.

One of those who'd hurt her.

But who'd left before the others had their fun.

I stepped out, kept my head down, and hugged the shadows to follow him into the darkened hallway on the other side of the club. My footsteps were silent and my pulse was steady and slow as I reached around and slipped my blade free.

Hinges squealed from the men's bathroom door. The spill of bright light made me slow. He disappeared inside and a second later, a stall door closed with a *bang*.

I followed, carefully pushed the bathroom door open quietly, and scanned the line of stalls for occupants before I turned to the sink and twisted the faucet. A smile was still on his face when he exited the stall with the noise of the flush behind him. He glanced my way but he didn't linger, just moved to the sink... until I lifted my head and turned toward him.

He froze, then carefully, slowly looked my way.

I didn't speak, just raised my arm high in the air and lunged, driving the blade down into the bastard's neck. *Stab...stab. Stabstabstab*...then I sucked in a hard breath as I met his wide eyes. He'd never had a chance...not with me. None of them would.

His blood spurted into the air to splash against the stark white bathroom tiles.

"You?" he spluttered as he desperately clutched his throat to try to stem the flow.

But it was impossible. It flowed in a torrent, spilling through the gaps of his fingers and down his perfect white shirt.

"You touched something that wasn't yours to touch." I lowered my gaze to his hand around his throat. "So I'll make sure you never touch anything...ever again."

He tried to scream as I stepped forward, but his knees gave way and he crumpled to the floor. There was no fight, not even when I pulled his hand from around his throat and gripped his wrist. Only then did the hate rise inside me.

I used it as I carved the knife through flesh and tendons, as I hacked and sawed until the hand dropped free...to hit the floor with a *plop*.

A whimper came from the bastard as I bent and picked it up. "A souvenir," I said as I cleaned my knife on his shirt, then met the dullness in his stare.

He had turned ashen by now and slipped away from me with no more than an exhale. I tucked the hand into the pocket of my hoodie as I rose, then strode out of the bathroom.

I stayed in the shadows and had made it halfway across the room before a guttural roar of horror came behind me. By the time I left through the back door, they'd know...

They'd all know...

You didn't touch what belonged to us.

I pushed through the door bare minutes after I'd entered. I headed back to the Explorer, tossed the knife on the floor of the passenger side, and climbed in. By the time they checked the cameras, it'd be too late.

Harrison Bolune would be dead…

And his buddies would be next.

That crawling sensation came at the back of my neck as I pulled out of the parking lot. I didn't need to look, I knew they were there…watching me. I turned the car, headed two blocks away to the offices of Burton and Bourke Family Lawyers and pulled the four-wheel drive into the parking lot.

There was blood on my hoodie. I tugged it off, cast it aside, and climbed out, then made my way through the front door of the prestigious offices and across the foyer. It'd do no good to have the cops on my case before I was done…I didn't want to have to kill them too.

But I would.

And I wouldn't flinch, either.

A pretty receptionist looked up from her seat behind the desk. She had red hair in tight ringlets against puffy cheeks and a perky smile. "Can I help you?" she asked.

I didn't answer, just shifted my focus from her and kept on walking, headed to an elevator and pressed the button for the third floor. Cold, unflinching blue eyes stared back at me from the steel doors. I didn't flinch, didn't look away, just stared ahead until the doors slid open and I stepped out into a busy reception area.

The phones rang.

The receptionists were busy.

I strode past, headed to the director's offices.

"Excuse me," one receptionist called out. "You can't go in there!"

I reached around to the gun in the small of my back and caught movement behind the office doors up ahead as I turned toward the large corner office of Martin Bourke. I gripped the door handle and turned as my pulse picked up pace while I scanned the area and stepped inside.

But he wasn't there, nor was he in the adjoining bathroom. Footsteps sounded behind me.

"You can't be in here. I'm about to call security!"

I walked back to his desk and found a single golf tee in the middle of the black leather desk pad. The desk reminded me of the one I'd shot to hell in that fucking house. "Don't bother." I glanced back at that tee. "I'm leaving."

I lowered my hand from the gun at my back and strode past her. I was out of the office before she had a chance to stop me and stepped back into the elevator as rage seethed inside me.

I wanted to kill him.

I wanted to kill them *all*.

I expected security to be waiting for me when the elevator doors opened. But there was no one as I headed back to the Explorer and climbed inside. That golf tee stayed with me as I backed out and headed out of the city to where the exclusive golf estates were tucked away from everything else.

Trees lined the road, but gave me glimpses of rolling greens hidden behind the lush pines. I pulled the car into the entrance and past the towering stone pillars of the Ashdale Country Club.

I headed for the sprawling club made for rich old assholes. Zipped up waterproof jackets and haughty expressions met me as I pulled the Explorer around to the rear of the building. The place was big...big enough to get lost in.

I settled my gun against my back and glanced at the hoodie. It was too bloody to wear here...but I didn't have anything else. I clenched my jaw and climbed out into the blustery wind, then headed toward the pathway to the greens.

My eyes watered as I scanned the idiots who were still out in weather like this. The room where we'd found her burned in my mind. I held onto that image when I spied Martin Bourke near a clump of ash trees. Three of the other vile bastards on my list had been with him. Of course they'd be here together.

Like attracts alike.

I reached around for the gun as Martin compensated for a sudden gust of wind, took a swing, and launched the ball through the air. My gun was out in an instant. I raised the muzzle, adjusted my aim, and fired.

Bang.

Martin dropped where he stood, a neat bullet hole punctured the back of his head...and had blown out the front. The three others spun as I swung the gun.

"No!" one screamed, his eyes wide.

Bang!

He dropped to the ground as Dale Landers unleashed a roar and charged me, swinging a golf club through the air like a weapon. Something snapped inside me and gave birth to something savage. I threw out my hand, took the blow of the club across my palm, and ripped it from his hold.

"You *motherfucker*," I roared as I swung and hit him on the arm. "*You fucking touched her? You motherfucking TOUCHED HER?*"

I swung again, and that time I caught him on the side of the head. He stumbled backwards and fell. It was all I needed. I yanked the club over my head and my muscles howled as I drove it through the air.

Crunch.

I swung again as blood splattered, tearing open his eye...and I couldn't stop.

I sucked in heavy breaths, consumed by the momentum as I hit again and again...*and again.*

Until I was lost in the blood and the movement. I couldn't get enough.

I wanted to kill and keep on killing. But the bloody, broken mess under me had stopped screaming and fighting. I stopped swinging, lowered the club, and stared at the body...and slowly felt that nagging feeling at the back of my neck, urging me to lift my gaze.

He was there...the *Son, with his* arms crossed as he leaned against the trunk of the ash tree, watching this all play out. He gave a slow jerk of his head toward the line of trees that led back to the club. "Missed one."

I barely caught the words, but they snapped me to attention.

There were three bodies, but there had been four of those motherfuckers. The Son reached to his waist, pulled a long switchblade free, and tossed it toward me. "I want it back."

Then before the knife landed, he turned and strolled away, headed in the opposite direction of the way I'd come. I looked at the steel knife that shimmered against the bright green grass and bent to pick it up.

I didn't understand him.

Nor at that moment did I care. I just gripped the knife and tossed the bloody, bent club into the trees as I started running. My muscles were cold and burned with the stretch as I pushed into a run. By the time I spotted Peter Sidcome flailing his arms and screaming for help, I was sprinting.

Flick.

The blade shot out with the press of my finger.

I'd promised her the hands of her attackers and I wasn't about to break that promise.

No...I'd break them instead.

He seemed to sense me as I bore down on him and turned at the last moment to fling his hands into the air. "*NO!*" he screamed.

I drove the point of the blade all the way through his palm. His screams sounded, even as he hit the ground.

But they didn't last long.

I was the man they were terrified of.

The man who was once a boy.

Until they'd made me into what I was now.

A cold hearted, killing machine.

A...son.

By the time I was done with him, he wasn't a man anymore. It wasn't just his hands I wanted this time. I lowered my gaze to the bloody mess at the front of his pants. I'd seen what the Banks brothers had done to avenge Ryth Castlemaine. At the time, I hadn't understood, not the depths of their rage...or the hunger they'd had for her.

Wide, perfect brown eyes filled my mind.

I'm not afraid of you, Carven, she whispered in my head.

I hadn't understood before. But I did now.

An ache filled my chest, plunging deeper than any blade could.

Yeah...I knew now.

I turned around, went back to where the bodies had bled out on the green, and used the knife once more. Hands...cocks. I carved the word *rapist* in each scumbag's chest before I wrapped the body parts in a windbreaker and rose to look down at the massacre in front of me.

They'd put it together in an instant. Hale would, at least. I turned around as the hate seethed inside me with the name. I wanted his blood on my blade more than anyone's. But I couldn't...not yet.

Ophelia's face rose from the back of my mind as I strode to the four-wheel drive and climbed inside. I was numb from the inside out and my fingers shook as I started the engine, turned on the heat, and aimed the heated air toward me.

Blood seeped from everywhere. My palm stung from the blow of the club, and it was almost impossible to get my phone from my pocket. But the screen was empty, not even a message back from my twin.

I punched in the tenth message I'd sent today and hit send:

Tell me what to do and I'll do it.

Then I closed my eyes, inhaling the stench of blood. "Just please don't tell me to stop wanting her."

I didn't think I could do that, not now she was under my skin.

But I'd try...for him, I'd try.

I'd cut her out from under there...if that's what it took.

TWENTY-FOUR

London

THE DEAD MAN IN FRONT OF ME JERKED AND TREMBLED, staring at me with wide, glazed eyes. His chest was bare, the once white shirt now bloody and wrapped around the stump that was once a hand. I lowered my gaze to the text message on my phone, the one I'd received bare seconds ago.

Hale:

Do this and I'll ruin you.

Ruin.

I lifted my gaze to Daniels. It was such a subjective word. How much could one carve out until they were considered ruined? Did it matter which part they took? A hand...a heart...*maybe a tongue?* I gripped the knife in my hand and stepped forward—I guess I was about to find out.

"I gave you everything you asked for!" Daniels screamed.

I widened my legs, straddled the chair he was bound to, and grabbed his jaw. I was beyond redemption now, my rage debased and cruel, stoked by the image of her beaten face as I growled. "Not anywhere near what I wanted. Now open."

I drove my fingers into the sides of his jaw, grinding flesh against teeth until he had no choice but to yield. The moment he opened, I drove the blade into his mouth and through that foul fucking thing lying there.

The thing that had given orders.

The *thing* he didn't deserve, not after what he'd done.

I hacked and yanked the blade down. Daniels bucked wildly and his screams turned to thick, wet gurgles until I reached in, grabbed the muscle, and yanked it free.

The pink flesh turned ashen almost immediately. It twitched in my hand as I released my hold on his jaw and stepped backward. Daniels howled, only now it wasn't much more than a sickening hiss of air.

"I promised her you'd die screaming," I informed him as I reached into my pocket and pulled out my perfect, white embroidered handkerchief and wrapped the tongue inside it. "Let's see how you'll scream with no tongue."

Daniels's head rolled back and his mouth gaped as he gasped and fought to survive. But he didn't look at me, just closed his eyes and slumped low against the hard-backed chair.

It was strange how the body still fought to survive...until the spirit broke.

We were getting close to that.

Real goddamn close.

But not yet.

I turned and found Marcus leaning against the wall as he watched the entire thing. But there was no disgust in his eyes, just that same hard glint I saw in my own.

"Send it." I held out the tongue. "Make sure the bastard has to sign, as well."

A nod and the former Navy Seal pushed forward to take the wrapped item. "Will do."

He left me there as I watched the man who had been seconds away from raping the only woman I'd every loved. I walked over to the bolted-down table near the small kitchen that held no water and no food—not for him, at least—and picked up a rag and wiped my hands and the knife before I pushed the blade back into position.

You could show me you at least care a little bit, can't you?

Those words rose out of nowhere.

They were the words she'd screamed at me the night they'd taken her.

Christ, I was a callous bastard.

I turned around to find Daniels's eyes open, his chest heaving as he sucked in air. "You will never touch her again." I closed the distance to stare into his eyes. "Do you hear me? She doesn't belong to you...she is, and always *will* be, *mine.*"

There was no panic in his stare, no fear. Maybe I'd already broken him? I hoped not...he had a lot of body parts left for me to send. And I couldn't fucking wait for Hale to receive them. I stepped away and glanced down at the rag. "I'll take this with me, can't have you choking on it now, can we?" His chest stuttered. "No, I still have plans for you. Be seeing you real soon, Daniels."

I left then, locked the door to the storage room behind me, and made my way back along the hall, then slowed near the room where Jack waited. A twitch came at the corner of my eye. I didn't want to see him, especially not after the Vault.

He…unnerved me.

But I found myself outside the door and punched in the code before I slipped inside. He stood near the wall, arms by his sides, and stared at me as I stepped through the doorway. His gaze moved to the knife in my hand as I slipped it into my pocket.

"I take it he's still alive?"

I didn't answer, not yet. Instead, I closed the door and made my way through the space, taking in the bed and the neat pile of clean clothes. "For now." But idle chatter wasn't what I wanted. "Are you ready to tell me everything you know about King?"

"I've told you all I can," he responded. "As I've said every time you've asked."

"Ryth—"

"Is safe," he interrupted, not moving a muscle. "You won't hurt her. I know that now."

"Oh, do you?"

He nodded as his focus shifted to the blood still visible on my hands. "Any man who loves her sister like you do wouldn't allow that to happen."

An ache bloomed in my chest as I crossed the room to stand in front of him. "Don't think I owe you a goddamn thing," I warned. "Nor should you believe any preconceived notions you might have, especially about where my heart lies."

There was a twitch at the corner of his lips. "I won't."

"Good."

"Good," he repeated as he held my stare. "I wonder if you've found the third yet?"

"Third?" I questioned as my gaze narrowed in on him.

"There was a third sister, older, if I remember correctly."

I shook my head, my mind racing through all the DNA tests I'd conducted over the years on every founding member. "No, there isn't."

"Hmm," the smug bastard murmured. "Maybe she wasn't a daughter of The Order?"

Not a daughter?

I shifted my gaze to the wall. *Not a daughter, not a...daughter.* If that was the case, then—

I turned around and left Jack Castlemaine behind. *Sonofabitch.* If King had another daughter, then she could be the entire key to all of this. There had to be someone keeping him safe. Someone who could get in and out of The Order...someone who was there with Vivienne and Ryth.

I closed and locked the door to the room behind me and made my way out. By the time I climbed into my car, I was furious at all the possibilities. Was that the person at Killion's house on the night of the killing? They could've been...leaving me to ask myself was King even alive at all?

I ground my teeth and pulled my phone out. It didn't matter what bombshell I'd just had dropped on me, there were far more important things I was dealing with.

Number one was my son who wasn't answering any of my messages...

And a missing goddamn chip.

I swiped my thumb across the screen and typed out a message, praying to God he answered this time:

I need to know you're okay, Colt. Nothing else matters to me. Please call.

Then I hit send.

It wasn't a lie. I needed to know the son was okay, more importantly, I needed to know if he'd looked at what was on that chip. My hands clenched around the wheel, drawing my focus to my fingers. *Please God, don't let him know.*

I shoved the car into reverse, backed out of the parking spot, and headed for home.

The city streets blurred as I waited for my phone to vibrate. But it remained silent all the way home...

This wasn't like him.

This wasn't like any of us.

Caged. Separated. Exposed.

That's how we were right now and I couldn't do a damn thing to stop it.

Desperation stayed with me as I drove home, turned into the driveway of the gothic mansion, and pulled up near the garage.

Armed guards patrolled the grounds and gave me respectful nods as I climbed out and passed them. I responded, but my focus was on Vivienne as I punched in the code and stepped inside, my words still ringing in my ears.

You will never touch her again. Do you hear me? She doesn't belong to you...she is, and always will be, mine.

Hunger ached inside me as I made my way past my study and the kitchen and turned toward the east wing hallway. I was already unbuttoning my shirt by the time I hit the entrance to the wing. I couldn't get to my bathroom fast enough, desperate to wash his vile fucking blood from my skin.

"London?" Vivienne called as I opened the door to my bedroom.

I stepped inside as I yanked the bloodsplattered shirt off. "Not now, pet."

"Not now?" she repeated carefully as she came down the hall.

I should've known she wouldn't listen. The woman was a pain in my ass...and the object of my desire. I kicked off my shoes as she pushed the bedroom door open behind me. But I had already yanked down the zipper of my trousers and was headed for the shower. She wouldn't want to touch me, nor would she want to look at me, not like this.

"What's going on?" she asked as I stepped into the shower.

"Nothing," I forced out the word under the freezing spray.

But she wasn't going to let it go, just stepped into the water with me, still fully dressed. "You're lying. You're fucking lying to me, London, and I don't like it. No, not 'I don't like it'. *I won't have it.*"

She won't have *it?*

Her gaze shifted from my eyes and trailed down my body. I saw the doubt, saw it like she was the one with the knife carving out pieces of me...starting with my heart.

She thought I'd been with Ophelia...

The thought rocked me. I saw the tenseness of her jaw and the pain in those big brown eyes. Pain because of me.

"I haven't..." I started, and then stopped.

The water warmed and ran down my back and over my chest. She lifted her hand and spread her fingers over my muscles.

"You don't want me anymore, do you?" she asked, her brow pinched. "After the attack."

I stiffened. "What?"

"You barely touch me. You haven't...fucked me." She licked a bead of water from her lips. "You're always distracted when I'm around. I don't think you've come to terms with that night. You avoid it, just like you avoid me."

I held her beautiful, soul-destroying stare. "You seriously think that?"

"Yeah," she answered. "I seriously think that."

Water ran down my arms and washed the blood away. It wasn't enough, but it had to be...for now. I turned around, hit the faucets, and ended the spray. "Then allow me to prove you fucking wrong."

Her eyes widened as I surged forward, picked her up, and gripped her ass against me. "You want to be fucked, pet? Then I'll fuck you until you forget everything else but the feel of my cock and the strength of my goddamn desire. How about that?"

I didn't wait for her to answer, just carried her from the bathroom and out into the hall. It was too early, two, maybe three days too early. But this moment wasn't meant to tame that savage need inside me. It was for her. *Like everything was for her.*

Water dripped from our bodies as I strode to that room and pushed open the door.

It wasn't the basement...it was better.

The black studded bench was perfect height for the machine sitting at the end, its twin arms gleaming steel. I carried her inside and kicked the door closed.

"London?" she murmured.

Those brown eyes widened as she turned her head and took in the room.

I carried her to the bench and laid her down. "You remember what to do?" My voice was harsh and raw.

Her wet hair dripped and rivulets ran down the leather to plop on the floor.

But she gave a nod even as I leaned down, slid my fingers through her wet hair, and softly fisted the strands. "I'm not soft right now, pet. Not kind. I won't hurt you, I'd...*never* hurt you. So I need you to tell me if this isn't what you want."

I didn't need to ask, I saw it in her eyes as she whispered, "I want everything."

She did...especially from me.

All my desperation...all my pent-up rage.

All my hunger. I lowered my gaze and spread my hand low over her belly. *Mine*...that desperation rose. *They will all know who she belongs to.* I closed my fist around her shirt and yanked, safely tearing the buttons free.

Her body jerked at the assault. A cry ripped from her. *No...no, this isn't going to—*

"Green," she whispered. "*Green...green...green.*"

Those words unleashed that darkness inside me. I straightened and looked down at her. In my head, she was splayed out on the dining table, defiance and seething anger in her eyes. I fucking wanted her as much now as I had then...maybe even more.

No, not wanted.

Needed.

I yanked her shirt upwards and she responded by lifting her arms until the sodden garment pulled free. The pink lace cups of her bra were almost see-through and glimpses of dusky rose nipples peeked through. *Jesus...*

"It's okay," she murmured. "I want this."

I jerked my gaze to hers, then gripped the straps of her bra and wrenched it down as I watched her breasts spring free. I was on her in an instant and lowered my head to take her cold, peaked nipple into my mouth.

"Yes," she whispered. "*Yes.*"

My cock hardened instantly as I dropped my hand to the button of her slacks and tugged it open. I shoved them down as I gave her nipple a lick and rose. The same aching need burned in her eyes. Christ, as if I needed to be enticed. I tugged her slacks down while I held that stare.

Think about the goddamn complications! The damn doctor's nagging voice rose as I tossed her wet slacks aside and moved to her panties.

This was about more than complications. Still, the doctor was too goddamn forward. I gripped the sides of the pink lace G-string and dragged it down her thighs. He didn't know a goddamn thing when it came to me, or her.

I turned to the machine, lifted the steel piston, and bent to pull a black steel case from underneath.

Snap.

She flinched at the locks as I pulled a thick, flesh-colored dildo out and snapped it in place. I'd never hurt her. Fuck her until she was senseless, maybe...but I'd never take a chance with her body or her fucking heart.

Those I'd fight to the death to protect.

"Do you want the handcuffs, pet? Or do you think you can restrain yourself?"

She licked her lips and parted her thighs. "Try me."

My lips curled as I picked up the remote. "Oh, I will...believe me."

I pressed the button and leaned forward, grabbed the thick cock, and aimed it at her entrance, then stopped as plastic kissed flesh. "Wider," I commanded.

She obeyed...her thighs gaping until the tendons were taught.

"Wider. I want to see all the way inside."

Her chest rose with a deep breath before she slowly reached down and spread herself wide.

"That's my good girl, look how wet you are." I licked my lips and looked down, that perfect fucking slit just ached to be filled. I reached out, ran my fingers along her opening, and pressed the button, slowly driving the thick plastic cock all the way inside. "Don't move, Vivienne, not even a twitch. Do you understand?"

I met her gaze and caught the small nod.

"Good girl."

My pet was learning.

Her eyes closed and her breath escaped as the dildo slid free, then pushed deeper this time.

"You think I don't want to fuck you?" I murmured as I slid my hand over her abdomen and gently pushed down. "All I think about is fucking you. Owning you. Making you *mine*."

Her fingers still spread her cunt wide, but I caught the pressure as she pushed down, rubbing herself against the dildo as it slid inside.

"That's it, pet. Look how good you take it."

"Oh God," she whimpered, and bit her lower lip.

My cock thickened. The pulse throbbed as I watched her before I leaned down low and pressed the button to slip the dildo all the way out, until the piston rested against the machine.

"Now do you understand?" I murmured, and licked her fingers before driving my tongue deep into her core. "Now do you see I can't get enough of you?"

She unleashed a primal sound and lifted her leg for me to gain better access. I slid my hand underneath and grabbed her thigh as I pushed my face against her quivering core.

I will have you, the words echoed in my head. *I'll have you so much I'll fill you with me.*

I licked her and sucked her clit until she cried out. "London, *please.*"

My cock kicked with her plea. "Fuck, I love it when you beg."

She lifted her head as I raised my head, swiped the back of my hand across my mouth, and climbed onto the bench big enough for two. "Next time, pet." I gripped her thigh, positioned my cock at her entrance, and growled. "I'm going to both fuck you and use that dildo to stretch your ass."

With a savage buck, I drove my cock all the way inside her.

I swear to Christ, it was like coming home.

The warmth of her.

The scent of her.

The way she moaned. "I love you."

I love you.

I rammed my hips forward, the words stuck in my throat as I lowered my head and lost myself in the feel of her.

"*I...*" I grunted and thrust before I lifted my head to find her stare. "*Love...you...*"

She reached for me and clawed my arms until I lay forward against her. Still my hips thrust and drove all the way inside until, with a groan, I succumbed to her.

My body spilled and filled her pussy. "You look so good beneath me." I lifted my hands and caged her in. "*So fucking good.*"

I closed my eyes.

You'll look even better when you're round with my baby.

Colt

No...

NO!

No more!

NO FUCKING MORE!

I snapped awake and kicked out, driving myself back in the driver's seat of the four-wheel drive. Horns blared from passing cars, their headlights blinding me. In the white sparks, I saw her. The dark, predatory eyes. A cruel slash of a mouth. Menacing, that's the stain she'd left behind. One that was growing now, festering and diseased.

The bitch. I want her.

Those fucking words came back to me.

The ones printed out from the conversation between Ophelia and Hale.

The ones I'd found on London's desk.

Fear was a clenched fist around my throat as the rest of the world faded away. She would. I knew that. She'd take Vivienne, just like she tried to take everything else. Ophelia didn't want to just hurt us...she wanted to *destroy us*.

My throat ached, clenched tight around the scream trapped in my chest. I winced as I slowly came back to reality. All my screams were there, every roar I'd swallowed, every tear unshed.

Violent and vengeful.

Like a bomb set to explode.

Lights glittered from the cocktail lounge across the street. I stared as the thrashing sound of my pulse quieted while I watched those from the bar spilling out onto the sidewalk, still clutching flutes of expensive champagne.

But I didn't linger on them, just shifted my gaze to the dark sedan parked out in front of the bar. *Her sedan.*

She was still in there, smiling and plotting.

I winced. That's what she was doing. She was scheming right now, spreading lies and whispering filth, giving orders to take from me the only thing I wanted.

The bitch. I want her.

Pain cut through my palm. I looked down to see my white knuckles clenched tight. A bead of blood slipped along the lines of my fist and fell, hit my black jeans and disappeared. I eased my hold and slowly unfurled my fingers.

The small chip glistened with blood.

A chip which held every vile piece of information about her.

I wanted to know it all, and yet...I was frozen with fear, unable to move forward and too terrified to go back. I worked the edge from my flesh and stared at it. Stared until my mind conjured fragments of my past and morphed them into a fantasy of the future.

A future where Vivienne was back there...with the men who wanted to use her...and hurt her. They'd hurt her so bad she'd be scarred, *just like I was scarred.*

A shriek of amusement rang out and made me flinch. Heavy breaths consumed me as I turned my head. But the bar blurred. I blinked, trying to soothe the sting and closed my eyes, just for a second. God, I was so tired...so fucking tired.

Still, I was snatched from the car and pulled back to the restaurant.

The restaurant where I'd almost ended it all.

I could still feel the *thud...thud...thud...*of my boots, still feel the movement as I reached around to the gun at my back. Her two bodyguards were standing outside, but my movement triggered them. One turned and his gaze narrowed on me as I stepped up onto the sidewalk. The wide glass doors to the restaurant were right in front of me.

That's when I looked...

Past the guards, to the real danger.

To her.

She turned at that moment as she talked to someone near the front. For a second, the mask she wore slipped and the predator was there. That icy stare. That look of *disgust.* Her lips curled before someone called her name and she snapped the pretense back into place.

But that one look was enough.

Enough to make my steps falter...and my pulse race.

Rain beat down as I stumbled forward and my hand slipped from the waistband of my sodden jeans.

"You fucking drunk?" one of the bodyguards muttered.

I kept going as I reeled from the panic inside. The thud of my boots faded. The awful roar of my pulse was just background noise, smothered under the sounds of my brother's screams at ten years old. Shrill screams. Terrifying screams. The ones I held onto as her men kicked and punched and unleashed their cruelty and rage onto my body.

That was all I heard as I stumbled forward until I hit the darkened alley.

Acid burned along the back of my throat.

Faint groans of disgust came from her bodyguards as I lurched forward, grabbed the edge of a building, and expelled the scant contents of my stomach. I retched and heaved as I tried desperately to dislodge the horror of the past along with them.

Still, it stayed with me, even as saliva dripped from my lips onto the ground.

"That's fucking disgusting."

I closed my eyes.

"Goddamn bum."

Rage flickered and my hand slipped. I fell forward and hit my cheek against the bricks. Pain radiated through my face. Pain that stayed with me now. I looked down to the thing I hated and needed all at the same time.

I could use it.

Use it to keep us safe.

My fingers were numb, and slipped as I pulled the door handle. I scanned the faces and found the same two bodyguards from the other night.

I had to be careful.

No doubt after what had happened, they'd notice me.

I scanned the crowded footpath, found the service alley that ran down the side of the building, and strode forward. Desperation drove me forward. I clutched the chip in my hand and lowered my head as I stepped onto the sidewalk. From the corner of my eye, I watched her men scan everyone.

They didn't see me as I slipped past into the shadows.

My boots crunched on bits of gravel, but it couldn't be heard over the traffic noise as I made my way to the back of the bar and the service entrance. The place was packed, so busy no one saw me as I opened the security door and slipped inside. The roar swallowed me instantly, laughter so loud it was almost deafening.

I moved amongst them like a ghost.

I'd never know what it meant to be that happy.

Not like they were.

But I was safe.

And loved.

And I had Vivienne...

I would *not* lose her, not now. I lifted my gaze and found Ophelia instantly as she stood amongst a group with her back to me. I gripped the chip, the one I'd bargain for Vivienne's safety. But the moment I saw her, I froze. She lifted her glass and sipped the champagne. Diamonds glinted from her fingers clutched around the stem.

Do it...

Do...it.

The blood rushed from my face as she tilted her head back and throaty laughter spilled from her lips. I saw her smile, and it was a smile I'd seen before, one that said she *always* got what she wanted. She turned to her fake London and her eyes glinted cruelly. She'd never made any sacrifice that wasn't in her favor. Never bargained. Never made a move. If she wanted it, she *took* it, and damn the consequences.

My pulse leaped as that realization hit home. There could be no 'deal' with her, could there? Only her sick greed and thirst for fucking brutality existed.

Please, not Carven! My own screams were faint as they resounded from the child I'd once been. *Hurt me! Take ME!*

My throat thickened and an ache throbbed. I remembered how I'd begged her not to hurt him, but it had never really been Carven that she'd wanted, had it?

The charcoal paintings surfaced in my mind. The wide, blue eyes from the child she wanted to hurt more than anyone lingered.

It was me...it had always been me.

My pain was sweeter, and she'd used the threat of hurting my brother to taste it. She'd used Carven then...*just like she was using Vivienne now.*

And I'd almost played right into her hands...*again.*

Adrenaline rushed, tearing through my veins like a drug. My breaths raced...

The bitch. I want her.

She was biting once more, sinking her fucking fangs into my vein to drink my torment. She turned back to her party, laughing and grinning as I watched.

"No…" The words spilled free as I stared at her. "You can't have her. *She's mine.*"

The world faded as I lowered my hand and slipped the chip into my pocket. There could be no bargaining, I knew that now. There would be no deals, no pleas. I didn't know why I'd ever thought there could be. I scowled as she reached out and grasped the arm of the man next to her, a man with dark hair and a strong physique. A man who looked amazingly like…*London.*

The man is unpredictable at best. Hale's words from the transcript rose. *Pity you couldn't control him.*

No one can control him. Ophelia had answered.

Except for her.

Yes, except for her.

I took my hand from my pocket and reached around to pull the gun out as I stepped forward.

Motion came in the corner of my eye as someone stepped backwards right into my path. I slammed into him as I started to lift my gun. There was a flare of anger.

"Watch where you're fuck—" he started, then stopped.

But I wasn't even looking at him. I was watching *her* as she turned and strode away, her hold still around the man's arm.

"Colt?"

I flinched at my name and turned my head, to see a familiar stare as Theo Ares grinned at me. He swayed a little, drunk like he'd been before, only this time there wasn't the rim of cocaine beneath his nose.

"Didn't see you there," he murmured, scowling.

Then his eyes flared with concern, sobering him as some friends laughed and called to him. But he didn't respond. Instead, he carefully lowered his gaze to the gun in my hand. "You here for me, Son?"

No one else knew what I was...

Not his friends, or the others partying around me.

But he did.

And it terrified him.

I stared into his eyes, my chest heaving with heavy breaths. "No."

Relief visibly swept through him as he gave me a nervous smile. "If you're not here for me, then who are you here for?"

I looked past him, to where she was striding out of the bar and heading for her waiting car. Theo followed my gaze and flinched the moment he realized.

"You go after her and you're dead, you get that, right?" He turned back, and the knowing was a stony stare. "There's no going back."

"There never was," I answered. "Not from the moment they tried to take her."

I turned, slipped the gun back into my waistband, and strode away.

"Colt," Theo called behind me.

But I didn't stop, just kept going, and headed back the way I'd come until I shoved through the back door and into the alley.

My breaths were savage. Still the acid didn't come as I lengthened my stride, then pushed into a slow run. By the time I tore out of the service alley, the dark sedan was gone...and so was Ophelia.

Anger tore through me.

The kind that came from all the terror I'd swallowed my entire life. There was no fear now...nothing but a bestial need to rip the world apart. I saw them...their smiles and their masks. They all wore them, wore them until they lost themselves. I closed my eyes, trembling as I clenched my fists.

I couldn't stop the white-hot rage from spilling out and unleashing a terrifying roar. The sound filled the alley and spread out. Laughter halted. They all stopped, turned, and stared. Music was all there was now as the smiles turned to fear.

The thud of footsteps came behind me.

"Colt?" Theo asked behind me.

I spun around and met that tormented stare. But it was the Explorer across the street he stared at. "Carven...is he here?"

That rage turned dangerous. I clenched my jaw and my fists followed. Carven was the one they were scared of, the one who was dangerous...the one out of control. I was the *mute,* right? The forgotten one, the one they never noticed at all.

I turned around and strode across the street as they all stared. Heat rose to my cheeks as I yanked open the door and climbed behind the wheel. A stab of the button and the engine came to life. I shoved the four-wheel into gear, punched the accelerator, and tore away from the bar...and the one chance I'd had to keep her safe.

TWENTY-SIX

Vivienne

L ONDON'S BIG HAND SLID OVER MY KNEE AS WE SAT IN THE study, then moved higher to massage my thigh as he snarled into his phone. "I need his location immediately, Jacob. I don't care how many men you need, just make it happen. Find my fucking son and find him tonight."

He was nervous, I thought sex would calm him, but only made him more possessive.

He didn't wait for a response, just lowered the phone, his gaze fixed on the rear wall of the study. Still, that hand didn't stop moving, it just slid higher to push the opening of my dress wide. His thumb stroked my bare skin, the movement born from the need to control *something*. Right now, that something was me.

I lifted my hand and slid my fingers along his arm as I sat cross-legged on the end of his desk. "They'll find him."

"Will they?" he asked as he turned his head and looked at me.

He was panicked now, panicked and dangerous. His messages and calls to Colt had gone unanswered. At first, he'd thought

Colt was pissed about Carven. But as the hours passed, he realized this was more.

I'd never seen him this cold...this *deadly*, not even when he'd strode into the middle of the gun battle between Ryth, her brothers, and The Order.

His grip clenched around my thigh, then slid downwards.

No, he'd never been this...*out of control.*

He held my stare as those demanding fingers drove deeper, until they brushed black lace and slowly, that look turned predatory. "Look at you, so pliable, so *needy*. Open your legs, Vivienne."

My breath caught, because I was still tender from the machine... and then his body. But I couldn't fight him, not now...maybe not ever. My thighs parted on their own.

"Wider," he commanded.

I took in a deep breath as my tendons tightened and my knees spread open to give him what he wanted. An ache flared as he stroked down the crotch of my panties, up and down...*up and down*, each time digging in a little deeper, pushing the tenderness away with the lick of heat.

His jaw flexed and the muscles went tight as he slipped his finger under the elastic. "So willing to please me, just to get what you need. Such a blissful form of torture, isn't it, relinquishing your control to me. And I do control you, don't I, Vivienne?"

His finger curled to circle my clit. I swallowed a moan. "Yes."

He gently pinched my clit, making me shudder. My mind was a mess. But under the panic and the desire came a thrum of terror.

I braced my hands against the desk edge beneath me as he pushed inside.

"So, you'll tell me anything for one more thrust of my finger, won't you?"

I bit down on the inside of my cheek and nodded.

"Use your words, Vivienne."

"Yes. *God, yes.*"

"So tell me, then, how do you know the Ares girl?"

Ares...

Ares?

My mind raced as I tried desperately to tear myself away from the feel of his fingers and *think.*

"I want you to tell me everything you know about them," he demanded. "Leave nothing out."

"I...I know her," I panted.

"How?"

"I've seen her there....at The Order." I squeezed my eyes shut. "*Oh, God, London.*"

"Focus."

I was trying to as he pushed two fingers inside and slowly thrust, then took them away, glistening. I looked down to where my panties were bunched against his hand.

"You've seen her at The Order. Who with?"

I slowly shook my head as I came apart under the brutal strength of his control.

"No one...I don't know. I...I *never saw her with anyone other than The Teacher,*" I moaned and closed my eyes as my hips rocked to meet that slow thrust.

"How many times?"

I squeezed my eyes shut tight as the need to come slammed into me. "Five, maybe six times, I *don't know*."

But he didn't ease up, just stretched me out as he thrust. "Over how long a period?"

His touch hit me deeper, harder, and made me fist my hands. "London, *please*."

"How. Many. Times, pet?" he asked again, his tone unforgiving.

I hated him at that moment.

Hated him and loved him all at the same time.

I lost myself when I was with him.

My control. My will.

I was nothing more than *this*.

"Since I was there."

His strokes stopped cold, tearing me from the peak of release.

"The entire time?" There was no playing in his tone now.

I met those dark eyes as they bored into mine. "Yes."

"And you never saw Dante with them? Just her."

"And the mother."

He scowled. "Are you sure?"

I gave a nod and expected him to slip from my panties and leave me wanting, now that he had what he'd wanted, which was me, panting and desperate. His brow furrowed, but his fingers didn't slip out, still deep inside me.

I lowered my head to stare at his hand cupped against my sex, until slowly...his fingers moved.

"Good girl, pet," he praised, as he curled his fingers to stroke me. "All it takes is two fingers to get what I want. Now lie back...and let me finish what I started."

My elbows trembled, then collapsed, and sent me thudding to the desk. He moved fast to grasp me under my shoulders, then lowered his head.

Warmth licked and wetness slid between his fingers.

I didn't care that I was exposed in a house full of armed men.

I didn't care that I was wet and needy.

"Fuck, you're beautiful," he moaned as he licked deep. "So fucking beautiful."

I lifted my leg to thrust against him. It didn't take long, not when I was...so...goddamn...*close*. I dropped my head back and unleashed a guttural moan as he sucked. My pussy quivered and sent shudders through me as the rush hit me.

"My beautiful plaything." He kissed the inside of my thigh as he eased my panties back into place with a brush of his fingers.

He had me whimpering.

"Just wait until it's all three of us." He lifted his head to meet my stare. "This perfect cunt is going to be dripping."

I carefully eased my thighs closed. The thought of all three of them made me throb while I tried to find the strength to push upwards as London's phone beeped. He pulled a handkerchief from his pocket and wiped his hands before he answered. "Yes."

I slid to the edge of the desk and pulled my dress into place as relief descended across his face. "You saw him two hours ago? Where? Okay. That's good. That's real fucking good. Yes, I appreciate it. Thank you, Jacob. Okay."

He lowered his hand and turned to me. "He was spotted two hours ago downtown."

I released a pent-up breath as a pang tore across my chest. "Thank God…" I whispered. "Thank—"

But my words were cut short as London's phone beeped again. He glanced at the screen, then answered. "Parker?"

Seconds…that was all it took, before London's spine stiffened and that hard look of rage to return. "You fucking what? You can't *be associated with me?* We've been in business together for twenty fucking years, and you're going to cut me out? *Why,* you at least owe me that."

My pulse raced as the heavy thud of boots echoed along the hall coming toward us.

"Well then," London snarled into his phone. "Let me refresh your memory about where I stand. You're either by my side, Parker, or you're against me. So, if I were you, I'd take this opportunity to look very fucking carefully where you are right now. You do not want me as an enemy." Then he ended the call.

A second later, Guild stepped into the room as London lowered his phone.

"Have you seen this?" He stepped closer and offered his own phone.

London glanced at the screen alight in Guild's hand and stared at his own image. "What the fuck is that?"

"Press play, London. You're going to want to see it."

He didn't want to…and neither did I. I shook my head as my body still hummed from London's need as he reached out, grasped the phone, and hit play.

We have the scoop at Lead Investigators. According to sources, the police are launching a brand new full-scale investigation into the death of Killion Dare. Due to an anonymous tip, detectives are looking at billionaire London St. James as a person of interest into the brutal slaying. We can't wait to have more information on this as it unfolds."

"Team three to base. You've got three detectives pulling up outside and making their way to your front door." The call came over the two-way strapped to Guild's belt.

I sucked in hard breaths and slowly turned my head as hard *knocks* sounded on the front door.

"No." I shook my head as London turned toward the door. *"London...no."*

Thud...thud...thud.

"It's okay, pet."

He was so utterly calm as he strode through the doorway and left me behind. I jumped to my feet and rage tore through me as I hurried after him. "Like fucking *hell* it is."

The world seemed to stand still as London opened the front door to three plainclothed detectives waiting.

"London St. James?" one asked.

"Yes."

"I'm Detective Gerald Brown and these are my officers Justine Shale and Marcus Brownstone. We'd like you to accompany us down to headquarters to answer some of our enquiries in regards to Killion Dare's death."

"Am I under arrest?"

The detective said nothing, just shifted his gaze to Guild, who strode forward and grabbed my arm.

"I said, am I under arrest?" London repeated.

I shook my head as the detective stepped forward. Silver cuffs glinted in his hands. Ones he slapped around London's wrist with a *snap*. The sight of that tore something inside me. I unleashed a moan and surged forward.

"Get them off him!" I screamed, even as Guild pulled me back. He didn't belong in cuffs. He didn't belong *with them!* "London...*London!*"

But my stoic protector didn't fight, not even when they yanked his hand behind his back and locked the other cuff in place.

Instead, he called quietly, "Guild."

"With my life, London," he answered beside me, his grip tight around my arm. *"With my fucking life."*

I didn't understand what they were saying.

Not until the police began to pull London away.

I strained forward even as Guild tried to hold me back and managed to yank my arm from his hold as it hit me.

London hadn't called Guild's name to protect him, he'd called his name to make sure *he protected me.*

With my life.

That's what London had made sure of, that our bodyguard would protect me *with his life.*

My heart leaped and slammed in my chest as the cop car door opened and London was seated. Tears came as I tore out the front door, my dress billowing as the car door closed with a *thud*.

"NO!" I lunged at the car and slammed my fists against the window as the engine started.

All I could see was London sitting in the back, that stony mask securely in place…until he turned his head and looked at me.

Then I saw it.

For a fleeting second, the man *I* knew surged to the surface. His brow creased as a look of fear flashed across his face.

I love you, he mouthed the words as the vehicle moved forward, slipped away from my fingers…and left me behind.

I love you…

I threw my head back and swiped my tears aside as Guild's heavy steps approached.

"You need to get back inside, Viv." He pulled me, but I couldn't move.

I was pinned to the spot by my pain.

First Colt…

Now London.

Who was going to leave me next?

I closed my eyes as I swayed. "Bring them back to me," I pleaded. "Do whatever you want with me, but please bring them back."

My tears finally fell, drawing lines down my cheeks…

Until slowly, they fell to the ground.

TWENTY-SEVEN

London

I CROSSED MY LEGS AND SWALLOWED THE TASTE OF BLOOD in my mouth from biting my goddamn tongue. The detective sat across from me, the other two stepping in and out of the room, no doubt trying their best to find something on me, like they'd been doing for the past six fucking hours.

Six hours I'd sat here.

Six hours *without her*.

Vivienne must be going out of her goddamn mind.

I clenched my jaw as I imaged the kinds of fucking hell she was enduring right now. First Colt was gone, and now me. I only hoped Carven and Guild were there to protect her, even if it was from the torment of her own damn mind.

"So, you're trying to tell me that you're *acquainted* with Killion Dare but not in a business sense, nor are you friends?"

Six hours for *this?*

Where the fuck was Major?

"Trying being the operative word there, detective," I responded as I uncrossed my legs, only to slowly recross them the other way.

There was a flicker of annoyance in his eyes. They didn't have a fucking thing on me and they knew it. Meanwhile, Hale was enjoying picking me apart, thread by fucking thread.

"I'm still not getting the big picture here, London."

I winced at my name on his tongue and my mind drifted to another tongue. The one I'd cut out of the bastard who'd used it to hurt someone I love.

"How on Earth are you connected to Mr. Dare?"

There was a sharp knock at the door. This one sounded different, more urgent. *It better be you, Major, or I swear to God...*

"As I've said countless times now, detective, through a mutual associate." *The same fucking dead man who'd put me here.*

And they knew it, too.

Not once in the last six hours had Hale's name crossed their lips. Not fucking once.

That alone spoke volumes.

The detective rose, slowly pushing out the chair with the backs of his legs as he took the opportunity to look down at me. *Twitch.* The nerve jumped at my temple as I forced the words through clenched teeth. "If you're looking for a motive, detective, you'll find none here. I have about as much to gain by Mr. Dare's death as I had when he was alive."

Knock!

I glanced toward the door as the detective took a step. He knew. The motherfucker knew and he was drawing this out for as long as he could, hoping to find any dirt he could.

A look of annoyance crossed his face once more, no doubt from the ass chewing he was getting in the earpiece he wore. With a snarl, he crossed the rest of the room and opened the door, to find my very pissed off, *highly* expensive attorney waiting impatiently on the other side.

Major Copeland pushed into the room, his eyes flashing with fear the moment ours connected. The purse of his lips said it all, but I wasn't in the fucking mood to hear excuses.

"We're leaving," he announced.

I was already rising. "Yes, we are."

The detective said nothing, just watched as I tugged the cuffs of my shirt, then strode over and stopped beside him. "Tell me, detective, what on Earth made you look at me for this?"

His brow pinched before he looked away. That was all the confirmation I needed.

"I apologize that this has been a waste of your entire night. I do hope you can track down whoever caused it. Sounds like a perfect deflection on their part."

A bitter curl of his lips followed. His eyes flashed with a look that said more than his lying tongue ever had.

I turned and followed the lawyer, who cost me seven figures a fucking year to waste my goddamn time with this bullshit, out of that foul fucking room. Other detectives waited, one dressed in a uniform and wearing more medals than I'd ever seen even on a soldier, and I'd seen a lot of soldiers.

He stared at me and gave a slow nod as I passed.

I knew him instantly.

My pulse pounded as I barely nodded in return, then kept walking.

He was the reason I was here, and why Hale's name hadn't even been mentioned once. The fucking bastard was yanking on the collar around my neck, determined to make me heel. I strode along the hallway beside my attorney all the way out into the large expansive foyer of the city's police headquarters.

The only problem was, if you didn't know the beast on the other end of the leash, it might just turn around and tear you to fucking pieces. Daniels' face came back to me, with that empty, shattered stare.

They had no idea who I was…

But they'd soon find out.

I reached into my pocket and grabbed my phone as I strode out the door of the headquarters and into the faint yellow light of the rising sun.

"Mr. St. James!" someone called from a small crowd waiting at the foot of the concrete stairs.

"This way," Major called as the reporters rushed forward.

Major did his best to step in between us, guiding me toward his waiting midnight blue Mercedes, before he turned, his arms stretched toward the onslaught.

A flurry of movement followed from the scavengers. Phones were shoved into my face as desperate questions followed.

"There will be *no* questions answered by Mr. St. James," Major declared forcefully. "No charges have been made by the police and we are doing all we can to help—"

The door unlocked with a loud click. I had already pressed the icon on my phone as I yanked the passenger door open and climbed inside.

Goddamn motherfuckers!

Two rings later, the call was answered. "What do you need me to do?" Carven's words were chilling.

I glared at the fucking reporters as they swarmed outside like vultures, turned my face away, and kept my voice low. "I want you to send a very clear message with Mr. Daniels, one that says *I* don't fucking heel for anyone, especially not *Hale*."

"My *absolute* fucking pleasure," Carven answered instantly.

I could hear the brutal delight in his tone, the excitement that the beginning of the end was here. Only it had to be Hale's end, because there was *no way* I was dying for that piece of shit.

A woman headed toward the car, her head down, her hair flowing behind her. I turned my attention back to the only important thing on my mind. "Vivienne?"

"You might want to get yourself home...as fast as you can."

He said nothing and everything all at once.

I winced at the image that arose. She'd be pacing. *She'd be pissed. She'd be tearing herself apart.*

"I'm on my way," I answered and ended the call as the approaching woman came closer, then lifted her head.

Brown eyes met mine through the windshield before they turned away and she melted into the cluster of reporters.

I flinched.

My heart hammered.

Blood drained from my face.

Those brown eyes stuck in my mind...ones that were eerily familiar.

I wonder if you've found the third yet?

Jack's words resounded.

A third sister, older, if I remember correctly.

Then it hit me like a blow. I jerked my gaze past the crowd of reporters as the driver's door opened and Major climbed behind the wheel.

"London?" Major called behind me as I left the passenger door open and lunged out.

Those eyes called to me, ones I knew better than anyone, ones I'd lost myself in over and over again.

Those were Vivienne's eyes.

I rushed and slammed into the waiting reporters who shoved their phones into my face as though I'd somehow changed my mind and was ready to bleed all my fucking secrets out to anyone who'd listen. The hard brunt of the collision knocked me sideways before I straightened.

A roar of protest came as I pushed forward, raced up the first, second...and third stairs. My pulse pounded in my ears as I searched for her. By the time I hit the top, I was sucking in hard breaths as I scanned the foyer of the police station...but she wasn't there.

There was no one in the foyer. The glass doors were still closed from when I'd walked through. She had to be here...*somewhere.*

King's third daughter.

The one who would lead me right to him.

I unleashed a roar as I charged toward the side of the building. Shadows waited for me. Shadows, but nothing else.

"What the fuck is going on?" Major called, breathing heavily behind me. I turned, and found his panicked stare. "Are you fucking falling apart on me?"

I scowled as I stared at him, then slowly shook my head.

He lifted his hand. "Then let's get the fuck out of here before those assholes decide they want another fucking bite, shall we?"

He was right.

I *knew* he was right.

But that didn't stop me looking over my shoulder one last time before I followed him, scowling the whole time at the reporters, who stared back at me with wary, confused expressions as I strode to the open car door and climbed back inside.

My damn hands shook as I fastened my seatbelt and stared up at the darkened building.

"Christ, you look like you've seen a goddamn ghost," Major snapped as he started the engine and shoved the car into reverse.

But it hadn't been a ghost that had just revealed itself.

It was the connection I'd needed…

To save myself…

And my family.

Exhaustion hit me as I leaned back against the headrest and my stomach churned with pent-up rage. "Just get me home, Major," I murmured, knowing what was waiting for me. "Just get me home."

TWENTY-EIGHT

Colt

Rage ripped me apart and pieced me back together. I climbed back into the Explorer and started the engine. But my fucking hands were shaking...shaking so bad I couldn't grab the gearshift. I wrapped them around the wheel instead and tried to hold on to my last sliver of sanity.

Still, they stared. Their wide eyes fixed on me from across the street where they spilled around Theo Ares as he watched me. I reached down, shoved the four-wheel drive into gear and punched the accelerator.

The vehicle surged forward, tires howling as I tore past the bar. I needed to get out of there. I needed to...

Tear something apart.

I clenched my grip and turned the wheel to zoom around the corner of the building. Dark, empty streets waited for me. I should be home...I should be anywhere except for here. But I couldn't go back there, not yet. Not while she...while Ophelia was *here*.

The green street lights blurred under my vision. I swiped my eyes and exhaled slow and hard. I didn't know where I was driving, all I knew was I couldn't go back home...not yet, at least.

Not with that rage so tight and explosive inside me.

I wouldn't do that...

Not with her.

I pushed the SUV harder, tearing along the city streets until the towering buildings slowly gave way to a star-speckled skyline and boarded-up, ruined buildings. I didn't know why I was here. Not at this place...

Carven came here.

Carven and his fury.

Not me.

But the wheel turned almost like it drove itself and I found myself braking as three guys leaned with crossed ankles against the fenders of a gleaming black Maserati, watching me as I drove past.

"No," I whispered out loud as I pulled into the driveway of the construction site and stopped beside the armed guard.

My voice was scratchy and hollow as I gave the code and waited for him to step aside.

A nod was all it took.

One nod and I knew I'd arrived in Hell.

"Don't do this," I muttered to myself as I pulled the Explorer alongside gleaming Lamborghinis and brand new Bentleys. "This isn't me."

I was under some kind of spell as I killed the engine and climbed out.

"Jesus Christ! HIT HIM, FOR FUCK'S SAKE! STOP DANCING AROUND!"

I flinched, drove my fists into my pockets, and looked to the ground as cries rang out from the rich assholes who'd paid their money to see blood. But I wasn't here for them...I was here for me.

I knew that.

Even if I didn't want to admit the truth.

I made my way to where the guard stood at the door as he slowly stepped aside to let me pass. My boots crunched on concrete and rubble. Remnants of bricks were all I saw as I made my way through the construction site and skirted the area where four fights were being held. Cheers followed a brutal *thud*. Gleaming black paintwork and the license plate *ARES 1* caught my eye.

I didn't want to look up. I wouldn't have, but a familiar snarl drifted to my ears. "Yeah, yeah, I see him. He's here...no, alone. How the fuck should I know?"

Slowly, I lifted my gaze and met the critical stare of Silas Ares. He leaned against the closed door of his sports car as he stared. But I lowered my head and kept walking to where snarling growls came from the ring in the barbaric spectator sport.

I caught movement at the edge of my view as he tore his gaze from the fight in front of him to glance my way.

"No...*fuck no!*" he snarled. "I told you before not to fucking step foot in here. *What the fuck do you think you're*—HIT HIM, FOR FUCK'S SAKE!" he roared at the fighter.

"It's me," I mumbled as I stopped in front of a big man.

Brutal thuds echoed from the fight mere inches away from me. Iron quieted, then slowly turned back to me, leaving me to lift my gaze to meet his stare.

"What the fuck?" He scowled, glancing behind me for the twin that wasn't here, then turned back. "I thought you were deaf?"

I flinched, then just stared back as he grew awkward before he turned back to the fight. "What the fuck do you want?" he flung over his shoulder at me.

"I want to fight."

He didn't shift his stare, but I knew he heard me. His eyes closed for a second as he muttered something under his breath. "Go away, kid. Your brother would fucking murder me if he knew I let you get beaten to a fucking pulp."

"I'm not here for him. I'm here for me."

Iron opened his eyes, then jerked that glare my way. "He know you're here?"

I shook my head.

He licked his lips, then turned to where the guy in front of us was getting annihilated. "Jesus fucking Christ, my sister hits harder than that asshole." He glanced toward the other three other fights that filled the area. "My sister hits harder than all these goddamn losers."

I waited...

Waited for him to turn back to me.

He finally did, but still glanced to the doorway behind me. "You sure he doesn't know you're here?"

I didn't answer and he didn't wait. "How much have you got?" There was a wince as the fighter in front of us dropped like a stone.

"What a fucking waste of money!" Someone called out behind me.

"You know what?" Iron snarled. "You can't be any fucking worse than these idiots."

With a jerk of his head, he motioned me in. "Get yourself ready and let's see what you've got."

I took a step, grabbed the plastic tape that wrapped around the barriers, and stepped in to the ring, where a guy twice my size sucked in hard breaths while he stared at his competitor, out cold on the ground in front of him.

"What the fuck is this?" he growled, glancing at Iron.

"Kid, don't you want to take off your jacket? Or warm up, or—I dunno, *hell, do something?*" Iron muttered, his voice sounding warped and strange.

But I wasn't looking at him, I was looking at the ground.

The building seemed to...fade.

I was slipping back there, to the pain and the rage, to the echoes of my childhood that never seemed to let me go. Roars filtered to me, cheers and calls. But I was standing in a vacuum, one where all the air had been sucked from my world.

My opponent stepped closer, his mouth moving as he lifted his hand, pointing to me then to Iron. But I wasn't listening, not to the sounds, or the screams. I was listening to my heartbeat, to the *thud...thud...thud* of life coursing through my veins, as I watched *everything*.

I saw the moment Iron commanded the big guy.

Saw the moment his look of frustration turned deadly.

The scowl smoothed from his forehead.

His jaw flexed, as did his fists.

I saw Iron motion to the others, and the three remaining fights around me stopped, then they all turned toward me. I didn't tense, didn't curl my fists, just stood there as Iron gave a slow nod. Then it started.

The first blow came hard, swinging through the air to land against my cheek with a brutal *crack!*

I stumbled sideways. My knee buckled for a second before I caught the fall.

Agony ripped through my cheek and radiated along my jaw. Still, I straightened and sucked in hard breaths.

"What the fuck is this?" The guy in front of me glared. "Fight back."

I said nothing, just waited for the next blow to come. I didn't have to wait long.

With a roar, he drove his fist upwards, connecting with the underside of my jaw. My head snapped backwards and my teeth gnashed with a *crunch.* Stars collided behind my eyelids and blazed neon white as I stumbled backwards.

The crowd screamed.

Iron was howling.

But in the middle of the chaos came her.

Beautiful brown eyes.

A smile that made me feel invincible and worthless all at the same time.

"Colt, baby," she whispered, and it was like I stood in a bubble, one that was entirely made up of Vivienne. Her throaty, erotic tone swallowed everything else around me. *"Colt, I need you."*

I stumbled from the blow, then straightened. The big guy in front of me drove his boot against the concrete and charged forward, his eyes blazing with determination.

"*Colt. I NEED YOU!*" she screamed.

The sound of her fear shattered something inside me. Shackles of my past broke and fell away as I moved at the last second, causing the fighter to pitch forward. Momentum took him and I used that to swivel around to grab him and unleash my fists.

Thud...

Thud.

THUD!

I became nothing but fists, rage, and movement. Blood came, I don't know from where or who. All I knew was there was movement as others rushed forward. But that same momentum gripped me now...and there was no turning back.

THUD.

THUD.

CRUNCH.

Someone tried to tackle me, but he ended with his back on the ground and me straddling him. Something wet smacked my face as I drove my fist down over and over *and over again.*

"*Colt.*"

"*COLT!*" she screamed inside my head.

And stopped me cold.

I looked down at the wide, terrified eyes of the guy underneath me. But he wasn't a fighter. Blood streamed from the broken nose of Iron's bouncer.

"Get the fuck off him!" Iron screamed.

But the rest of the crowd was quiet. Not just quiet...*stunned.* Deep moans came from behind me. I glanced over my shoulder at the massive guy who, seconds ago, had charged toward me. But he wasn't charging now. He was writhing, clutching his shoulder, groaning in agony.

"You fucking *broke it!*" he moaned. "You *fucking broke my shoulder!*"

"Get the fuck off me," Iron's guy hissed underneath me, his voice nasal through his broken nose. "Just get the fuck off me, man."

I slowly rose off him, my fisted hands bloody at my side. He stared up at me in fear, the kind of fear I knew well.

"You're fucking broken!" he snarled as he shoved away, cupping his nose with one hand. *"Motherfucker!"*

I stared at him...at all of them, knowing I'd done this...but I didn't feel it. I felt nothing.

I felt nothing but her.

Only her.

Iron stumbled forward and roared. *"Look at what you fucking did! Get the fuck OUT OF HERE!"*

I followed the wave of his hand to where three other guys slowly rose to their feet, each of them staring at me with a look of terror. I stumbled backwards, trying not to look at all the others who sat on their cars, watching me in silence.

But it was Silas Ares that stepped forward. "Colt," he called as I tried to step around him.

With the movement, came agony. A tsunami of pain slammed into me as I staggered toward the demolished door and the exit.

With each wave of pain, those sparks came, exploding inside my head. I groaned as I hit the cold night air and tried to focus…to find the blurred outline of the Explorer.

I took a step toward it, and the moment I did, my knees gave way.

"*Colt,*" Vivienne called inside my head.

I had to get to her.

I had to get—

I hit the ground hard and agony ripped through my knees. I lifted my head, and surged upward, desperate to get to the car. Shadows shifted, blurring against the neon glare behind my eyes. I took three more swaying steps before I reached out, desperate to grab the handle of the door, but my fingers slipped…

And I fell.

The darkness blurred and shifted around me. I stared up as a shadow moved closer. "You're reckless," the shadow snarled. "And so is your brother. I thought you might be different, thought you might be like us, but I can see now you're not."

Someone grabbed me and lifted me from the ground.

"*No.*" I lashed out, trying to fight.

Faces blurred. I looked to the lights and the expensive cars, finding hardly a glance my way. Silas Ares and the others around him stepped back and watched as the shadows closed in around me.

"Get him inside," the voice commanded.

I bucked and kicked out with my boot. "Get the fuck *off me.*"

Silas glanced at the men who grabbed me and I caught the scowl in a blur before he turned around, giving me his back...and the others followed, *refusing* to see.

"Fuck you," I forced through clenched teeth as that agony continued to roar in my head.

They carried me to a car and pushed me onto the floor. I tried to hold on, fought the wave of darkness. But it was consuming, leaving me to drift into the gloom. Car doors closed with *thuds* all around me before an engine started.

"Who...who the fuck are you?" I whispered.

But no one answered...

Because I was gone, plunging headfirst into nothing.

"WAKE UP."

A kick came at my side. Pain followed, radiating as I cracked open my eyes. A stranger stood above me, and stared down. Dark, unflinching eyes pierced mine.

"You won't just get her taken back, you know that, right?" He slowly squatted onto the balls of his feet. "There're men out there that make Haelstrom Hale look like a fucking boy scout. They 'll take her, the ones we call the Others, and you won't find her again. Do you want that?"

I sucked in hard breaths, staring at him.

My pulse boomed.

He scowled, his lips curling.

He knew about the Order.

You're reckless. His words echoed back to me. *And so is your brother. I thought you might be different, thought you might be like us, but I can see now you're not.*

Like us...

Like us.

I slowly turned my head, finding others who stood in the shadows. "Sons," I whispered as my stomach sank. "You're Sons."

He lifted a knife, the blade gleaming under the light. "I did tell your brother I'd go through him to get to her, but it looks like I won't need to go to the trouble." He settled that hostile stare on me. "I'll go through you instead."

He lunged forward and drove the knife through the air as I swung. I grabbed his wrist, knocked the blade free, and kicked out.

The sharp blare of a two-way radio sounded, filling the air with frantic chatter. But I didn't listen. I swung instead, driving my fists into the side of his head.

Get out of here...

Get the fuck out of here now!

This fight was different. It was realer somehow, like everyone else wasn't a threat, but this asshole was.

"You stay the fuck away from her!" I roared as I drove him backwards.

"We have to go," came a frantic call from one of the others.

"Kane! *We have to go NOW!*"

Gunshots came, tearing through the metal shell from the abandoned warehouse, leaving gashes behind, ones wide enough to let the bright glare of sunlight through. Was it morning? How long had I been here? The asshole in front of me shoved me. He sucked in hard breaths as he rose and staggered.

He looked down at me, scowling. "Why the fuck do you fight so hard for her?" he growled as a *bang* came from somewhere outside.

The others were already moving, grabbing whatever they could and running in the opposite direction.

"Colt!" a familiar voice called.

I tore my gaze away from the retreating group to the team of former Navy SEALs as they headed toward me, their guns aimed at the Sons as they slipped away.

"Harper?" I croaked.

He came closer and reached out his hand even as he had his sights trained on the distance. "It's me, buddy. Come on, let's get you out of here."

I took his hand and let him haul me up to a stand.

But I followed his gaze...to the Sons who'd disappeared.

Sons, who'd warned my brother.

Sons, who wanted the one thing they'd never have.

The daughter who belonged to us.

TWENTY-NINE

Vivienne

———

"Vivienne...stop!" Carven grabbed my hands and pulled them from the tangled mess of my hair. "You're going to make yourself fucking bald."

Strands pulled and snapped as I fought him. He snarled as he unfurled my fingers and pulled my hair free. But I couldn't just *stand there and wait,* I had to *do* something. Because I was going insane.

I pulled my hands from his and turned to pace the length of the study, my gaze flashing to the empty doorway. "He should be here by now. He should be back."

Back and forth. Back and forth...*back and forth.* I waited for the click of the lock...and the heavy thud of their steps. My eyes stung and my vision was grainy as I fixed on that empty doorway, until I *hated* the fucking sight of it.

Agony carved open my chest and hacked out my heart.

It was somewhere out there.

Somewhere, clutched in London's controlling grip.

Cradled in Colt's chest.

Leaving a hollowness inside me.

"Where are they?" I turned and found that unflinching, icy stare. "Where the fuck are they, Carven?"

Beep.

He yanked up his phone and stared at the screen.

"What?" I stumbled forward. "What is it?"

"They found him," he muttered. "They found Colt."

A trapped breath escaped me as my shoulders curled. "Thank God. *Thank God!*"

I staggered and reached out, desperate to grab something as the study seemed to sway...only *something* caught me.

Carven lashed out and grasped my hand, his focus still fixed on the screen as he typed, before he lowered the phone...and turned to me. "They're safe. They're both safe, Wildcat. You're okay now. You're okay."

He pulled me close, the...cold, cruel hunter dragged me against his chest as he rose. His hands were awkward when he gripped my shoulders tightly, as though he didn't know what to do...and yet he wanted to do *something*. I knew his words weren't just for me, they were for him, too.

My throat thickened. His grip clenched as a tear slipped down my cheek. The movement was so fast, I barely saw it as he flicked the drop away with a slide of his thumb, then stared at it shimmering against his nail.

Then he slid it into his mouth and turned that chilling stare my way.

My breaths froze, then in the silence I heard the faint *thud* of a car door.

Carven's gaze moved to the door. He dropped his hands and stepped around me as the *snap* of the lock sounded. Heavy steps followed. I'd know that gait anywhere.

"London," I cried as I spun and lunged for the doorway.

I was out of the study in a blur. My heart drove against my chest as I gripped the doorway. His white shirt was open, sleeves rolled high. There was a look of utter exhaustion as I rushed toward him, making him seem older, colder...and *desperate*.

But he wasn't too exhausted to catch me as I lunged.

His arms were around me in an instant, sliding up my back as he clasped me hard against him. A huge exhale and he murmured, "Fuck, I missed you."

I clung to him as I buried my face against his neck. His rich scent invaded me in an instant. I sucked in deep breaths, desperate to fill that empty void inside me once more. "I was so fucking scared," I croaked. "So fucking scared."

His strong arms tightened. But underneath the desperation there was a taut, trembling rage. The sound of an engine came as it drew closer to the house. Carven turned at the sound and listened to the rumble of the engine as it pulled to a stop.

The heavy thud of car doors came, followed by the sound of the vehicle pulling away. I stepped back from London and turned my head at the faint sound of the lock of the front door. Heavy steps echoed, mirroring the boom of my heart. From around the corner came Colt, looking horrific.

There was dried blood on his face. His clothes were a mess, crumpled, torn, and dirty. But it was his eyes that gripped me. They were fixed, empty, not like the eyes of the man I knew at all. He looked at the floor as he came closer, his hands shoved into his pockets.

Carven and London didn't say a word. They didn't go to him, didn't move at all. But I wasn't so contained. I strode forward, then lunged to wrap my arms around his neck. He grabbed me and pulled me close. I could feel the tension in his body and the discord in his soul. I could feel the sheer weight he carried...the only question was, *why?*

His arm dropped from around me as he stepped close to the others and dragged his other hand out of his pocket, then reached out to London. Nothing was said as Colt placed the small chip in his hand. London looked down, then clenched his fist around the thing.

London scowled and lifted his gaze to Colt's. But Colt turned around and walked away. I stared, feeling that same emptiness as though he was still gone.

He wasn't here, not really. Somehow, I'd lost him, just when I thought I'd found them all. I took a step forward before my arm was grabbed.

"Don't, let him go," Carven growled.

Only this time, I wasn't following orders. I yanked my arm from his hold. "Don't tell me what to do," I snarled, and surged forward.

Tonight was too raw.

Too bloodthirsty.

I'd almost lost more than one of them.

I wasn't going to take another chance. Not for all the safety in the world.

I pushed into a run and caught up to him as he hit the entrance to our wing.

"Wait!" I called and grabbed his arm as he kept walking. "Colt...*stop*."

He did, then just stood there, facing away from me. The side of his head was a dried, bloody mess.

My heart was in my throat. "What have I done?"

His eyes tightened and there was a tiny shake of his head. It was all he was giving me.

"Then why are you pushing me away?" I whispered, running my hand along his powerful arm. "I need you."

He flinched at those words and turned instantly to grab me and yank me close.

I wrapped my arms around his neck and rose to pull his mouth to mine. "I need you, don't you get that? You can't leave me, you can't *ever* leave me."

He kissed me, turning me around to drive me back against the wall. He was hungry, so fucking hungry. His big hand slid around the back of my neck and held me in place. My lips were crushed against my teeth, but I didn't care. I pulled him harder against me, desperate for more. Until he broke away, scowled, then drove his hand out to brace against the wall as he swayed.

"That's it." I pushed forward and grabbed him around the waist. "Into my bathroom, now."

I expected him to fight me. One look into those blue eyes and I saw the spark of defiance. But he didn't argue. He let me wrap my arm around his waist, steadying him as I walked him to my room. I threw the door open and it hit the wall with a *bang* while I helped him into the bathroom. Under the white light of the bathroom, his head looked even worse.

"Sit," I commanded as I eased him toward the toilet.

He let out a snarl, then opened his mouth to speak. I cut him off with a glare, and he slowly closed his mouth once more. "That's what I thought."

I gave a jerk of my head, and the dangerous son slowly sank down.

"Good boy," I murmured, and earned a glare.

One I ignored as I set to work to see what damage there was to my pain-in-the-ass, stubborn-to-an-infuriating-level lover. He didn't wince when I parted those thick brown curls, didn't pull away. Instead, he leaned forward and pressed his forehead against my belly.

"I can't see a damn thing with this mess," I grumbled as I tried to find the wound under all the blood. "You need to shower so I can see better."

He lifted his head, grabbed his shirt, and pulled it off. The firm muscles of his chest flexed and the light hit the thick, crisscrossed silver scars. On anyone else they'd be gruesome. But on him...they were beautiful. Even beaten and bloody, this man was mesmerizing. He rose to tower over me. Those intense eyes nailed me to the spot as he reached down, unbuckled his jeans, and pushed them low.

My bloody, silent protector was breathtakingly naked in an instant.

And for a second, I forgot how to breathe.

I swallowed hard and fought the urge to look down as I realized I was staring like an idiot. "We'd better...we'd better get you in the shower."

He just stood there. "You're going to need to move for that."

"Oh?" I looked down, to see I was standing in his way. "Yeah, of course."

I stepped backwards, then instantly regretted it. Because the view from the back was just as spectacular as the one from the front. His thick shoulders flexed as he opened the shower door and stepped in. I traced his body down to his tight ass and powerful thighs. He was scraped and bruised almost all the way. On instinct, I grabbed my shirt and tugged it over my head, kicked off my shoes, then shoved my pants off.

I joined him in my underwear. This wasn't about sex, although, Christ, it was hard to focus as he turned around and tilted his head back. There was something insanely erotic about watching the tendons of his throat flex, something that made my pulse race. He was exposed to me, like a powerful predator giving in to his mate.

There were no walls here.

No pretense...

Not at this moment.

I stepped forward and slid my hand along his arm. "Let me wash you."

Water ran down his chest in rivulets as he lowered his head and looked at me.

"If you want me to, that is?"

A careful nod and I bent, grabbed the washcloth, squeezed it in the palm of my hand, and massaged his head carefully. I found the gash. It was small...but gushed like a torrent the moment the water washed away the partially formed scab.

If I hurt him, he didn't say.

Nor did he flinch.

But he inhaled deeply when I ran my hands over his hard pecs and his eyes glinted when they moved lower.

"I'm not injured there, Wildcat."

I stopped, very aware I might trigger him. "Do you want me to stop? I can."

He reached out, grabbed my wrist, and pressed my hand against his hard cock. "You stop now and we're going to have a problem. You feel me?"

I smiled instantly. "Yeah." I curled my hand around his thickness. "I do."

He forced a smile, even if it was haunted. "Good, because tonight I'm sleeping in your bed."

THIRTY

Carven

___

I GRIPPED THE VANITY AS I LISTENED TO THE WATER RUSH in the bathroom next to mine. I knew he was in there, knew *she* was in there, too. I clenched my jaw as I imaged exactly what they were doing, her hands all over his body, his mouth on hers. Jealousy seethed inside me. But if I was honest, it wasn't just him fucking her that had me riled.

It was *him*, his moodiness, his *silence*.

He was never silent.

Not with me.

I was his fucking brother.

I sucked in deep breaths and lifted my gaze to the ruthless motherfucker in the mirror, the one with stark white hair, dark roots showing, and unflinching, murderous eyes. I stared into those eyes, ones that others thought were like my brother's. But they weren't.

They were colder.

Cutting.

And nothing like the stare which had settled on me when Colt came into the hallway minutes ago. He'd barely looked at me, just pressed that fucking chip in London's hand and walked away like I hadn't spent the entire fucking night worried out of my goddamn mind about him.

That wasn't like him...

Not at all.

The muscles of my jaw flexed. My grip on the vanity tightened until I pushed back and yanked my shirt over my head, then kicked off my boots. The jeans were the same as I'd had on before, but the shirt was one I'd grabbed from the warehouse after disposing of Daniels' body...

Because the other one was *soaked with blood.*

I tossed all my clothes into a heap on the floor, then stepped into the shower and switched on the spray.

There was blood under my fingernails. The shit had worked into the edges and stained the cracks. I closed my eyes and tilted my head back. Screams still rang inside my head, and guttural husky hisses of air from a man who had no tongue.

I opened my eyes and turned to pump shampoo into my hand and lathered my hair. The *thud* of the water being switched off sounded next to me, causing me to glance at the wall. Moody bastard. He could fucking have her if it was that important. I reached down and grasped my cock as a savage burn of anger rose.

He could have her.

Pain flared like a fucking knot in my chest. One that worked its way deeper. I braced my hand on the wall, then leaned forward and unleashed a moan. *Jesus.*

I tried to suck in air as the bathroom darkened and swayed.

My hand slipped on the tiles, and I crashed against the wall.

I was having a fucking heart attack.

My damn knees wobbled. I jerked my gaze up and slammed my fist against the wall. *Thud.* "Brother," I croaked, but the word was a whisper...under a howling need.

What the fuck is this?

As the bathroom grayed, I tried to focus. I needed to go to them. I needed...

I slapped the faucet and ended the spray. The moment I did, that strangle-hold in my throat eased. Air rushed in and drove away the darkness, a little bit, at least. I stumbled out, grabbed a towel from the rack, and wrapped it around me as I lurched toward the door.

My senses sharpened in the hall. Every one of them zeroed in on her. Her energy, her anger. Her fucking desperation. I made for her bedroom door and pushed it open. Inside, movement came from the bed. Him...and *her.*

Blue eyes flashed my way as I quietly closed the door.

She didn't even notice me. Her eyes were closed and her head was tilted back as he slid his fingers through her hair. Saying nothing, he watched me approach the bed before he turned back and kissed her.

She gripped his arm and her lips parted as he took her. The way he dragged her against him mesmerized me. I'd seen him kiss her before, seen him fuck her, too...*but nothing like this.*

This was desperate and consuming.

This was...

Love.

That's what this was.

She must've sensed me then. The panicked catch of her breath came before she jerked her gaze my way and found me standing at the foot of her bed.

Silence…that's all there was between us.

I waited for her to say the words. *Get the fuck out, Carven, or leave.*

I'd pushed her to say those words before.

I'd wanted her to say those words.

But fuck me…

If she said them now—cruel fucking terror slammed into me—*if she said them now, they'd destroy me.* Goosebumps raced along my arms. I'd once thought she was pathetic and weak. *Jesus, I couldn't have been more wrong.*

She was more ruthless than any Son.

With one word, this *daughter* could tear out my fucking heart.

But she didn't say the words I was terrified to hear. Instead, she shifted closer to Colt, then lifted the sheet on the opposite side.

I was moving before I knew it, aware how fucking desperate and needy I looked. But I didn't give a fuck. I dropped the towel to the floor, rounded the bed, and climbed in.

She reached for me instantly…her arm slid around my waist. I looked down at her reddened, swollen lips from my brother's mouth. Then, I gripped her jaw and kissed her.

She yielded.

Eased back against the pillow.

Gave herself to me as I plunged my tongue deep.

While my brother watched.

His hand skimmed her ribs and cupped her breast. Fuck me if the sight of that wasn't a shot of adrenaline. I broke away, sucked in a hard breath, and looked down.

"You like this?" I watched my brother's fingers slide over her tight nipple. "Like my brother's hand all over your breast and my tongue down your fucking throat?"

She swallowed, then whispered. "Yes."

My pulse thundered. "You want us both?"

Her eyes widened. "Yes."

I lifted my gaze, meeting that careful fucking stare.

He said nothing, but that wasn't a no, was it?

It wasn't a fucking no.

I lowered my head and moved down, licked the tight peak of her other breast, and shoved the sheets aside. "Legs open, *daughter.* We're gonna need some prep here."

She complied. So. Fucking. Fast.

Her legs splayed. Her pussy was already wet as I pushed my fingers inside. "Brother?" I managed as my cock hardened at the feel of her.

He hesitated for a second, then lowered his hand and dragged it down her body to find her clit.

"Oh, God." She shuddered under our touch.

I looked down and watched his big thumb brush over that tender little nub as my fingers fucked her.

Him.

Her.

Me.

We were going to share her, just like we'd shared everything, including the body of the woman who'd given us life. The vein under my cock throbbed at the thought of that, driving all the way to the head. She was practically dripping as my brother shifted lower in the bed.

I slid my fingers out, caught all her moisture, and rubbed it against the tight ring of her ass.

"Fuck…" she whimpered, and closed her eyes as Colt licked her nipple.

Her body clenched and shuddered as I slowly pushed in. "Open your eyes, Wildcat," I commanded. "Look down."

She did, tilting her gaze to watch us. My brother lifted his head, found her gaze, then rubbed his finger over her clit as he slid down in the bed.

I carefully pushed my fingers in deeper as I stretched her. "Look at how fucking well you take us." Her body clenched as he slipped two of his big fucking fingers inside her. Slick coated his knuckles as he thrust.

"Look at how your greedy cunt needs him. You fucking need him, right?"

Her answer was a tortured moan.

I liked the sound of that.

My wildcat opened her legs wider. "That's it, my perfect fucking whore. Lift your knees."

She opened all the way for us as I lowered my head, worked the spit in my mouth, then dribbled it down. It ran between my brother's fingers when he opened up her cunt. The sensation made her catch her breath.

I thrust my hips on instinct, humping the goddamn air. Christ, I'd never felt anything like this. I was out of my fucking mind with the need to fuck. But I had to take my time...I had to *make it good for her.*

I licked my lips as my spit combined with her wetness and slipped around my fingers, then I pushed two fingers back in. Her ass clenched around the invasion as her body worked to take it. But it was softening with the stretch, and warming. "That's the girl." My words were husky. "Open that ass for me, baby."

She dropped her head back and drove her hips down, which caused me to reach deeper inside her. Colt spread her wide, then spat himself, and watched the trickle run the length of her cunt before he gripped her shoulders and pulled her toward him.

I used the momentum, slid her leg over his thick thigh, and moved behind her. "Breathe, Wildcat," I urged as I grasped my cock and pressed against her opening. She pushed her ass against me, letting me ease the head in.

"Jesus...fucking, *Christ,*" I moaned as I slipped back out, only to push in once more.

She took it all that time, that tight fucking muscle like a fist around my cock. She bucked, then moved out and back. Something rubbed the head from the inside, stroking, pushing. It took me a second to realize what it was...

It was Colt.

He thrust deep inside her. The pressure collided against me. I gripped her hips, held her steady, and timed his thrusts to meet the pace, and I tried to keep it together. But every time he drove inside her, it nearly sent me over the fucking edge, caressing me through her.

My fingers dug deep into her flesh. I knew it was bruising, but I couldn't stop...I couldn't...

"Harder," she moaned. *"Carven...fuck me harder."*

Her words were all I needed. I reached up, grabbed a fistful of her hair, and yanked her head back, hard enough to shock her... but not to hurt. *I never wanted to hurt her again.* "Tell me, *Wildcat*," I grunted. "How does it feel to be fucked by both of us?"

Her body clenched and trembled around my cock as Colt thrust harder, and unleashed a growl. She bucked and jolted with the impact. I drove deep, forcing her body down around him. "Christ, you fuck so good. You were made for this, Wildcat. You were made for *us.*"

"Oh, God...oh—" My little whore stilled, and her ass pulsed around me as she came. *"Jesus..."*

I held on, my fist in her hair, the other on her shoulder as I drove her body down hard and rammed all the way in to the hilt. "Fuck... *me*," I moaned as my cock kicked and I came hard. Colt lowered his head and released a grunt as he slammed home inside her time after time. He was relentless, desperate and powerful. Her body jolted with each thrust, until he gave one loud growl, deep and guttural, and filled her pussy with warmth.

I felt that warmth.

Felt it all.

Stars collided behind my eyelids, blinding white. I lost myself in the neon glow, the aftershocks of her body milking every goddamn drop from me.

I eased my hold from her hair and dropped my head forward to kiss her shoulder, then nuzzled the side of her neck. I couldn't stop the need to touch her, not even if I wanted to...and for the first time in my life, I didn't want to.

Her asshole gaped when I slid out. Cum coated my cock as it pressed against her ass when she eased against me.

"You okay?" Colt gasped.

She tried to catch her breath, then nodded instead and whispered, "Very much okay."

He wedged her between us as she dropped her head beside his and tried to catch her breath. The room was filled with those raspy sounds as we all came back to Earth.

"You do NOT fucking leave me, do you understand that?" She lifted her head and met that deep-blue stare. "Because if you do, it'll kill me."

My brother searched her eyes and it was as though, in that second, he was a stranger. I'd never seen that desperation in him, not in all the years we'd been together. Not even when he'd taken those beatings in Hell had he looked at me the way he looked at her.

"I promise," he answered carefully.

I waited for her to nod and close her eyes...but she didn't.

"Carven," she whispered, and turned her head to me.

My heart thundered and panic bloomed as I met her desperation.

"I need you to say it," she urged. "I need you to say you'll never leave me."

BOOM. BOOM. BOOM.

The world seemed to stand still.

She wanted me? She...really wanted *me?* "I promise," I managed the words.

She made sure they were the truth, too. Whatever she saw eased her fear. A breath escaped those lips, lips I wanted.

I leaned forward, cupped her cheek gently, and kissed her more tenderly than I'd thought I had in me, then let her go. That act alone terrified me. I'd never cared before, hadn't even wanted to look at them. Sex had been a battleground, one where I took without consequence and left them broken after. But not her... not *my Vivienne.*

For her, I'd be different.

I gently released my hold as a look of exhaustion washed over her. She closed her eyes and exhaled softly. Tonight had been brutal, for all of us.

"Good." Her hand grasped mine and dragged my arm around her waist. "That's real good. Just need to...have a sleep n—"

She was out cold in a second. I'd never seen someone fall so goddamn fast. One minute she was talking, then the next, she was gone. I stared at her for a second, mesmerized by the rise and fall of her chest.

Then I slowly became aware of him.

That unflinching stare was already fixed on me. But he said nothing, as though he hadn't yet decided if I was worthy. Maybe I didn't know if I was either. Still, the seconds stretched between us and the...the push-pull intensity grew. *What the fuck is going on with you?*

The words rose inside my head.

I wanted to say them, but they never came.

The feel of her body against mine turned hypnotic, drawing me into how fucking perfect this was. I didn't dare move, terrified I'd break the spell. Instead, I watched him, knowing this was what touching Heaven felt like for a soulless bastard like me. Until she whimpered, then jerked.

Colt swung his focus to her barely a second before I did. We stared at the woman who fucking terrified and transfixed us both as she fought demons in her sleep. My arm tightened around her and Colt shifted closer.

"No, get away from me," she whimpered, making Colt freeze as she shook her head. "*Carven,*" she moaned. "*Carveeennn...*"

My pulse thundered at the sound of my name. Panic rose at the frantic speed of her breaths. At first, I thought I was her tormentor...I sure as fuck deserved the title, until...

"*Carven, help me. Help me, please...*"

I clenched my jaw, that savage part of me roaring to the surface. Give me someone to kill.

Give me *anyone...*

I needed to—

I froze, stopping myself cold. How the fuck could I kill the monsters inside her head? I didn't know. But I had to find a way. Fuck. Me. I'd find a way. "I'm right here, Wildcat," I whispered, finding my brother's gaze once more. "I'm right here."

Her breaths slowed as she cracked open her eyes. She wasn't awake, not fully, at least. Still, she was aware of me. "Am I worth it?" she whispered.

I scowled. *What?*

Then it hit me. That day at the Four Seasons, the one when I'd hated the fucking world. Those were the words I'd spat at her... *you'd better be worth it*. Jesus. That was what I'd said to her.

Agony rushed in, ripping me apart rib by rib to get to that festering, pulsating thing in my chest. "Yeah," I answered as I stared at Colt. "You are."

With one hard exhale, she closed her eyes once more and drifted.

I knew then...

Knew we were so fucked.

There was no going back now.

Not for him.

Not for me.

Not without her.

THIRTY-ONE

Vivienne

A LOUD SNORE IN MY EAR WOKE ME INSTANTLY. ANGER flared as I lifted my hand to swat whoever it was away, until the soft, glorious ache of hard sex registered. My ass clenched and my pussy pulsed, as a deep sense of exhaustion washed through me. Then I remembered what had happened. I cracked open my eyes to find soft dark curls right in front of me and my pulse skipped.

Colt...

I turned my head to see stark white hair behind me.

And Carven.

Jesus...the both of them...at the same time.

Something fluttered inside my chest.

I softly bit my lip, then jumped as a heavy hand landed against my waist. With a sudden *yank,* I was pulled backwards. "Sleep, Wildcat," the groggy growl came in my ear.

"I was trying," I sniped back. "But you snore like a damn trucker."

One blue eye cracked open. "*What* fucking trucker?"

That sent my pulse racing. "No one...it's just an expression."

He scowled, then closed that eye again. "Better be. Don't make me murder someone before breakfast."

I couldn't help but smile. Because he would, wouldn't he?

He'd murder another man just because he *thought* I might've slept with him. I snuggled hard against his body, letting him tether me against his chest as I listened to the hiss as air escaped his mouth and realized just how much trouble I was in here. Carven wasn't just demanding in bed...he was jealous and controlling, as well, enough to give London a run for his money. The soft sound of his heavy breaths lulled me back to that perfect bliss. I closed my eyes, ready to drift off...until the human chainsaw started behind me again...and this time it didn't fucking stop.

You've got to be fucking kidding...

I opened my eyes, listened to the sound, and knew sleep was over for me.

I waited just long enough for me to be able to gently grab his hand. The moment I adjusted him, the snoring stopped. This time he didn't mumble, but I knew he was aware of my every move.

It was like being tracked by a predator. Only this predator didn't want to kill me.

He wanted to fuck me.

And keep on fucking me.

That ache flared deeper as I eased out from around him and slowly made my way to the foot of the bed.

"Do not go outside, not without me," he murmured. "That's an order."

I spun around, scowling. *That's an order? Who the fuck did he think he was talking to?*

Even as the words seethed in my head, I knew there was no arguing, not with him, not anymore. I picked my battles, and this wasn't one of them. Instead, I clenched my jaw, walked to the massive walk-in closet, and found a pair of gray sweats, a soft t-shirt, and a pullover before I tugged on thick white socks and headed out.

A yawn escaped as I eased open the bedroom door and closed it quietly behind me, leaving them alone. I needed coffee...like, stat. I made my way to the kitchen, but found it empty. The clock said it was after one p.m. and, for a second, I had to adjust myself.

I slipped a mug under the coffee machine and pressed the button. A yawn escaped. It made sense, after we'd spent all night in a whirlwind of emotional torture. I gripped the counter as the machine gurgled and the sharp, seductive scent of coffee filled my nose.

I yawned again, then reached up to grab a second cup and turned my focus to London. That heaviness took hold. I removed my cup and filled his as I added cream and sugar. I carried them into the study, knowing where I'd find him.

There were only two places he'd be...behind his desk...or asleep on the sofa. The door was cracked open. I eased it aside with a gentle push and found him stretched out on the black leather sofa. I placed the mugs down, then turned back and eased the door closed.

The desk was a mess, with pages scattered all around.

That lone computer chip drew my focus. I hated how it triggered a flare of jealousy. I wanted to grab the heaviest thing I could find and grind it into nothing. Maybe if I did, the bitch it was about would follow as well.

The screen on London's phone lit up as it vibrated and the ringer went off.

I glanced over at him, unmoving, before I approached it.

I wasn't the kind of woman who snooped.

But the second before the screen went dark, I caught the message.

Congratulations, you're now fertile.

Fertile? *What. The. Fuck?*

I turned my head, then quietly picked up his phone. I knew his passcode by heart, since I'd watched him punch it in time after time. My fingers flew across the screen before it unlocked in front of me...

Leaving me to stare at the app where the message had come from. It was an ovulation app, with the profile listed under *my* name, *Vivienne Evans.*

Today: Congratulations! You're highly fertile and will be for the next 2-3 days.

Heat rushed through me as I scrolled down and found my details, from my last period, to my height, weight, and date of birth, driving home the fact that this man knew everything about me.

Now he knew a little more.

What the f-u-c-k was he planning?

He gave a grunt, then shifted his weight. I quickly closed the app and placed his phone down gently before I picked up his mug. My mind was racing when I moved closer, making my steps hit a little harder. He cracked open his eyes as I neared the foot of the sofa and held my focus.

"Vivienne," he said carefully.

"I figured you'd need one as much as I did."

"Maybe not as much," he murmured as he scratched his head and scanned my body. "But I appreciate the effort."

Heat flushed my cheeks as he rose from the sofa and took a step closer. Even dressed in the same clothes he'd worn yesterday, he was devastatingly handsome. An ache filled me, one that seemed to grow claws the closer he came. I realized in that moment how deeply I'd fallen for him. "If you have a problem with me and the sons, I need to know, London."

He took the mug from my hand. That dark, possessive stare didn't once move from mine. "If I had a problem with that, pet, I would never have brought you to live with us in the first place." He brushed the back of a curled finger down my cheek. "You belong to *us*. Never worry about that."

He took a sip and the softness of his mouth transfixed me. Fuck, I'd never wanted to kiss someone as bad as I did in that moment. My body was sated, but this was about more than sex. I wanted him. I *wanted him*.

He sensed the hunger between us instantly and lowered his cup to move even closer.

Strong fingers slid through my hair as he took my mouth.

I forgot everything at that moment.

Including how to breathe.

The slow kiss deepened.

My hand slowly lowered.

Without missing a beat, he took my cup from my hand and drove me backwards toward the wall as he kissed me hard enough to make me feel like I was falling. I was. Because I was falling for him.

Heavy steps outside were headed toward us. London broke away to turn toward the sound. Guild strode into the study a second before the familiar echo of Carven's boots followed behind him.

"You need to hear this." Guild glanced from London to me as he held out his phone.

London scowled, then stepped backwards to hand me my coffee as Carven came into the room, still tugging his black turtleneck sweater down. The muscles of his stomach flexed before they disappeared. That piercing stare moved to me instantly before he muttered. "What's going on?"

"Your guess is as good as mine," London muttered, then took a sip of his coffee.

Colt came in a second later. His thick curls were a mess as he yawned and tugged down his sweater. He glanced at me, then London as Guild pressed play on his phone...and the news report began.

"It looks like the investigation into billionaire Killion Dare's death has taken a gruesome new turn. Reports just in have discovered the badly mutilated body of Macoy Daniels, who sources say was a close personal friend of Mr. Dare."

I stiffened at the name, then slowly turned my gaze to Carven.

He didn't flinch.

Didn't look away.

But that icy mask of rage flickered under the surface. One that was utterly terrifying as the reporter continued:

But that's not all. The location of the body outside the tight-lipped religious community of The Hale Order has brought a fresh wave of attention by local law enforcement to the founder and president, Mr. Haelstrom Hale. Mr. Hale is now being investigated after it was reported he misled police to interview Mr. London St. James, which sources say was nothing more than an unfounded witch hunt. Mr. St. James has now been cleared of all enquiries.

London's lips twitched at the corners.

Those dark, knowing eyes sparkled.

But none of that made me feel safe. Instead, I felt more exposed than ever. I knew better than anyone that when someone like Hale was pushed into a corner, everyone had better be scared.

"Are we going to run now, London?" The words just slipped out. "Do we hide now?"

His brow wrinkled as he settled that careful stare on me. "Run, pet? No, we don't run. *We don't ever run.*"

Those same words echoed back to me from the night they'd rescued me.

I don't fucking run. Not from them, not from anyone. The moment you do, you're dead. You know that.

I inhaled deeply as those words hit home.

Beep.

London's phone chimed, instantly breaking the tension. He stepped around me, snatched it up from the desk, and punched in his code. My cheeks burned as he stared at the screen. There came that twitch again in the corner of his mouth. Was it another reminder of just how fertile I was right now? How this moment was the perfect moment to put a baby in my belly...

You're fucking mine, you get that? Everyone will fucking know by the time I'm done...they'll...all...fucking...know.

My heart raced as I relived that moment.

Had that been his plan all along?

Was that why he'd bought me?

To have...his children?

My pulse raced. But he didn't lift his gaze from the screen and he didn't look my way. Instead, he lifted the phone and answered the call. "Parker. How are you?"

There was silence...on his end, at least. But I could hear the shouts from the other end...threats boomed, shrill and howling.

But he didn't flinch, if anything, he grew colder, harder...those lips I'd kissed a second ago twitched at the edges before he spoke. "You've known me for over twenty years. Twenty years of using my connections, of using *my* name to your advantage, what did you think was going to happen when you cut me out? You were there because *I* allowed you to be there. You were wealthy because *I* allowed that too. That multimillion-dollar house you just bought at the Cove? *I own that house now.* That new Bentley you purchased? That's *mine, as well.*" He leaned forward and braced his hand on the desk as his voice turned colder and more threatening than I'd ever heard. "I now own fucking *everything*. So I'm giving you until the end of the week to get your things and get the hell out. You will not get another chance with me. Do you understand what I'm saying?"

Carven's brows creased.

He knew.

I knew...

London was about to unleash the sons on *everyone.*

They'd never stand a chance, would they?

"With me, Wildcat," Carven murmured carefully, without taking his gaze from London. "You stay with me."

I swallowed hard, fully understanding now. We weren't going to run...because to London, this was war.

He lowered the phone and swiped the icon. The study was filled with silence. Even Guild looked at him carefully, and that cold shiver of fear I'd once held for him resurfaced. I'd forgotten what he *truly* was here. In his arms, I'd forgotten how dangerous he could be.

Now I remembered, with chilling clarity.

"The information from the Vault," he murmured, then looked at Guild. "I want it. Because I'm about to destroy them all. To hell with waiting for King."

Beep.

He scowled and looked down, read the caller ID, then answered the call. "Mickie?"

Mickie? The name was familiar. I tried to place it.

"What do you mean, he's missing?" London snapped. "You let him escape?" He stilled, then stiffened...and went pale. "No doors were open. No walls breeched. You're telling me Jack Castlemaine has just fucking vanished? Jesus fucking Christ. I want the grounds searched. I *want him fucking found. Do you understand me? Find him...now.*"

Anger seethed in him after he ended the call.

More than there'd been even seconds ago.

"You wanted to know if we run, pet?" I shivered with the chill in his tone. He lifted his gaze to mine. "Not even when our backs are against the wall. We hunt. We control. We strike fear in anyone who even *thinks* about making a move and we do it without fucking flinching. We're not going to run, Vivienne. I want you to shower...I want you to look every bit the woman I know you are...and put on the dress I bought you, because I'm taking you out."

THIRTY-TWO

Vivienne

"You can't be serious?" Guild muttered as he shook his head and stepped forward. "You want to go out in the middle of all *this*?"

London yanked his chair out and sat down. "That's *exactly* what I want." He punched in the log-in code to the Mac and clicked the screen.

"Think about it for a damn minute." Guild stepped closer. "First, Killion, now Daniels. They'll be watching you, London. The whole fucking city will be watching."

But that's what he wanted, wasn't it?

Everyone will fucking know by the time I'm done.

Those were his exact words.

They'll know because he plans on rubbing it in their faces.

The heavy *tap, tap, tap,* of his fingers smacked the keyboard before he fixed his attention on the screen. "Carven," he called the son.

But the dangerous hunter didn't move, not right away, at least. Silence grew as Guild glared at London. Both Carven and Colt were still, until they shifted their stance in unison and moved a little closer to me.

Warm arms brushed mine, their bodies pressed hard against me just like they had last night...and the entire study noticed. The hairs on the back of my neck rose as London looked our way and fixed on the two sons next to me. I waited for anger, for an ultimatum that had never been there before.

Because they'd *always* done what he wanted, no questions asked.

Now they weren't just asking...

They were speaking loud and clear.

London glanced from Carven to Colt, then to me. My breaths raced as the corners of his lips twitched, then curled. There was a slow nod of his head before that hard expression softened.

Good. His stare said.

Because this was what he'd wanted. Their loyalty wasn't just to the man who'd saved them from the Order anymore. It was to me, too, to the woman he'd watched forever, the woman he'd brought home for them.

You belong to us. Never worry about that.

I did belong to them.

They also belonged to me.

"I want them scared," London said. "I want them so fucking scared they scramble like rats in a sinking ship. They'll run and they'll make mistakes. I want them to see me. I *want* them to see *us*. Then they'll know," he murmured and turned back to the screen. "They'll know to never look at us again."

He said to us...

But what he really meant was me.

They'd never look at *me* again.

This wasn't just about retribution. It was about strength. About power. About hitting them when they were already falling, to make sure...they...*never*... got...up...again.

"Whatever you want, London," I heard myself say. "I'll do it."

He met my gaze. Hunger, love, and desperation burned between us.

Heat rushed through me. *Yes, Daddy,* I whispered as that sexual tension between us grew.

Until Guild shifted uncomfortably and cleared his throat. "What exactly do you need us to do, London?"

He took a deep breath, then glanced at Guild. That connection we'd had was dying away in the room. "What I need is to find out where the fuck Jack Castlemaine is."

His focus shifted to the screen again. We all felt it, that eerie sense that something wasn't quite right, and it drew us closer. Carven moved first and strode toward the desk as Guild followed, then Colt stepped behind me. The recording London had called up played out on the Mac. It was the inside of the storage sheds where London had kept Daniels...and Jack.

My breath stilled as I focused in on the image on the screen and watched as London rewound the footage. Light turned to darkness, then to light once more. His brow tightened as he pressed play. On the screen, I saw Jack slowly pace across the room, only to halt in the middle.

He stared at something out of view, then he slowly lifted his gaze. Goosebumps raced up my arms, making me shiver as the lights flickered inside the room before it plunged into darkness.

London leaned close and his lips curled in a sneer. It felt like a lifetime of darkness...but it was only seconds before the lights flicked back on to reveal an empty room.

"What the fuck?" Guild muttered.

London said nothing as he grasped the mouse and rewound the footage once more.

Once again, we watched as Jack paced the cell and glanced sideways at something or someone out of view. "He's waiting for someone," Carven muttered. "Look at him, pacing and watching."

The lights flickered, then went out. Darkness, that's what we stared at, nothing more than shifting shadows. London leaned close again, his gaze riveted the moment the lights came on. But there was nothing, no open door, no exploded wall. Most importantly, there was no Jack.

London reached up, flicked the camera, and pressed rewind until the words flashed across the screen *NO SIGNAL.*

No signal, what did that mean?

"Sonofabitch," London growled. "It's King. It has to be. That *bastard.* He waited until now? Of all the fucking times to get Jack out, he waited until *now?*" He stiffened. "The police station. The goddamn police station. I saw her...I saw—"

"Who?" I whispered.

London slowly turned his head and those eyes grew darker and more dangerous as they settled on me. "His eldest daughter."

Eldest daughter?

It took a second before it hit me. I shook my head. "No, you said—"

"I didn't know," he interrupted as he rose from his seat. "There was no information in any records I'd seen, no way that anyone other than King could know. But the moment I saw her, I knew…"

"How?"

He fixed that stare on me. "Because I'd know those eyes anywhere." He brushed the back of a curled finger along my temple. "They're exactly like yours."

I shook my head. But inside, I was reeling.

Sister?

I had another sister?

Exactly how many were there?

"If there's another Daughter," Guild started, but London shook his head.

"She's not a Daughter. That's what Jack said."

Guild narrowed his gaze. "And you believe him?"

"Why would he lie?" London asked, then turned back to the empty screen. "Why would he lie, indeed?"

I stepped away, needing space to think. Colt and Carven watched me as I walked out of the study. I left them to the mysterious disappearance of Jack. I couldn't help them with that, even if I'd wanted to.

Another sister?

One London had seen…close enough to look into her eyes. A flare of jealousy tore through me. Had he looked into her eyes like he looked into mine?

He wouldn't.

There were many things London St. James was. Dangerous, hungry, and the most infuriatingly erotic man I'd ever met in my entire life. He took my breath away. He scrambled my mind. He made me feel things that were detrimental to my mental health…and yet…I couldn't stop.

One taste of him.

Of that power…

And that need.

One kiss of those lips.

And the feel of his hands on my body, and I knew I was done. Me. My needs. My desires. My wants all revolved around him… and now the sons. But he wasn't a liar and I knew now he wasn't a cheater.

I'd trust him.

Until he broke that trust.

What would happen after that? A shudder tore through me as I stepped into my bedroom. I didn't know and I sure as hell didn't want to find out. The familiar slow, steady thud of footsteps echoed along the hall. I knew he'd follow me. Because I knew them all too well now, didn't I? Better than I knew this desperate, consumed version of myself.

"It's okay," I murmured as I felt his energy behind me when I stopped at the foot of the messed-up bed. "I just needed a second, that's all."

He didn't touch me, not with his hands, at least. Warm breath blasted against the back of my neck, as an icy, malevolent whisper filled my ears. "Are you afraid of me now?"

I stiffened and closed my eyes.

My mind conjured images of what had remained of Macoy Daniels before I quickly shoved them away. Nope. No freaking way...not gonna do that. Not going to—a tremor rose and with it, I became aware of my racing pulse. "Yes," I whispered. "Yes, I'm afraid of you."

"I hurt people. That's all I'm good at." The faint brush of a finger came against my neck. I tilted my head to the side, knowing this was what it felt like to be submissive to a predator. Your life in their hands. One bite. One stab. One...*word...and you were over.*

His hand closed around my neck and his strong fingers grasped tight. "Know this, Wildcat. I will *never* hurt you. I'd rather you run than to ever see that terrified look on your face again, especially when it's aimed at me. So, this is me promising you with all I have to my name, that I will never lay a hand on you. That I *will* protect you with this pathetic excuse for a life...until you no longer want or need me."

No longer want?

I turned around and faced that chilling stare. Only it wasn't so chilling now, was it? It was darker, deeper, the depths taking me all the way down. "Then it looks like you have me for all time, unless you have a problem with that?"

The corners of Carven's mouth curled. "I'm sure I'll suffer through it."

I scowled when he reached around to the small of his back, but when he opened his hand, I froze, then frantically shook my head as I stared at the tracker. "No...*no fucking way.*"

"You have to."

I jerked my gaze to his. "I said *no.*"

"You. Have. To." But his growl wasn't cruel, it was desperate. He searched my eyes. "I *have* to be able to find you. I have to know who I need to kill to get to you."

My voice was so small. "That didn't help me before, did it?"

He flinched. "You're here, aren't you? You're here, and Daniel's isn't. Like London said, they'll never look at you again."

I lowered my gaze. "Then I won't need that, will I?" I met his stare. "I won't need that because I'll have you. You won't let them take me. They will not hurt me. Before that ever happens, you will kill them all." I stepped closer and pressed my body against his until I looked up at him. "Won't you?"

He inched his head down until those hard lips brushed mine. "Until my last breath."

Then he kissed me.

His hand gripped the back of my neck and held me in place.

He might not have said the words...but Carven had just told me he loved me.

When he broke the kiss, he knew it, too. He held my stare until, with a snarl, he grabbed his phone and looked down. "I have to go. You have my number, Wildcat. I want you to text, call, whatever you need, got it?"

I nodded as I met his gaze.

He took a step backwards. "I'll be back as soon as I can."

He left then, striding from the room. I knew wherever London was sending him was important. But it didn't make me feel better as I watched him go. I pulled off my sweats and tugged off my socks before I stepped into the bathroom and started the shower.

London wanted to go out.

It'd be the first real outing since the mall, and I knew how well that had turned out. I stepped under the spray and tried my best to push it all away. Maybe London was right? Maybe this *was* the end of it all. With Hale arrested, the cops would start looking into the Order and they'd never stop.

He'd go away forever...

And the entire festering pit would crumble.

I washed and let the thought of that flow right through me.

And hoped.

THIRTY-THREE

Carven

FIND HIM.

Find him and get back to her.

The need made me feel dangerous as I climbed into the Explorer and started the engine. The guards stared as I punched the accelerator and the four-wheel drive responded, kicking up rocks as I tore along the driveway and hit the road hard.

My teeth gnashed.

But I didn't care. I was hunting now with a purpose...and that purpose was *her*. I flew along the streets, then headed to the storage shed, careful to take the long way around and watch the rear-view mirror. I leaned forward to look up at the washed-out gray skies, then settled back and hit the seat warmer.

At least this time, I'd grabbed a jacket, because I knew sure as hell I was going to be out in the cold, unless I cleared this up fast. It had to be a guard. There was no way around it. I'd known that the moment I watched the footage the first time, and I was even surer of it now.

One of them had betrayed us by switching off the lights and opening the door. There was no way around it. London could be pissed all he wanted, but it was right there with blinding clarity...and the empty goddamn cell where Jack Castlemaine had been.

I pushed the Explorer harder. The sooner I was there, beating the shit out of the guard who'd stabbed us in the back, then the sooner I'd be with London and Wildcat when they went out.

Goddamn stupid idea.

But it wasn't my call to make.

London knew better...he'd better.

My tires slipped on the icy road. I eased my foot off the accelerator and let the momentum take me until I'd pushed the car back within the lines and turned the wheel as I lifted my gaze to the storage shed. But instead of driving in, I pulled over and watched.

The guards' cars were parked toward the back of the lot. I caught glimpses of a dark Chevy and a sleek red convertible, and winced. Way to stay invisible. But there was nothing else. The empty lots around us gave me no answers.

Get this done.

That hunger drove me. I shoved the four-wheel drive into gear and pulled into the driveway. I barely stopped long enough to punch the code in and drove through. I was parked and climbing out before I knew it, that same desperate need to get back to her howling in my veins.

I'd never feel this ache before.

Never felt this fucking *wired.*

It was dangerous.

I was dangerous.

God help those who stood in my way.

I pushed through the doors. The guards already stood there as I walked in, staring at me with pale faces and wide, terrified eyes. They knew why I was here. "I want to see everyone who was on shift today and I want to see them now."

Mickie gave a nod and lifted his phone. "Already on it."

"Good." I scanned the foyer of London's little rat cage. "I'll be in the room."

I headed along the hallways to the storage units that housed cells. But I didn't go straight to the one where Jack Castlemaine had been. No, I stopped at the one where the air was still tainted with the smell of blood and the desperate hiss of a dying man.

I stopped in the hallway and shoved the door open. The room was empty and had been scrubbed clean. But I could still feel it, that nothingness that had consumed me...that chilling *rage*. All I saw was her. Her bruises. Her fear. The monster that lived inside had taken control and it hadn't stopped.

Even now—I closed my eyes—I wanted to kill all over again.

I'd find new ways to make him piss himself.

New ways to deliver him to Hale that'd sicken and terrifying anyone else.

I yanked the door closed and stepped away.

Find him...find him and get back to her.

I headed for the room where Jack had been, punched in the code and opened the door. There were no marks on the locks, no signs of forced entry anywhere.

Beep.

I scowled, grabbed my phone, and looked down.

Wildcat: Tell me this is a good idea.

I clenched my jaw. Hell no, it wasn't a good fucking idea. But London was a shark in the fucking water and right now all he smelled was blood. Only, I couldn't tell her that, could I? I couldn't tell her that because it'd only panic her more and she was scared enough. I punched in a reply.

I'll be back before you know it. I'm going to be right there with you. So the only thing you need to worry about, Wildcat, is to make sure you fucking stretch by the time you get home...cause I plan on fucking you well tonight.

My pulse was racing as I sent send and it had nothing to do with the promise of destroying that sweet fucking ass. It had *everything* to do with the need to get back to her. I scanned the room and stepped inside.

There was nothing.

In fact, there was less than nothing.

No screams.

No scent of blood.

And no Jack Castlemaine.

The heavy thud of boots sounded as they neared. I tracked the movement as Mickie stopped in the doorway behind me. "Sebastian isn't answering. I'll keep trying."

"Sebastian isn't answering," I repeated, then slowly turned toward him. "Why do you suppose that is?"

There was a flare of concern in his eyes, then a shake of his head. "No, he's not that guy. I vetted him personally."

"So you admit you fucked up?"

His scowl deepened. "I didn't fuck up. He wouldn't betray you and he wouldn't betray London."

I stepped around him and headed into the hall. "We'll see about that, won't we? If you let him know I'm coming, I'll be seriously pissed."

The former SEAL said nothing as I headed out. I pulled up Sebastian's address, when I backed out of the parking lot and headed for the townhouses on the edge of the city. A heaviness filled my stomach as I slowed the four-wheel drive and scanned front yards littered with kids' bicycles and overflowing trash cans.

Most times, I didn't care I was the fucking dog London released. I did what I had to...what I was *trained* to do. But there were those times when I didn't want to wear the stain of another person's blood—I pulled the four-wheel drive over to the side of the road and killed the engine while I stared at the cramped, ugly two-story house—and this was one of those times.

I palmed the switchblade, climbed out, and caught movement in a window above as I locked the car. Anger rose inside me. If that asshole would've answered his fucking phone, then I wouldn't have to be out here. I wouldn't have to walk along the concrete pathway and scuff the fucking chalk flower outline his kid left behind.

I wouldn't have to climb the stairs and force my way in.

I wouldn't have to leave the man fucking bleeding...or worse, dead.

I wouldn't have to be the killer I needed to be.

I stopped outside the front door and waited without knocking.

Whatever happened inside was his own fucking fault.

The lock snapped and the door cracked open. The guy I stared at was sick. Pale and shaking, his eyes bugged out.

"You going to let me in?"

There was a moment of hesitation. No doubt the asshole had a gun in his hand. I'd slice him between the ribs before his finger could touch the trigger...and I'd leave him to bleed out.

He knew that, I saw it in his eyes, saw the way he looked at me before he took a step back while tucking his hand behind his leg. "I didn't answer Mickie's calls 'cause I'm sick."

I stepped inside and looked around. The place stank of sweat and fear. I knew the tang well. My senses picked up no movement from the bedroom. The kid wasn't here...good.

I turned and faced him. "Want to tell me what happened?"

"I dunno, man. I think I picked up some kind of bug." He scratched the back of his head, careful not to make eye contact.

He knew that wasn't what I meant. The awkwardness grew. I watched him look around everywhere but at me.

"You have a nice family," I murmured as I glanced at a photo of him, a pretty redhead, and a daughter who had to be about ten.

"Don't," he protested, his voice deeper. "Not them."

"Then tell me what happened and make sure it's the truth. I'll know if you're lying."

He winced and his eyes darted around the room before he went still. Here was the battle, and the only advantage I had. My reputation sometimes preceded me...and was the only thing that kept some schmucks like this guy alive.

"It wasn't my fault."

He waited for me to say something, to ease him somehow. It didn't happen.

"I *was* telling the truth. I picked up some kind of fucking bug and this morning I was feeling like hell." He reached up, scratched the back of his neck again, and that drew my focus.

Then I saw it.

The raised red lump on the side of his neck.

"I switched off the alarm and unlocked the fire door, just for a second. I didn't know if I was gonna barf or fill my damn pants or both. Then it hit me."

"What hit you?"

"The fucking bitch."

I scowled. "What. Bitch?"

"The bitch that was fucking waiting. She was just there, man. I stumbled out, about to hurl my guts up, then the next thing I knew, I was fucking blindsided. I went down, then the next thing all I heard was footsteps. She must've taken my card, it was gone when I pushed to my feet."

I took a step closer. "And you didn't say anything about it?"

He jerked in response and took a step backwards, then met my gaze. "I fucked up. I knew I'd fucked up. I just...panicked."

"You. Panicked."

Agony tore across his face. "I don't want to die...and I don't want my family hurt."

I crossed the room in an instant, grabbed the incompetent asshole by the throat, and drove him backwards. "Then you should've opened your fucking mouth and set off the fucking alarm. Do you know how much damage you've caused? All because you can't keep your fucking shit together."

"It must've been the coffee. There was a new girl and, I dunno, she must've fucked up my order. They know I'm lactose sensitive."

I stiffened. "You're telling me you stopped at some fucking cafe, spouted your damn mouth, and then drank some swill that was most likely drugged."

"No." His eyes widened and he shook his head.

"They knew your name, right?"

He slowly nodded.

A nerve twitched in the corner of my eye. "And I'm guessing you broke the fucking rule that said you don't wear your uniform in public?"

He was almost gray.

"So, she was waiting for you and you walked right into it. What kind of fucking incompetent asshole are you?"

"I didn't know..."

I unleashed a snarl, then shoved him away.

"How was I to know? She took my card and let herself in. They were gone before I knew it."

"Where's the fucking card now?" I snarled as I turned away. I might be able to get Harper to pull a print.

"I dunno. She must still have it. I never got it back."

I swung back. "She still has it?"

My pulse kicked. The sound thudded in my ears as he nodded. I grabbed my phone and strode from the sight of the fucking moron, before I punched him in the goddamn throat.

"Carven?" Harper answered on the second ring. "What do I owe—"

"I need you to trace a chip that's in one of the access cards. The name is Sebastian Poole. I need to know its location and I need it now."

"Okay. Want to tell me what's going on?"

"If I'm right, then King's other daughter just broke Jack Castlemaine out and if she's running, then she might still have the access card she used to do it with her."

"Jesus..."

"Yeah."

"Give me a second," Harper muttered as I strode down the stairs and trod on the fucking chalk outline again as I headed back to the car.

By the time I climbed in, he was back. "I got it," he announced. "Sending the location to your phone now."

"Thanks," I acknowledged as I started the engine.

Beep.

I lifted my phone as I snapped my seatbelt in place, expecting it to be Harper...but it wasn't.

Wildcat: Will you meet us at the restaurant?

My damn hand shook as I stared at the text. I shouldn't be here. I should be with her. I should be calling in backup to get this over and get the hell out of here. But the only backup I'd ever had was my brother...and the way he'd looked at me tonight, he may as well not be.

He'd looked at me like I was a goddamn stranger. Not one he particularly liked, either. I closed my eyes for a second as my phone vibrated again in my hand.

I opened my eyes and looked down to find the text from Harper and scanned at the GPS marker on the secure tracking app before I stilled. "What the fuck?"

The card wasn't at the storage shed, that's for sure. It was somewhere near the goddamn marina. They'd ditched the access card, or some idiot had stolen it. That was the only way it could've ended up anywhere near there.

This was a total waste of my time.

I needed to get back home.

Back to...*Vivienne.*

I left her text unanswered, desperate to get this done. She wouldn't even know I was gone. The longer I stared at that goddamn marker, the more pissed off I became. I pulled out, headed into the city, and followed it all the way toward the water until I pulled over in front of the marina. The card had been tossed in the water. That was the only way—

Until the damn marker moved.

Right in front of me.

I stared at the screen, then lifted my gaze to the heavy steel gates that blocked off the entrance to the multimillion dollar ocean cruisers that were docked there. But that wasn't where the beacon was pointing. I yanked the handle, climbed out, and followed the blinking light to a massive shed in the middle of a compound next door.

I adjusted my jacket, checked my gun, and locked the four-wheel drive behind me. I didn't know what this was...some kind of boatyard. I headed for the gate, grabbed the bars, and heaved myself over.

The sooner I confirmed this was a dead-end, the sooner I could get out of here. I lengthened my stride as I headed along the boardwalk, then turned. The marina was packed with boats, luxury cruisers that glinted and gleamed even in the pathetic washed-out gray sunlight.

I shifted my focus to glance down at my phone before I lifted my gaze to the towering boat shed behind a locked gate in the distance. I reached around, grabbed the all-in-one tool I'd slipped into my back pocket, and found the cutters.

The place didn't look like it was alarmed. One scan of the grounds, and I knew there were no guard dogs. I glanced over my shoulder and scanned those who laughed and partied on the boats behind me, before I rounded the side of the compound, then dropped to the ground.

Seconds.

That's all it took before I cut the wire and was through the fence. Jagged metal ends snagged my goddamn jacket and tore a jagged hole in the fabric as I stood. *Motherfucker.* I ignored the hole and turned my focus to the looming shed in front of me.

The massive overhead rollup door was open, so I was free to stare at the expensive as fuck luxury cruiser docked inside. The closer I came, the more I saw. Two cars were parked in the space, a black Bugatti and a midnight edition RAM. The vehicles were fucking impressive. But I wasn't here for a fucking tour of the place. I was here for Jack Castlemaine.

I scanned the huge shed as I stepped inside and kept to the shadows. The place wasn't just a 'rent by the fucking day' hideaway, that's for sure. I rounded the side of the mammoth cruiser to find a wall packed with guns and weapons and a bench full of power tools.

I stopped cold.

The same screen we'd found in that abandoned apartment sat there, the one I'd stared at as my fucking woman was being taken.

Thud.

I jerked my gaze to the cruiser. My senses sharpened and narrowed in on the boat. There was someone in there. I reached around, grabbed my gun, and scanned the machine the boat was moored to, then headed for the ladder and climbed.

I was too loud, no matter how hard I tried. So I moved faster and vaulted over the rail to land on the boat with a *bang*.

"Fuck," I muttered under my breath and headed for the cabin.

The hinges were silent as I opened the door and stepped inside. There were men's clothes on the floor...clothes I knew instantly, Jack's. A white access card lay next to them, one fitted with the chip I'd tracked. I didn't touch it, just turned my focus to the door leading down into the living compartment and lifted my gun.

This motherfucker would be lucky if he came out of this alive. Sister or not, I'd had enough of this cat and fucking mouse game. I'd had enough of being away from Vivienne.

I stepped down and saw Jack's fucking trousers on the floor of the living space, then lifted my gaze to the sleeping compartments toward the back and kept moving. The air shifted in the boat and I was aware of it. Goosebumps raced along my arms. For a second, a flicker of worry rose before I lifted my gun and reached out to grasp the door handle.

A quiet turn and I pushed the door inward and stared into the murky light. My eyes adjusted in time for me to catch a hint of movement. Light from behind me spilled into the room to show glinting silver eyes from the biggest fucking black cat I'd ever seen. The beast arched its back and hissed like a fucking snake as fear kicked in my chest.

Something was wrong.

Something was—

I spun around in time to catch a blur of movement.

Crack! The brutal blow crashed against my head.

Sparks exploded behind my eyelids.

In the blur, I saw her…her big brown eyes and those fucking perfect lips.

"Wildcat?" I whispered before my knees gave way and I crumpled to the floor.

She moved closer and stood over me. "I don't think so, asshole," she murmured and lifted a rifle, the butt already swinging at my head. "Nighty night."

I tried to lift my arm, tried to move, but the end of the weapon bore down on me and slammed against my head once more.

Darkness came.

One so black that it swallowed everything.

Including the one face I needed…

And I was gone.

THIRTY-FOUR

Vivienne

I CLASPED MY BRA, THEN ADJUSTED THE SHEER BLACK French panties London had bought for me. The dress was next, lying ready for me on the bed. I took one last look at the blown-out, untameable curls of my hair, then the sultry kohl outline of my eyes.

I looked good...really good.

Pity I was a fucking mess on the inside.

My pulse was erratic and out of control as I strode to the bed, glanced at the Louis Vuittons waiting on the floor, then grabbed the dress and stepped in. The heavy thud of footsteps approached. I braced myself as London came into my room and moved closer.

I knew it was him without turning...and God, my heart wasn't ready.

But it didn't matter. One look at him in his black-on-black suit and I was rendered speechless. He *knew* he looked good, too. Those dark eyes glinted even darker. Carven said he was like a shark on the hunt...and it looked like it as he placed a long jewelry box on the foot of my bed.

"Pet," he said carefully as he stepped around me.

I shivered at the brush of his fingers along my spine. My breath caught as he leaned down and kissed my shoulder. 'You look ravishing."

"You don't look like a hot mess yourself," I murmured as I closed my eyes.

His deep chuckle made my body clench. Christ, he could do things to me with his amusement alone. The smile returned; the one he'd given me days ago when I was strapped to that bench, his machine driving all the way inside.

I lived for his smile.

For his laugh...

For his *everything*.

He gently tugged the zipper up, and I opened my eyes as he stepped around me, then this formidable, dangerous man slowly sank to his knees.

My pulse skipped.

"Use my shoulders, Vivienne." He slid his hand along the back of my leg.

I did, gripping the strong muscles, lifting my foot and waiting for him to slide my shoes into place, one after the other. He took his time rising, then skimmed those big hands over my body until he met my stare. "Are you ready for tonight?"

I swallowed. "No."

That grin grew wider, but he searched my eyes as he brushed a strand of hair from my face. "Do you trust me?"

That question made my stomach clench. To trust this man was a very dangerous thing to do...*but then, so was loving him.*

"Yes," I answered.

That made him happy. He stepped away and leaned down to grab the box he'd placed on the bed.

"Another anklet?"

Excitement burned in his stare. "Not exactly."

I looked down as he slowly opened the case. I thought it'd be diamonds, or gold. But I hadn't expected *leather.*

He pulled out the sleek black leather choker with a black clasp, and as he tilted his hand, the light caught the deeply etched words.

Property of London St. James.

I flinched, then jerked my eyes up. He wasn't serious...*was he?*

Oh...he was deadly serious. I looked at the choker in his hand once more. *They'll know.* Those words rose in my memory. *They'll all know by the time I'm done.*

Heat moved through my face. I felt his focus, his...*excitement.* He wanted this. He wanted me and he wanted the world to know who I belonged to.

My pussy throbbed, sending a wave of desire through me. I couldn't stop this sickness inside me. I couldn't stop from wanting to be craved by this man. A slow nod, and his eyes widened. He knew what this was for me...

The ultimate level of trust.

Do you trust me?

I stared at his look of utter delight as he stepped closer. The seductive scent of his cologne washed through me as he reached around and fixed the choker into place. I *did* trust him, so much it scared me.

"There." He pulled back, met my stare, and lowered his gaze. His chest stilled at the sight of the leather around my neck. "It's perfect," he murmured. There was a look of pride on his face before he lifted his hand. "You ready?"

"As ready as I'll ever be."

That made him laugh as he took my hand and led me out of the house. Guards swarmed around us as we headed to the car already waiting for us. The driver opened the rear door and I climbed in. Headlights bounced off a soft fog that swept around us, leaving me to shiver in the cold.

I scanned the others, searching for Colt, but I couldn't see him anywhere. He hadn't come to see me after Carven and he hadn't left, I knew that. I winced, grabbed the phone London had bought me, and opened my messages.

I stared at message after message I'd sent to Carven...

Ones he hadn't replied to.

Movement from the house captured my attention as Colt walked from the house. He didn't look my way, nor did he look toward London. Instead, he climbed into the driver's seat of the Explorer alone.

I typed out a message:

I need you.

I waited for a reply as London gave our driver directions then climbed inside. He took one look my way, then at the phone in my hand. "Everything okay?"

"He's not answering his messages."

"Carven?"

I nodded.

"Don't worry. Sometimes he can be...busy."

I winced at the word, my mind conjuring all sorts of terrifying images. He wouldn't kill Jack. He knew how important he was to Ryth and to London. I turned to him as we pulled away from the house. Jack was important, but then that meant little when you were dealing with men like this.

They were violent and unpredictable at best.

Thud.

The car jolted as we hit the street and accelerated. London eased back, growing colder and more distant as we drove. I glanced at my phone once more, then shifted my gaze to the darkness outside. We drove into the city, toward the busy clubs and bars, and kept going.

Surprise rose as I glanced at London. "I thought we were going to some club?"

"We are," he answered. "A very *special* club."

I turned back to the view outside as we slipped away from the busy streets, then turned into a discreet driveway behind a towering, darkened building. If it wasn't for the five other cars lined up at the dimly lit entrance, I would've thought we were at the wrong place.

But one look at the immaculate tuxedos and floor-length designer gowns of those heading through the massive black doors illuminated by soft white lights, and I knew we weren't.

Something brushed my hand. I flinched as London entwined his fingers with mine. I realized this was important for him. Maybe tonight more than ever. I met his stare and grasped his hand as we pulled forward. Before I knew it, the car was stopped and our driver was out, opening the door for us.

I slid across the seat and followed London out. He waited, gripping my hand, his focus only on me. I shivered both at the attention and the night air that throbbed faintly with a heavy beat of music. Then we headed inside.

The black door led us to a hallway where a low white floor light illuminated the way until we came to a set of stairs. Others climbed casually, some chatting to companions. I glanced at London and followed. His hand went to the small of my back as he matched his pace with mine.

Servers greeted us with flutes of champagne. London took one, then held it out to me as he motioned toward the immaculate glass bar that seemed to stretch the entire length of the room.

I followed him to the bar and waited as he ordered for himself. No money was exchanged, no cards charged. What kind of party was this? The moment I turned around and followed him to where the other guests mingled, I knew exactly why we were there. Every one of them stopped, turned, and stared as we neared.

We were here to be admired and feared...to be seen, more than anything.

Because London St. James didn't cower from anyone.

"London," one of the men called, then shifted his gaze to me. "I'm glad you could make it."

"Wouldn't miss it for the world," he answered, his hand tightening against my back.

Heads turned, watching another group as they stepped from the stairs.

"Dante," the man who'd greeted us murmured.

I followed their focus to the Mafia leader and his stunning wife. The moment I saw her, something clenched inside me and a panicked feeling gathered like a storm. Dante followed London exactly, taking a glass of champagne for his wife before he headed to the bar. But unlike me, Meredith Ares wasn't too shy to scan the room.

The moment our eyes locked, that panic rushed, making my pulse race. She held my stare, even as her husband joined her. One look our way, and Dante guided his wife toward us.

"Dante," London murmured.

"St. James," he answered as he glanced my way and gave me a careful nod. "Vivienne."

But there wasn't the usual undressing me with his eyes, unlike the other men who gawked. Instead, Dante turned his attention to his wife, who was still staring at me.

"Meredith." London glanced her way. "You look beautiful, as always."

She smiled, yet it didn't quite reach her eyes.

"Dante. London." The man who I assumed was our host drew their attention. "Allow me to introduce you to Kennedy Romanoff."

"You okay?" London asked, leaning a little to meet my gaze.

"Sure, go ahead."

He leaned closer and his arm slid around my waist as murmured in my ear. "I'll be back in a second. I have something I want to show you."

I watched him leave, and so did every other woman around me. Husbands left, but they all paled in comparison. But London didn't go far, just enough to be out of earshot.

"Nice choker," Meredith commented, drawing my focus. She stared at the leather around my throat, no doubt reading the inscription. "You're a very lucky woman."

A sentiment that burned in every jealous stare directed my way. They all wanted him. I could see that, even Meredith looked twice before returning her gaze to her husband. I focused on downing my drink before the waiter passed with more.

Heat rolled over me. I glanced at London who, even though he stood amongst the other powerful men, still stared at me.

The intensity in his stare was breath taking. Every dark, depraved thought he conjured was aimed at me. That hunger swept me away until there was no club, no room, no others standing around staring.

There was just him and me.

"Jesus, he is perfection," one of the women muttered, jerking me back to reality.

I turned back to him as heat raced into my cheeks. He turned back to his colleagues, muttered something, then headed my way.

"Ready?" He held out his hand. I couldn't take his fast enough. "Ladies," he greeted, glancing their way before he turned back to me.

"London," gushed the one who panted like a dog in heat.

But we were already leaving, headed for the rear of the room. I glanced over my shoulder to the stairs. "I thought we were leaving?"

"Not just yet. There's another party I thought you might enjoy."

He took my hand, leading me to another set of stairs that took us down this time. His hand on my back, with his body so close to mine, only added to the bliss I was feeling.

"This way." He motioned, leading me along a dimly lit empty hallway.

A tremor coursed along my spine. But London was in his element here. He was the one in control. He opened a door toward the end of the hall and motioned me inside a smaller room.

I searched the dark corners, finding us alone. "London, what is this?"

He bent down, grabbed another glass of champagne for me, and held it up. "You trust me, right?"

I took the glass, unable to see the truth in his eyes as he cracked an unopened bottle of Scotch and poured it into a tumbler.

"Trust and apprehensiveness are two different things."

He moved behind me, slid his hand around my waist to slide upwards, and cupped my breast. "So how can I ease that, pet?"

Through the gloom in front of me, the wall shimmered. His strong fingers brushed my nipple, sending desire coursing through my veins. I bit my lip and stifled a moan, my gaze fixed on the movement in front of me as what looked like black curtains slowly drew aside.

Lights were on in a room beyond ours, revealing men and women having sex. The glass wall between us was the only barrier. I stiffened at the sight, watching bodies entwined, cocks driving deep.

"London..."

"It's okay," his murmur was against my ear. "It's a one-way glass, they can't see us."

His breath came against my neck, his focus not on the orgy in front of us...but on me. Jealousy flared. "Do you come here often?"

"Often? No."

I turned around to face him. "But you have been here before, right?"

My insides clenched.

The excitement in his eyes seemed to dull. "Yes."

My pulse was booming, imagining all the kinds of women he might've brought here.

"Once," he continued coolly. "And I never wanted to come here again...until you."

A pang tore through my chest at the pain in his tone. Whatever had happened clearly hadn't been an enjoyable experience. "Why bring me?"

A spark of lust sparkled in his stare as he moved closer and slid his other hand around my waist. "I assumed that was obvious." He lifted his gaze to the display in front of us. "I want you to experience everything when it comes to desire and lust."

"As long as it's between us and the sons, right? I don't share, London."

His smile was instant as he brushed my hair from my shoulders. "You never have to worry about that, pet. No other woman could compare."

I gave a slow nod, finding ease in his focus. "You thought I might like...watching others?"

He gave a shrug, pulling me against him. "I think it's good to see what doesn't turn you on."

I shifted my gaze to the display in the room and watched as one man sank low and settled between a gorgeous redhead's thighs. A surge of excitement rose at the sight of her legs splayed wide and his mouth on her pussy.

I was transfixed by the sight, slowly sipping champagne as London moved behind me. But it wasn't the others that drew my focus. I was aware of his hand on my hip and the warmth of that strong chest against my back.

Those fingers moved lower until they traced my abdomen. I knew what he was thinking.

"I know you've seen the app," he whispered against my ear, his hand rising to brush the leather choker around my throat. "I know you understand what the vitamins are for, as well. I plan on taking you home tonight and putting a baby in your belly, Vivienne. I plan on making you mine in all the ways I can."

I turned around, my breath catching.

"What do you think?" He bent, placed his glass down, and waited, searching my eyes.

From the moment I'd met London St. James, he'd been demanding and possessive, never once had he asked, *'what do you think?'.*

But here he was...his hope hanging on my reaction.

His brows tightened as he tried to read me.

I hadn't allowed myself to think about it, to dream about it. But the idea of carrying this man's child made me feel...intoxicated, and it had nothing to do with the champagne. "Yes," I whispered. "That's what I think...*yes.*"

His chest rose and fell with a huge breath. Surprise followed before he grinned. "Yes?"

I laughed. "Yes."

The smile gave way to that carnal hunger as he captured my face in both his hands, staring deep into my eyes. "A baby," he repeated. "*Our* baby."

Our baby...

And our family.

Him, me, and the sons.

He pulled away, breaking the contact. "You're not really interested in the display, are you?"

"No," I whispered. "How can I be when I have you?"

He smiled, then took my glass. "Want to get out of here?"

I breathed a sigh of relief. "I thought you'd never ask."

THIRTY-FIVE

Vivienne

He wasn't going to let me go, was he? His hand gripped tighter as the car pulled over to the curb. I stared at the lights of the expensive restaurant. "I thought we were going home?"

"I'm going to need to make sure you're fed well, pet." His tone was dangerously erotic. "And I plan on making you nice and round. This place has the most delicious salmon you've ever had in your entire life."

My pulse quickened at the thought. I'd hoped to go back home and make dinner for the four of us, but before I could say anything, he opened the door and pulled me with him. I followed, smiling at our driver before climbing the three stairs as London opened the door and ushered me inside.

The smells hit me instantly. My belly snarled in anticipation as London walked toward the host.

"London St. James," he announced quietly as he glanced around the restaurant. "I'd like a table toward the back."

But the host didn't move. Instead, his eyes widened as he turned to some important looking guy in a black and white tux, who rushed over.

"Mr. St. James," he murmured carefully, glancing around at the packed restaurant. "I'm afraid we've given your table away, sir."

"You've given my table away," London repeated, narrowing his gaze in on him. "Tell me, Jackson, why would that be?"

The guy was beyond flustered now, he was moving into full-blown panic territory. I reached for London's arm. "It's okay."

"No. It's not."

That deadly stare seemed to grow colder as London leaned closer. "I've been coming here for a long time, Jackson. I've helped you and Xavier personally. I think I deserve an explanation."

The guy was white as a goddamn sheet. "Mr. Hale…" he started before he gasped to a stop.

London stiffened as he took a breath. "You do not want me as an enemy," he said carefully. "Especially not tonight."

I didn't know if the restaurant manager's movement was a nod or he was just shaking. "The deluxe table toward the rear," he ordered as he turned to the host. "Make sure, Mr. St. James gets everything he needs. Complimentary, of course."

London eased back, tugging his jacket. This wasn't the end, not by a long shot. London was collecting bodies tonight and he didn't care who it was. He slid his hand around to the small of my back and led me away as we followed the poor, shaken host who led us toward the rear of the restaurant.

Heads turned toward us as we passed.

Critical stares picked me apart.

Head up, Vivienne...

London's words echoed in my mind.

Always walk with your head up, watching everyone around you. It makes you less of a victim.

I lifted my chin, ignored the stares, and kept walking. London hadn't just been overbearing, he'd been protecting me from moments just like this. Pride swelled inside me as I walked with the man other men envied and women lusted for.

He wasn't anything like they imagined he was...*he was so much more.*

The host stopped at a table for four discreetly placed against the wall and carefully pulled out a chair for London. But he wouldn't sit, not until I did. My bladder gave a twinge, those few glasses of champagne now suddenly a bad decision. I glanced around and spotted a discreet doorway with a ladies' sign illuminated. "I'll be right back."

London scowled, glanced at the restroom, then nodded. "Of course."

I left him, fighting the urge to quicken my steps as I hurried toward the restroom. I pushed in, raced for the stall, and fumbled with the damn lock before I shoved those sexy French panties down and sat.

"Jesus," I whispered as relief hit me. "How the hell can I have a child when I have the smallest bladder in the world?"

I closed my eyes as I waited, grabbed a wad of paper before I wiped, then slowly rose and flushed. Sultry dark eyes met mine in the mirror as I washed my hands then dried them. "Just get this done and you're home," I whispered as I listened to the soft drone of the diners in the restaurant.

I gave a sigh and made my way out. My thoughts were distant, trying to block out everything around me as I headed back to our table...until movement caught my gaze. I lifted my head...and found my seat had been taken.

Ophelia sat across from London.

The sight stopped me instantly.

I stood in the middle of the hallway and watched her lean across the table to touch his hand. He flinched as those dark eyes darted to mine. Rage roared through me, deeper than anything I'd ever felt before.

I was cold...all the way to the core, as I forced myself to move. She didn't lift her head, didn't look my way. *You're in my seat,* I wanted to say, but I doubted the ugly fucking cunt would even respond.

My gaze went to the jagged edge of the knife in front of her. I'd love nothing more than to drive it through her goddamn chest, but I wouldn't find a heart. She was more than London's former lover...she was the sons' private tormentor, one determined to break them.

Colt's haunted stare came back to me as I stepped past her, then turned, sliding onto London's knee. "Ophelia," I said coldly, staring down at the bitch. "I figured you'd be scurrying along with the rest of the rats...you know, fleeing the sinking ship."

My anger was in control, making me feel dangerous.

It wasn't London she needed to be wary of...*it was me.*

Only then did she lift that cold stare, to find the choker around my neck. I'd forgotten all about it, but now the importance of it came rushing back to me.

"Nice to see you put this one on a leash, London."

Fuck you.

I couldn't stop myself as I gripped the edge of the table and leaned close enough that she had no choice but to look me in the eyes as I murmured, "And a baby in my belly, you ugly bitch." I sneered down at her. "Which is something *you'll* never have."

Rage drove to the surface in that cruel stare. There was a slow twitch of her lips before she glanced back at London, but I didn't dare take my eyes off her. Instead, I stared her down, watching as she desperately sought my lover's attention.

But he didn't give it to her. Instead, he ran his hand along my arm and leaned forward. "Ophelia, it's been a pleasure, as always." He dismissed her like the afterthought she was.

She waited for a second as pain tore across her face, then she pushed upwards.

"Bye-bye now," I growled as I watched her turn and stride away.

My pulse was pounding, making me feel dizzy. I gripped the table edge tightly, no way was I letting that sick fuck get the better of me. But I was well beyond being on fucking display. "I want to go home, London. *Now.*"

His thumb brushed my hand. "Whatever you want, pet."

I gave a nod and slowly rose.

The lights and the sounds of the restaurant were too much. I stepped away and held out my hand. London was there instantly, sliding his fingers between mine. "Easy, kitten. I'll get you home."

It couldn't be fast enough.

The moment we took a step, a man sitting at a table near ours called out. "London." He placed his napkin down and extended his hand, smiling. "I thought that was you."

Only, his gaze was on me and took its time taking in my body.

Suddenly, the floor-length black gown wasn't protection enough, not from these people...or this world. I fought a shiver and glanced toward the entrance as Ophelia walked through the door and disappeared.

"Angus." London shook his hand and shot a glance my way. "Nice to see you."

"I was hoping I'd run into you. I was wondering if I could have your opinion—"

The conversation started before London lifted his hand. "You'll have to excuse me. It seems the night got away from us. Maybe another time."

August flinched. It looked like he wasn't used to being cut off, but luckily London didn't give a fuck.

"Vivienne." He motioned. "Until next time, Angus."

"Sure," the guy muttered, staring as we walked away.

"Goddamn," London murmured under his breath.

We made another three tables before it happened again. It seemed you were either fighting for your life in this fucking city, or fighting to beat the leeches off with a stick.

London unleashed a low growl before shaking the guy's hand who rose and stepped toward us this time. A panicked glance my way and London mouthed, *sorry*. I glanced toward the door and scanned the front of the restaurant outside as London tried his best to get away.

By the time he grabbed my hand and muttered low enough for only me to hear, "Walk and don't stop," it'd been ten to fifteen minutes and I couldn't wait to get out of there.

I all but lunged down the stairs, not bothering to wait for London to open the door. My hands were shaking as I shoved the handle and stumbled outside. The cold air rushed in as I sucked in a deep breath and spotted the familiar dark Explorer. The driver's door opened and for a fleeting second, I thought it was Carven.

Colt strode toward me with two of our men close behind.

An icy chill washed through me as a whisper urged me to turn my head.

In the distance, Ophelia watched, before she turned and slowly strode away.

The shrill sound of squealing tires pierced the night.

London jerked his gaze toward the sound as what looked like a beat-up blue van hurtled toward us and the side door was thrown open. Two men were dark shadows inside until I caught the flash of something metal.

"GET DOWN!" London roared.

Something hit me, driving me toward the pavement.

Crack

Crack.

CRACK!

CRACKCRACKCRACKCRACK...

Gunfire followed...and it didn't stop.

I didn't dare lift my head, too terrified I'd find the end racing toward us.

All I could do was slam my hands over my ears and scream.

THIRTY-SIX

Carven

Agony radiated through my head. I blinked, unleashed a low moan, and tried to open my eyes. Then the jackhammer started, tearing through my goddamn skull. The fighter in me forced me to shove against the floor and slowly stand.

"Motherfucker," I whispered as I touched the back of my head and my fingers came away wet.

Lights shone. At first, I thought it was behind my eyes, until it came again.

My phone lay face down, the screen's light smothered. I ground my teeth and bent to grab the damn thing.

Wildcat: I need you.

Fear kicked me hard, driving the agony away. I looked around, trying to remember where the hell I was and stared at the tiny inside of...*a boat?*

In a second, it all came rushing back to me. The guard. The tracker...the image of Jack Castlemaine's clothes discarded.

Nighty night.

The throaty female tone rushed back. My fucking pulse spiked as I remembered her. Vivienne...

No.

Not Vivienne.

But someone who looked an awful lot like her. I shoved my hand out and stumbled forward, making my way to where I hoped was the front of the boat. I wanted out of this fucking thing...*and I wanted to get back to her.*

Bright sparks detonated in my head as I climbed. I clenched my jaw and kept going, past the discarded men's clothes tossed on the floor, and out the open cabin door.

I should stay, should gather every scrap of information I could on that bitch, knowing full well she was the closest we'd come to finding King. But I didn't care about that now. I gripped the railing and heaved myself over to the machine that braced the luxury cruiser and slowly climbed.

My boots slipped. I fell and the steel railing hit hard across my cheek. My teeth gnashed and the agony was blinding. Still, I let myself fall, anything to get to the floor faster.

The impact when I landed was brutal. My breath tore from my chest and left me reeling. But it was nothing compared to that desperate howling inside me.

Get to her.

I shoved against the concrete floor and stumbled into the yard. Darkness smothered the marina, leaving the lights of the boats to glimmer and shine, but that only ratcheted my desperation higher. I searched the fence, then stumbled forward, yanked the cut wires, and shoved through.

My fingers were trembling as I hit the numbers on my phone and stumbled along the dock to the gate. But it wasn't Vivienne I called, it was my brother. "Answer your fucking phone," I snarled.

"What?" he answered.

Relief hit me. "Thank fuck. Where the hell are you?"

"At the restaurant."

I exhaled hard, slowing my steps. "Okay. *Okay...*" I breathed. "I thought there was a problem."

"No problem."

But the way he said it made that fear inside me writhe. "Just hold on a second," I muttered, then shoved my phone into my pocket.

My goddamn head was pounding as I grabbed the gate, then heaved myself upwards. The faint crack...*crack...crack* of what sounded like gunfire made me turn and look around. But there was no one there, just the yachts that bobbed in the water and the soft slaps of waves against the hulls, so I turned back.

It was fucking messy swinging myself over the fence before I hit the pavement on the other side. I grabbed my phone and lifted it. "I'm back."

But he was gone. I glanced at the blank screen. "Asshole." Then I raced for the Explorer.

That nagging feeling grew inside me as I unlocked the damn thing and climbed inside. I started the engine, shoved the heater to blast, and pulled out, accelerating hard. The GPS put me about twenty minutes from the restaurant.

I glanced at my phone, then pressed the button, and listened to it ring...and ring...and ring.

This time, he didn't answer.

I glanced at the GPS, then my phone, pressing the button for the main guard on duty and listened to the same annoying fucking tone. It rang...and rang...*and rang*. "Come on, Clarence. Pick up your goddamn phone."

But he never did...

I pressed London's number, driving the accelerator all the way to the floor as that nagging sense that something wasn't right started screaming...

No...

It was screams...

Her screams.

"Carven!" London roared as the *crack...crack...crackcrackcrack* of gunfire filled my ears. *"GET HERE NOW!"*

That shrill sound swallowed out everything else.

The sound of the woman I loved...in trouble.

I dropped the phone and it hit my thigh and bounced. But I didn't care, not anymore. I gripped the wheel and yanked, taking the corner on two wheels. All I saw was the street ahead and the blinding glare of headlights.

All I heard was her terror.

"VIVIENNE!"

The roar ripped from me, bestial and bloody.

Whoever they were...*they were fucking dead.*

THIRTY-SEVEN

Vivienne

THE GLASS WINDOW OF THE RESTAURANT SHATTERED WITH a resounding *BOOM!*

Something heavy hit me from behind and drove me to the ground beside our parked car. I couldn't move, could only turn my head, to find a dead man on the pavement. Not just *a* dead man...*one of ours*. My pulse spiked as I took in his body. Blood covered his chest and splattered his face. His mouth was open, his eyes—I winced and turned away from the sight.

Screams came from inside the restaurant, but I didn't dare look. I couldn't care about them now.

"Colt!" London roared, the gun kicking in his hand as he fired... *crack... crack...crack! "Get down NOW!"*

That heaviness left me as London pushed to his feet. I jerked my head up to watch him lunge toward a gunman who stumbled onto the pavement and lifted his gun, aiming at Colt.

London shifted his gun.

BANG!

BANG!

I jerked and screamed, unable to take my eyes off the gunman as both shots sounded.

There were too many of them now, two vans filled with men who spilled from the open doors and scurried out into the street. I turned my head and found the wide, unblinking eyes of our guard before I glanced at the gun in his hand. One hard shove and I scrambled forward, snatched the weapon, and spun.

My dress billowed out, almost making me trip.

Only it wasn't the dead gunman I found. He was dead on the pavement at the steps of the restaurant.

London wobbled and his face was unnaturally pale as he met my stare.

"London?" I whispered, searching his eyes.

"Get behind me, pet." His voice was strange, *shaky*.

There was a hole in his jacket. A hole that shimmered...*his blood*. I shoved forward and grabbed hold of him as his knees gave way.

"London!" I screamed, clinging to him.

Crack!

The thunderous sound of gunfire made me flinch. I jerked my head upwards as more of the men came, scurrying around the parked cars like rats. Only these rats had come for the kill. Reflex took over and forced me to lift the gun in one hand and take aim.

Crack!

The gun bucked and the bullet shattered the window of the Mercedes in front of us.

"No," London growled as he lifted his own.

Crack.

He squeezed off the shot while pushing me behind him.

Crack!

They went down, hitting the ground hard. But there were more of them coming. Colt unleashed a roar. The sickening sounds of fists on flesh filled the air.

"We have to get out of here." London jerked his gaze to me, then glanced at his men.

He looked behind us, to see two more of our bodyguards dead on the pavement. Desperation filled his voice. "Can you run?"

Fear gripped me tight.

"Vivienne...*can you run?*"

I nodded. "Yeah. Yeah, I can run."

He turned around, lifted his gun as the *crack...crack... crackcrackcrack* of automatic fire peppered the other side of the car. The hiss of the tires followed, leaving us stranded as three more gunmen came.

We were going to die here.

We were going to—

The roar of an engine grew louder. I jerked my gaze as a black Explorer mounted the curb and shot clear across the intersection. Tires shrieked as the four-wheel drive skidded sideways and stopped in the middle of the street.

Crack!

London took aim. *"Carven!"* he roared. *"Your brother NOW!"*

But the deadly son was already out of the car and racing toward us.

I'd never seen anything so terrifying. Carven slammed into Colt's attacker, his hand driving down over and over and over...*stab stab stab...*

Blood shot high as the assailant slumped to the ground, and Carven lifted his other hand and stepped away from Colt, swung that deadly glare my way, then shifted his gaze behind me. "Wildcat...get down."

His command was so calm...so...*chilling.*

He lunged forward, took aim, and unleashed shot after shot.

Boom!

Boom!

BOOM!

The window in front of me shattered. London grabbed my arm, shielding me with his body as he dragged me from the destroyed Audi and toward the dark alley beside the restaurant.

Crack!

Colt charged forward as another enemy came from the other side of the van. Everywhere I looked there was chaos and blood. It was too much. Too much blood...too many deaths. I shook my head and stumbled backwards, hitting a wall.

London lunged forward, lifting his gun and stumbled around the ruined Audi as Carven charged around the other side of the van.

Boom!

BOOM!

I jerked and moved back, desperate to get away, and hit something hard...and warm.

Something that reached around and clamped over my mouth.

"Sh...sh...sh..." A deep growl echoed against my ear. "I've got you, *Daughter.*"

THIRTY-EIGHT

Carven

HEADLIGHTS SHONE, BLINDING ME FOR AN INSTANT AS TWO four-wheel drives screeched to a stop behind the stolen vans. I raised my gun and lunged around the first one, barrelling into the three motherfuckers hiding behind the clapped-out piece of shit.

"You *come after MY FAMILY!*" I drove the hilt into the closest bastard's face.

His head snapped backwards and slammed into the dented driver's door with a *dong*.

He wobbled before I grabbed him by the shirt. "No you fucking don't." I yanked him in close to snarl. "You don't go down until I make you."

Crack...

Crack.

CRACK!

London *unleashed,* charging forward until I lost sight of him through the van windows. I swung my gaze back and drove the muzzle of my gun into the scumbag's face. The sight carved into flesh, tearing open his cheek. I hit him again...and again...and again, until white bone splintered.

"You fucking piece of shit!" I snarled.

His head rolled backwards, and the whites of his eyes showed as his buddy lifted his gun, taking aim.

But I didn't care...

I was past it now.

Rushing headlong into that part of me that fucking *liked this* as I turned to find the asshole with the gun. Vivienne's screams resounded in my head, Just like the ones that'd echoed through my phone moments ago. The need to protect her was more elemental than anything I'd ever felt before. God help those in my way.

The ballsy fucker let out a scream and shoved backwards as I charged. But he was too slow. *Way too fucking slow.* I grabbed his hand, driving the gun upwards.

"Should've pulled the trigger, motherfucker." I pressed my muzzle into his chest and squeezed.

BANG!

He jolted with the impact and slid down the dented side of the van, leaving a smear of blood behind.

Two more came rushing toward me. I took aim.

Crack!

CRACK!

They went down in an instant. I kept moving and rounded the rear of the van as London drove one of the attackers to the sidewalk and stabbed the muzzle of his gun into the bastard's eye before he pulled the trigger. *BANG! He* blew the bastard's brain across the pavement.

I lifted my gaze to his.

Those dark eyes sparkled with rage.

"Colt," he grunted. "There's something wrong."

I lifted my gun and squeezed off a shot at another sneaking figure, then narrowed in on my brother behind me. Colt drove his fist into a bastard's face on the ground in front of him, then straightened. His hands were bloody and his eyes were wild, but he didn't turn to face the two fuckers that were coming for him across the street, he was staring into the darkness, watching the sidewalk from the restaurant.

"What the fuck?" I roared, unloading as I charged toward the goddamn thugs.

Crack! I squeezed off a shot and hit one before I lunged and slammed into the second.

"*Colt!*" I screamed as he just fucking stood there. "*COLT!*"

He flinched, but still stared into nothing.

Which only pissed me off even more.

I turned back to the dazed fucker I'd knocked to the ground and drove my gun against the side of his head. "Who sent you?"

His eyes were wide and blood smeared from his split lips as he stuttered. "I-I d-don't k-now."

"You don't know," I repeated.

Adrenaline roared through my veins, making me want to tear the fucking world apart at the seams. But under that rush came something else. That heaviness at the back of my neck. One I knew all too well. I scanned the cars, searching...

"Who?" I snarled again, and lifted my gun.

I scanned the cars across the street, and the alley, too. But I couldn't find the fucker I knew was watching.

I couldn't find the *Son.*

I turned back to the dead man I straddled. "Last chance. Who. Sent. You?"

"I—"

Bang.

His head dropped back and bounced. I rose to my feet. Blood splatter cooled against my cheek. Every breath I sucked in held the stench of blood. But I shoved that all aside and turned, scanning faces. He was here somewhere...*he was—*

The alley next to the restaurant was empty.

Vivienne...

That sinking feeling swallowed me whole. "No," I moaned. *"No!"*

I took a step, then another.

"Carven!" London barked as I lunged, sinking back into that cold darkness.

My boots thundered as I left them behind. All I cared about was her.

Shadows, cold...and *him.* That's all there was here. That's what I *hunted.*

I raced along the alley to the building at the end. Black on black waited. I blinked while my eyes adjusted to the deeper darkness found a door to the right barely cracked open. The hinge howled as I shoved it open and raced through. I didn't stop, just kept running, keeping my intuition in the driver's seat.

A cry tore out in the distance, faint, muffled...*female.*

I clenched my jaw and kept pushing, as I zeroed in on the sounds just out of sight.

"*Get the fuck off me!*" she screamed, followed by a heavy male grunt filled with pain.

I smirked. *That's the way, Wildcat, kick the bastard in the balls.*

"*Fuck you!*" She fought...

Until her battle cry was followed by a groan of pain.

That wiped the smile from my face.

I lowered my chin and drove forward, scanning what looked like a hallway. I kept my mind fixed on the moment I met up with them.

"*You think you're a big man, huh?*"

Her rage grew faint. I scanned closed doors and spied an exit light at the end of the hall. The place was some kind of storage facility. Some of the walls were old and decayed. I slowed, twisted the handle, and shoved through the door at the end into more ruin.

The stench of wet, rotting cardboard was fucking rank. I gagged and tried to breathe shallowly as I charged forward. Movement came through a hole in the ruined wall up ahead.

The bastard's grunt was audible as were her muffled screams.

He had his hand over her mouth, that was obvious.

He'd touched her...

He'd. Fucking. Touched. Her.

I dropped my shoulder and crashed through the hole in the wall with a *boom!*

The Son swung his gaze toward me as Vivienne thrashed in his arms. Her eyes were terrified as the black dress bunched around her legs and made her fall back against him. Only then did I see the gun.

Steel glinted in his hand from moonlight that spilled in from holes in the roof.

I sucked in a deep breath as I lifted my gun and took aim. "Let her go."

"You gonna shoot in the dark like this?" He jerked her around in front of him.

Fear tore through me. He was right, I couldn't see well enough to be sure of not hitting her.

Bang!

I flinched and fell forward as pain ripped across the side of my head and I hit the filthy floor. A swipe of my hand and I found the shallow gash.

"Motherfucker." I lifted my gaze to him as he stepped backward, using her as a goddamn shield.

I shoved to my feet. "Last chance. Let her go."

"I told you before...you and your brother. The Daughter is coming with me."

I didn't make a sound, just rushed the bastard, hurled my body through the air, and hit both of them. Air ripped from her with a *grunt* a second before we all went down.

Dress.

Fists.

Someone kneed me in the goddamn balls...

I let out a growl and shoved forward as he rolled away, dragging Vivienne by the goddamn hair. "Up, Daughter."

She screamed as she reached over her head to grab his hand.

The sight of that did something to me.

I lifted my gun, took aim, and fired.

BANG!

But the bastard must have dodged at just the right moment because he didn't seem to be hurt. I lunged and grabbed her as best I could, but the bastard had her hair clutched in his fingers and she slipped from my grip. She screamed again, the shrill sound a fucking knife to my chest.

"Uh, uh," he taunted, and yanked her backward as I took aim again.

"You gutless *motherfucker!*" I roared.

He looked around him, searching the shadows, and I knew instantly why...

He was looking for the others.

Once they got here, it'd all be over.

She'd be gone in an instant...and there wouldn't be a thing I could do to stop them.

He swung her around as I rushed him. I stumbled, but grabbed her again while he scanned the darkness. White teeth shone in the darkness as he reached for her. I caught the glimmer of steel on a blade a second later.

"No!" I lunged sideways without thinking, caught another handful of her dress, and flung her behind me.

The slice was fucking brutal as it tore open my shoulder. A cry ripped from me for an instant, until I swallowed the sound.

"Carven," Vivienne cried as she wrapped her arms around me.

I pulled her against me, making sure she was safe, not once taking my eyes off the fucking Son. "Stay behind me, Wildcat."

She moved with me, sidestepping a razor-edged sheet of steel that was a beheading in the making. I tested my shoulder, taking comfort in the gruelling agony that followed.

"You're fast, I'll give you that," the Son murmured. "You sure you don't want to join us?"

I unclasped her arms from me, but kept moving, making him step backwards, to put as much distance between him and her as I could, and slowly lifted my gun with one hand, watching as he did the same, only using both hands.

My fingers gripped steel and pressed the button of his own blade before one flick of my wrist sent it sailing through the air, flipping end over end.

"I think they call this checkma—" He jerked as the blade buried itself deep into his stomach.

There was a second of confusion. His brows pinched before he looked down.

BANG!

He jerked as the bullet found its mark. But I was already moving as I strode forward, wrapped my hand around the hilt of the knife, and yanked it free.

He unleashed a cry as the steel came away and raised his head.

"I tried to warn you, but you didn't listen..." I shoved the knife in once more, once...twice...three times, then jerked upwards as I stared into the Son's eyes. "You touch her and you die."

Those dark eyes of his sparkled.

Right before his knees gave way and he crumbled to the floor.

I stood over him, sucking in some deep breaths.

I didn't waste another second on him, just turned around, to find her staring at me in the darkness.

I searched for horror and disgust...I searched for fear.

But there was none.

Instead, she flung herself toward me. I jerked the knife away at the last second before she slammed against me.

Her arms were around me in an instant, her face buried against my neck.

I wrapped one arm around her. The other was shaking uncontrollably. "You're okay," I murmured. "You're okay now."

She didn't cry, didn't scream, just held on tight enough for both of us.

"Vivienne!" London roared from nearby.

She pulled away and for a second, I would've given anything to feel her warmth against me and her breath on my skin. But the sound of heavy boots approached.

"We're here!" I croaked.

The wall crashed in as London tore his way in. His eyes found her, then he shifted his gaze to me.

If that act alone didn't speak volumes.

It's how I felt, too.

I looked toward her. She was first. *Always and forever.*

"Let's get out of here." I reached down and grabbed her hand with my good one.

The movement drew London's gaze. He narrowed in on the shake of my other hand, then met my stare.

One nod was all he needed. He stepped forward and reached for her. "Pet."

She moved toward him, but turned her gaze at the last minute to mine.

"I'm right behind you," I assured, and urged her forward.

As they moved, I looked behind me at the dead Son bleeding out on the filthy warehouse floor.

That could've been me...

The thought slammed into me. An ache in the back of my throat followed as I turned back to the heavy thud of steps as London led Vivienne out. I'd never allowed myself to think about all the things this man had done for two skinny kids he didn't even know.

Now I did...

And it hit me harder than I was prepared for.

I tried to take a step, but my knees wouldn't hold me, and I fell.

Vivienne stopped instantly, as though, somehow, she knew. She spun around and saw me as I hit the floor.

"Carven!" she cried out.

Tears sprang to my eyes at the sound of her rushed steps.

But it wasn't the pain in my shoulder that had me in its tight fist...it was *love.*

The kind of love a Son should never have.

And yet here it was, wrapping its arms around me and helping me to stand.

"I got you," she whispered, clutching me against her side.

I managed to walk, leaning heavily on her as we made our way out of that derelict building and back into the alley.

The sound of sirens was shrill in the air.

"This way," London called as a door opened to the building on the other side of the alley.

One of our men stumbled out, shining a light from his phone. We followed him and made our way to the back of the building to a parking lot. The Explorer was there, with the engine running and the headlights illuminating the dark.

"Colt?" I croaked.

"Waiting in the car," the guard answered.

I recognized him now. The smartass guard on duty. He met my stare as he opened the door. Blood splattered his cheek. He wore the same shell-shocked gaze as us now, the same haunted reflection that'd stay with him.

He gave a slow nod as I followed the others to the car. I didn't even flinch when he opened the door for us. All I did was find my brother sitting in the back seat, staring out at nothing.

"Colt." Vivienne climbed in and slid over to wrap her arms around him.

He turned at her voice, leaving me to climb in beside her and close the door. But there was something not right with my brother, something that made that broken little boy glimmer in those blue eyes.

She nestled against him as London climbed into the passenger side and the guard slipped behind the wheel. We were out of there in an instant, watching as red and blue lights filled the night as they raced past us.

They'd come for us.

Maybe not tonight.

But soon...

THIRTY-NINE

Vivienne

THE HEADLIGHTS BOUNCED AGAINST THE ORNATE WINDOWS of our home as we pulled into the driveway and came to a stop in front of the garage. I couldn't move. One arm was wrapped around Colt's, and my other hand was clasped in Carven's, so I was tethered between them while London shoved the passenger door open and climbed out.

He slammed the door behind him with a *bang,* making me jump. But then Carven opened his door and held me as I climbed out, even though he was the one wounded. Those bright blue eyes were darker than I'd ever seen before, as he turned them from me to his twin.

"Colt," he called.

I looked over my shoulder and found my quiet protector staring into nothing, just like he had the entire way here. Pain tore through my chest at the sight. I was so tired, so...*empty.*

But he needed me.

I pushed all that away and lifted my hand. "Baby," I whispered, watching carefully as he turned his gaze to mine. "Let me take you inside."

He looked past me to his brother, then to the house, as though he'd only just realized we were here. Slowly, he scooted across the seat and climbed out, letting me take his hand to guide him.

The moment we were inside, London shoved the study door open and slapped on the light. *"Who the fuck was it?"* he roared.

Boots thundered as Guild rushed around the corner and stumbled into the room. "Jesus fucking Christ!" He scanned all four of us with a panicked stare.

"It was *someone!*" London roared, dragging his fingers through his hair. "I want them found. I want them...*dead!*"

Sparks detonated in his eyes as he swung around, grabbed the heavy glass paperweight on the desk, and hurled it across the room. It hit the wall with a *CRASH* and shattered to the floor. There it lay while we all stared, numb and empty.

"I want them found." He turned slowly, finding Colt, then Carven. *"You hear me? I want them dead. No one touches my family*...no one touches—" His voice broke as his gaze settled on me. "No one touches those I love."

We all trembled in the presence of the man.

Of his rage.

Of his promises.

Of his need.

His hand went to his hair once more, only this time I saw the tremble, until, with a guttural growl, he strode across the study and lifted me from the floor.

"I thought you were dead." He pulled me close and buried his face against my neck. "*I thought you were all fucking dead.*"

My hands went to his strong arms and slid over his shoulders as I turned my head until my lips met his to whisper. "Not while I have you."

A wounded sound ripped from him as he kissed me. I wrapped my legs around his waist as he turned and carried me out of the study, ending the kiss. "Colt...Carven," he called.

Steps sounded behind us as together we left Guild and the study behind and went to London's bedroom. Black, silver...red. The colors all melded together as he strode toward the massive king-sized bed in the middle of the room.

He kissed me as he lowered me to the bed, gripped the strap of my dress, and tugged it aside to kiss the top of my breast.

"Rip it," I urged.

"What?" he questioned as he met my stare.

"I said, *rip...it.*"

A deep breath, and he yanked, jolting me as the expensive fabric tore. The sound shattered something inside me. Some barrier that had held me frozen was now fractured, allowing me to sit up, grab the open collar of his shirt, and yank.

All I saw was blood...

Blood that had seeped into his shirt under his jacket. I stared at the mess, then lifted my gaze to his. "London, you need a doctor."

He shrugged off his jacket and looked down. I shoved against the bed, rising...

"No, you don't."

He stopped me instantly, lifted that demanding stare, then yanked his shirt. Buttons popped and flew across the room before he yanked his belt. "You're not going anywhere."

He was nearly crazed with rage at that moment.

But underneath that was...

Desperation.

It was that which made me still, *that* which held me transfixed as he shoved his pants low and grabbed me around the waist. "Carven," he murmured without looking away. "Take her hand."

The son moved, rounded the bed, and climbed up beside my shoulder.

"Gonna put a baby in your belly, pet," London's voice was chilling. "One way or another."

Carven's hand clasped mine as London reached down, slid one arm under my knee, and yanked upwards. My body jerked as my hips tilted to the side. He slid his hand along my thigh, pushing my dress up until he exposed the black French panties he loved.

"My family," he whispered as he reached under me to yank them down. "My fucking heart."

My pulse leaped and skipped as he dragged my panties down and tossed them aside. His hands, so warm...so familiar, slid along my skin. I closed my eyes at the contact. "Do it."

I felt the room still.

Warm breath rushed and followed the trail of his fingers as London parted my thighs. We'd almost been killed tonight... what a better way to celebrate our survival? "Fuck me, London."

I opened my eyes as he kissed the inside of my thighs. "Fuck me and fill me with your child."

He sucked in a shaky breath.

The hunger in his stare had roared to the surface.

But he was so gentle as he kissed me, moving along the inside of my thigh until he closed his mouth over my sex. I moaned at the contact and arched my back. My hand wrapped tightly around Carven's.

London stopped, then turned his head. "Colt...*son?*"

But my protector didn't move. He just stared at me...

No.

He stared *through* me.

I kept my eyes on him as London turned back and parted me with his fingers.

He wanted them to be a part of this, any way they could. His fingers slid inside me, and his tongue followed. I grasped Carven's hand and gave my body over to them. Heat rushed through me, making me spread my legs wider and look down as London rose. He didn't care about the bullet in his shoulder, nor did he care about the pain.

Instead, his focus was on one thing...

Me.

He slid inside with a sure thrust that caught my breath as he dropped his head and unleashed a moan. "Fuck, you feel like Heaven."

He pushed against me, gripping my leg higher as he drove all the way inside.

"Uh...*uh...uh.*" My cries jolted as desire roared to the surface.

I shouldn't be coming...

Not this fast.

But adrenaline punched through me, driven on the tip of his cock driving inside me.

"Harder!" I arched my back, my legs as wide as I could get them. *"Harder, London!"*

He gave a roar, crushing me against the bed as he pumped his hips.

I was lost in the impact. Empty and full all at the same time. A vessel for him...for all of them.

Lightning tore through my body as he stretched and fucked me like a man possessed. I surrendered and let the rush sweep me away. My body clenched and pulsed as I unleashed a moan of desire.

"You. Are. Fucking. *Mine,*" he grunted, jerking those dangerous eyes to me. *"You understand that?"*

I shoved upwards, grabbed the back of his neck, and pulled him down low enough to stare into his eyes. *"You're MINE too, do YOU understand THAT?"*

With a low moan, he stilled deep inside me. My leg was pushed higher as warmth spilled inside me and I released his head and fell backward.

Mine.

Mine...

Mine...

The word resounded through my mind. He stayed there as he sucked in deep breaths and held my gaze.

I thought he was done, but he didn't pull out. Instead, he thrust again. That incensed look was sparking as he shoved his softening cock inside, then finally withdrew. His gaze lowered and found the mess.

"You will have *all* of me," he grunted as he slid his fingers through the slick to push it back in. *"Every...last...drop."*

An ache tore across my chest.

He wanted me pregnant.

But did he truly want *me?*

"Then marry me."

He stiffened, then jerked his gaze to mine. "What did you say?"

I released Carven's hand and shoved upwards on my elbows. "If you want me so bad, then *marry me.*"

He shook his head as a look of horror crossed his face.

I tried to hide the pain, but it was too close.

It was *all* too close.

Agony roared as he stumbled backwards, and with that came rage. I shoved upwards, not caring about the warmth that slipped out between my thighs. "You want to *fuck* me. You want to put your child in my belly, but I'm not good enough to wear your ring. Is that it, London?"

"No," he groaned.

His knees wobbled as he turned gray.

"Oh, the *fuck you do!*" I barked as I practically jumped from the bed when he turned toward the bathroom. "You don't get to play me, London. You don't get to."

He stopped walking and spun around *"WHAT THE FUCK DO YOU WANT FROM ME?"*

I froze and flinched as though I'd been slapped. The bedroom faded. In that moment, there were just the two of us...

"What do *I* want?" I whispered, forcing myself to move forward. *"What the fuck do I WANT?"*

I lunged, driving my fist into his good shoulder as tears filled my eyes. "I want YOU, *YOU STUPID FUCK!"* I moved closer. "I want *you. Don't you get that? I want...you."*

He stepped back into the darkened bathroom until he hit the basin.

There was nowhere for him to run now.

No one to fight.

Just me.

I moved closer, hating how desperate he made me feel, and slid my arms around him. "I just want you, all three of you." I pressed my head against his strong chest as the words spilled free. "You forced me into your life, into your home. You forced me to love you and now that I do, you can't shut me out."

"I'm not..."

I lifted my head as warmth slipped down my cheeks.

He was sickened at the sight, giving me a shake of his head.

"No, *Vivienne."*

"Marry me." My voice was hoarse. "Love me the way I love you."

His brow creased and that empty stare was a knife to my chest.

I knew then...

Knew there was no changing him.

My arms slowly slid from him. "I get it now," I whispered. "You truly are a cold-hearted bastard."

He jerked at the words and his eyes widened. "I—"

I didn't wait for him to say another word, just stepped backwards until I turned. The room swayed as I slammed into Carven, who stood there, watching everything.

"Wildcat." He reached for me.

I shook my head, tore my arm out of reach, and stumbled into the bedroom. "Don't...just...*don't*."

I left them there, walking as fast as my legs could carry me and headed for my room.

"Colt?" Carven called. "*Colt?*"

I stopped, looking at his closed bedroom door.

"He was just here," Carven growled as he tore past me. "This is all we fucking need."

I stood in the middle of the hallway and felt London's cum slide from my body as I listened to the heavy thud of Carven's boots that only grew more frantic. I tracked them as he raced from the kitchen to the rear of the house and back again.

London gently pushed past me, not giving me a second look as Carven strode back.

"He's gone." He shook his head and panic roared in his stare. "*The FUCKER is gone!*"

London grabbed his phone and punched the numbers. But the phone only rang twice, then went to voicemail. "Goddamn him." London hit end, then tried again.

Only this time, it didn't even ring.

Not once.

Like Colt had switched his phone off…

Like he was *gone*.

The hallway blurred. I stumbled to the side and slammed against the wall.

"No," I moaned, remembering Colt's vacant stare as I'd led him inside.

My knees buckled and I crashed to the floor.

I hugged my knees as I leaned against the wall.

Defeated.

"No," I whimpered. "No…"

FORTY

Colt

____

Ophelia will go after her.

Just you wait and see...

We did...didn't we? We waited and we saw. Now we were dealing with the aftermath.

Gunshots cracked inside my head and the tormenting sound of Vivienne's screams followed.

I'll protect you.

I'll protect—

"It's okay," I whispered, and stared into her eyes as London thrust deep inside her. "I'll protect you."

She jolted with his impact and moaned with pleasure, unable to hear a word I said.

But I did...

And that's all that mattered.

"Then marry me," she groaned.

"What did you say?" London asked.

But I was already slipping away, unable to bring myself back, even when heartache roared into the room.

Movement came, blurring everything out of focus.

Because I was back there with the crack of the gunfire and the screams of rage.

In my head, I stared at the dark blur as *she* scurried along the pavement outside the restaurant. Cold plunged into my chest at the memory, the ice gnawing until it consumed me. *Ophelia will go after, just you wait and see.*

I turned away, unable to stay in that room a second longer. I was already gone from here, plunging back into that darkness. Sounds came from the far end of the house.

I tracked the movement and sensed Guild moving away as I stopped at London's study. Keys for the Explorer glinted on the corner of the desk, drawing my focus. I snatched them and made my way back outside. No one saw me climb into the vehicle and start the engine. No one saw me quietly back out of the drive.

I'll protect you.

I'll protect—

I sucked in hard breaths as I lost myself again. Streets blurred and headlights blazed. But I kept going and made my way through roundabouts and across the city until the bright lights of the bars blurred in my rear-view mirror. I turned then, slipped down a familiar street, and scanned the curb.

There was no driver waiting outside now, no party for her to go to. It seemed that tonight, Ophelia was all out of excitement. I flinched as movement came from behind the curtains. I switched off the engine, yanked the handle, and climbed out.

My body was exhausted, my mind numb as I slowly made my way across the street to the side of her house. I knew the layout of the townhouse, knew the combination of her locks. I knew *everything*. Except what was on that chip.

But that didn't matter.

Not when I stopped at the high brick wall, grabbed the top, and heaved myself over.

"I *need you!*" Her shrill scream was far too clear as it came from a cracked open door above me on the second floor. *"He's going to come after me, don't you get that?* He'll find out. He'll—"

Her voice went quiet as I rounded the bottom of the stairs and began to climb.

"Okay. You're right. They're all dead. No one can trace them back to me. It was just a coincidence I was there. Just a—okay, okay, yes. Just come and get me and I'll spend the night, and Haelstrom...*thank you.*"

My gut clenched with the words.

Thank you?

THANK YOU?

I gripped the steel banister as I swayed.

She thanked him for protecting her.

All vipers.

All snakes.

I opened my eyes and kept climbing, catching the light spill from the cracked open door. She didn't know she'd left it ajar as she ran for her life—I caught the movement as she paced, her phone still clutched in her hand—but soon she would.

The door hinges were silent as I pushed the door and stepped inside.

Her back was to me, her gaze fixed on the window. She took a step, brushing the curtains aside to stare into the night. Did she see my car parked in the dark alley? Did she feel me breathing down her neck?

I took another step inside and scanned the counter, finding partially folded white cloth coverings and an open tool box. Newly hung artwork decorated the gray concrete walls. Charcoal and blue beckoned at the edge of my vision, just like the ones we'd burned.

I didn't look...I didn't dare.

I wasn't here for them...

I was here for her.

Steel dragged along the counter as I gripped the hammer and pulled it free. She turned then. Her eyes widened as they fixed on mine. That cruel fucking mouth pursed tight.

"You," she said, then gave a chuff as she glanced at the hammer in my hand. "What the hell are you doing here?"

"You shouldn't have touched her." I stepped closer. "You should've stayed away."

I wasn't me...I wasn't here.

I was someone else, someone *empty*. "You...should've just...*RUINED ME INSTEAD!*"

She jumped at the roar. But then that *fucking mouth* curled. "You think you can escape me?" She stepped forward, completely ignoring the weapon in my hand. "You *think* you can *ever* escape *me?*"

I sucked in hard breaths as she moved closer. "You can't, don't you *get* that? No more than I can escape you. He never told you the truth, did he? All he gave you were lies and silence. You swallowed it all down, every single drop of it."

"You shut the fuck up."

"Lies, lies, lies."

"I said *shut the fuck up!*"

She slithered closer. "London and his *whore* daughter and his *bastard* sons."

I swung my fist. *"I SAID SHUT UP!"*

The hammer hit her in the side of the face with a *crack*. She jerked sideways, then stumbled until she hit the wall. Her hand went to her cheek, then she looked at her fingers. Her chest was rising and falling with her panted breaths. "You...you bastard." She lifted her gaze and I saw blood on her cheek. "You fucking bastard."

She shoved against the wall, but stumbled before she straightened. I saw it then, saw that *serpent* behind her eyes. It blinked and fixed on me.

"I'll fucking ruin her," the serpent spat. "I'll drag that *cunt* into the club and I'll stand by and watch every man there have his turn. And then I'll put her out onto the streets. I'll shoot her veins with so much heroin she'll forget her own fucking name. She'll wear red until that's all she knows. All she'll remember is bright blue eyes. Bright blue eyes and the memory of what she once had."

I charged forward, grabbed her by the throat, and shoved her backwards. *"I fucking HATE YOU!"*

Her head hit the wall with a crunch. The whites of her eyes shone for an instant as they rolled backwards and then closed. My gut clenched as a sickening chuckle spilled from her slips.

"You don't get it." She opened her eyes. "You were mine before you were anyone's. Mine to have, mine to torment, mine to destroy if I wanted to. You were mine when you were conceived and you were mine when I gave birth to you."

I stiffened.

Her gaze burned into mine. "My flesh. My blood."

"No." I shook my head, my hand falling to my side as I stepped away. *"No."*

"He never told you because he wanted you for himself. He was so fucking weak and pathetic when it came to the both of you."

"You're a liar. That's what you do...you *lie.*"

She yanked up her blouse, exposed her abdomen, and shoved down her slacks. All I saw was the white slash of a scar across her belly. "You came from me, implanted from one of the founders of The Order. He gave up his rights to you, but *I* never did. I *never did!*"

"You beat us," I croaked as pain ripped a jagged blade through me. "You *beat* us *and you tormented us!*"

I focused in on her. It all came rushing back now. Every boot to my back, every fist to my face. "You beat and starved and ruined us."

She jutted her chin high in the air. "I made you the man you are today."

"YOU BROKE ME!" I roared. *"YOU BROKE US! YOU TURNED US INTO NOTHING...YOU...YOU—"*

I had my hand around her throat before I knew it. Corded muscles clenched tight along my arm. "But I won't let you ruin her. I won't let you destroy her. She'll be happy. She'll marry London and she'll be happy."

That same sick gurgling sound vibrated against my grip.

She didn't fight, just stood there with those *knowing* eyes boring into mine. I gripped the hammer with my other hand. The tool felt heavy in my grip.

"He can't. Marry. Her." The words were just hisses of air. "Because...he's married to *me*."

The words were a kick in my gut. I shoved her away, until she slid along the wall.

"No." The room blurred with the shake of my head.

She stumbled and fell. Her gaze moved to the window and the darkness outside.

I couldn't think. I couldn't...I clenched my fist and punched the side of my head. Pain throbbed deep.

"That was the condition when he took you. He married me. He obeyed me. But all this time he was looking for a way out. He thought he found it in her...he was wrong."

"No." I clenched my eyes closed. "No..."

I sensed movement, but I couldn't react. I couldn't do a damn thing as that *numbness* crawled along my spine.

"You always were pathetic, Colt."

"Shut up."

"Pathetic and soft. You think *daddy*—"

I snapped open my eyes. Only, she'd managed to stand, and she was close...too close, her gaze fixed on the open door. There was only one way out of this now. Only one way for those I loved to be safe. I clenched my grip and swung.

She threw her hands up to protect her face. But it didn't matter. Steel hit her palm and drove it into her nose. Bone crunched. Her screams followed, shrill screams as I yanked my arm back and swung once more, impacting the side of her face.

There was only that numbness now.

Swing.

Hit.

Swing.

Hit.

Swing...

I blinked and she was on the floor in front of me.

Her face was bloody, her hair a mangled, blood-matted mess.

"I'll protect you." My grip slipped with the blood, so I had to clench tighter as I lifted the hammer high above my head. *"I'll protect you all."*

I swung down, driving the steel through the air as hard as I could.

Crunch.

Embedded deep into bone. There was only the hiss of air now.

Only the white of her eyes and inside her skull.

I sucked in deep breaths as I slowly rose. Warmth cooled against my skin as bright lights flared along the street. The sound of a car grew louder until, through the gap in the curtain, I watched it turn into the drive.

Just come and get me...

Her words surfaced as reality slammed into me. I looked down at my hands smeared with blood...then glanced at the broken thing in front of me.

I did that...

I...did.

I did.

I—did...

My hand trembled as I reached for my phone. Blood and flecks of white brain matter smeared across the screen as the engine outside died. I stabbed the numbers, praying...

"Colt," London answered.

The *thud* of car doors sounded. "I did something," I whispered, staring at the ruin in front of me. "London...I...I killed her."

"You *killed her?*"

"The fucking bitch who tried to kill you. I killed...*Ophelia.*"

Silence. Then a hard breath.

"Hale's here. He's just pulled up in the drive."

The *boom...boom...boom...*sounded. I thought it was my heart.

But it wasn't. It was London...*running.*

"Stay right there," he roared. *"Do you hear me, Colt? STAY RIGHT THERE. I'M ON MY WAY."*

I jerked my head up at the sound of boots thudding. My stomach sank. "Tell her...tell her I lo—"

Grab the bonus scene with Carven and Viv here!

Preorder Claimed here on Amazon

They came...

They took...

Now it's time to destroy them from the inside out.

But first I need to get him back...my son...*Colt*.

Click the QR code or click here to find the Blood Ties signed trilogy and more in my store.